CUBAN ROOTS

by

Michael A. Pyle

1655 N. Clyde Morris Blvd.
Daytona Beach, FL 32117
Contact: mike@armstrongmediagroup.net

Dedication

Cuban Roots is dedicated to all Cuban-born people,
no matter whether they remained in Cuba or not,
and regardless of their beliefs about political matters
or the history or future of their country.

Credit

I give special thanks to poet Richard Blanco,
author of *The Prince of Los Cocuyos,*
among others, for granting me permission
to use a quote from his book in dialogue.

Foreword and Acknowledgements

I owe thanks to a great number of people and organizations.

<u>Early Seeds - Close family who helped me learn and understand:</u>

The seed that germinated into *Cuban Roots* began to sprout in the late 70s or early 80s after I met Maria L. Pyle, born Maria Luisa Lopez Cueva in Santiago de Cuba, Cuba, to whom I was married from 1979 until 2018, and her family. I learned that she and her brother had been sent to another country at age seven because of a rumor spread throughout Cuba that the Castro regime planned to send children ages six and seven to Russia. Many of those children were sent to the United States, on what were called the Peter Pan flights.

I began writing this novel over 25 years ago. Over the years, I learned, in general conversation, about the long-term psychological effects of separation of family members, the loss of comfort and personal items, and the longing for one's home country even when one has left.

I asked relatives of Maria in Miami, particularly Waldino 'Waldy' Sierra and his family members, to help me understand the geography of Santiago de Cuba, La Socapa, and Cayo Smith, now Cayo Granma, and I still have the drawing he created for me. I also asked him and others, including Maria's sister Emma 'Yiyi' Lopez, about their memories, including whether residents of Vista Alegre neighborhood could hear gunfire from the Cuartel Moncada the morning of the attack, and what it was like to remain in Cuba as a child during the early years of the Revolution.

<u>Research after 2009:</u>

In 2009, the U.S. government opened the door for me to go to Cuba to research in person, by allowing U.S. persons who had family in Cuba to travel there. Maria knew of a second cousin, Mario 'Mayito' F. Rodriguez Tamayo, whom she'd never met. She asked him to babysit me on my first trip to Cuba in January 2010. We spent almost a week walking through Havana and visiting museums. He and I flew to Santiago de Cuba where we also walked for miles and visited museums at the Siboney Farmhouse and La Moncada army barracks.

We found other family members of Maria living in the Vista Alegre neighborhood of Santiago de Cuba. Lilian Sierra, first cousin of Maria, still lives in her family home. We met her daughter Lili Acevedo and her niece Leonor Sierra Salas. Lilian's husband Jorge was away at the time, but I met him later. Lilian took us to where Maria and her family had lived. Some years later, I took Maria to visit Santiago de Cuba and we stayed in the home with Lilian and her family, and she, Lili, and Jorge provided me photographs of the city in early years, as well as information about historical occurrences. Leonor introduced me to local historians and provided information, photographs and books.

During those early trips, I was sometimes confronted by Cuban officials questioning what I was doing in Cuba and by U.S. officials, usually those of Cuban heritage, in Miami on my return. U.S. immigration would ask me for my specific license allowing me to travel to Cuba. I would explain that I was on a general license 'close family visit'. Immigration officials would sometimes state that I was not allowed to do that without my wife. I would explain that I had read the law and yes, I was, because under our law, Maria's family is my family. They would argue with me and berate me. In the past couple of years, I have had a couple of caustic discussions with our immigration authorities, but not recently. In recent years, Cuban officials interrogated me on every visit and investigated me, but now it seems that they are satisfied that I am not in any way a threat.

<u>Readers of very early drafts, providers of insight and /or support of my work:</u>

I give particular thanks to a number of people who read drafts, some long ago and some more recently, and / or gave me insight and information, and / or have consistently supported my writing efforts. They include: my daughter Michelle M. Mills, Maria L. Pyle, Kenneth McGee, Louis Roppolo, Julie Adams, Susan Moseman, Donna Beemer, Donna Edwards, John Williamson, Debra Bennett Jung, Roger Larson, Guy Emerich, Eric West, Neil Oslos and Brooke White.

<u>Others who supported me by inviting me to give talks or in other ways:</u>

A number of local people involved in writing, publishing or organizations about those activities have provided much support to me, asking me to speak about a book that I could not say was about to be published. Donna Gray-Banks and her 'F.R.E.S.H. Book Festival', Milton McCulloch and his 'Conversations Literary Series', Deborah Shafer, Davita Bonner, Sue Kopald, Cinematique Theater, Daytona Beach, Friends of the Daytona Beach Regional Library, City Island Branch, Volusia County Libraries, members of several local book clubs and the Pallet Pub at 816 Main Street, Daytona Beach.

In the past couple of years, I have sought input from people living in Cuba for a better understanding of their points of view on matters related to the book. My cousin Mayito, mentioned above, told me he used to work at the Institute of Cuban History in Havana. He introduced me to an executive of the organization, Aurea Veronica Rodriguez Rodriguez. She introduced me to the president of the Institute, Rene Gonzalez Barrios. She and others read the text and gave comments, approval and support. They invited me in 2018 and 2019 to present the book at the annual event of the Institute.

At the presentation, I met Kenia Herrera, an employee of the Institute, who also made a presentation. She introduced me to Katia 'Katya' Arias. Katya reviewed the text and provided some comments. She has begun translating the text into Spanish. Both hold degrees in studies of Cuban history. Katia also assisted greatly in trying to get us authorized to present at the Havana International Book Fair. I've been to a number of historical sites in Havana that I had not seen before with these two and Katya's daughter, Keily Neky, also a student of Cuban history. Kenia arranged for us to gain access to the top of the Bacardi Building in Havana, thanks to having been the professor of a class in which security guard Yosmel Biquillon Agüero was a student. The building is closed, but he got special attention and arranged to take us up. I also have been assisted in my research by docents at the museum that is the room where Hemingway lived as he wrote books in Hotel Ambos Mundos in Havana and docents at the museum in the Siboney Farmhouse.

Through all these people involved with the Institute of Cuban History, I have learned what the Cuban people believe about the Embargo as we call it, the *Bloqueo* as they call it, and a great number of atrocities they believe were committed by the U.S. CIA. One specific one, which I had never heard from Maria or her family, is that the rumor about children being sent to Russia was a ruse created by our CIA. I was given a copy of a book named *Operación Pedro Pan*. Whether these beliefs are true or not, I tried to show both sides of the various stories in this book.

Other Cuban people have assisted as well. Luna Perez, who owns a rental unit in the Playa area of Havana, Cuba, gave me access to important books on history. Daniel Cruz Nasiff has been my friend and driver in Holguin, Cuba for many years now and drives a blue Willy. Yanette Novoa invited me to her home in Miami, Florida and allowed me to interview a relative, and Dolores Salas Tort provided me much information including many copies of Cuban newspapers.

Starting about six years ago, Leonor Sierra Salas, of Santiago de Cuba, Cuba, offered to assist in providing more historical information than she provided on that first visit. Since her job at the La Universidad del Oriente in Santiago de Cuba included being an editor for the scholastic press and magazine, she began editing the manuscript, while still fact-checking and providing information on history. It was difficult because at that time the only access available allowed one megabyte at a time to be transferred via email from the old computers at the university, and one hour a month of Internet. Leonor 'Leo' edited the book through several versions for a few years.

Then, I engaged Veronica H. Hart, "Ronnie", to edit as well and also to assist with various other matters about publication of this and other books published by Armstrong Media Group. She and her husband, Bob Hart, together worked on the final review.

I am very grateful for all the assistance of both Leo and Ronnie, which has been a years-long effort. The combination of editing by two very distinct professional editors, with different native languages, has been very, very helpful.

I also wish to express gratitude to Brandy Winston for creating the cover and performing many additional tasks for this and other books, Chris Holmes for her technical work on the final publication as well as prior work on this and other works, and Marie McIntyre for reviewing the text before submission.

Finally, I want to express my appreciation of some businesses that I frequent in Havana, where I sit for hours, writing and editing, including *Elizalde* restaurant, on the corner of Empedrado and Avenida Belgica (Monseratte), the bars of Iberostar's *Hotel Parque Central* (both buildings), and a restaurant / café called *Lo de Monik* at Chacón y Compostela, all in Habana Vieja, 'old Havana, in Cuba.

Cuban Roots

Saturday, November 26, 2016
Shortly After Midnight

Chapter 1
Luis Morales

Foggy with sleep, I lumber along the tiled hallway as fast as my old legs will carry me toward the distinctive rings of both the home phone and my iPhone.

I huff. "I thought we decided not to have phones in the bedroom so we wouldn't be disturbed. And I thought my iPhone was automatically set at night to *do-not-disturb*."

Sylvia has been helping me along, but, being much younger than I, now sprints ahead, calling back to me. "Your DND is overridden by more than one call from the same person."

I realize I've been leaning forward as I walk, like an old man. I pull my shoulders back and raise my head. "What time is it?"

"Just after midnight."

She reaches the phones and points at the digital screen. "It's a five-three country code. That's Cuba, isn't it? Should I answer?"

"No, don't. It would cost her a fortune." I catch up to her. My sister's home phone number in Havana shows on the display. I log into my mobile, pull up the application that allows calls at reduced rates and tap the icon. The computer voice says, "You have twenty-five minutes remaining on this call."

"*Se murió*," my sister wails.

As I try to escape the sleep fog, Sylvia, looking fresh, her light brown hair sliding across her blue, silk-like pajama top, takes my arm and helps me to sit.

I ask in Spanish, "Who died, Emma?"

"Fidel. Fidel is dead." She bawls loudly.

I know she expects me to react, but I say nothing. The news of Fidel's death is no great surprise to me. People have been convinced he was dead several times. I question myself and come to the conclusion that I feel no emotion one way or the other. I'm not far behind him in age. My friends and acquaintances have been dropping off one by one for years, and the number is accelerating. Who knows how much longer I have.

Sylvia touches my shoulder and whispers, "What's the matter, honey? Who died?"

Emma continues sniffling and blubbering. I hold the phone away from my ear, put my hand over where I presume the microphone is and whisper, "Fidel Castro died."

Sylvia scrunches her brow in surprise. "She's crying about Castro? I thought everybody hated him."

I whisper, "Not everybody, especially in Cuba."

"Emma, is it really true this time?"

Emma's daughter Maribel talks through sobs in the background. Emma says, "Raul made the announcement on television."

The home phone rings again. Sylvia says, "It's Clara."

I'm sure my other sister, who lives just around the corner from our house, is calling to express joy at Castro's death. I whisper, "Answer and tell her I'm on the phone with Emma. I'll call her back."

Emma continues to pour out her desolation. "Luis, are you coming to Havana for the services?"

"Emma. I'm sorry to hear the news. I just got home to Miami a few days ago. I go to Santiago at the end of this week."

"Luis, you aren't even upset, are you?"

I glance at Sylvia and shrug to indicate I'm trying to extricate myself. "Yes, Emma, of course I'm upset."

Sylvia raises her eyebrows at me.

I hold my hands up in an *I don't know what to say* gesture and shrug again. She smiles.

"Listen, Emma. Clara is calling. I'll talk to you tomorrow."

I disconnect and take the home phone from Sylvia. "Luis," Clara's voice shrills through the line, "Fidel is dead." She laughs out loud. "The son of a bitch is finally gone. Gone. I'm so happy."

I cringe. I hold the receiver away from my head again, and again Sylvia looks confused.

"Luis, come on. People are going down to *calle Ocho* to celebrate."

I frown. "There's nothing that would get me out on the streets at this time of night, especially to celebrate a death. And I would hope that you'd stay home too."

"You sound like an old man. I hope I don't go downhill like you when I reach your age."

"That gives you six more good years, Clara. I'm going back to bed. Good night."

As we amble back toward the bedroom, Sylvia says, "How can two people have such opposing feelings about this?"

"The difference is that Emma stayed in Cuba and Clara left."

"You knew Castro, didn't you?"

That's the last thing I want to relive or discuss with Sylvia right now. I nod. As I sit on the bed, she gives me a light, sweet kiss on the lips.

It takes me a while to get to sleep. I doze but am periodically startled awake as I find myself wake-dreaming. Fidel, dressed in a khaki-colored uniform similar to those of Batista's army, stands on a wooden box in the dirt driveway of a small, white-washed, wooden farmhouse on the highway between Santiago de Cuba and the beachside town of Siboney. Before him, over a hundred men, dressed in similar uniforms, although the uniforms of many fit them poorly and are wrinkled and stained, smile, grimace and nod their heads in interest.

Most of the audience appear to express a zealous interest in his words, as they shout in response and raise their arms periodically, while a few appear to doubtfully linger on the outskirts of the group. He raises both arms and proclaims, "Comrades, in moments, we will depart to attack the Moncada army barracks, with the intention of seizing control of the government. We may win, or we may lose, but in the end this movement will triumph. If we overcome, July 26, 1953, will fulfill what Martí aspired to. If we don't, the gesture will have set an example for the people of Cuba."

I jerk in the bed. "Louis. What's the matter?"
Where am I? What is happening? Who would pronounce my name Louis instead of Luis? . . . Sylvia. I orient myself. "I'm sorry. I guess I was dreaming."

My dream swerves from the driveway outside the farmhouse to Fidel's arguing in a courtroom where we were tried together, to his developing and practicing his speech denouncing Batista in his jail cell and later in prison—standing like a giant, in uniform, his riveting eyes, his endless speeches, his voice, high and almost melodic, echoing in the night air and then through concrete hallways, as he raises his arms and points his finger to the sky.
"Ow, Louis. That hurt."
"I'm sorry, Sylvia."
I look at the clock. Four a.m. Not wanting to disturb her sleep any further, I rise, slip on my slippers and move toward the door.
"Where are you going?" She sounds concerned, not annoyed.
"I'm sorry. I'm having a restless night. I'll let you sleep."
"Hurry back."
I trudge down the hall to my study, move papers on my desk, glance at the clock, and glance through my agenda for the meeting with my son six hours from now. I need to be alert then.
I grasp a folder with the label "Company Documents" and sit in my comfortable chair. I review and sign a stock certificate, by which I am transferring some of my stock in the law firm to my son, Franklin. Then I sign the stock power I've prepared to allow him to vote my shares in the law firm in the event I cannot.

I rise, hesitate a second for my equilibrium to catch up and take a couple of steps. I open the safe, pull out a folder with a label saying 'estate planning documents' and peruse my health care documents and durable financial power of attorney. I affix colored sticky flags to the front pages of those documents and various pages of my will and my trust indicating changes I wish to make.

Sitting again, I evaluate how the documents protect Sylvia and my children. I hope my children do not resent what I am doing for Sylvia, but if they do, so be it. I'm not trusting her livelihood to chance. I think Franklin will be more open to it than Elena will. I am also sure he will take care of our employees and clients, and the people of Cuba. I hope Franklin and the others grasp that I'm being so meticulous because I lost control over my own destiny too many times in my life. I cannot leave things to chance.

I also need to impart the evidence I have compiled that raises concerns about my law partner Braxton Doolittle, and Elena's husband Kalvin. These two menaces to the good reputation of the law firm must go. Elena will probably have a fit when her husband is booted out, but it is his own fault. I'm not so sure their marriage is going to last anyway. I've protected her in every way I can, but I cannot continue to let Kalvin create havoc in the firm.

I again consider Fidel's death. At our ages, death arrives and should never be a surprise. Every day one remains alive is a gift, and when life ends, it ends. I briefly consider whether there is an afterlife, a heaven, or not, and knowing something about Fidel's religious beliefs, I ponder his thoughts as he died and where he or his spirit may be now.

I also evaluate the feelings that people hold in relation to him. While he is hated by many who have left the Island, and his decisions affected my life and my family's lives very much, I am unable to take it personally or to hate.

I will never stop delivering remittances that Cuban people have inherited, my own gifts, and gifts I've collected from others, including members of the vocal and angry 'Cuban exile community' who would never want their identities known. Regardless of what happens with the government, the Cuban people on the Island are my people. My deliveries are vital to meeting the financial needs of those I can help.

Again, Castro's smooth voice swirls through the halls of the jail as he struts back and forth. "It was not the revolutionaries who were judged there; judged once and forever was a man named Batista— *monstruum horrendum!*"

Chapter 2
Sylvia Morales

Sylvia awoke and glanced at the other side of the bed. Empty. Darn it. He needs his sleep. Could these phone calls have upset him so? Could he be suffering over Fidel's death?

But how did he know Fidel Castro? Had they been friends, classmates, or colleagues? He loves his country, his Cuba, as he says it, but why won't he discuss it?

When she tried, always unsuccessfully, to pull information from him, she sensed bits and pieces of suffering. Because of his reticence to discuss his feelings, Sylvia had searched for information about the history of the country. She'd studied books and articles about trauma to the children who were sent to live with strangers in the United States on what people in the United States called the Peter Pan flights, and the trauma also suffered by those who were left behind.

She'd also read that the Cuban people who remained in Cuba had a negative idea about the flights. She'd read that they referred to it as 'Operation Peter Pan' and blamed the United States CIA for creating the false rumor that children would be sent to Russia, which lead to Cuban parents sending their children away. As a result of that fear, Franklin's parents sent him to a boarding school in Spain instead of to the home of non-Spanish-speaking strangers in the United States. Elena had remained on the Island without her father and brother for years. It was likely that all aspects of the separation had traumatized the entire family.

Sylvia flicked on the light and glanced at framed photographs of the family. The photo of Franklin, his wife, Diana and their son, Miguel showed strikingly similar faces of father and son. She studied a photo of Louis, dressed in a suit when in his thirties, looking thin and athletic, just like now, and just like his son and grandson. She studied the photo of her husband. Almost jet-black hair. Light skin. Strong jaw line. Dark eyes under strong dark eyebrows. Those eyes had pulled her in.

7

At this point, Louis' hair was thin and white. Franklin, a bit past sixty, still had strips of black among silvery gray patches. Miguel had a full head of deep black hair, looking much like Franklin in the photo from some years before. Other than some creases of the skin, the eyes of the three men didn't change with age.

She again thought of Franklin's attitude. He and Louis seemed to get along well enough together. Probably the distance she felt from Franklin was because of her marrying his father and being younger than he.

Two days before, at Thanksgiving dinner, Elena was surly, as usual, but Franklin was in good spirits. Franklin's wife Diana was fairly sweet, as usual, giving her a light hug. When Franklin's son Miguel swept into the kitchen, carrying little Alisa, he kissed Sylvia on the cheek, as did his wife, Jordan. Franklin's daughter Michele also kissed her on the cheek and gave her a half hug, as did Elena's son Pedrito as he entered with Elenita. At least the younger ones treated her like family.

At the table, while cutting and serving turkey, Louis said, "I remember our first Thanksgiving in this new land, struggling to figure out how to choose and prepare turkey and stuffing. We wanted to assimilate ourselves, to make the United States our country . . . to adopt everything, including this strange culture and this rather bland food."

Franklin said, "Do you know of a Cuban-American author and poet named Richard Blanco? In his book, *The Prince of Los Cocuyos*, there's a chapter called, 'The First Real San Giving Day.' Get it, 'San Giving' instead of 'Thanksgiving'? It reminds me of us that first Thanksgiving. I'd like to read an excerpt. I hope you won't mind just one bad word at the table, papá."

Louis granted permission with a nod, coupled with a half shrug.

Franklin smiled. "Cover the ears of the young ones. Blanco wrote that the grandfather looked at the cranberry jelly and said, 'What's this *mierda roja* for?' Blanco writes that he didn't know what it was either. Then the grandfather says, 'Well, it must be for *el pan*,' and he began spreading cranberry jelly on buttered Cuban bread. Then everybody did the same."

Silence surrounded the table for a moment. Then, Louis laughed, and the rest of the family followed suit.

Sylvia was embarrassed not to know what some of the Spanish words meant. She knew what *el pan* was. She whispered to Louis. "What did he say about the cranberry?"

He looked at her kindly and leaned in, whispering, "red . . . uh . . . uh . . . well, the other word is a bad word." He'd lifted his hands and grinned. "The grandfather asked what the disgusting red stuff was."

She smiled. Then, she realized that others at the table were silently smiling. Elena smirked. Did their expressions reflected enjoyment of what Franklin had read, or amusement that she knew little Spanish? She wasn't sure how much Spanish the younger family members knew, but she figured they knew more than she.

Sylvia was filled with memories of warmth and family comfort experienced in Thanksgiving meals and the remainder of the holiday periods of her youth. She pictured her mother, grandmother and aunts lovingly basting the turkey and preparing all the accoutrements, the aromas and love pouring from the kitchen and surrounding the extended antique dining room table, and her grandfather and later her father propounding expressions of thanks and good wishes. Sylvia had never thought about the fact that the beloved Thanksgiving holiday was purely a U.S. tradition that any foreigner would find strange.

Louis asked everybody to hold hands as he said grace, thanking God for allowing them to arrive in the U.S. Elena's cold and clammy hand in Sylvia's broke the spell of togetherness for Sylvia.

"Sylvia," Franklin said as he served himself seconds, "This turkey is very moist and flavorful. And the stuffing and gravy are delicious. Excellent meal. Nothing like our first experiences at cooking it."

Most of the others nodded and said something nice. Elena did not.

Sylvia said, "It's a joint effort. Your father makes the herb concoction, slides it, garlic and bay leaves under the skin and injects a liquid mojo into the meat. He also adds his magic to the stock and stuffing."

Franklin said, "In Richard Blanco's story, he also said the grandfather put the sauce of *el lechon asado* on everything, because the turkey was so bland and tasteless. But this turkey is perfectly moist and has its own delicious mojo."

She often asked Louis to describe the dwellings he visited on his frequent trips to the Island, what kind of food they were able to buy and how they cooked. He explained how the Cuban people suffer from lack of money to purchase many food items, and that they often cooked with old United States small appliances.

In his study hung photos of Louis and his family in the city where he grew up. She'd inquired about those locations and had gotten a bit of information. He would answer deliberately, with some hesitation in his voice and words.

She'd thought of asking if she could join him on a trip someday, knowing that in recent years she would have been allowed to do so under United States legal restrictions, but she knew his trips were work. However, she had her job at Abraham and Sons, P.A., and she was not sure she wanted to take vacation or personal time for such a trip instead of enjoying time with Louis that would be relaxing for both of them.

One day a few months ago, she said, "Louis, tell me, Cuba is a communist country, right?"

He nodded. "People describe it as communist or socialist."

"What's the difference?"

"It's complicated. There's not much difference."

"Louis, would a visitor recognize that it's a communist or socialist country?"

He looked at her. "Good questions, my love. You probably would not realize that it is not a capitalist economy. Raul Castro has made some changes, so it seems more capitalistic than in the past, but he says the changes are improving socialism."

She said, "I've read about how people left the country without permission, many by water, on boats and homemade rafts. For a time, that was quite common, wasn't it? Now though, people are allowed to travel and return, right? Do people still want to leave?"

"Yes, Sylvia, Cubans who have the money now can travel to various countries. Some still want to move away, but for different reasons than in the past. Generally, they want to leave for financial reasons, or to join family who have left. But even though Cuban people are able to travel and return home easier than in the past, the United States does not readily issue visitor visas to Cubans because once a Cuban arrives in the United States, they can become residents, according to the wet foot/dry foot rule."

She frowned. "I read that the Cuban government doesn't like the wet foot/dry foot rule."

"Correct. In their view, the Empire, as the Cuban government calls our country, encourages Cubans to leave their country by telling them it's better here, but when they arrive, they cannot find work in the area of their training."

She freshened up and walked toward the kitchen. She glanced into his study, where he sat with his eyes closed. She crept close, heard his deep breathing, glanced at the clock and decided not to awaken him. There was time before Franklin was scheduled to arrive.

Sylvia went outside, retrieved the two copies of the Miami Herald lying on the wet grass, one in Spanish and one in English, returned to the kitchen and placed both at his place at the table. The striking front pages contained only the word "DEAD" in the English version and "MUERTO" in the Spanish edition, each over a full-page photo of Fidel Castro, with the dates 1926 – 2016 at the bottom. A small notice at the top of the page stated that detailed stories would appear in the Sunday edition.

She removed food from the refrigerator, deftly cracked two eggs over sautéing red peppers, spread cream cheese and guava paste on toasted Cuban bread, and sliced bananas, mango and papaya. As the dark liquid began rising from the spout of the espresso maker, she poured a few drops onto sugar already in the cup, the Cuban way Clara had taught her, and whipped the slightly brown, moist sugar furiously. She poured the remaining espresso into the cup, which rose to a beautiful, light-brown foam.

Louis entered and kissed her.

"Good morning, Louis, my king."

"Good morning, my angel." He inhaled the coffee aroma, smiled, picked up the cup and sipped. "Mmmm."

Louis moved to the table and sat, staring silently at the front pages of the two papers. He flicked on the television, changed the channel to local news in English, opened the Spanish version of the paper, and ruffled and folded it backwards to prop it up.

He periodically glanced through the paper and back at the television screen. He grimaced at a video on the local news of a small band of revelers celebrating in front of Versailles restaurant on *calle*

Ocho. Sylvia always found the restaurant so calming when she passed men downing Cuban coffee on her weekly trek to purchase guava pastries for Louis. Now, the raucous crowd seemed out of place, reminding her of the craziness during the fiasco with Elian.

She delivered Luis' food and sat opposite him, watching his pained expression.

Chapter 3

Franklin Morales

Sweating profusely, Franklin returned from his morning run, snatched the newspaper off the dew-dampened lawn and entered the house. Late November and eighty degrees at this time of morning. As was his weekend ritual, he zipped around the kitchen, plating scrambled eggs and smearing an English Muffin with raspberry jam. He set them on a tray, along with espresso coffee topped with milk foam, and carried it to the bedroom. "Diana," he called into the bathroom. "Breakfast is here."

Picking at his food and sipping coffee, he saw on CNN in Spanish and Facebook that Fidel Castro had died during the night and that those of the Miami based 'Cuban exile community' had already taken to the streets to cheer.

He wondered what his father wanted to discuss this morning. A text message from Franklin's son popped up on his computer. "Dad. U hear about Fidel?"

"Yes." Franklin wondered whether Fidel's passing would have any effect. Each time he was rumored to be dead, this vocal and resentful group acted like his passing would cause collapse of the government, allowing them to return and resume their lives as they'd been before 1959. But now, with Raul as president for some years, and having made changes, some of which Franklin was not so sure adhered to Fidel's wishes, he didn't think much would change because of Fidel's death. He answered. "Probably nothing."

He could see his son typing. "I'm on FB chat with cousin Adriana in Havana and Luz in Santiago. They both say their mothers are sobbing."

"Interesting. But they aren't?"

"No. How's Abuelo taking it?"

Franklin didn't imagine that his father would react one way or the other. He'd never expressed any of the hatred that festered in so many 'Cuban-Americans' of Miami. "Haven't talked to your grandfather yet.

13

Going there in a few, but this meeting was already scheduled. It's not about Fidel's death."

Miguel said, "Pedrito and Aunt Elena went to *calle Ocho* last night to celebrate."

"Your grandfather would say that's a lack of respect."

Diana came out, dressed in tight jeans and a thin, bluish blouse. Her recent short haircut over her light-bronze, Latin features suited her. He still saw the remnants of the cute pouty-lipped look and twinkling eyes that he'd fallen for many years ago.

She leaned down for a kiss. "Remember, we have dinner guests. Can you pick up steaks and sausage to grill?"

"Sure."

"Give your father my love, babe."

Franklin clicked through various posts from Cuban-Americans and Cuban residents on Facebook, trying to gauge the feelings in the two locations. He went to the *Cuba Debate* Facebook page and found a running commentary. He saw that cousin Ignacio was online via WhatsApp. He wrote, "Ignacio, how are you?"

"*Hola primo*. I'm fine. You hear about Fidel?"

"Yes, I just heard. It was late last night, I guess. How are people taking it there?"

"Raul announced it about eleven. Many are taking it hard. My mother and sister are crying non-stop. They called your father. The streets are eerily calm and quiet."

Franklin wondered whether Cubans in Cuba were united in their feelings. Did age make a difference? Ignacio and his sister were about Franklin's age. Yet, Ignacio didn't seem so shaken up.

Ignacio was typing. "Has Trump said anything yet?"

"Trump? He's only president-elect. But that doesn't mean he wouldn't act like he's already president. He's probably tweeted. Let's see . . . . Yes, he did. Nothing nice about your leader, of course."

"I don't understand how you could elect Trump. How about Obama? Has he given condolences?"

Franklin didn't bother stating that he himself did not vote for Trump. He Googled for an answer. "Can't see that Obama's said anything yet. He's probably trying to find something polite to say that doesn't indicate our government is in favor of yours or that he admired your leader."

"Presidents from around the world are expressing sorrow and planning to come for services. We should have known the U.S. wouldn't. And those people celebrating. That's not going over well."

Franklin had mixed feelings about the U.S. government's hesitation to acknowledge with sorrow the death of a well-known international figure. He understood that some politicians believed it was vital to have the support of the vocal South Florida Cuban exile community. Yet, politicians also sometimes had difficulty pleasing that group, who were entrenched in the belief that the U.S. should do nothing to support Cuba or Cubans and that any involvement benefited the Castro government. Now, a great number of U.S. citizens wanted to see Cuba and had no concern at all about how they spent their money there and who might benefit from it. It seemed that presidential candidates in the past few months expressed somewhat contradictory views on the Cuban situation, Obama's normalization efforts and the Cuban exile community's beliefs. "Ignacio, do the Cuban people understand that we, the people of the U.S., do not necessarily share the stance of our government?"

"Franklin, your government, *El Imperio,* has always tried to rule the world and destroy Cuba. Martí pointed that out long ago."

"Not all of us believe that our country should rule the world."

"You tout the concept of democracy and the fact that you elect your leaders. So how can you not agree with your government?"

"Ignacio, our leaders are elected by a majority of the people, not all the people by any means. We do not all like or agree with what our elected leaders say or do."

"I know, Franklin. I'm just kidding with you. Your recent election shows your system isn't perfect either."

Franklin laughed. "I never said it was perfect."

Chapter 4

Sylvia Morales

Sylvia had reported to her husband that a young, pretty reporter named Yamila had arrived and was waiting for him in the kitchen. As she put the finishing touches on a *cortadito* for the guest, Louis came in, shook Yamila's hand and sat next to her at the kitchen counter.

Sylvia slid the tiny coffee cup and saucer across the countertop. Yamila took a sip and smiled. "Oh my God. This *cortadito* is more Cuban than they serve at Versailles."

Louis sipped his coffee. "Yamila, this is a surprise. I do not believe we have an appointment, do we?"

She hesitated and smiled, as her cheeks reddened. "I'm sorry, Sir. I was hoping you wouldn't mind. I did not have your home or cell phone number."

He frowned. "All right. I have a meeting in less than an hour. Let's get to the interview."

"May I record?"

Louis nodded.

"Mr. Morales, do you have an opinion about Fidel Castro's death."

"Hmm. An opinion? Let's see. In my opinion, he's probably really dead this time because all the news outlets say so and my family from Cuba said they saw Raul say so on television."

Yamila laughed. "I'm sorry. That wasn't a very good question. Do you have a reaction about his death?"

Louis looked at her, a frown on his face. "I have no reaction. He was old, and he died."

"Are you celebrating like other Cuban-Americans?"

Louis shook his head. "I do not believe in rejoicing any person's death. I understand that those who celebrate suffered loss and disillusionment after the Revolutionary government took hold in 1959. Hatred has festered ever since they escaped the Island. A Cuban on the island would be offended that I use that word, 'escape', but that's how the people who left Cuba in the 60's see it. They call themselves exiles,

16

as opposed to emigrants. They've been waiting for this day for a long time, expecting a significant change. Their children, who were born here, or came when they were too young to even understand, have heard their parents say, 'We will return to our homeland only when Fidel is gone.' Those people have waited bitterly for Fidel's death for all these years. I can only speak to what people in Cuba think. If you want to talk to the partiers, go to *calle Ocho* and interview them."

She smiled. "Understood. We'll focus on the Cubans in Cuba. Have you spoken to people in Cuba since Fidel Castro's death, and if so, can you describe their reaction?"

"So far, I've spoken only to my sister, who lives in Havana. She was very sad."

"Can you state how it is that you have recent knowledge of the people of Cuba?"

"As you know, I've been making deliveries of money to Cubans for about eight years now. I go every other week. I started doing that pursuant to a court order, allowing inheritances to be delivered incrementally to heirs of U.S. residents. Later, I began donating my own funds and what I receive through a not-for-profit foundation I created.

"Initially, I had to obtain specific authority from the U.S. and a multiple entry visa from Cuba. In 2010, Obama opened the ability to visit family members on the Island. Later, it created other ways that U.S. citizens could travel to Cuba, and this year, expanded it further."

She wrinkled her brow. "Don't Cuban-Americans frown on all visits to Cuba?"

"Yes, many are outraged that I travel to Cuba. These radicals say when a person stays in a hotel or eats a meal in Cuba or gives money to Cubans, he benefits Castro and the communist government. I say," he made quote marks with his fingers, "Should I let these people who have inherited money suffer because some think it somehow benefits Castro or the government?"

Sylvia had never heard her husband speak so passionately about Cuba or his trips there.

Yamila made a note and looked up. "Do you not believe your travels and delivery of funds to Cubans benefits Castro?"

Louis' eyebrows rose and dropped. "I don't stay in hotels, which are owned in whole or in part by the government. I sometimes stay with family. To do so, I must obtain special permission from the Cuban government, because it deprives the government of tax income. Everywhere else, I stay in private homes licensed to rent, called '*casas particulares*'. I pay about twenty or thirty dollars in their money, *pesos convertibles*, in shorthand stated with the letters 'CUC', pronounced as 'say oo say' or as 'Kū', each night and five CUC for breakfast. Staying in *casas particulares* helps the people. People who rent dwellings pay tax, but I understand it's nominal, and I believe it benefits the government less than staying in a hotel would."

Yamila tapped her pen on her white, perfectly arranged teeth. "I take it your trips will continue?"

He set his palm firmly on the counter. "I will not cease these trips, until I'm unable. The people are counting on me and deserve to enjoy the money they have inherited. Next week, I'm taking my son Franklin, to teach him what I do and where I go, and to introduce him to the people I visit."

The reporter nodded and jotted some notes. "Do you know if others share your sister's grief?"

Louis cleared his throat. "I've seen on one T.V. network a report that the people are very solemn, that a feeling of incredible loss permeates the country. That's what I hear from family as well."

The reporter looked pensive. "Why would that be? Is Castro not the demon he is portrayed to be, or did he somehow brainwash his people?"

"Perception. Indoctrination. Patriotism. Most Cuban citizens and residents have never known anything other than the current government. Many do not believe, as our country holds, that their previous lack of modes of communication, such as cellphones, e-mail and the Internet, was intended to keep them in the dark. Internet is still not very accessible, but at least now one can buy hours for a couple dollars and go to a Wi-Fi hotspot park to access it. That's still a lot of money for somebody who makes twenty dollars a month, but it is available. Cell phones too. The people think of this difficulty as just one more aspect of the common saying, *life is hard in Cuba*. And they believe much of their difficulties are the fault of the U.S. Embargo.

"Many people in Cuba, young and old, are extremely supportive of their government. As they see things, Castro did what he said he would at the outset of the Revolution in ending the graft and corruption of Batista. When asked about good things that Fidel Castro and his government created, the government and the people tout the tremendous efforts to equalize benefits among the races, the literacy effort, free, quality education, as well as the provision of excellent, free medical care for all people."

She wrote, while speaking. "Did the people embrace the change at the beginning?"

"Initially, the populace had great hope because they hated Batista. Some became disillusioned after the Revolutionary government took hold, because it changed more than they expected. Many fled, but many stayed and devoted themselves to helping the country achieve its goals. Despite the weak economy, Cubans on the Island believe to this day that everybody is obliged to do all they can to construct a better country through socialism. They expect the youth to support the country. Some criticize youth leaving the country, even for study, because they think they are abandoning the socialistic principles."

"Do the young people who reside on the Island strongly support the government?"

"Many do. Some criticize financial matters. Yet, even the youth who might complain follow the ideals of their parents, although not with their parents' fervor."

She looked at him. "Are you saying they do not believe their form of government is the cause of their poverty?"

"I do not believe the people in general believe financial difficulties are caused by the form of government. In addition to free education and medical care, the people pay nothing to live in their homes, and very little for utilities. There's no cable or satellite T.V., but they can receive a very good signal with a digital box, for which there is only an up-front fee. With the ration book, which they call '*la libreta*', their basic food supplies are provided for almost nothing. But generally, meat of any kind is rarely available in the stores that sell under *la libreta*, and household items, like soap and toothpaste are no longer listed there, and, thus, are usually quite expensive. As I hinted a few minutes ago, if you ask a Cuban living there, even a younger one, about the country's third-world economic status, the answer will likely be that the economic challenges are the fault of the U.S. Embargo, what Cubans call 'the Blockade', in Spanish, '*el bloqueo*'."

She frowned. "Our government and our news sources tell us that Cubans live in a very restricted environment, and lack human rights. We hear the prisons are full of dissidents who are outspoken against the government. What about human rights? People in prison? The *Ladies in White* being prohibited to protest?"

Louis nodded. "Many Cubans on the Island believe that human rights are very much honored in their country, and that anybody who is in jail is there for a reason. The government talks about human rights as a positive, necessary aspect of the government there. But most people in Cuba know little about people being detained unless they know protesters or have seen it happen. Those arrests are not reported news."

"Do Cuban people love their government and their country?"

"Cuban people love their flag and their country, whether or not they love their government. Politics and governments are one thing. A country is another thing."

The doorbell rang, so Sylvia left them, still talking, now of what Castro's death would mean, and whether it would change Raul Castro's handling of things. She opened the door to find Franklin standing there.

"Good morning, Sylvia. Is my father here?"

He was cordial, as always. Simply cordial. Nothing more. She took him into the kitchen where Yamila and Louis still talked.

Chapter 5

Franklin Morales

Franklin entered the kitchen of his father's home to find him talking to a woman.

"Hola, papá." He hugged his father lightly.

His father introduced them, saying she was a reporter who posted articles on an Internet news site.

When she'd left, Sylvia asked if he'd like coffee.

"Yes, please. A *cortadito* would be great. I stopped at Versailles, as usual, but there was too much activity and no parking spaces."

"Louis, would you like another?"

"No, thank you, honey."

Franklin always wondered why his father didn't teach Sylvia to say his name as 'Luis' instead of the North-American-sounding 'Louis.'

Franklin swallowed the coffee in one gulp. His father took his water glass and then ushered him into the study. "Son, I asked you to come today to discuss a number of topics." He pulled out his leather-bound notebook and opened it to a page. "The first topic involves my estate planning documents."

He set copies of the documents on the table. "These have been in effect since before I was married to Sylvia and before you came to work at the firm. They designate George Murphy to make the initial decisions about general health matters. But if it is determined that I am not getting better, or if the living will provisions are being considered, then you and another step in with him. The other person was Lansing Armstrong, God rest his soul. Roosevelt Harris is the alternate for anybody who cannot serve."

Franklin knew both Lansing and Roosevelt well, having represented them and their restaurant group, Roasted Oak Grill and Roasted Oak Holding Company, in many business matters. He knew that Lansing was one of the first to help his father when he arrived in Miami. Roosevelt was Lansing's trusted right-hand man, and the senior-most executive in the company.

21

"The originals of these documents were in Lansing's firm safe. His son, David, who is now a lawyer, has them."

Franklin nodded.

"I want to remove non-family members, and add Sylvia, so that she has a voice."

Franklin felt an instant distaste but fought it down. She had been married to his father for the past fifteen years and was obviously in it for the long haul. He managed, "Yes, I understand. I would have involved her even if she was not designated, but that's fine."

"I am replacing George Murphy partially because he's close to my age. I trust Roosevelt, but it's time to name family. I doubt that Elena could handle it. I'm thinking of naming you and Sylvia. I think a third would still be a good idea. I would name Miguel but having both you and your son involved might be seen as giving you two votes. I want to name Pedrito as the third person. I don't know how Elena will take it if I name her son instead of her. What do you think?"

Franklin could be jealous that his son wasn't named, but his father was right. This was the best way to keep peace. "Yes, papá. I think that makes sense. Elena would never be able to participate in a decision. Pedrito is a mature young man. You could name Miguel as an alternate for any of us if you wish. But it's your plan, and your decision."

His father nodded. "That's what I want to do. Name Miguel as alternate for any of the three so that three will serve together. Can you draft all my documents doing that?"

"Yes, of course."

"Fine."

"Papá, our trusts also now include a trust protector. I suggest naming Sylvia, Pedrito and me, but also add Miguel to that, so there would be four to make any changes on the vote of three of the four."

"I agree. Now, one more thing. I've learned some things about Braxton Doolittle and about your brother-in-law Kalvin that concern me greatly. I'm gathering documentation and reviewing facts to be sure I am correct. But if I am, we need to eliminate both of them from the firm before they cause further damage. I've put that documentation in a compartment hidden by a false back in the credenza in my office. Here's a drawing of where it is and how to open it."

"Papá, all this planning seems a little extreme for this particular moment. Are you ill? Is something going on I should know about?"

His father shook his head. "No, it's just time. I've been dilatory, like many lawyers, about my own documents. I'll be eighty-five soon and I don't expect to live forever.

"There's one more thing related to that . . . a stock power. I still own the great majority of the shares. I'm granting you a stock power to stand in my place in case I'm unable to participate. I'm also gifting you stock in the firm. Here." He handed the two documents to Franklin.

Franklin felt awkward receiving this gift and the stock power, especially in conjunction with all this other discussion.

"Next," his father said.

"More? Papá, you are making me very nervous. Do you have a medical problem?"

"I already answered that. Nothing has happened. I'm old and getting older."

"It's just that you've never brought up any of this before."

His father waved an arm, brushing him off. "You know about my trips to Cuba. If it's all right with you, and with Diana, I would like to take you late this week and three weeks from now to train you and introduce you to everybody I deal with there. If I am unable to continue to make these trips for any reason, or if I just decide to slow down, I need you ready."

"Yes, papá. I'll talk to Diana and clear it. She won't mind."

"If Diana gives her blessing, we will leave Saturday, December 3 and return Tuesday, December 6. We fly to the city of Holguín and deliver in the easterly region of the country. Two weeks later, also if you and Diana are in accord, we go to Havana for the same number of days to visit all the western provinces."

Franklin nodded. "Does the court order have to be amended to include me?"

"No. I haven't needed the court order since 2010. That's when the Obama administration opened the ability for U.S. persons to travel under what it called a general license to visit family. A general license means the traveler only has to make an affidavit. No application is required. The law says a U.S. person can visit family in Cuba if they are related within three generations of a common ancestor. Therefore,

23

you qualify as well. There are other licenses that fit what we do, but they require that you document how you spend your time, while the family visit license does not."

His father consulted his list. "I think that's about it for the day."

Franklin laughed. "You still have me concerned, papá."

They stood. His father put an arm around him. "Let's go tell Sylvia about the changes."

In the kitchen, Sylvia had spread out roasted pork, ham, Swiss cheese and condiments to make Cuban sandwiches. She held up a long loaf of fresh Cuban bread, wafting its aroma. "Can I interest you gentlemen?"

"Sure," Franklin said.

His father pulled out two bottles of beer from the refrigerator. Franklin took one. They helped Sylvia assemble the sandwiches. His father rubbed some garlicky oil on the tops and put them into a sandwich press. "Much better for the health than the butter they use in restaurants."

As they ate, his father said, "Sylvia, some things for you to know. I am adding you to a committee of people, including Franklin and Pedrito, to handle things for me if I pass away or become incapacitated."

Franklin was surprised that tears sprang from her eyes. "Louis, don't you even talk like that."

His father said, "I'm just updating, to involve you and family rather than others."

Sylvia frowned. "Is something the matter? Is there something you aren't telling me?"

Franklin said, "I asked that too. He insists that there's nothing going on."

"That's right, Sylvia. It's just time. I'm also taking Franklin on my next two trips to Cuba. At some point, I hope to slow down and, if he's willing, let him take over."

Sylvia smiled. "I would love to have you here at home rather than traveling those four or five days every two weeks."

Chapter 6

Elena Morales Lennox

Elena sat in the kitchen puffing on a cigarette.

Pedrito walked in. "Mom, why don't you quit? Or cut down. Or at least smoke outside. I don't want Elenita inhaling second-hand smoke."

She shot a hot glare at her son. "I don't smoke around my grandchild."

Pedrito scowled. "Yes, you do, Mom. And my ex says she smells it on Elenita and all her clothes. She's threatened to not let me bring her here anymore."

Elena scowled back. "You tell her mother I won't let any smoke come close to her."

Pedrito grabbed a beer from the refrigerator. Elena sipped red wine.

"Son, are we going out to celebrate again tonight?"

"Sure, we can. But mom, I've talked to my cousins. It seems people there are really sad."

"That's bull, Pedro."

He grimaced. "They say people are crying."

"Are you trying to tell me everybody in Cuba is sad?"

"Well, no. I saw a prostitute on a Facebook video who said her life is horrible, and it's all his fault. And I saw a guy standing in front of the art museum, *Bellas Artes*, saying he'd shown a lack of emotion about Fidel's death and had lost his job as a result."

Elena felt her insides sizzling. "Like the guy who lost his job said, people act sad because they have to. They don't believe it. When I was a girl, the CDR *chivatos* would report you if you said the wrong thing. We thought they could even read our minds."

"What's CDR, and *chivato*?"

"Committee for the Defense of the Revolution. There are national chapters, local chapters and one person in each neighborhood. *Chivato* means somebody who turns on you and reports you. Believe me, if those people don't cry and carry on, the CDR *chivatos* will report them."

"I don't know, Mom. The sadness of the people seemed sincere."

"That bastard. He took everything. They're brainwashed. Good goddam riddance. Now, if we could only get rid of Raul."

"Raul's made a lot of positive changes, Mom, and now that Fidel's gone, he's likely to continue."

She glared at her son. "You didn't live in that environment. Raul was right there from the beginning of the so-called Revolution that never ends. You sound like your grandfather. If you support the Castros, why are you coming out to celebrate?" She lit another cigarette, then looked at it, saying, "*mierda*," and walked outside. The smoke wafted into the room through the window. "Your grandfather is still going there all the time, putting money into the government's hands."

"The court ordered him to do that, didn't it?"

"Oh no. He *wants* to. He's treated like royalty there. Going in like a prince on a white stallion to save the poor people whose lives are ruined by their favorite dictator."

Pedrito turned from the window. She was sure he was rolling his eyes.

"Gotta go, Mom. I'll pick you up later."

Elena lit another cigarette, inside her house. Her house, where she could do whatever she damn well wanted.

Chapter 7

Luis Morales

Sylvia removes plates from the table and puts them on the countertop of the kitchen island. "Do you want to go to a movie tonight? It's Saturday, movie night."

"If you don't mind, I'd rather just stay at home. We can drink some wine and relax. How's that?"

"Fine. I know it's been a stressful day."

The phone rings. She picks up before I can say not to. She says something to the caller, hits mute and says, "Your brother in law. I never know how to pronounce his name . . . Clara's husband."

Sylvia holds out the cordless home receiver to me. I hesitate. I know what he'll say.

I take the receiver. "Hello, Humberto."

"So, how's the communist doing today now that your leader is dead?"

I want to use a bad word and slam the phone down. But I don't use such words. Disconnecting a cordless doesn't have the same effect as slamming the old kind of home phone. I know my blood pressure is rising, my pulse quickening. "What do you want, Humberto?"

"You aren't still planning to go down there as the great gift-bearer now that he's gone, are you? The government will surely fail now if you'll just stop injecting funds."

"I'm not addressing your faulty logic, Humberto. I'm going to hang up now." I press the red symbol to end the call.

Sylvia says, "What was that about?"

"Son of a . . . that man. I don't know how Clara puts up with him." My stomach flips.

She comes around the kitchen island, hugs me and kisses me on the lips. "Who could imagine that Castro's dying would cause tumult in your life?"

"I sure didn't imagine it."

27

"I know what you do for the Cuban people is very important to you."

"Next to you, it's the most important thing in my life. It's my purpose."

The phone rings. She looks at the caller ID. "It's Silvestre."

Even though he's an old friend, I'm not willing to listen to his diatribe. "Don't answer."

The doorbell rings. I whisper, "If it's for me, I'm taking a nap," and walk to the bedroom.

Sylvia comes into the bedroom as I lie sprawled on my back, fully clothed. "It was Pablo, smiling like a Cheshire cat."

I pat the bed as an invitation. She lies down and leans over me. "He stood, waiting, but I said goodbye and closed the door."

She leans down and we kiss. I hug her tightly. She is so even tempered, always pleasant, always smiling.

We lie together, dressed, for a good while. I don't know about her, but I drift off a few times.

I awaken to find her face above me, smiling. Her green, inquisitive eyes glisten. "Good morning."

"Is it morning?"

"No, I was teasing. It's about nine o'clock, still Saturday evening. Would you like something?"

"Only you . . . here," I say and pull her on top of me. Her hair smells delicious.

When we finally rise for dinner, I say, "I'm surprised we haven't gotten any more calls."

"I unplugged the phone and put your iPhone on silent."

Together we prepare an extravagant salad. Sylvia tops it with her homemade dressing, containing crushed ginger, honey and lime juice. She sears fish and scallops. We feast. No phone. No doorbells. Then, we clean up the kitchen together.

I pick up my iPhone, seeing that I've missed calls, texts and e-mails, but before I can click into any app, Sylvia struts up and snatches it away. "No. Absolutely not."

I put my hands in the air, indicating surrender.

"Louis, do you want to watch the news or skip it?"

"I could skip the news for the rest of my life. If it's not about Cuba, it's still about our election and our new president-elect and his alleged ties with Putin. For the rest of my life, I could instead do what I'm about to suggest. Let's have some sparkling water with that ginger and whatever you put in that infusion you made and climb into that giant Jacuzzi bath that we don't use nearly enough."

"Deal."

Chapter 8

Elena Morales Lennox

Elena and Pedrito stood on a street corner near Versailles restaurant, both waving Cuban flags and shouting, "*Cuba libre*," along with the rest of the crowd.

People banged spoons against pots and pans. Others shook maracas, rang bells and chanted. They waved small and large Cuban flags. Some wore the Cuban flag as clothing. Revelers had unfurled a large flag and carried it horizontally down the street. A man opened a bottle of champagne, spewing the cool liquid on Elena and others around her. The chant pulsated through the raucous group, over and over.

A hand grabbed Elena's shoulder. She turned to find an elderly friend of her father, puffing on a cigar. He leaned in and they shared kisses on cheeks. "Elena, *¿cómo estás?*"

She lit a cigarette from his fire. Sprinkling words of two languages, she answered, "*Hola*, Silvestre. *Muy bien, y tú?* Celebrating. *Gracias a Dios* that he's finally gone."

He yelled above the din. "*¿Y tu papá?* And Franklin? Aren't they coming to join in?"

Elena laughed at the thought of her father or brother's position on this activity. "Neither would ever be found dead standing on the streets to celebrate Fidel's death. They would not approve of sharing joy over this historic and joyous event."

"Have you talked to them?"

"No. Not since the death. I saw them on Thanksgiving. But I know them. They wouldn't come even if they did agree."

Silvestre nodded. "I know. I called your father, but he didn't answer. Did you see that article he was quoted in?"

"What article? No. I didn't know about it."

"A pro-Castro article encouraging readers to weep for the poor socialists."

Elena shook her head.

Pedrito returned to where Elena stood and greeted Silvestre with a hug.

"Mom. Let's walk up this way to be in front of the T.V. cameras."

The three marched along the street, all videoing from their cell phones with one hand while pulsing a flag toward the sky with the other. *"Cuba libre. Viva Cuba."*

A group of youthful dark-skinned musicians spewed out rap-style words in Spanish about the tyrant Castro being dead.

Silvestre said, "Elena, will your father continue to travel to Cuba? Will you go now too?"

"No. I will not go. Absolutely not. Not until Cuba is *libre* again. Not until Cuba is *libre.*"

"Your father is not well-liked because of his missions there."

"I know. He's an embarrassment. A total embarrassment!"

"We still need to fight. We need to continue the battle to rid our country of Raul, so we can return to a Cuba *libre.*"

"Yes. Yes. Yes."

"Cuba libre. Cuba libre. Viva Cuba. Viva Cuba."

At the next corner, a band played Cuban music of old. Elena danced with Silvestre in the street.

Chanting got louder. Then, they were in front of television cameras, waving and making more noise.

"I hope mi papá isn't watching this."

Silvestre said, "I hope he is."

Chapter 9

Luis Morales

Sunday, November 27, 2016
Before Dawn

After the bath, we enjoy together-time in our bed, which then leads to a deep sleep, for a while. Then, dreams of the past start seeping through. I start and relax, shudder and relax.

Crash, tinkle, tinkle, tinkle. I gasp and sit up. *Where am I? What was that?*

Sylvia grabs my arm. "Louis. Was that glass breaking?"

I glance at the clock. Four-twenty in the morning. I grab my robe and stick my feet into my slippers as Sylvia dons her robe. We creep down the hall. I glance at the phone, but it's still dark, as is the answering machine. Ambient light reflects on glittering shards of broken glass covering the floor.

Crash, tinkle, tinkle. Sylvia squeals and grasps my arm. A rock rolls across the floor and stops near the rock from the first crash.

I stoop down and move toward the rocks.

"Louis, be careful. Another one can come in."

Tinkle. Another narrowly misses me and crashes against the wall. I pick one up. Rubber bands are wound around the rock and a piece of paper. Sylvia grabs one of my legs and slides me toward her. I read the hand-written note aloud. "Morales. Communist. Stop making pro-Castro announcements in the news. Stop taking money to the communist government. OR ELSE."

Sylvia takes the paper from me. "What are they talking about? What did you say?"

"You were there when I talked to her. I didn't see what she published, but people get what they want to out of what they read."

I'm going to get pierced by glass if I keep moving like this. I squat and waddle toward the other rocks, grab them and return.

The notes are similar. I crawl to the phone, plug it in and wait for a signal to come up. I dial 911. "Hello, this is Luis Morales," and I give my address. "Three rocks have come through my front windows. They have notes with threats."

Soon, I hear several police cars arriving and a heavy bang on the door. I stand, walk to the door and open it. Numerous blue lights circulate and tinge the sky.

I back up as the young, dark-haired, Latino-faced officer sweeps into the room. He looks at me with what I take as disdain. In Miami-Cuban Spanish, he says, "Where are the rocks?" I motion toward the counter, where they sit, disassembled. He glares at me, continuing in Spanish. "You touched them all? You've ruined the chance of getting prints. Let me see a note."

I hand him the first paper I removed.

He keeps scowling at me. "You made pro-Castro comments? This week? How stupid are you?"

Sylvia pipes up. "Now, wait a minute, officer . . ."

I put up a hand to pause her and glare back at the man. I speak in English, because we are in the United States, where, even in Miami, English is the official language. "Officer, I did not make such comments. I called you here because somebody threw rocks at my house. I did not call you to debate about my beliefs or for you to insult me. Get out of my house."

He glowers at me. "You called the police, so here we are. You interfered with the evidence. You apparently brought the rock-throwing and notes on by making pro-Castro statements."

I place my hands on his shoulders, turn him and push him toward the door. He sticks a foot out, knocks me off balance, reaches one arm back and pushes me to the floor, onto the broken glass. He pulls out a device and aims it at me. Sylvia screams. My hands, legs and feet bleed from falling on the broken glass.

Sylvia runs to the door and yells. "I demand a supervisor. This officer has just assaulted my husband. My husband is the victim."

The officer pushes past Sylvia and marches out, bellowing, in English now, "I should arrest the old fuck for putting his hands on me. Battery on a law enforcement officer."

Two other male officers, one a tall African-American and the other a chubby Caucasian, come in and help me up. One radios paramedics. Soon red lights flash into the front room. Paramedics put me on a gurney, pull slivers of glass out of me, and cleanse and cover some of the tiny holes.

The Caucasian cop says, "Did you put your hands on the officer?"

I nod. "Yes, I did. He accused me of being the cause of the attack on me. I asked him to leave and he refused. He said I had called 911 and invited him in. This is my home. He was not making a report. He was making prejudicial accusations. I believe I have the right to remove a trespasser . . . any trespasser . . . from my home. And all I did was put my hands on him and turn him to the door."

Chapter 10

Franklin Morales

"Franklin", Sylvia sobbed, "Your father needs you. Please come."
Franklin shook off sleep and focused on the clock. After five a.m.
"What happened?"

"Three rocks with horrible notes crashed through windows."
Franklin could hardly understand her words. "Your father called the police, but an officer attacked him."

"A police officer attacked him?"

"Yes, can you come?" She sniffled loudly.

"I'll be right there."

Franklin turned onto his father's street. A number of flashing blue and red lights imbued the area with a surreal texture. Police cars blocked the driveway, so he parked on the street.

A cop had planted himself beside Franklin's car door, blocking his ability to open it. In Spanish, the cop said, "You're his son, aren't you?"

Franklin answered, also in Spanish. "Luis Morales is my father. Will you let me out of my car, please?"

The man remained in place, his jaw set.

Franklin switched to English. "Will you please let me out?"

Finally, Franklin started honking the horn and flashing his lights. He also dialed 911. A woman answered. "Ma'am, I'm trying to get out of my car to see if my father is all right after an attack. A cop is preventing my exit."

"Sir, you must abide by the police officer's instructions."

He spoke louder. "The officer is not instructing, ma'am. He's blocking my exit."

"Calm down sir."

"Oh, fuck it. Never mind." Franklin pushed the red panic button on his key fob, causing the lights to flash, the horn to honk and an alarm to sound.

Two other cops, one Caucasian and one Latino, approached the car. The cop blocking the door moved away. Franklin turned off the panic button.

"What's the problem, sir?"

"This guy wouldn't let me out of the car."

"Who are you?"

"I'm Franklin Morales, the son of the man who lives here. His wife called me and asked me to come over. She said a cop attacked my father. I'll bet it's the asshole right there."

The cops looked at the other one.

Franklin continued. "I had half a mind to shove my door into that asshole, but I knew he'd arrest me. Damn, man. Now, may I go in and see my father?"

The cops nodded and moved toward the other one.

Inside, Franklin found his father lying on a stretcher, being treated by paramedics. One worked on his knees. Another worked on an elbow. Another treated a hand. Spots of blood dotted the ground where broken glass was scattered. He looked at Sylvia, then took in his father's pale, sagging face, eyes focused on the ceiling.

Franklin looked at the police officers. "Has anybody taken a statement from my father?"

"You mean about the rocks. We don't need him to tell us."

"I mean everything that occurred, including his being attacked by a police officer."

The officers smiled. One said, "That's not the way we heard it."

"You have an obligation, officers, to take a statement from my father, to preserve the record. Who's the senior-most officer here at the scene, including inside and outside?" The tall black cop acknowledged that he was.

"Then, will you please take a written statement from my father?"

The senior officer nodded to the other man, who reluctantly began an inquisition of Franklin's father.

When the interview was finished, the black officer said, "Sir, we are not going to charge you for touching the police officer. Do you wish to file a complaint against him?"

"No."

Sylvia said, "Are you sure, Louis? That man was nasty."

Franklin's father said, "Yes, I'm sure. I have no ill will. Maybe this man will come to understand that there are two sides to every story. Nothing will be gained by attacking him for acting out his emotions."

Sylvia piped up, looking at the officer. "Sir, I believe you should write him up. This kind of attitude will progress if you don't check it."

Chapter 11

Luis Morales

Monday, November 28, 2016

After a rather tumultuous night's sleep, I wake on Monday morning determined not to talk to any reporter ever again about anything.

In the kitchen, Sylvia, in silk-like, light-blue, short-sleeved pajamas, grins and pops a kiss on my cheek. "Good morning, Louis." I smile at the way she pronounces my name, kiss her, sip my coffee and take in the news. Television news displays more videos of the action on *calle Ocho*. I switch channels. All the same. I flick the television off. Many of the articles and full-color photos in the newspaper are the same, quoting the Miami Cuban 'exile' group.

I find some articles in which Associated Press reporters have interviewed Cubans in Cuba and accurately described the sorrow of the Cuban people. I know a lot of people in the U.S., especially the Miami Cubans, won't read those articles.

I click on a Spanish news channel. Several men and a woman mope silently along the deserted sidewalk just across from *El Capitolio* in Havana.

Sylvia brings me food. She says, "I already ate, hon. I'm going to finish getting ready."

"So early?"

"Yes, we have an early staff meeting."

"I'm sorry I couldn't keep you as my secretary once you and I became an item, but Abraham sure lucked out. Anyway, I love having you here as my wife. So, the sacrifice was worth it."

We both laugh.

"Yes, you, Mr. Senior Partner of your prestigious firm, have a life of leisure and can stroll in whenever you want, play with a few papers, look important, flirt with the girls and leave when you want."

I grin. "You know I never flirt with the girls."

She smirks. "Yeah. That's what you said when you got me."

"Well, anyway, I'm glad you work because I would not want to leave you alone here today in case more crazies come out."

We kiss, and she exits the room.

I study an article about the foreign presidents and other dignitaries already arriving in Havana and review photos of crowds of people on the streets. I pass through the pages, read more articles, and then get ready for my own leisurely work, as Sylvia calls it.

I leave our home and drive through the historic Coral Gables area of Miami, past sumptuous, well-landscaped yards and nicely-kept, mostly older homes, then east along Coral Way, under the forest-green, oak-tree canopy, toward Biscayne Bay. I pass Latin American Cafeteria, and, as always, think of the *lechon asado, congrí*, and other true Cuban food I enjoyed during my youth in Cuba.

I turn north on Biscayne Boulevard, passing tall buildings on the left and the Intercontinental Hotel on the right. As I near the end of Bayside Park, I gaze up at the cupola over Freedom Tower, the tall building in which I was examined and processed before being allowed to stay in the United States, and nod, as always, just to say thank you.

I pull into the ramp leading to the parking garage of my office building and make my way upward, tires lightly squealing with each turn, until I reach my floor and my parking space, beneath a sign saying, "Luis Morales." I exit my car and walk toward the door.

"Mr. Morales."

I turn to find a man with a microphone rushing toward me.

"No." I keep walking.

"Mr. Morales, your words have caused quite an uproar. I'd like to delve further into your feelings about Castro."

"No comment." I rush through the door and into the hallway.

"But sir, you expressed feelings yesterday."

"I did not. I have no feelings about the subject." Then, I regret that I've said that much.

I enter the back door into the rear of the law office, pull the door closed and latch it. The employees wouldn't expect me to come in the back door. As I turn the corner toward the reception area, I see a man standing at the desk. The receptionist sees me and makes an odd facial expression. I slink behind the wall.

The man says, "I'll wait for him."

"Sir, you may certainly have a seat, but don't expect to go beyond this area."

My heart is pattering. Why did I grant that interview? I reiterate to myself that support of the Cuban people is my mission. I will not abandon them.

I nod and say a quiet "Good morning" to staff members and attorneys on the way to my office. They look at me questioningly since I am known to greet them with more gusto.

As I sit at my desk, Ruth places files into my in-box. I arrange my fountain pens and note pads and open a real estate transaction file from the stack. I glance at the calendar, noting that I have only one client appointment. It's wonderful at my age to have my son Franklin and other junior attorneys handling the workload and appointments.

As the sun glints off the water of Biscayne Bay outside the floor-to-ceiling window, I check my unread e-mail list. One arrives from the receptionist. "Mr. Morales, since I told this man you are not here, I also had to say that to a caller. Mr. Goyanes wants you to call him."

I'm aggravated that she didn't give me the phone number, but I suppose she was flustered. I use the legal computer program to locate it.

"Mr. Goyanes, please. This is Luis Morales returning his call."

"Hey Luis. What the hell is going on? What was that article about?"

I'm caught off guard. "It wasn't an accurate quote. It was an excerpt."

"An excerpt means you said it. Listen, I've been defending you here for too damn long. You take money to the Island. You represent interests that want to get rid of the embargo. You know the culture of this company and where ninety percent of the executives came from. I've fended them off you time and time again. Now, they've had it. You've lost this account. After all I did for you." The line goes dead.

I shake my head. I'm surprised they didn't do that long ago. But I'm tired of defending myself, of trying to explain how the people of Cuba suffer because of the useless embargo, and why I must take them money. The discussions always ended with his saying, "Luis, don't flaunt this. The executives of this company will not do business with you if you keep it up. I do my best to sweep your activities under the rug."

I always respond, "I'm not interested in hiding my convictions just for business. I'm sorry if they don't like it."

I peruse the checklist Franklin has prepared on a real estate transaction. He's correct that a dirt road bisects the property, but neither the plat nor the chain of title reveals an easement.

I buzz Franklin on the intercom. "Good morning, Franklin. Can we discuss the Wilkinson survey?"

"Sure, *papá*. I'll be right there." I smile. He calls me that when no employees can hear. It's common to hear Spanish and Spanish-accented English among staff members. But Franklin and I usually work in English.

"No, that's fine, Son. I'll go to your office."

I close the file, with the survey, title search and checklist on the outside, and stand. I think again of the reporters and others hounding me. My breathing intensifies.

After taking a couple of steps, I'm frozen by an intense ache constricting my chest. The agony deepens, into my upper back, like a boulder is plowing its way into me, while a vise squeezes my shoulders together. Burning pain radiates into my arm, neck and jaw. I perspire, shiver and shake. My vision dims. The pain squeezes my brain. I try to call out. In seemingly slow motion, I collapse to the floor. Everything goes black.

Chapter 12

Sylvia Morales

Rushing into the surgical waiting room at the hospital, Sylvia Morales found her step-son Franklin pacing back and forth. He looked up, anguish on his face. They moved directly to each other. She thought for a moment they might even embrace, but they both halted in an awkwardly hanging moment. He dried his eyes and nose with a tissue.

She did the same. "What happened, Franklin? Tell me, please."

"He buzzed me and said he was coming to my office. I heard a grunt, and then a thud. I rushed in and found him on his back, arms wrapped around his chest. His eyes were clenched shut, his face contorted in pain.

"When the paramedics arrived, they took action as though they believed it was his heart. But his face was distorted, and his cheek hung down on one side, so it may be a stroke as well. When we arrived in the ambulance, they rushed him back. Nobody has told me anything."

Sylvia dabbed her tears. "Did you call Elena? Is she coming?"

Franklin nodded, frowning. "Yes, right after I called you. She was hysterical. She knows where we are. I hope she comes."

Franklin and Sylvia talked, speculated, paced and wondered for hours. Then a man dressed in green scrubs entered. "I'm Doctor Mackey. I performed the surgery on Mr. Morales."

Sylvia sensed wisdom and years of experience in his eyes, visage and silver hair. "I'm his wife Sylvia, and this is his son Franklin."

The doctor grimaced and looked directly into Sylvia's eyes and then into Franklin's. "Your husband . . . your father . . . suffered a massive heart attack, caused by a complete blockage of the left anterior descending artery. We had to open his chest to create a bypass so the blood could flow. None was flowing from the moment of the attack until we were able to restore the flow. He suffered loss of oxygen to the brain, causing a number of significant cerebral accidents, or strokes."

Franklin and Sylvia peppered him with questions, which he tried to answer, looking back and forth between them.

Franklin said, "Doctor, was the surgery successful?"

"I deal with the mechanical process of the heart pumping blood. Other specialists address the brain and other parts of the body. Although we corrected the vascular blockage that caused the attack, that does not reverse the deprivation of blood-flow to the brain, nor the effects of the strokes."

Sylvia tried to grasp the depth of the issues. "Will he live? Will he recover?"

Dr. Mackey shook his head. "We can't say at the moment. There's so much swelling that it's hard to determine the extent of damage. A neurologist will have to assess the brain function and prognosis. It will take a while before the medical team can compare notes and issue any kind of prognosis. At this time, his condition is grave. Generally, visitors are not allowed in the Intensive Surgical Care Unit. Nevertheless, you may enter."

Chapter 13

Luis Morales

I jolt to alertness. Lying motionless on my back, I try to focus on the ceiling. Where am I? Is this my recurrent nightmare of the long days and nights in prison? Sickening pain. In my chest. In my head. Is that damn guard, *El Asesino*, my name for the bastard prison guard I despise, pressing on my chest?

No. That's not it. Ceiling tiles. Not 1953. Not the same texture or tone. Weight. Pushing me down. Heavy. Not human.

Discordant buzzing, clicking, humming, suctioning and beeping sounds bounce around the bare room. I can't seem to move my head or my eyes.

A bag of fluid hangs on a metal pole above me. Drip, drip, drip. In the periphery, I see a large square shadow, with little lights blinking. Equipment controls me. Wires and tubes lie on my skin. Something sticky holds contacts in place. I understand. I'm in a hospital. It's— what is it? 2016? Yes.

I fight to move an arm, a leg, a foot, a finger, my jaw, or my tongue. Nothing. I try to control my eyelids, to turn my eyes, or to move my head. Nothing. I tense. I struggle. I urge myself to move. Impossible. The hopeless vibration of panic takes over.

I try to swallow. I cannot. A hard object fills my mouth and throat. The convulsive urge to gag keeps pushing its way up my raw throat. Is the hard thing intruding into my body holding me in place?

Am I dying? Am I paralyzed? I analyze the pain in my chest and head, the numbness and tingling of my limbs. I cannot come to a rational conclusion.

Something presses on my chest, sounding like the pneumatic machine that inflates tires. With the sound comes violent, agonizing pressure on my chest. Push, push, push. Periodically, bands inflate and deflate on my legs, pressing and releasing. A heavy weight pushes down on my pelvic area.

I want to move—to stop the machines from pushing and holding me. I'm trapped. I tingle with alarm. Try to think. What has happened? A heart attack? A stroke? An operation?

Click. I look up to the plastic bag above me. Fluid drips, clouding my brain, making me woozy.

Machines pump life into me. My body chokes and sputters like a failing outboard motor struggling to impel a boat mired in a muddy river bottom. A lead weight feeling seems to push me into the mattress. A smell. A taste. Is it the medication, or impending death?

People murmur and chat in the hallway. The clatter of metal on metal reverberates through the halls and into the room.

Where's Cari? Cari? Where are you? Her face comes to me. Enticing lips. Sparkling eyes. Oh. Wait. Her face has shifted from youthful to aged. We aren't young lovers anymore. I see her on the bed, face wrinkled, facing the sky, just like I am. I'm crying. Yes. Cari, my first and forever love, is gone. Is she beckoning me? I feel an invitation. No, Cari. Not yet. Let me understand what's going on.

Oh, yes, I'm in a hospital room, alone. Nobody is hovering and worrying. Does Sylvia know I'm here? She must be terrified. I wish I could hug her, to tell her I'm all right. My sweet Sylvia. Her smiling face, reddish hair and light freckles. At my age, I should never have married her—so young. Why did I do that to her? Well, I didn't feel so old fifteen years ago.

I strain to remember what happened. One minute I was in my office. Then tiny, squeezed, extra-terrestrial-like sets of eyes surrounded by tan skin and varying widths of eyebrows, wrapped in mint-green cloth, looked down at me, as hands worked furiously. One of the alien-looking beings put something over my hair, as another inserted something into the tube leading to my hand, while somebody put a mask over my face. Darkness fell.

I awoke, in a fog, trying to understand, pushing and willing myself to move. My heart pounded like the rat-tat-tat of machine-gun fire, as I lay motionless and terrified. The more I tried to calm myself, the more afraid I became. I perspired, shivered and vibrated, while I could not voluntarily move anything.

Where are my children? I hope they aren't too concerned. I worry that they may be in a waiting room with Sylvia. Franklin and Elena

45

have always had such a strained relationship. And the two of them and Sylvia do not see eye to eye either.

I dwell on the decisions I made when my children were young. Was I wise to send Franklin alone to Spain and to leave Elena and Cari behind in Cuba while I tried to make a home for us here in the U.S.? Six long years apart. How they must have suffered. Is it any wonder the relationship between my son and daughter is strained? And of course, my marrying a woman younger than either of my children hasn't helped either. But I do not regret marrying Sylvia, so fresh, young and vibrant. My only concern is that I don't want her to suffer.

I felt so helpless when Cari lay dying.

I slide back to the day that I first came into the presence of the mesmerizing Cari at the beach, in a calm, protected waterway, right below our families' summer cottages. Later encounters and budding love while swimming there and across the inlet at Ciudamar Yacht Club bounce around in my memories. Then, in the cool water at Siboney Beach, where we were pushed around in the rough waves, holding each other, bouncing up and down as our feet tapped the multiple round, smooth, slippery stones on the bottom.

I dwell on the weekend—the interviews—the article—the harassment. Fidel's death means nothing to me. Does it? So how is that affecting me so?

What about my office? My employees? My clients? Will everything be okay in my absence? I think Franklin will hold the fort.

All the people in Cuba that I am scheduled to see. When? This week. Oh, no. I've got to recover in time for that. They are counting on me. I met with Franklin about going with me. But how could he go alone the first time? He may have to. Ruth will help him. Daniel has been driving me for so long he knows the route and people as well as I do. If I cannot make this trip, hopefully I can make Havana on the next round.

Is everything else set to operate properly? I think so. Whether I live or not, I have designated people I trust in my estate planning documents. I spoke to Franklin about changes I want to make. When was that? Oh, yesterday, I think. We haven't had time to make the changes, but it's all right. I think I can relax. Whatever happens, all is well.

Drip. Drip. I think calming juice is entering me. This time maybe it will take effect.

Chapter 14

Franklin Morales

Discomfited by the sterile smell, mechanical sounds and pumping of machines, Franklin held and rubbed his father's hand, across from Sylvia, who was doing the same with his other hand. He gazed at his father's gray skin and drawn-back cheeks and chin, seeking any sign of understanding or recognition. He supposed the heavy medication and brutal surgery had taken its toll, and hoped he'd improve as he healed, and the drugs wore off.

Sylvia cried quietly. Although he'd placed a hand on her trembling shoulder as they entered the hospital room, their constant unease with each other remained. He wondered why he mistrusted her so. Was his mistrust of her the cause of her attitude toward him? Were his feelings caused by her being not only younger than his father, but also ten years younger than he? Was it that Sylvia had replaced his mother in his father's life? She seemed to exude genuine concern. But was it concern for her husband or herself? He tried to think well of her.

Glancing out the window, he saw streetlights dancing in the dark.

Jittery and drained, he reviewed this morning, which seemed so long ago. Hearing his father's voice making that awful guttural sound and the thud as he crashed to the floor, Franklin ran, panicking, to his father's office, called 911, and sat holding him. Knowing his father would not want to be seen like this, he told the crowd of staff to return to their desks.

A man held a cell phone above them. Franklin jumped up and scrambled toward him. "Hey, who are you? Turn that off."

The man said, "Morales. I knew you were here. Would you like to make a statement?"

Franklin shouldered the man's chest, knocking him into the wall. Staff members gasped and moved away. Franklin grabbed the man's cell phone. "Delete it."

The man leaned against the wall, holding his chest. "Who are you? Morales junior? You'll pay for this." He looked at the onlookers. "Call the police."

Franklin located the video and deleted it, saying "Get this guy out of here." He knelt again beside his father.

Franklin was startled back to the present by a voice. Two uniformed police officers, one dark-skinned, and one light-skinned, stood at the hospital room door.

One light-skinned officer said, "A Mr. Oswald wishes to file a complaint against you for battery. Did you strike him?"

"I don't know anybody by that name."

"He says you struck him while he was at your office for an interview."

"I know nothing of an interview."

"Did you strike a man in your office this morning?"

Franklin clenched and unclenched his jaw before responding. He drew a deep breath and explained. "A trespasser entered the office without permission. I made him give me his phone, so I could delete the video he was taking of my father. I did not raise a hand to him. I have the right to protect my family, my employees and my property from an intruder. That does not constitute battery."

The cop looked pensive. "All right, we'll talk to the gentleman again and see if he wants to pursue it."

Franklin scowled. "That man was no gentleman."

The dark-skinned officer spoke for the first time, with what seemed like a Haitian accent. "Will your father be all right?"

"Do you know him?"

"Yes, he helped many in the detention center for free when we arrived in this country."

Franklin had heard the stories, but they never failed to touch a warm spot in his heart. "Hmm. Well, to answer your question, he had a heart attack and perhaps something more. His condition is very serious."

"May God be with him."

The officers left.

Chapter 15

Luis Morales

Something vibrates below me. I'm on a seat of a bus, heading toward prison with those convicted in the attack on the Moncada barracks. Fidel Castro sits shotgun, chatting up the driver and the guards like we are kids on a school field trip.

The bus stops several times along the route. As guards stand with rifles ready, five prisoners at a time are allowed to move just a few steps into the woods to urinate. I have trouble voiding under the pressure of being rushed and having rifles pointed at me, but I don't seem to be alone in that concern.

Eventually, we arrive at a small port, where a vehicle ferry waits.

A guard smiles. "Almost there. *El Presidio Modelo. La Isla de Pinos.*"

Castro announces, "A boat ride. See what I do for you men?"

A boat ride, in this bus, with these men, to prison. Great.

The bus moves onto the ferry. Deck hands cast off. Waves immediately begin banging the vessel. The hard bench beneath me pounds my behind as the chassis of the bus takes the rough sea. Most of the guards are standing on the deck, taking the pounding in stride.

Across the chop of the white caps, an island begins to take shape. Then we move into a calm strip of water and dock.

The bus pulls off the ferry, cruises along a road and turns into the prison grounds. We pass buildings on both sides of the front gate and then continue past immense, imposing circular structures. I glance upward, seeing fingers gripping bars and arms hanging through barred openings.

At the end of the large complex, the bus stops outside a low, rectangular building. The men roll slowly off the bus between two lines of guards with rifles. I look around, trying to determine if there's a way out. Although we are not handcuffed, we are in a large barren area with few trees, bounded by a high hill on one side. Even if I escaped the prison grounds, swimming across the rough water would be impossible.

I stand in line. Prisoners are processed one by one and directed through a door. I try to glimpse what is inside.

Finally, I am directed through the door and into a long dormitory with two rows of beds. Is this where we will be? Permanently? Not in those huge buildings we passed?

Men chat in small groups as I enter. "Morales," one shouts. "There." He points to one end of the row. "Last bed."

They will never consider me part of their group, since my lawyer argued that I was an unwitting non-participant in the attack. But many of them disclaimed involvement too. The only difference is that I really was not part of their plan.

Needing to use the toilet, I creep down the corridor past the beds and several groups of prisoners and look behind a half wall into the toilet and shower area. Men are sitting on the two toilets. I pause and lean against the wall, facing away from the beds where the other prisoners congregate.

Fidel's smooth diction seems to resonate through the room, drowning out the others' gruffer voices.

Chapter 16

Elena Morales Lennox

Words had failed Elena when Franklin called to inform her of their father's medical crisis. Shock and fear began deep within her and rose, taking hold and freezing her. Tears poured through squeezed eyelids.

"Sis, did you hear me?"

"Yes."

"I can hardly hear you. You must come."

"Where did it happen?"

"The office."

"Did you call *her*?"

"Yes, she's coming."

Elena hung up without a word. She found herself in the kitchen dumping Coca Cola and Bacardi into a glass. She cut a lime and squeezed it in. She lit and dragged on a cigarette, downed the drink, picked up the phone and punched in a number. "Pedrito, your grandfather has had a heart attack."

"Is he going to make it?"

"I don't know." Shuddering, she tried to hold sobs back.

"I'll ask to get out of work. And I'll skip my Bar exam prep class. Want me to pick you up?"

"No, you go and tell me."

Elena smoked a couple more cigarettes. She'd had the television on all morning. Now the news was showing crowds in Havana attending activities regarding Fidel's death. Black and white photos and videos of Castro kept popping up. "Son of a bitch. That son of a bitch," she said aloud.

She found herself dozing and waking. She shut off the television, made another drink and sat on the couch, stuck in the awful churn of worry. Fidel's voice kept coming to her from those long, long speeches the television always showed when she was young. Stressful memories of being stuck in Cuba as a child, left behind by her papá, haunted her.

She closed her eyes again and tried to relax.

The sun is just peeking past the curtains of her grandmother's large home. Her mamá is scurrying around, packing belongings into a cloth bag.

Outside, *tío* Alejandro is loading things into a car. Elena tugs at his pants leg. "Tío, where are we going?"

He kisses her. "An adventure, *mi sobrina favorita de ojos verdes.*"

She laughs at the constant little joke about her being his favorite green-eyed niece. "You always say that, tío. I'm your only niece with green eyes."

He musses her hair and laughs.

She and her mamá climb into the car with tío Alejandro, tía Yiyi, and cousin Amelia and drive out of Vista Alegre, to Nona's home. Nona, tía Clara, tío Humberto and cousin Berta are standing next to some large canvas bags on the sidewalk. Tío Alejandro and tío Humberto get out and cram objects into the car.

Berta comes to the car window, looking bewildered. She whispers, "Cousins, where are you going?"

Elena and Amelia look at each other and shrug.

"I don't know," Amelia says.

Elena watches her uncles loading the car. "Mi mamá says to see mi papá. Tío Alejandro says it's an adventure. Aren't you coming?"

"No, only my father."

Tío Humberto kisses and hugs Nona, Aunt Clara and Berta and gets in the front seat of the car. Everybody weeps. Amelia and Elena share a look. Amelia looks as frightened as Elena feels.

Tío Humberto says, "I'll send for you. Don't worry. You'll join me soon."

As the car moves away, Elena watches Berta, standing with her arms around her mother's leg, bawling. Amelia grabs Elena's hand and gazes into her eyes. Elena is sure her eyes reflect only fear.

Tío Alejandro drives out of town and along the Siboney Highway. Elena looks out at trees, roadside stands and homes she recognizes from when they've driven along the same road to swim at Siboney Beach. The sun peeks between points of the hills to their left. As they roll along the road, her uncles keep glancing around, looking nervous.

How could we be going to see my father? Where could he be? Where could we be going? And why? If we do find my father, will we go with him, or then return home alone again?

Just before Siboney Beach, her uncle turns to the left and travels along another highway, with a sign that says *Baconao*. The sun, now shining through the windshield, begins to brighten the vegetation and rocks on the mountains to the left. After a while, the highway veers downward, close to the water and then along the coast.

A few minutes after passing a sign indicating the distance to the city of Guantánamo, on a stretch of road where trees and bushes separate the highway from the water, her uncle pulls to the right and stops on a sandy area. Both uncles again glance around. Then, the car bounces along a path of white sand, between trees and bushes, jerking to avoid exposed roots and ruts in the ground.

Eventually, tío Alejandro parks. The adults tug supplies out of the trunk and carry them to where blue water slaps the white sandy shore.

Her uncles yank palm fronds off a flat contraption of inflated inner tubes, canvas and worn wood, all tied together with rope.

Elena watches, bewildered and afraid. Are they really going into the ocean in that flimsy thing? Where will she find her papá? She shivers.

The men tie more pieces of wood onto the structure. Elena's mother cuts canvas bags into pieces with a machete and sews them to what is already attached.

Amelia and Elena sit on the ground, glancing at each other from time to time, as they pick up and crack dry, brown leaves and drop the remnants to the ground.

The adults struggle to insert a wooden pole into a knothole in one of the pieces of wood. Finally, they jam it in and quietly cheer.

As the sun rises and heats the sand, the adults lug the raft to the shore and place it into the water. The men help Elena's mother, her aunt, and the girls onto the raft. They trot into the water, pushing the raft and tripping over rocks. Finally, they leap on from different sides. The men pick up poles with flat pieces of wood tied on the bottoms and paddle.

Against a strong current and wind, the grown-ups battle the sea, trying to fight their way away from shore. Sweat pours down the men's faces and soaks their shirts.

The sun climbs. A large tanker and a freighter creep along on the misty horizon.

Elena's aunt says, "We must get clear. We are going to be seen and reported."

As the men continue struggling, the waves intensify. They try to catch wind with the make-shift sail, but the current pushes the raft back toward the shore.

"Watch the swinging boom," says tío Alejandro. Everybody ducks repeatedly as the long cylindrical wooden piece that holds the sail taut violently swings to and fro. The women yank the sail back down.

Her uncles paddle desperately. But it's a losing battle. The wind, waves and current force the raft toward shore.

Trembling, Elena and Amelia grasp hands.

Tío Alejandro says, "We must get away from shore. We must find a favorable current."

They struggle harder, trying to increase the distance from shore.

Tío Humberto says, "*Caramba*. This is a bad day."

The waves pick up in size and intensity. Elena's mother works to retie loose knots. Blood from cuts on her hands smear the ropes.

The shore keeps appearing closer and closer. The men groan and paddle harder.

Elena huddles with Amelia. Water splashes through gaps in the fabric and soaks their clothes. Elena's entire body seems to vibrate, from fear, or from the battering of the raft, or both.

Tío Humberto's paddle separates from the pole. "*Mierda*."

The raft spins. Tío Alejandro holds the lone surviving paddle straight off the stern, trying fruitlessly to control the direction.

Tío Humberto says, "We're heading in. There's no way avoid it. Look. Rocks ahead. The raft will break apart."

Amelia and Elena look at each other, wide eyed. Elena shudders. Her tears blend with the ocean water splashing her face.

Elena's mother points to an area of beach. "There's a little sand there, and the waves are smaller. Try to get there."

Tío Humberto nods. "Steer to that beach. Swing the paddle from left to right. Harder. Harder."

Tío Alejandro can't control the raft.

Waves break over them, pushing the raft faster. The ropes keep coming loose and hanging limp. Pieces of wood rattle and bang together as the raft rushes toward shore.

Two pieces of wood snap together, pinching the skin of Elena's arm and cutting her. The salt water burns the wound. She puts her hand over it and cries silently, watching the torment on her mother's face and on the faces of the others. Amelia looks at her with horror in her eyes.

Nearer and nearer to shore, large waves crash and rumble in front of them. A wave grabs hold and pushes the raft into the churn. The raft roars down, hitting bottom with one corner.

Suddenly everybody is flying in the air. Time seems to stop. Amelia and Elena hug as they hover and fall. Elena worries she'll hit the rocks just under the surface, breaking her head open or shattering bones. How should she hit the water? She releases Amelia, but Amelia clamps on tight. They hit the water hard and roll. A wave smashes them down to the hard bottom, but it's mostly sand. Elena's foot hits a rock. She struggles to stand. Her head and shoulders break out into the hot air. She coughs. The inside of her throat and nose burn.

Pieces of wood patter and bang as the raft separates. Some planks are still attached by torn pieces of canvas. Pieces of the raft float all around.

"Elena," shouts her mother.

"Here."

Amelia's mother shouts. "Where is my Amelia?"

"I'm here, Mamá."

Tío Alejandro swims over and grabs Amelia. Tío Humberto takes Elena's hand.

Amid pieces of broken wood, deflated tires and supplies, they wade to a small patch of sand surrounded by sharp rock formations and collapse. Everybody weeps, even the men.

Elena awakened, soaked in sweat. Where was she? On the goddamned couch. She jumped up. That nightmare again. She grabbed a cigarette and flicked her throw-away lighter. In spite of her shaking hands, she finally lit up.

What the hell time was it? Shit. Pedrito's ex, the bitch, would arrive in minutes. She waved her arms to rid the air of smoke remnants, turned on the big fan, opened the windows, sprayed Lysol and went to brush her teeth.

Uncomfortable feelings churned through her midsection and her mind. Why did she resist seeing her *papá*? Did she love him or not? If he hadn't left her and her *mamá* alone, they wouldn't have tried to leave on that damn raft. But that wasn't fair. It wasn't his fault. She found herself crying. She grabbed a cigarette. No, the bitch would walk in and catch her.

She thought again of going to see him. She couldn't stand the thought of him dying without a last visit. Yet, she didn't want her brother or her stepmother, or even worse, both together, scrutinizing her words and actions. She called the hospital.

"Patient Information, how may I help?"

"My name is Elena Morales," She intentionally omitted her married last name. "My father, Luis Morales is a patient. Can you tell me his condition?"

"Let me look." After a few minutes, the woman said, "We have no condition yet."

Elena trembled. A vibration overtook her. She should have gone to the hospital. She should go now, shouldn't she? No, she could not. She would not.

Chapter 17

Luis Morales

"Morales. *Pendejo*. Answer." The jeers of the other Moncada prisoners echo in my brain.

Flat on my back, I gaze into the eyes of *El Asesino*, as he presses on my chest so hard I cannot answer. I know why the other prisoners deem me to be the enemy, but why does this bastard prison guard favor them and persecute me?

At the other end of the long, foggy barracks, near the showers, the other Moncada prisoners congregate, all facing me.

"*Coño,* Morales. We want to eat. Say you are present."

In the middle of the group, Fidel Castro stands tall and statuesque, illuminated like a shrine by light from the window above him. His melodic voice seems to emanate from all sides. "Morales. Be a comrade for the Movement for once. Just say you are present so the men can go to the mess hall."

The others' voices reverberate. Then, Fidel's comes through again, drowning them all out. "Come on, Morales."

I struggle to get enough breath. "*Presente.*"

The weight doesn't leave my chest, but *El Asesino* is gone.

Medical noises return. I'm cold, wet with perspiration. I try to move my eyes or head again, but I can only see the blurry ceiling above. I try to break through the fog and understand.

I again push and will myself to make some limb, some digit, my lips, my eyes, or anything move. Here, in the hospital, in Miami, just as trapped and lacking control as I was in the prison.

I need to calm down, to slow my breathing. Concentrate. How can I do that with that machine pumping me? I feel that I'm taking shallow breaths more rapidly than its steady pump. Does that mean I am breathing on my own?

El Asesino forces himself back into the nightmare I've suffered so many nights of my life. The pain in my chest continues, but he's not pushing. My thoughts are vacillating too rapidly. It must be the medication.

Voices rumble from the far end of the barracks. "*Carajo*! Why does this bastard Morales, who disavowed us in trial have to be here?"

A couple of them amble down the barracks pointing at me. "Send him to the general population. Not here with us. Or put him in solitary."

Yes, please, I silently bid. Send me to solitary permanently, to be in peace. All alone in the small, quiet cell, adapted from a closet, on the other side of the courtyard. Anything, anything to be away from these thugs.

Fidel passes the men and sits on my bed. "Morales, I know you never intended to be involved with us. I'm sorry it ended up badly for you." He raises his voice. "Men, he's not the enemy. Give him a break."

The others turn back.

The fog lifts briefly. A young, blonde, female nurse takes my vitals. A dead weight is pushing me down.

I feel Sylvia's hand rest on my left wrist. She smells of Shalimar. Franklin clasps my right hand. They sniffle. I sense no tension, at the moment.

Chapter 18

Sylvia Morales

Sylvia sat with her husband as a nurse inspected contacts of electrodes, took his pulse and blood pressure and wrote in a chart.

She looked at the nurse's name tag. "Hi, Felicia. I'm Sylvia, Louis' wife. Do you know the results of the neurologists' examination and when they are doing more tests?"

"Uh-uh."

"There's nothing in the chart?"

"Nope."

"I'm seeing movements and reactions. Are you?"

The nurse scowled at her like she was crazy. Sylvia decided that either she or Franklin needed to try to gain information at the nurses' station. He might have more pull.

She wondered what Louis was thinking, if he was able to think anything. She expected him to squeeze her hand and bust out in that special grin that spread from his lips to his dimples and extended to the laugh lines at the corners of his eyes.

She allowed her mind to wander back to when she'd moved to the large, metropolitan city of Miami years ago, after landing a job as a paralegal with Louis' law firm. Living throughout Florida her entire life, the largest city she'd worked in had been Cocoa, some three hours to the north. She'd gasped with delight upon reading the engagement letter, which stated that she would be the personal legal assistant to Mr. Louis Morales, Esquire, founder and senior partner of Morales and Doolittle, P.A.

She thrived in the new environment, laboriously pouring out his dictation, creating his files and getting to know his clients, habits and beliefs. She was confident that he felt as fortunate to have her in the position as she felt having landed the job.

Toward the end of her first month of work, Louis appeared at her desk late one afternoon as other employees were leaving. She could not identify his facial expression. "Ms. Woodruff, may I see you a minute?"

He moved to the threshold to his stately office, held his hand out like a maître d', and beckoned her to enter. He shut the door behind them, walked to the front of his desk and turned the two client chairs to face each other. He motioned for her to sit as he sat opposite her.

This informal gesture was completely out-of-character for Mr. Morales. Despite the informality, all she could imagine was that she was about to be fired. As she tried to figure out what she could have done to displease him, her mind raced through her work and their interactions. She always tried to perform her work professionally and perfectly. She was certain that he found her work and her behavior exemplary. But something had to be wrong. She simply could not imagine what he could have found unsatisfactory.

She sat, rubbed her palms on her pants and squeezed her hands between her knees, waiting for the dreaded words. Realizing she was staring at the floor instead of making eye contact, she forced herself to look up at him, but as she did, he diverted his eyes.

The stern, all-business boss to whom she was accustomed, fidgeted and avoided her look. She guessed he didn't like firing or disciplining employees.

"Uh, Ms. Woodruff, I have a dilemma."

Again, she caught herself looking at the floor, looked up and found his eyes darting back and forth.

"Ms. Woodruff, I'm not sure exactly how to say this." Now, he was the one rubbing his palms on his pants legs. "Um, I wish I had met you before you worked here."

Beads of perspiration emerged at the top of his brow and above his lip. She wondered why he would act like this if he were firing her. But why would he say he wished he'd met her before? She wasn't sure what he was thinking.

"Ms. Woodruff, this may be completely out of line, and I apologize in advance." He cleared his throat. "Here it is. I would like to invite you on a date, but I never, ever date employees. I don't know if you'd accept dating me or not. I don't know whether you'd consider a second date if we had a first one. I don't want to put you in fear of losing your job. I don't want to make you uncomfortable or put any pressure on you, one way or the other. But I also don't want to do nothing. I don't want to be silent and regret it."

He stopped, looked down and then back up at her. She was relieved, although shocked. An invitation to go on a date with him was the last thing she'd expected. Notwithstanding his stern-looking eyes and grim frown, she now was seeing a soft side. She'd never even considered a personal relationship with him, but she did find him handsome and distinguished, with an air of elegance.

Now, he looked like a nervous school kid, anxiously waiting for permission to do something. She didn't know what to say.

He said, "I guess I haven't asked a question. Since I don't see horror on your face, here goes. Would you consider having a meal with me at a private yacht club? You would not be likely to see any other employee there."

Although still speechless, she managed to nod and listen to the details of when and how they would meet. "Yes, sir."

"You can't call me 'sir' on a date."

"Well, uh, Mr. Morales, you probably should not call me Ms. Woodruff on a date."

They both smiled.

At the dinner, he said, "What would you like to drink?"

She shrugged, unsure if she should order a drink, or wine, or something non-alcoholic.

"Do you drink wine?"

She nodded.

"What do you like?"

"Well, I'm not a connoisseur or anything. I like Chardonnay."

He smiled.

She tried to discern his attitude. "I suppose you drink something more elegant."

He grinned. "I'm not a wine snob. But if you'll indulge me, I'll order a bottle of something similar to the taste of Chardonnay and we'll see if you like it."

She'd only been in a couple of restaurants where the sommelier had pulled the cork, given it to the customer to sniff, poured a touch into the glass and waited as the customer swirled it, took a sip and nodded approval. She'd thought the whole production was a bit odd, but Louis seemed to like that ritual.

They both tried the wine. She found its light, smooth flavor much more desirable than any wine she'd ever tasted.

As she studied the menu, he said, "Do you like seafood?"

She nodded.

"Do you like lobster?"

She nodded. "I'm embarrassed to admit I've eaten lobster only a few times in my life. I'd rather have something light. Fish or scallops or something like that would be fine."

He pointed out seafood items on the menu, one of which was broiled mackerel with scallops and shrimp. He said, "They cook it just enough, not over-done. They toss a splash of white wine on it. It's superb."

She nodded and put her menu on the table. "Perfect."

He grinned. She gazed into his eyes, which now appeared kind, cheery and devilish. His frown was replaced with a constant half smile.

As they ate Caesar salad and then the main course, he gazed into her eyes and asked insightful questions about her family, early life, schooling and prior work. The brownish-greenish hue of his lively eyes riveted her. She did not feel that he was prying or testing her. He listened. He watched as she answered. He responded. He paused and thought. He asked more questions.

She couldn't recall anybody ever spending so much time and effort trying to know her. She felt as though she'd left the mundane earth and glided upwards, buoyed by his words, his interest and her growing feelings for him. She wondered what such a man could possibly see in her, an unsophisticated woman who knew nothing about fine wine, fancy food or even which kind of fork was used for which type of food. She even thought the fish knife was a bread knife, until he gently advised her.

By the time her mango sorbet and his decadent, molten chocolate cake arrived, she'd begun to think she could enjoy spending a lot of time with him. Then she felt silly and immature for even thinking that. One meal with a man, and she was thinking of a lifetime. Ridiculous. But then she'd get pulled into his eyes again.

When they finished, they walked together along the wooden, oily-smelling docks of the yacht club, as boats stood still, or rocked gently, with occasional tiny slaps of water hitting wood. He stopped walking, took her hands and turned her to face him, again looking like a scared school kid. She felt like one too. He said, "Would you permit me to invite you out again?"

"Oh, yes. It was a beautiful dinner. I enjoyed your company very much." She was embarrassed by her sudden, overly-enthusiastic response.

Sylvia was startled by Pedrito and Miguel, Louis's grandsons, entering the hospital room, looking shaken. They acknowledged Sylvia with nods. She stood, pointed to her chair and the one across the bed. "Please, take a seat and be with him. Talk to him."

She went out into the hallway, where she found one of Louis' doctors. "Excuse me, Dr. Orwell, may I speak to you for a moment?"

The extremely young man stopped and whirled around.

"I wanted to ask you about my husband's condition."

He looked surprised. "Yes?"

"Well, I've been wanting to learn what's happened to him and whether he'll get better."

He paused, pursed his lips, looked away and then back at her. "I'm afraid you're not the designated health-care decision maker."

She glared at the man. "Has anybody with authority talked to you?"

The young doctor looked around, as though seeking help.

"Look, Dr. Orwell. I'm his wife. I am the one who should be consulted."

"I'm sorry, but I'm unable to discuss this with you," he said and marched away.

Chapter 19

Luis Morales

I wake from a slumber and take in my dark hospital room. I again try to move my head and my eyes, wanting to see more of my surroundings. Were my eyes closed when I slept, or are they fixed in the open or partially open position?

I have two different hands on me. Who could it be? Elena? No. I hear voices. Pedrito and Miguel. Speaking English. Fine boys. Smart boys. As they've just graduated from law school and will likely pass the Bar exam on the first try, we will soon welcome them as members of the firm. I suddenly remember how disenchanted I was when I realized that my first U.S. law firm employer was planning to make only family members partners, but now I have the same intentions. I need to rid the firm of Doolittle and Kalvin before they join.

My thoughts are muddled and slow. Everything feels heavy—my body, my arms, my legs, my head, my eyelids and my brain.

I doze off again.

I move vegetables around on the heavy, white plate at the dark-wood dinner table in our home in the Vista Alegre neighborhood of Santiago de Cuba. My father lights a cigar.

My younger brother Miguel hasn't eaten much of his meal. Eyes fluttering, he keeps glancing at our parents and then fixing his gaze on his plate. I'm wondering whether he's in trouble. He looks like he's working out a plan. He sighs.

Finally, he speaks. "Papá, I am joining a group that has splintered from the Ortodoxo Party. I am committing to the new revolutionary movement to make Cuba a better place, with new leaders. Batista has turned out to be worse than Prío."

Enraged, our father's fist bangs on the table. "How dare you! Fulgencio Batista is our friend. He's eaten meals with us right here at this table. My company and President Batista are arm-in-arm. What do you know of government? Of political parties? What do you know of revolution? You are a naïve teenager."

My brother cowers just a bit. His voice drops. "The people of Santiago de Cuba are discontented. Your Batista government oppresses us. The new party is strengthening."

My father bangs his fist again. I jump, in my mind, at the table at that time, but not in reality today.

Our mother looks around nervously, gathers some dishes and takes them into the kitchen.

My father's voice rises with each exchange. "Why do you think we need revolution? What is wrong? Nothing. We are a strong country. We raise sugar. We raise tobacco. We have active nickel mines. People from all over the world come to play in our casinos and enjoy our fancy hotels and nightlife. The products and the tourism support us."

My brother's voice starts to strengthen again. "You would mention sugar, just because it's your business and where grandmother's money came from. If everybody is so happy, why are there riots?"

My father sneers. "You exaggerate. When have you seen a riot? I think never." He looks at me. "Luis, weigh in on this. Tell your brother he's wrong. Have you ever seen a riot?"

I stay quiet. Politics and loud voices do not appeal to me.

My brother's jaw is set. "We work for *los habaneros*. The people of Havana take advantage of us. They have all the money, all the political clout."

This time when my father bangs, the coffee cup and saucer rattle together so hard I think they will break. "That is not true. A strong part of the government is right here in Santiago. What do you truly know about the party to which you profess your faith? What do you know about revolution? Do you even know anything about the youngster who's behind the new party, this Castro boy? What is he? In his twenties? He's just become a lawyer. He's always been rebellious. Luis, Castro graduated from colegio Dolores. Have you heard anything about him at the school?"

I shake my head no.

My father continues. "According to administration of the Dolores school, he was troubled. He wasn't well-thought-of. His mother was a maid. His father married her long after his birth. He was an outcast because his father was *nouveau riche*, so he did not have the same cultural background as the other students. He was a rebel. He never wore a tie, which is strictly against the rules. Is it not, Luis?"

I nod.

Our father is now consistently pointing a finger at Miguel. "That boy deliberately developed his speaking skills to get beyond his troubles. He took charge of everything in school. He was the organizer. That gave him a name. As an adult, he promotes and somehow maneuvers himself to the forefront. His popularity is not natural. He creates it."

My brother glares at my father. "His oratorical skills make people pay attention." His voice rises. "Of course, he's different. Yes, he is a rebel. That's what we need. A rebel who will fight against the corrupt government."

My father glares back. "This group you want to follow consists of a bunch of uneducated, disenfranchised young people, following a gangster."

"He's not a gangster," Miguel shouts. "And his followers are students."

Our father bangs his fist again. "No, they are not. Very few are students. Castro attracts socially marginal, angry, alienated young people he can mold."

My brother shakes his head passionately. "Words, words, empty words. This country needs honest government, economic independence, political liberty and social justice. The Ortodoxo party has said it promotes these things, but it is weak. I am part of the group that separated from it."

Our father stands and leans on the table, looking directly into Miguel's eyes. Our mother opens the kitchen door slightly, peaks into the dining room and quickly retreats. I'm thinking our father may be about to strike my brother. "He broke away from the party only because it would not support him as a candidate for the National Assembly."

Miguel continues. "The group broke off because Fidel Castro is a revolutionary. He is against graft and corruption."

My father laughs deeply. "He said those words just to try to get the support of the full Ortodoxo Party. Even the communist newspaper ridiculed him. Chibás himself called Castro a gangster and a deceitful, resentful bully."

My brother glares at my father. "I believe in the Revolution that is going to come." He marches out of the room.

Our father levels eyes at me like I'm supposed to do something about this.

Why can't I have nice dreams? Maybe it's the drugs in my system. The boys are gone. Sylvia hasn't come back in. Where is Elena? I don't think she's been here at all. Has George been here? I vaguely recall hearing his voice late one night or early one morning talking to a doctor, speaking in his usual matter-of-fact, unemotional way. Did I dream it?

Chapter 20

Elena Morales Lennox

Pedrito's ex brought Elenita in and dropped her and her things off. She said goodbye to Elenita, kissed her on the head, and silently shot a sneer at Elena as she marched out. Elena put a children's video on the TV, fixed herself a drink and lit a smoke.

That damn nightmare had upset her. She kept reliving pieces of it now that she was awake.

On the sand next to the water, as pieces of the raft and provisions floated around the shoreline, tío Alejandro rubbed his head. A stream of blood oozed from his dark hair, rounded his ear, and slid down his cheek.

"Humberto, take them to find the car. It can't be more than a couple of miles away. I'll try to salvage what I can and hide the raft, so we'll be ready for another day."

In the sultry heat, Elena plodded behind the others through the heavy brush, swatting mosquitos and gnats. Tío Humberto pointed to the water. "The shoreline is the best guidepost."

Eventually, they found the car. For a few minutes, they sat, still as corpses, their heads back, roasting in the unforgiving sun. When tío Humberto started the car and began to move, the hot air inside stirred, offering slight relief.

He drove quickly back toward where the raft had broken up. After a while, he slowed. "I think this is the place. Can you see the water?"

They all craned their necks. Elena pointed to a faint line of blue. Tío Humberto stopped the car, stood and yelled out, "Alejandro," several times. No answer.

"Stay here, I'm going to walk toward shore to see if he's there."

He limped like an old man toward the water, calling. After what felt like a long time, he returned to the car. "I don't know where he could have gone. He cleaned up the debris and hid it. Maybe we'll find him on the road."

Tío Humberto drove homeward. By late afternoon, Elena and her mother dragged themselves into Mima's home in Vista Alegre and collapsed.

The following morning, her mamá pulled her from a deep dream of her papá. "Let's go to Nona's to see if they've heard from your tío. Elena trailed after her mamá through the streets of Vista Alegre and then the few additional blocks to Nona's house.

Nona answered the door. Tío Humberto, tía Clara, Berta, Nona, tía Yiyi and Amelia stood behind her.

A tear rolled down Nona's cheek. "Have you seen or heard from Alejandro?"

Elena's mamá said, "We thought he'd have come here."

Nona said, "I hope he didn't try to go on his own."

A stain of dried, dark blood appeared near tío Humberto's hairline. "Not by raft. That's for sure. I found all the fragments. He may have walked toward the base at Guantanamo and swum over."

A knock sounded on the door. Elena's mother opened it and backed up, as a uniformed army officer and a uniformed police officer entered the room.

Nona nodded toward the police officer. "Captain Marrero, how are you? How is your family?"

"Well, Señora. How are you?"

"Well."

The officers looked from person to person, standing in a semi-circle around the large room. Amelia took Elena's hand, as they hid among legs of adults.

The army officer focused on Elena's mother. "Where were you yesterday?"

"Out looking for food, like every day."

"Liar. You never have to do that. The servants do it. Your husband is a criminal who left the country long ago. We know you were trying to leave too. Isn't that right?"

"No," she answered.

"Liar," he said again, sneering and imposing his face close to hers.

Nona moved closer. "Leave her be."

Still holding Amelia's hand and trying not to cry, Elena grabbed her mother's arm with her other hand. She would have told them where her father was, so they would leave her mother alone, but she didn't know. All her mother had ever told her was that he had gone to make a new and better life for them.

The officers looked at Nona, who stood, jaw set, but shaking slightly. "Where's your son Alejandro?"

"I don't know."

The police officer looked back at Elena's mother. "We are certain that you were with your brother yesterday, and that you all tried to leave."

Elena's mother shook her head.

He looked at tío Humberto. "And what about you?"

He shook his head.

He returned his gaze to Elena's mother. "We know you were. We have him in custody; he confessed."

The women wailed, "Oh no. Oh no."

The entire family stood, silently trembling, shedding tears.

Tía Yiyi banged on the police captain's chest. He laughed.

Then, apparently sensing that Elena knew something, the army officer turned his attention to her. He grabbed her arm and pulled her from behind her mother's legs. She lost the touch of Amelia's and her mother's fingers. He squeezed the top of her head with one hand. "Little girl, weren't you with your mamá and your uncle yesterday?"

She did not know what to say.

"Did you go in the water?"

She cried, shrugging. "I don't know."

"You don't know if you were with your uncle yesterday? You don't know if you were at a beach yesterday?"

She shrugged again, shivering. "I don't know."

Her mother reached out and clenched her hand, trying to pull her back.

"No?" He put his face so close that she smelled his disgusting breath. "Did your mother tell you that the CIA of the Empire has tainted the sand where you would land at the military base with poison to kill you?"

Elena shrunk back with the thought of the words *poison* and *kill*.

Her mother sprung at him. "Leave my daughter alone, you...."

The officer pushed her in the chest.

71

"Mamá," Elena cried, as her mother swatted at both men with a windmill action of flailing arms.

The army officer smiled. "Maybe we should take all of you in."

Nona turned to the police captain. "Capitan Marrero. Please. Leave us alone."

Capitan Marrero shook his head. He looked around the room. "You know that the homes of everybody involved can be confiscated, don't you?"

"That's a lie," Elena's mother said.

"Oh, you want to see what can happen?"

The police captain pointed to Elena's mother, tío Humberto, tía Yiyi, Amelia and Elena. "You, you, you and you two young ones. Come to headquarters."

The officers pushed the family out of the house and marched them to two cars. Nona and the others who were not singled out wailed. Neighbors standing outside averted their eyes as they were led out. Nobody wanted to know them now.

Elena was left alone in a room for what seemed like an eternity. Eventually, her mother hobbled back in, pale as chalk, the bags under her eyes bigger and darker than ever. Her forehead and cheeks were smudged with dirt.

Her mother grabbed her arm forcefully and pulled her to the door.

Outside, Elena looked up. Her mother's jaw was set. "What happened, mamá?"

Her mother kept her lips a thin, tight line, as she ushered Elena home, where Mima greeted them, horrified, but silent.

Her mother went into the bedroom and cried so loudly and so desperately that Elena thought her heart would break.

Elena wiped tears from her cheek with the back of her hand. What had they done to her mother? She glanced at Elenita, playing with a Barbie doll, put an arm around her and pulled her close.

Chapter 21

Franklin Morales

The last time Franklin's father held his hand swirled into focus. He studied the lines in his father's face, recalling how he looked when Franklin was a child and his father and mother entered his bedroom late that night, their faces grim, and told him he would be leaving to live in a boarding school in Spain.

Franklin fought to hold in tears as each parent held one of his hands. How fitting, right now, that he and Sylvia were each holding one of his father's hands. Franklin wished his mother were still here on earth. She may be waiting for the love of her life to join her in Heaven.

Early morning a couple of days after the late-night announcement of his imminent departure, Franklin sat in the back seat of the family car as Elena knelt on the floor, trying to maneuver her crayon over a piece of drawing paper on the seat. They swayed as Rafael swerved and zipped through the streets of Vista Alegre and down into the city of Santiago de Cuba toward the train station. Franklin tried to picture the places he loved. He wondered when he'd be home again. Now, after wondering where playmates had gone so many times, he was the one leaving without notifying friends. He hoped they'd know he could not. Occasionally, he looked back to see the car in which Luisa, tío Alejandro, tía Yiyi and Amelia followed.

They all boarded a train for Havana. Franklin stared out the window as his mother continually touched his arm, held his hand and cried.

After many hours, the train stopped in Havana. Tía Emma, tío Horacio and their children stood on the platform, smiling, laughing and waving like they'd arrived at a party. The Havana family chatted happily as the men loaded suitcases and the women directed the travelers to an automobile for a drive to their apartment. Amidst the energetic chatter, Franklin and his family remained morose and silent.

As they entered the downtown area of *La Habana*, Franklin stared out at the flat, straight streets and ornate facades of the commercial buildings, so different from the streets of Santiago de Cuba.

That evening, after joining the Havana family for a large meal, which Franklin had trouble downing into his tense stomach, the adults continued talking. Luisa and Franklin tailed their cousins Ignacio and Maribel to the steps outside. Sniffling and silent, Luisa slid dark hair behind an ear. Franklin tried to be strong but found it hard to talk.

Ignacio said, "Why are they sending you two away?"

"They say bad things are happening, and we might have to go to Russia."

"That's stupid. Why would you have to go to Russia? And why only you? Why not your sister? Why aren't they sending me to Russia?"

"I don't know, but that's the reason."

Sitting in the still baking night air, with the hum of cars, music emanating from several areas, people talking and shouting and the other sounds of the city, Franklin said, "We never get to sit out like this at home. They say it's dangerous."

Ignacio shrugged. "That's stupid."

The next morning, they piled into cars again to travel to an office in order to obtain documents that would allow Franklin and Luisa to leave the country. After talking to their parents for a long time, two officers took Franklin into a room, and two others took Luisa someplace else.

An official asked Franklin, "Why are you going to Spain?"

Franklin concentrated on what his father had told him to say. He said not to mention school, because they might send him to Russia instead. "To visit my Godmother."

"What's her name?"

"Uh . . . tía Marta. I call her tía, but she's not really my aunt."

"Where does she live?"

"Madrid."

"How long is your visit?"

"A few weeks."

Franklin became afraid that he had not answered as his father had instructed. But the exit visa was issued. Then he wondered if he could have said something differently, so he wouldn't be sent away.

They returned to Aunt Emma's and Uncle Horacio's apartment for another meal. Franklin managed to eat a little more this time, telling himself that he needed nourishment before the long flight in the morning. Then he spent a sleepless night, petrified about the unknown.

Early the next morning, they sat in a waiting area at the airport as their families, dread sketched on their faces, watched from the other side of the glass. Other children said being in the waiting area was like being in a fishbowl, with people peering in at them. Seeing the mothers, especially his, crying so miserably made Franklin want to break down too, but he fought to maintain his composure.

A man in uniform announced, "All unaccompanied minors," and motioned with his hands for them to approach. "You children traveling to Miami, this door. You who are traveling to Madrid, this door."

Franklin gripped Luisa's hand as they alone went to the Madrid door.

As they neared the portal that led to the unknown, Franklin could hear their mothers crying and yelling, "Franklin . . . Luisa". He glanced up and saw their palms pressed against the glass, as though they could reach for them and pull them back. His eyes brimmed with tears, making it almost impossible to see the floor or anything else along the walk.

"Franklin?"

He lurched to the present. "Huh?"

Sylvia gawked at him, eyebrows raised. "We haven't heard anything about the neurologists' findings. We don't know if they've done any tests or when they will be. I'm wondering if they'll talk to you."

Franklin nodded, stood and marched down the hall to the nurses' station. A nurse looked at him askance.

"Is one of Luis Morales' doctors in the hospital?"

She picked up a chart and leafed through pages. "What's your name?"

"Franklin, his son."

"I'm afraid you're not the designee."

He held his temper. "I'm part of the committee."

"The charts do not say anything about a committee."

"I don't want to make a decision. I just want some answers."

A tall, blond man in blue scrubs entered and looked through papers in a folder. The nurse approached the man. Glancing at Franklin from time to time, she whispered to the apparent doctor. The man glanced up at him, shook his head, turned away and whispered something to the nurse.

The nurse returned to Franklin. "I'm sorry."

Returning to the room, he said, "I got nowhere. We need to find George Murphy."

Chapter 22

Luis Morales

The soft skin of a hand rubs mine. Is it Sylvia? I cannot awaken.

I'm floating. It's the hand of my fiancé, Cari. We are perched on the uncomfortable couch in the living room of my family's home in Santiago de Cuba on a Saturday afternoon in July 1953, under the intense gaze of my mother. Perspiration seeps down my sides, caused only partially by the still air and sweltering heat.

A maid comes in. "Señor Morales, Felipe Salvador Llorente is at the front door, asking to see you."

I excuse myself. As I leave the room, I hear my mother asking of Cari, "Dear, where were your grandparents born?" My blood boils.

Felipe pulls me away from the house. "Luis, I have important news. Your brother, Miguel, is involved in a revolutionary attack that is sure to fail. He's apt to get himself into serious trouble."

I'm instantly alarmed, knowing my brother's overzealous enthusiasm and trust, and as my father says, his naiveté. "Where is he?"

"I'm not sure. Dissidents are arriving from Havana and all over Cuba, mixing with the revelers arriving for *carnaval*. They're being housed in various locations. Later tonight they'll go to a small farmhouse on the Siboney Highway, which is the staging point for an attack."

I shake my head. I've traveled often on the highway that connects Santiago de Cuba to the village of Siboney and its well-known Siboney Beach. "What is the farmhouse to which you refer?"

"As I said, it's the preparation area from which the group will move out to attack *Cuartel* Moncada, the military garrison and barracks."

I walk past the Cuartel Moncada regularly on my way to the courthouse where I watch trials in action as part of my wish to become a lawyer. I've also visited friends and relatives in the Hospital Civil Saturnino Lora, across the street.

"Why attack a little fort like Cuartel Moncada here in Santiago de Cuba? What will that gain them as to the whole country?"

"They think it will enable them to stage a coup. They are also taking a fort in Bayamo."

"I don't see how taking control of a couple of forts here on the southeast part of the country will give them control of the government, seated in Havana."

Felipe says, "Nobody thought the silly little coup that last occurred would put Batista back in power either. These men think they can overthrow him."

"Won't the rebels be noticed as they come into town?"

"That's why they are doing it in conjunction with *carnaval*. Many partygoers are coming from afar, arriving by car, bus or train. Nobody will notice another couple hundred. They believe the Moncada soldiers will party too, and be drunk, and asleep, before sunrise, so the rebels can surprise them."

I laugh aloud.

Felipe grimaces. "It's an interesting plan."

"Interesting, yes. What does Miguel have to do with it?"

Felipe sighs and shuffles his shoes along the lush grass. "I guess he's joined as a fighter."

My stomach churns. Poor Miguel has no real knowledge of politics. He's chasing the excitement. I recall his stand against papá at the dinner table and his talk of joining the Ortodoxo rebels. "How can I get him away from this?"

Felipe shakes his head. "I don't know. We'll have to try to find him. Maybe at the Siboney farmhouse."

I hesitate only a few seconds. "I'm going to find him and pull him out of this."

"I'll go with you."

Back inside, Cari looks at me with concern.

"Cari, I'm sorry, but I fear my brother is in trouble. I have to go find him."

"I understand," she says, flushing and looking down.

My mother gives me the same look, and says, "Go save your brother. I will not inform your father, so bring him home soon and safely."

The streets of Santiago bustle with activity, as citizens carry on everyday activities, and others, already dressed in colorful costumes, put the finishing touches on floats, carriages and horses and scurry around with excitement. *La fiesta* will soon permeate the city, becoming wilder and wilder. Rum will flow everywhere. People will dance in the streets.

A few already intoxicated pre-revelers stagger along the streets. Teenage girls dressed up in flamboyant outfits skip down the sidewalks in small groups, ride in carriages, or sit on the backs of motorbikes. Brightly polished convertible automobiles float by with pretty women in dresses perched on the seat backs and the doors.

Cars move along the streets, some packed with yelling and whistling revelers dressed casually or in costume, and others filled with stone-faced young men dressed in t-shirts and other drab clothing. I point out such a car. "Rebels?"

Felipe bobs his head from side to side. "Probably so." He glances at me. "You and I look more like those revolutionaries than partiers."

I nod. "I'm not sure who it's safer to resemble."

"Oh, Louis." At first, I'm confused by the sound of Sylvia's light diction. She sniffles. I catch the sweet aroma of her perfume and the tender touch of her fingers on my hand and wrist.

The larger fingers of Franklin's hand rub my other hand. His voice breaks as he tells me he loves me. "Papá, *te quiero*."

I'm glad they are here again. I wonder if the doctors have told them anything. Will I recover? I am no longer panicked. If my life is over, then it's over. I know I've lived much longer than many men. I didn't want to retire earlier, to vegetate and die of boredom. I only regret that at age eighty-four, I expected to retire soon and enjoy traveling with Sylvia. I'd worried that Sylvia would have to care for me, since she's only fifty-two. But I didn't even fathom I'd be sick or maybe dying so soon.

I try to move my lips. If this hard thing that intrudes through me were removed, could I move them? Could I turn my head? I struggle to see through cloudy eyes. Are my eyes moving? Sylvia and Franklin do not appear to realize that I am awake. I feel a curtain falling over me again.

I am moving in and out of a dream, with the sound of a car's gentle rumble humming beneath. At first, I am back in my childhood, on the road toward the landing of the boat that would take us to our cottage. Then, I'm sitting in the back seat holding hands with Cari, while our chaperones, Ernesto and Margarita, supervise us from the front seat, Ernesto studying us in the mirror, as Margarita turns to say nothing, her eyes roaming over us. Then, I'm in the front seat on an evening out drinking with the boys.

Now, I realize where I was before, on the road to *La Granjita Siboney*, and my neighbor, Felipe, not Ernesto, is driving. I've skipped the effort to find out where we need to go. I shift back to my walk through the city streets with Felipe in search of information about my brother.

We mingle among undulating crowds of Afro-Cuban partiers rumbling through the streets, playing horns and banging worn bongo drums. Lighter-skinned people have also joined in the crowds, enjoying the party atmosphere and especially the rum. As darkness falls, throngs gyrate and sway in the streets, dancing in haphazard conga lines, grasping the hands of others and together spinning in circles.

We roll down through the city, trying to decide whether to go into the *Trocha* area, where the main *carnaval* activities usually commence, or to the train station, or to a park near La Moncada.

Ernesto, dressed in a white, collared shirt, stands on a street corner, foot propped behind him on the base of a lamppost, tugging on a cigarette.

"Felipe, stop the car. Ernesto has always been a follower of revolutionary movements."

We greet him and shake hands. He grins. Light from the street lamp brightens his face and teeth. "Young men. Are you partaking of the festivities?"

"Maybe. How about you? How is Margarita?"

He frowns and shrugs.

I decide not to inquire further. Felipe lights a cigarette and glances around, and then at Ernesto. "Ernesto, what do you know about Fidel Castro and his followers coming here tonight?"

Ernesto shoots a curious, suspicious glance at the two of us, and then skims the street. "Shut up. Don't say that name here."

I look around. "Nobody's listening. What's going on?"

He shuffles his feet and looks at me earnestly. "What do you mean, what's going on? It's party night."

I try to contain myself, but my worry over Miguel is intense. I put a hand on Ernesto's shoulder. "Listen my friend, you know my brother is, well, impressionable. I understand that he's gone somewhere, perhaps to a farmhouse where insurgents will prepare for an attack. I'm trying to find him and get him out of there."

Ernesto laughs. "Who do you think you are, my friend? The movement is stronger than you are. It relies on zealous young men like your brother. Young men are arriving from all over Cuba. They know little about the plan, other than that they must participate. Fidel will save the country."

My stomach turns. "Ernesto, a group that overthrows a government is rarely better than the existing government."

Felipe nods.

Ernesto says, "Batista himself promised to save us from the horrors of the prior administration, but he's worse. His arrogance in his second administration has surpassed that of himself, Grau and Prío."

I struggle to get words out. "I don't care about any of this political stuff. I only care about my brother. He is an innocent."

A gray Pontiac rolls slowly toward the corner and stops. Five disheveled young men nervously look in all directions.

I smile. "These guys sure don't look like they are here for *carnaval.*"

Ernesto shoots a look at me and turns away. He pulls a crumpled, folded paper from his back pocket and leans through an open window.

"Give me your names and group."

The man in the passenger seat speaks. Ernesto studies the list. "Yes," he said, "Artemisa. Where are the other members of your group?"

"Abel, Melba and Haydée are already here, aren't they?"

"I don't know. But where are the other cars that should be arriving with you?"

The man answers, "Some were told not to come. Some decided not to come or turned around on the way. We saw a lot of cars broken down along the highway. Also, we were told not to drive into the city all together."

Ernesto points down the street. "You are to go to the Hotel Rex. Look for a man with a large, red birthmark covering most of his face. That's Renato. He will direct you."

Ernesto returns to where we stand.

Felipe grabs his arm. "How are you involved, Ernesto?"

Ernesto simply smiles.

"Ernesto," I say, "Have you seen my brother? Do you know where he is stationed?"

He glowers. "I saw your brother, with three others from your neighborhood whom he appeared to have recruited. He's infiltrated himself into the local group of former *ortodoxos*, but they are not very organized or connected. Three revolutionary bands operate in Santiago, but I do not believe any is part of the attack. Your brother has attempted to join as an attacker, but he and his recruits are on their own. They would not be on my list. I greet only out-of-towners."

A car arrives with flags commemorating the 4th of September. It stops in front of Ernesto. He seems surprised by the flag that supports the Batista government.

He leans in. "May I help you?"

"We are the San Leopoldo cell."

"Nice flag," he says, smiling. "That'll throw them off."

He reviews his list and instructs the men.

Felipe puts an arm on mine and tries to pull me away. "Let's go."

I snatch my arm back and face Ernesto. "How do you say my brother is an attacker if no locals are involved?"

"Your brother seemed very knowledgeable of the plan. He asked about locations. I gave the address of 8 Celda Street, where certain cells are meeting."

"Garbage," I yell. "A lie. How could he be so knowledgeable? He's only a follower."

Ernesto laughs aloud. "Yes, that's why he's valuable to the movement. We need followers."

"Do all the groups convene at the Siboney farmhouse? When? Where is it?"

"Eventually, probably. On the road to Siboney, of course."

"How far."

"Not too far. Maybe a half hour along the highway, not far before the beach."

I shove the ingrate. Felipe grabs my arm and pulls me away again.

Ernesto laughs. "Luis, you are misguided. Hundreds of young men are arriving. Tomorrow will be a new day, a day of hope and the dawn of a new prosperity."

Felipe drags me away. As we turn down a street toward the car, he whispers, "Listen, let's check out the Hotel Rex and the Celda Street house. Maybe we can learn something or follow somebody toward the farmhouse. If we cannot, we'll just drive on the Siboney Highway and look."

At Celda house, we see a mass of young men moving around inside the house. Several groups of men drag suitcases to the door and inside. Then groups of men exit the house, also struggling with heavy luggage.

Felipe says, "That guy with the big glasses is coming back out. He seems to be a leader. Let's follow him."

After the man with the big glasses gets into the front passenger seat of a car, Felipe follows it to the bus depot and parks. I exit the car and follow the man. He walks directly up to five men leaning on a wall. I stay back, but within earshot.

"Comrades, I am Abel Santamaría." He consults a piece of paper, and points in a direction. "You two go to La Perla Hotel, over there."

He directs the others to his car. They try to cram their luggage on top of others, but finally, the men take bags on their laps. I return to Felipe's car and we follow.

The man drives to 218 I Street in the Sueño neighborhood. The passengers heft some of their luggage inside and leave other pieces in the car.

After a couple of minutes, I say, "Felipe, drop me at the Rex, and you go to La Perla."

On the way, I see the chief officer of the Moncada fortress, dressed in civilian clothes, wandering among early evening revelers.

"Stop the car." I get out. "Alberto, how goes it?"

"Luis, my friend, how are you?"

The odor of rum emanates from him.

"Enjoying the festivities, Alberto?"

"Beautiful women, music, activity. I love it."

"Alberto, what is the rumor about an attack?"

He brushes his hand at the air as though deflecting an annoying fly. "We are ready for anything. A small group of disorganized, unarmed men may try to infiltrate."

"Who's in charge of the Moncada?"

His eyebrows rise. He frowns. "I am."

"Alberto, you are out here, dressed like a civilian, and under the influence."

He brushes away the invisible fly again and careens away.

At the Rex, I see the man with the incredible red birthmark on his face, speaking to the bartender. "We need twenty orders of *arroz con pollo*," he said "*Plátanos, frijoles, café, ensalada, pan con mantequilla, agua, cerveza y postre.*"

I sit in a corner, attempting to look like I'm reading a newspaper. Several young men, dressed in wrinkled clothes and looking exhausted, pull in heavy luggage. The man with the birthmark directs them to different addresses. Like at Celda Street, men, some with suitcases, come and Santamaría, Renato and another retrieve the food and enter the elevator. I bound up the stairs and stop when the elevator door opens. The din of men's voices buzzes through open doors along the hallway.

Two men stand in the hallway. One whispers, "I believe there is a shortage of weapons and ammunition."

"But what of all the suitcases?"

"It's a ruse. They're carrying them here and there, trying to make it appear there are more than there are. Anyway, the ones I saw were 22 caliber rifles and discontinued Canadian rifles, the same as we used in practice. That's a joke."

"I understand that there are many more men and weapons at the farmhouse."

"They have bullshit weapons because they really don't think we'll have to use them. Did you know about the plan before you came?"

The man shrugs. "No, not really."

"I think we are a very small group, going against a trained and well-armed army. Many of our men have never shot a gun. It's ludicrous. I'm thinking of leaving."

I return to the lobby. Felipe enters. "I saw Fidel Castro," he says, "drinking coffee at the café in Plaza de Marte. Seemed like they'd just arrived. A man seemed to be arguing with him, saying he thought he was only to perform surveillance on the Moncada in order to understand the military strength. Finally, he said, 'Now I understand.' Fidel smiled and said, 'Don't worry, Lulo, it is all completely planned.' Lulo stomped away."

We resume our seats in the car, watching Ernesto direct men to specific cars. A parade of *carnaval* attendees dances by in a line. A couple of young men abandon the revolutionary cause and join the throngs in the street.

Following a small group of packed cars, we skirt the border of our neighborhood, and enter the Siboney highway. Dust rises and dulls the taillights of cars bouncing along the dark, tree-lined, road.

After twenty minutes or so, brake lights illuminate hovering dust particles. The cars turn to the right, past a yellow light standing on a lamp post next to a wooden gate.

Felipe slows to a crawl. Tires throw gravel and soil as the cars speed between bushes, past barbed wire strung between stands of twisted, dried tree branches, and into the yard.

Felipe speeds in behind the cars, passing a tiny white-washed wooden cabin, with a pitched red tile roof, red framing around the front door, and a white-tiled porch, also framed at the top with red. Through the windows, we see that the house is packed with people. We veer to the right and stop behind a wooden structure. A cloud of dirt particles rolls into the dark sky as men pile out. Some pull heavy-looking suitcases and canvas bags from car trunks and back seats. Loud voices and the grate of furniture dragging on tile floors inside the house overpower the noise of cars arriving.

A young man says to another, "What do you think we are expected to do?"

"Fidel will lead us. It's going to be a new world."

"What's the plan?"

"Trust Fidel."

The house seems to be overflowing with people. A man walks out and urinates off the porch. We follow two young men onto the porch and inside.

Inside the door, a man stops us. "Where do you come from?"

"*De aquí. De Santiago.*"

"Why do you come?"

I swallow, lick my dry lips, and answer, "To work for the Revolution," intentionally emphasizing the last word.

"Who will lead the Revolution?"

I glance at Felipe, who looks as nervous as I feel, and reply, "Fidel."

The man stands aside and lets us pass.

Chapter 23

Elena Morales Lennox

Elena sat on the couch, with an arm around her darling granddaughter, who sucked her thumb as she watched a DVD of the *Flintstones*. Elena felt a special joy in sharing this cartoon that Elena loved when she'd first arrived in the U.S.

Elenita tapped her hand and pointed to the screen. "Mimi, Pebbo," she said, trying to say the name of Pebbles. The Flintstones family's pet dinosaur appeared beside little Pebbles and barked. "Dino, Mimi. Dino."

"Yes, baby. Dino." Elena tousled her granddaughter's hair.

The phone rang. She glanced at Franklin's name. Her hand hovered above the green icon. Not wanting a ringing phone to go unanswered, she snatched it up. "Hello."

"Hey, sis. I haven't seen you at the hospital. Are you coming today?"

Her heartbeat accelerated. She tried to tell herself that there was nothing so offensive in those few words. But she was unable to think nicely.

"Franklin, mind your own business." She flicked the phone off and threw it across the room.

The doorbell rang. Elena's cousin Berta and another woman peeked through the wrought-iron grating that covered the window. Elena leapt up, flung the door open and kissed Berta on the cheek.

The other woman yelled in Spanish, "Elena, you don't remember me? Amelia. We just arrived here two weeks ago.'"

"Amelia!" Elena shouted. They cheek kissed and embraced, moving back and forth.

Elena offered a cigarette to Amelia, but she declined. Elena lit up. "Would you like a drink, or some wine?"

"Water would be great," Amelia said.

Elena said, "I've wondered about you and your parents for years and years. How's your father? He was always a hero to me. But that day he tried to take us away, and his going to prison for it. That was awful."

Amelia sat. "He's fine. He was released but ended up imprisoned again. He was finally released just months ago. Your father helped him somehow. More importantly, Berta was telling me that your father is quite ill. How is he?"

Elena felt her eyes mist. "I don't know." Suddenly, she gushed tears and sobbed loudly. Amelia hugged her.

"I haven't gone to see him. I don't want to see him in his current state. My asshole brother keeps pushing me to go."

Amelia pushed hair out of Elena's face. "Don't you and your brother get along? I'm sure Franklin thinks it would be good for both you and your father if you saw him."

Tension hit Elena. She tried to talk rationally, but her voice rose immediately. "Franklin's high and mighty attitude always gets me riled up. He thinks I'm just an uneducated housewife, who struggled through college and earned no advanced degree. I may not be a lawyer like he is, but my husband is." Elena was embarrassed that her Spanish, like Berta's, had the distinctive Miami Cuban flavor to it and wasn't perfect.

Amelia smiled. "I bet if you'd lived in the same home when you were young, Franklin would have been an important beacon in your life."

Elena laughed. "You sound like a social worker."

Berta said, "She *is* a social worker."

Elena shook her head. "Did he send you two here to gang up on me?"

Berta said, "No, we haven't seen or talked to him."

Amelia put a hand on each of Elena's shoulders. "What I mean is that you and Franklin were separated for a long time, starting when you were very young, under difficult circumstances. What were you, two when he left and eight or nine when you were reunited?"

Elena nodded.

"After Luisa returned to Cuba, we struggled with misunderstandings because of the long separation and her sudden return. I'll admit that I was jealous of the attention she garnered."

Elena felt herself getting anxious, as she always did when thinking of this time and her brother. "I understand what you are saying, Amelia. Being sent away was not his fault. But I feel like he enjoyed a cushy, relaxing existence in a plush boarding school in Spain, while I was suffering alone in Santiago where everything had become different."

Amelia said, "I bet Franklin's experience wasn't as nice as you think. I bet he suffered abandonment issues too. Kids who were sent here to Miami on the so-called Peter Pan flights often felt that way. If I can learn enough English, pass the tests and begin working in my field here in Miami, I hope to help patients who, even in their sixties, suffer from feeling abandoned and unwanted as children. They were too young to understand why their parents separated the family. I know Luisa felt that way, and I did too."

Elena wasn't sure she wanted to discuss this further. But she couldn't let it lie. "I was the one who had it hard. Franklin is very self-assured and totally arrogant. He can't be suffering because he left." She felt her voice rising and shaking. "I was the one who had it rough, because he was gone. My mother became sullen and withdrawn. I recall being very young, maybe four, and finding my mother in Franklin's bedroom, fluffing his pillow and smoothing his blanket, as I stood in the doorway wondering why. She sat on the bed, crying, 'Oh, if only Luis and Franklin were here. I wonder what they're doing now.' I felt like I wasn't enough for her. She'd stare at their photos. They were nothing more to me than phantom black and white images adorning the shelves. She thought only about him while he was gone. And when he returned, he took what was left of her attention away from me." Elena grabbed a paper napkin and wiped tears from her eyes. "Amelia, as kids, how could either of us even grasp the concept of having a father and a sibling we didn't remember? As we reached tiny milestones in development, when would understanding of family come? What about at four, five, or six? Do I actually remember any specific event, or is it an accumulation of later memories that makes me think I remember anything at all about those times? I'm not even sure at age eight I remember reuniting with my father here in Miami, or the following day setting eyes on my thirteen-year-old brother as he marched into the reception area of the airport, smiling.

Amelia put on her serious, social worker face. "Elena, you probably block memories as a defensive mechanism and piece fragments together. I may remember more than you because I lived in the same house all this time. Even you, Berta, stayed until just a few years ago, although your father was gone for years."

Berta nodded, grimacing. "Elena, your servants continued working for you. But in my family, we went together to find food. Inside a small, street-front, almost-empty-shelved bodega, mi mamá would point to a chalk-board on which the words beef, chicken and fish were scratched through.

"Mi mamá would see a neighbor appear at the door. She would say, 'Can I trade you something for some eggs?'

"The lady would nod her head. 'Canned milk.' They'd each purchase what the other needed that was available in their ration book."

Elena laughed. "I went out on those searches sometimes, but never with my mother. She only moped around and slept. I went sometimes with Abeo as she forged through the city like an elephant on a mission. You know she stayed with the family even though she was no longer paid, which is part of why my grandmother never realized things had changed."

Berta said, "Abeo! Could she be alive? My God, she'd be a hundred. She took care of your father when he was a child. I loved that accent, from Haiti or somewhere like that."

Elena said, "My father told me once he used to see her on his visits, but she passed."

Amelia said, "Your father brought us money every month too."

Elena was surprised. "Really? He never mentioned it."

"That's your father. He wouldn't."

Berta smiled. "We never had an Abeo."

Elena glanced at Elenita, talking to her dolls as she sucked her thumb.

Amelia said, "You think you were hungry in the early sixties? Things improved when the Russians were there, when we, as we referred to their contributions, 'sucked the breast of the Soviet Union.' During the *Special Period*, after the Soviet Union collapsed, that was hunger. There was hardly any food, even on *la libreta*. Unless you want to count sugar and rice as alimentation. There was a saying, "Nobody can live on what *la libreta* provides, but without *la libreta* many people could not live."

Elena lapsed into a daydream in which she followed Abeo down dusty, streets in the sweltering heat.

Chapter 24

Sylvia Morales

Tuesday, November 29, 2016

Sylvia sat with her husband in the quiet still of the night. Franklin had left a couple of hours before. Elena's and Franklin's sons had appeared in the early evening, but not Elena. Sylvia should get some sleep, but she was not willing to leave. It had been fourteen hours since she'd rushed into the waiting room.

Louis was attached to so many tubes and noisy pieces of equipment. A wheeze swirled in the room every time the pump pushed.

She could barely choke out words. "Oh, Louis, I hope you are not hurting. If you can hear me, I'm here with you." She brushed her hand across his forehead, fingering strands of silver hair. Was that a movement? A forehead wrinkle? She wasn't sure. "I've been remembering our early times together, my darling."

She closed her eyes and put a hand on his wrist.

She found herself and Louis seated at a table in the same remote corner of Louis' private club, three days after their first date. He'd never asked if she was single, or if she'd ever been married. She wouldn't have wanted to delve into the marriage she'd escaped.

He continued quizzing her about her parents, her younger siblings, her early life in New Smyrna Beach, Ft. Lauderdale, Cocoa, and West Palm Beach, her father's work and how it felt moving to new towns and new schools so often.

After he had delved into her history for a few more questions, she said, "I can't imagine there's anything else that could interest you about my awfully boring life. You haven't told me much about yours."

"My past isn't interesting." His eyes shifted. His slight smile became a tight horizontal line. "I, uh, well, I married young…to Cari, the mother of my children. She died five years ago."

His eyes focused on her and then softened and went to the table.

She felt that she had intruded into a sensitive subject. "I'm sorry. For your loss and for bringing it up. It seems that you had great love for her."

"Yes." He blinked. He swallowed several times. When he spoke, his voice was rough and congested. "That is true. We had difficult times, not in our relationship, but because of circumstances beyond our control, and a long separation . . . distance, not marital . . . but we weathered it all."

Silence fell on the table.

She studied his face. Lines deepened with sadness. "The depth of your emotional self is usually well hidden."

"Yes," he said, smiling again. "One of my gifts, or faults, depending on the circumstance, or point of view of the observer, is that my look is almost always expressionless."

"Louis, I see something in your eyes I never saw before. And I like it." Then, she felt her cheeks sizzle with embarrassment.

The devilish grin he never showed in the office emerged. "This look is reserved for you."

Before the end of the dinner, he'd turned serious again. "Sylvia, I enjoy our time together so much, I would be very dismayed to let it end."

A small tingle of alarm pinged in her chest. "I feel the same. Why would it end?"

He hesitated, then proceeded. "I would like to spend as much time with you as you will allow, but that one problem exists."

"You mean the problem that you never, ever date employees? Apparently, you do." Relieved that he didn't intend to end their relationship, she laughed, and he joined her.

"I hate to ask you to discontinue your employment." He shook his head. "Now, I feel guilty about dragging you into this. I could try to find you another position."

She said, "Louis, I worked hard to become a paralegal. I moved to Miami just to work in your law firm. I know I've been there a very short time, but I love my profession and my work at Morales and Doolittle." Should she even consider leaving a great job for a relationship that was only sparking? It's not like Luis had proposed or anything.

He scrutinized her.

She looked at a painting on the wall and tried to think. "Louis, I would like to spend as much time as possible with you as well. I'm overwhelmed by your respect and concern for me and my job and profession. Would you mind breaking your little rule about dating employees, which," she added, smiling, "as I said, you've already broken twice, for a little longer before making me choose a relationship with you over my job? We can date discreetly and behave ourselves in the office. You can be your stern, bossy self, and I'll be my obedient, hard-working self. Nobody will know."

He smiled, "Of course. I will be just as aloof and disinterested as always."

She took a final swallow from her wine glass. "I know you'll have no problem hiding your feelings, Mr. Morales, but I'll have to work on that a little harder."

Sylvia glanced at Louis, as he lay unmoving on the white sheets. She studied his lips, trying to discern movement. Do they reflect discomfort, pain, anguish? Or maybe happiness and peace? Was that a smile? She'd swear it was. Could he be reminiscing their past too? She hoped so.

After their second dinner, they began eating almost every dinner together in more casual, less expensive places. He introduced her to his favorite Cuban restaurants, La Carreta, Versailles, Latin-American Cafeteria and a Spanish restaurant, Casa Juancho. He invited her to his home and cooked a delicious, fresh-fish dish, along with cooked asparagus and a salad filled with a tasty combination of crisp vegetables, topped with a dressing he'd apparently made by hand. He refused her help.

Then, she invited him to her tiny apartment where she baked her specialty, lasagna, accompanied by toast topped with garlic, cheese and olive oil, and her homemade Caesar salad. He seemed to enjoy it.

Six months later, he proposed. "Yes," she'd said so quickly she was embarrassed that she sounded too eager. Then, she added, "On one condition. You must get me an interview at Mr. Abraham's office. Right where you started your law career in the States."

Shoes shuffled behind her. She opened her eyes, finding her hand still resting on her husband's. She blinked, trying to clear her vision.

She turned and found Franklin, the usual smug, cold look on his angular face. His dark eyebrows rose in a slant, just like his father's. He nodded at her. "Sylvia, you should have gone to get some sleep."

She was sure she looked a mess. But he seemed scruffy himself—unshaven—wearing running pants and a t-shirt—hair askew. "I couldn't leave him alone, Franklin. What time is it?"

"Four a.m. How is he?"

"The same."

She thought Louis' hand jumped in hers. She glanced around the room, lost, hesitating. She mustered up the courage. "Franklin, it was impossible to have the revised documents signed, right? I can't believe George Murphy is named instead of me . . . or you. Do you know him?"

Franklin winced. He and his sister had such a knack for acting like they thought she was a money-grubbing whore who had latched onto their father, that she didn't belong in their social class and that she was prejudiced against those below the class she now enjoyed.

"Mr. Murphy? Sure, I've known him ever since I arrived in the States. My father met him after he arrived. I think he let my father stay in one of his rental properties for free for months. You've met him, haven't you?"

She recalled meeting George Murphy at the Latin-American Café years ago. She was surprised to see Louis greet another man as fondly as he did, even embracing. Louis introduced her to his "dear friend." She thought Mr. Murphy's rugged Clark Gable face looked incongruous compared to his blue-collar-worker clothes and protruding gut.

"Only once. He's a plumber, isn't he?"

Louis seemed to stir. They both turned their gazes to him, lying like a phantom immersed beneath a bright white sheet.

Franklin sneered. "Mr. Murphy is a professional. He operates a very successful business. A finer man you will not find. And he cares deeply about my father."

She hadn't wanted to sound negative about Mr. Murphy in Louis' presence, so she dropped the line of questioning.

Chapter 25

Franklin Morales

Aggravated by Sylvia's words, Franklin tried to ignore her presence and concentrate on his father. He rested his head on his hands, propped up by elbows on the bed, as fatigue pulled him down.

The hum of engines played a tune as the plane cruised toward Madrid. Luisa dozed next to him, her cool, limp hand in his. She jerked from time to time. Stewardesses had tried to talk to her when they'd entered the plane, but she just silently stared back, wide-eyed. He wished he could sleep. The most-attentive stewardess, brown-haired, tall, thin and pretty, kneeled in front of him, put her hands on his knee. "You're a big boy, taking such care of your sister."

"She's my cousin."

"Oh, well, you're still a big brave boy. Don't worry. Spain is a lovely country."

The hours wore on. Every time he felt tears well up, the stewardess was there with a fresh drink or another snack. He would make up his mind that he was going to be stoic, for Luisa if not for himself. But tears still came.

After the plane touched down, they remained on the plane as everybody else passed their seats. Luisa remained mute. The attentive stewardess hugged both youngsters. An official from the airline escorted them. Franklin grabbed Luisa's hand and supported her as she stumbled with an uneven gait.

Franklin felt lost and frightened as they were led into the busy airport. Before long, a man dressed in priest clothing extended his hand and said, "Franklin, I am Father Francisco. I am here to take you to your temporary home and school."

Two nuns greeted Luisa.

Father Francisco rested a hand on Franklin's shoulder as they walked one way, while Luisa and the nuns went in the opposite direction. Franklin had wanted to hug Luisa and not let go. He again

97

did his best to be a man and not to worry about Luisa, his mamá and papá, his sister, and his grandparents.

The priest packed Franklin's suitcase into the back of an old Renault. On the ride, Franklin fought to stay awake, but the lack of sleep on the plane and the drive pushed him down. He periodically awoke with a start, realizing that his head was bobbing, and tried to appear like he hadn't been sleeping. He'd take in the vast countryside. He was very far from home and family.

The priest drove onto a narrow highway and cruised past pastures dotted with livestock, patches of trees, rambling stone walls and workers swinging sickles, punching pitchforks or jabbing hoes into the dirt. Occasionally they would pass small homes, silos and barns.

After some time, a village of older buildings appeared on a hill. The priest downshifted and braked, then climbed the winding, rolling roads. On the hilly terrain, haphazardly constructed stone walls separated the road from rolling pastures. Men swung sharp tools through greenery.

Eventually, the priest down-shifted one last time, turned and drove along narrow, cobble-stoned streets in a town.

They stopped in front of a majestic stone building. A man exited through a foreboding, heavy, wooden front door and took his suitcase as Father Francisco led him up the stone steps and inside.

He followed the priest, who walked with an odd twist, like something was pulling his back to one side, through a large hallway and then into a room with two bunk beds. Father Francisco pointed to a top bunk. "This is yours."

Then, Father Francisco guided him into a classroom, where a man with dark hair stood in front of the class holding a large heavy-looking book. Twenty or more students regarded Franklin.

The priest announced, "This is Franklin Morales. He has journeyed far and will be with us for some time. Please welcome him."

The boys silently eyed him.

The instructor set the book on the podium and pointed toward an empty wooden desk and chair. "Welcome, Señor Morales. Please have a seat."

After Franklin had sat and opened the notebook that lay on the desk, the instructor began lecturing about fractions, a subject that Franklin knew. The instructor had an unusual accent, much stronger than the

Spanish to which Franklin was accustomed. The professor used the sound *th*, which in Cuba would sound like *s*.

Franklin felt the watchful eyes of his classmates. The professor called upon students to work out mathematics problems he'd written on the chalkboard. Some did so successfully, with the same unusual manner of speaking. When a student didn't answer correctly, his classmates jeered and derided him. Franklin was petrified that he would be called upon to speak, not only because he might not know the proper formula, but also that he might be fodder for ridicule for his Cuban Spanish.

On weekends and holidays, chauffeurs and family members retrieved his classmates, leaving him behind, alone. Although Franklin's family had been financially comfortable, he understood that now he was a charity case. When school was in recess, he also could leave for short trips to see tía Marta, but she was too far away. He had no place nearby to go—nobody to see.

When the other boys returned after the *Semana Santa* vacation, they described parades and parties. Those from Seville described *La Féria,* Easter and post-Easter carnivals in which families set up fancy tents on a huge area maintained just for the purpose, as residents danced and marched up and down the cobblestone streets, many on horseback or horse-drawn buggies. The boys described beautiful girls in incredibly colorful long dresses and fancy hairstyles.

On Christmas holidays, when the last of the students had left the school to return to their homes and families, Franklin was again alone. The days were long and tedious. He tried reading. He tried studying. There was nobody with whom to play a sport. There was nothing to do, but sit for long hours staring into space. He would lie in bed thinking of his sister and his mother, wondering where his father was and what he was doing and trying to imagine how soon they could be free to return home, or someplace else. Franklin would cry and then put on his stoic, sober face.

With everybody gone, Christmas day was like any other day, he would have to go to chapel two or three times. On January 6, the Day of the Three Kings, there were no gifts. He sat alone on the pew in the chapel again.

He wandered the halls of the huge, cold, institution. He tried, often fruitlessly, to find a single station on the small transistor radio the priest had given him, hoping for any song to help the day go faster. From time to time, he walked outside and sat under the tree near where the boys played baseball and *fútbol*.

When school was not in session and the other students were away, Franklin often left the school property and wandered along the cobblestone streets of the historic city, past ancient architecture. He eventually befriended a baker and other shopkeepers, who probably thought of him as that odd little boy who spoke funny and had no family.

The first summer vacation that Franklin was in Toledo, a man came to retrieve him and drove him to a little village, where tía Marta had a summer home. When he entered the house, Luisa was sitting in the living room, and she ran to him and hugged him for what seemed like forever. He remembered their awkward separation in the airport and blinked his eyes to keep the tears from falling.

The old lady did not seem to have tolerance for children, but Franklin, sometimes with Luisa, enjoyed the outdoors, playing with other kids, swimming in a stream and walking around the town and in the woods. He'd thought that his visit to Spain would be for a few months, but he ended up at this summer vacation spot six times before he left.

One day, Franklin received a heavy envelope with a Cuban postmark and his mother's maiden name, Ortiz, in the return address. He opened it and carefully pulled out onion-skin paper with elegant writing in black fountain pen ink.

> *Dear Franklin,*
> *We miss you terribly and we trust that you are happy and safe. All is well here. Elena and I are healthy. We now live in the family home with your Mima. Your tío Alejandro, tía Yiyi and prima Amelia are fine. They miss Luisa like we miss you. Your Mima and Nona are well, although your abuelo is away for a while. Everybody sends you greetings and love. We've heard from your papá from time to time. He is well. He's doing what he can to make a home for us and help us to join*

him as soon as possible. Keep your hopes up. Keep your strength. We will all be together again before long.

Enclosed were four heavy, black-and-white photographs: one of Franklin, Elena and their parents standing in front of the old homestead, smiling; one of the family at the cottage, dressed in summer clothing; one of his parents on their wedding day; and one of the family with his *abuelo* and *Mima*. Franklin fought back tears as he studied every detail of the grainy photographs, trying to remember his parents' touch.

He worried that his grandfather was 'away.' What could that mean?

Franklin came back to the present. He shielded his eyes with his hand so Sylvia would not see his tears. He looked into his father's still face and wondered what he thought at the time the family was torn apart, and if he was thinking now.

Chapter 26

Luis Morales

I hear a new voice, high and youthful, and I feel a new touch, an almost hug. Right above my face, I see my darling granddaughter, Michele, with the straight, dark hair, olive skin and striking facial features of her mother, Diana. She embraces me delicately, due to the numerous wires, tubes and other contraptions in the way. I am warmed by her staying with me for a long while. She repeats, *"Te quiero, Nono,"* over and over. Teardrops splash onto my chest and neck. The feel of the tears warms me. Eventually she's gone, and I am alone.

The clamor of many young men moving around and talking heatedly inside the tiny, packed, front room of *La Granjita Siboney* is deafening. To our left is an open room, also packed. I scan the rooms in vain for Miguel.

Beneath the hundreds of dirty boots, I can make out small, square, red tile, separated by white lines of grout. The walls are white plaster, also trimmed in red.

To our right, a closed wooden door swings open. A woman in a long dress, her hair held back, comes out and turns toward the back of the house. A young man follows her, glancing around the room, and saying, "Wait, Melba. There's more to discuss." She glances at him and shakes her head but marches on without responding.

Straight ahead, three men organize wrinkled, dirty-looking, khaki-colored army uniforms on the dining room table. Melba grasps several uniforms from the floor and joins another woman, rapidly ironing and laying partially-pressed uniforms on the table and the floor.

A young, clean-shaven man in a white collared shirt approaches us. "Your names?"

"Luis Morales Ortiz and Felipe Salvador Llorente."

A young man turns around. "Luis, how are you? I never expected to find you here." He grins. "Miguel said you are too reserved to become involved."

102

I hesitate, feeling the eyes of the man who asked my name peering at me.

The man who asked our names moves closer. "Why are you here?"

"We are followers of the Revolution. We hope to participate."

He eyes us. "Let me introduce you to some people." He takes my arm and pulls me along, into another tiny room. Several men mill around. He stops in front of the man with large eyeglasses framed in black I'd followed earlier. "This is Abel Santamaría. What is your name again?"

We identify ourselves again. Santamaría's face is anchored on me, but I cannot make out his eyes through his thick glasses.

The walls are plastered with labeled drawings of the highway to Santiago, the streets around the Moncada and details of the two-story concrete-block Moncada barracks, the guard towers in opposite corners across the large parade ground in front, the officers' homes and the officers' club the nearby courthouse and civil hospital.

The planners have scribbled in pencil and crayon details of the routes to and away from the Moncada, locations of guards and names of dissidents who would attack in each location. Arrows point up the narrow concrete steps to the second floor of the barracks, and to the rooms inside.

Santamaría considers me seriously. "I met another young man not long ago with your surname."

"Miguel?"

"Yes, Miguel. How are you related?"

"He is my brother."

The others stop talking, focus on me and move closer.

Santamaría leans in. "Are you of the same political persuasion as your brother?"

I look at Felipe for help but get nothing. "Of course. We are followers of the Revolution, to save Cuba from the assassin Batista and his regime."

The man who brought us into the room raises his hand to stop me. "Your brother is a coward. Does it run in the family?"

I gulp. "Excuse me?"

The four men study us. Santamaría speaks up again. "I do not believe you have been involved with any of the rebel groups in

Santiago or elsewhere that have been planning this movement. Is that correct?"

I hesitate, trying to decide how to respond. "My brother has."

"Are you members of the Ortodoxo? Any other revolutionary group? Have you been recruited? Have you participated in any of the preparation activities? Did you even know about us before this evening?"

We shake our heads, dejected.

"Mr. Morales, I understand your family resides in the Vista Alegre neighborhood of Santiago. Is that correct?"

I hesitate, becoming more nervous. "Yes."

"That is an upper-class neighborhood, of more or less wealthy families, is it not?"

I nod silently.

He nods as well. His mouth and head move and twitch in an odd way as he formulates the next thought. "Would you be surprised if I told you it is unusual for the wealthy to be anti-Batista and in favor of the Revolution?"

Another squints. "Why are you a revolutionary? Is your life so bad? Living up there in Vista Alegre, looking down upon the people, the people just like the soldiers who are here. It makes no sense. Isn't your own father an executive in the sugar industry and a close friend of the assassin, Batista?"

"Well, uh," I stammer, trying to use some of Ernesto's rabid arguments. "Batista is a murderer. I do not follow my father's beliefs."

One of the men releases a high, light giggle, like a kid who's just won a monopoly game, "You don't even believe that."

Felipe finally pipes up with his contribution, a quote, or near to it, from Ernesto. "Batista makes Prío and Grau look like saints."

They all stand, still staring at us, heads shaking, mouths turned down.

The man who brought us into the room says, "How old is your brother? Seventeen?"

I nod.

"We only have a few so young. They are from the poor neighborhoods. On interrogation, we determined your brother did not actually have the cause in his heart. He lacked conviction and nerve.

You are even worse . . . You two are from rich neighborhoods, from a family of Batista followers, and have never been involved with any of the groups of revolutionaries. I see no reason for you to be involved."

Santamaría says, "Your brother and some others have been sequestered. They will not be permitted to join us."

I'm happy he can't participate, but uncomfortable at the same time. "What exactly do you mean by sequestered?"

"We have locked them up, for their own safety. They will be able to leave after we prevail."

That's why I have not seen him. I glance nervously at Felipe. My Adam's apple bobs as I try to swallow. "Where?"

One of the men snickers. Santamaría glares at us.

A man says, "By eight this morning, we will be in control of the government, and you will be freed. We don't plan to jail the sequestered ones under our new government, because they at least professed to be on our side."

A stern-looking man shuffles his boots on the floor, says, "Take them to the holding area," and lights a cigar.

I cringe, worrying that maybe we will be shot. Leaving Santamaría and the others in the room, the other three forcefully usher us out the kitchen door and across a dusty yard. Outside, we pass two men kneeling over a cistern. A soap crate with the top removed and some burlap bags full of rifles lie on the ground next to the cistern. One man pulls a rope as another kneels, grabs a canvas bag and pulls it up. Butts of rifles stick out of the top of the bag. Another man pulls rifles out of the bag and lays them on the ground.

I survey the area, looking for an escape. To the rear of the house I see flat, open grazing land below a steep hill, crisscrossed with walls constructed of stacked rocks and bounded by barbed-wire. In front of us is a two-story, three-sided structure constructed of worn, unpainted wood, similar to the one that shielded the property from view of the highway. This one has a small enclosed upper level.

One of the men smiles. "Welcome to the chicken coop. That's appropriate, isn't it?" The guards laugh. Two cars occupy the entire lower level. There are no chickens. I glance behind and see the men at the cistern pulling up more canvas bags of rifles.

One of the guards climbs a flimsy wooden ladder to a loft. Another pushes the barrel of his rifle into my back. I climb, with him following. The third follows Felipe. The trap door to the floor above is secured with a large metal bar, which the first man yanks loose and hangs on rafters. He climbs and stands up in the loft area and then aims his rifle back down at us. The guard behind me shoves me in. I trip on the slatted boards and fall.

The guards retreat quickly and jam the bar back into the trap door. It takes a few minutes for my eyes to adjust to the dim light in the room. Then I take in about ten or twelve young men, all looking dejected and afraid. At first, I do not recognize my brother, but then I hear a questioning voice say, "Luis?"

I turn and find Miguel cross-legged on the floor. "This is the Revolution, I guess," I whisper.

"And I wanted so to be a part of it," he mumbles.

"What happened?"

"The men pulled us into a room and quizzed us. Then they told us some details about the operation. There were holes in the plan."

"What did you do or say to end up here?"

"Some expressed fear or doubts about the plan. I did neither. I don't know why they doubted my devotion."

"Miguel, as soon as we arrived, they questioned our family's financial status, saying we were not typical followers. But more importantly they somehow knew that our father is a sugar executive and connected to Batista."

"I do not understand."

Of course, my brother wouldn't grasp how his stated idealistic goals would appear out of synch with the rebel cause.

I glance around. "What do they intend to do with you? . . . that is . . . with us?"

My brother looks at the ground. "I wish you had not come. We do not know our fate. I suppose once they leave for the attack we can break out of here. This structure seems to have been constructed just to hide the cars and this loft, to place people like us, for safe-keeping. I want to be part of the Revolution, not locked in a room like an enemy of the very Revolution I want to assist." Like everybody else inside the farmhouse, he emphasizes the word *Revolution* like it is something momentous.

A man in the corner looks at Miguel. "You are as crazy as them. They do not even have a plan. They think the soldiers won't be sober enough to realize when they replace them, dressed in supposedly similar uniforms. The soldiers outnumber them by hundreds and have working automatic weapons. All these guys have is lesser caliber or broken rifles and pistols, as well as being dressed in stinky, wrinkled, off-colored fake uniforms. Most have never shot a weapon in their lives. It's ludicrous."

My brother is incensed. "The master plan is brilliant. The soldiers will be drunk. They will be overpowered by surprise."

The man across the room laughs and speaks again. "*Bruto. Loco.*"

I put a hand on my brother's shoulder. "It matters not very much what you think. You are here, imprisoned with the rest of us. Imprisoned by those who you believe will set the people free."

My brother fixes his eyes on the straw-covered wooden floor again.

Now, in my hospital bed in Miami, Florida, in 2016, I try to see anything besides the ceiling above me. I wish they would raise the head of the bed, as they have done from time to time, so I can see around the room. Elevated, I can make out people as they move, sit and stand, like I'm squinting through partially translucent window shades.

If my eyes are open sometimes and closed other times, it certainly is not within my control. But if they are open, why do people act like they see no awareness? I want to control my movements. I want to show them that I am here.

I hear footsteps. Franklin says, "God, how aggravating."

Sylvia grips my hand. "What happened?"

"Nothing. The usual. The doctors won't talk to me. It appears that George Murphy has been here and has talked to them. I understand HIPAA law, but this is ridiculous. I'm going to find Mr. Murphy and get to the bottom of this."

Franklin and Sylvia continue talking, but their voices fade and become garbled.

I sway to another time. Days after I've abandoned my homeland, shredded the cohesion of family and arrived in Miami, alone, with no job and no money, I tramp in sweltering heat along Douglas Road near the airport. I find the address and knock on a door. A man with greased back hair and an early bald spot says, "Mr. Morales?"

I nod.

"I'm George Murphy. Come on in. Let me show you the place."

I follow him from the small living room to the bedroom. He shows me the tiny bathroom and kitchen. Then he announces the price and deposit requirements.

I look at the floor.

The toothpick in the man's mouth has begun bobbing franticly. "What's the matter? You wanted to see the place, didn't you? You don't have any money? Is that it?"

I hesitate. "Not yet."

"Well, when? I came all the way over here to show the place to you, thinking you could afford it." He looks exasperated.

I briefly explain how I'm looking for work in this new land. He says, "You Cubans seem to be moving your whole country here. I can't help everybody."

"Yes, sir. I apologize for bothering you."

Five minutes later, his manner has changed, and he says I can stay there for free for up to five months.

Suddenly, I remember I'm in a hospital room, with Sylvia and Franklin near me.

Sylvia sighs. "I so wish your sister would show up."

"I do too, but I can't control her. I tried talking, but as usual, it ended in a fight."

I understand their frustration. It's nice that they have a mutual concern.

Chapter 27

Franklin Morales

Franklin shuffled files on his desk, stewing over his inability to converse with his sister in a calm, rational manner, and trying to decide what to do next.

His cellphone rang.

"Franklin. It's Harold Jeffreys. I wanted to talk to you about your father. I'm sorry he isn't doing well."

Franklin knew this man had been his father's general practitioner for years. "Doctor Jeffreys, I'd love to know something. I keep hitting brick walls."

"Yes, I know. As his GP, I've gotten some information. George Murphy as surrogate, has been talking to the specialists. I haven't been able to reach him. The heart surgeon, Dr. Mackey, says as far as he's concerned the heart is operating normally now. The neurologists haven't yet figured out the extent of damage or why he's not regaining consciousness. They did an MRI, a PET scan and other scans this morning. They found evidence of multiple strokes and significant bleeding. They are trying to determine if the bleeding has stopped, in which case they need to remove the excess blood. They'll do more tests later today or tomorrow, I think."

"Thank you very much for that information. It's by far the most I've heard. I'll pass it along to Sylvia, who is just beside herself at the silence."

As soon as he'd hung up, the receptionist buzzed, and announced, in English, but with a Miami-Cuban-Spanish accent, that his tío Alejandro, tía Yiyi and cousins, Luisa and Amelia were in the reception area.

He rushed out to greet them. They leapt to their feet. He recognized all of them instantly, although of course they had aged. Their facial expressions, mannerisms and family traits took him back to the last time he'd seen any of them. He felt choked up with emotion.

Tía Yiyi grabbed his face and squeezed it. "Oh my God. You have your father's eyes and dimples. And that heavy, dark hair. I can still see the seven-year-old Franklin in you."

His uncle looked solemn. "We are so sorry to learn of Luis' illness. How's he doing? Can we see him?"

"It's quite serious. We still do not know much. But yes, you can see him. He seems to be in a coma, but I am thinking and hoping he is aware. I'm sure he'll appreciate your coming."

He ushered them into the large conference room. "After all these years, you all look great. I can't believe all four of you are here in the States, finally."

The receptionist came in and made espresso at the machine in the corner of the room, asking in Spanish how each would like it. She spooned sugar from a glass bowl into each cup. She set out little pitchers of cream in front of those who wanted it. She set a cup and saucer, a small spoon, a glass of cold water and a napkin in front of each guest.

Tío Alejandro said, "I managed to get a work visa to Mexico and was able to take them with me. Then we did the walk-across into Texas. It was a harrowing experience because it was days before Obama halted the wet foot / dry foot rule. The guards would let a few cross the bridge and then stop the rest. We were all camping out by the foot of the bridge, not knowing what was happening.'"

Franklin said, "It was so surprising that Obama killed that law. I expected Trump to do it, but not Obama. I think Obama just wanted to take the ability to gloat about having done it away from Trump."

The group laughed.

Franklin smiled. "I have no idea how my father managed to get you all out. But that's my father."

Amelia said, "I saw Elena this morning. She knows she needs to see your father, but she's afraid. I told her I'll accompany her."

Franklin was caught off guard, and struggled for words, not wanting to be negative. "If you can get her to visit, you are doing better than I."

Amelia glanced at Luisa, returned her gaze to Franklin, and smiled. "Franklin, Luisa and I understand exactly how you both feel. You and Luisa went away, and Elena and I were left behind, too young to even remember you. When Luisa returned to Cuba, I felt a stranger had come in and separated me from my mother." Amelia placed a hand on her father's wrist. "Papá was a distant memory to Luisa and unknown to me during those years, just like your father was to the two of you. I thought Luisa had a nice time in an expensive boarding school in Spain, while I was left alone. I know Elena feels she struggled, and you did not. It's a very common sentiment among the children who were separated, both the ones who were sent away and the ones who remained. Many resent their parents."

Luisa said, "It was very traumatic for me when you and I left for Spain, Franklin. I imagine it was for you too. But I thought of you as the rock. On the trip to Havana, the day we had to go and get our exit passes, sitting in the fishbowl as our family looked so distressed behind the glass, and the flight. You hugged me and patted my arm. You didn't cry. You were my strength."

Franklin shook his head. "I was no rock. I tried to keep it together, for you. But I was just as scared and bewildered as you."

He looked down, thinking of his sister. He raised his head and looked at Luisa again. "I don't want to fight with Elena. It just happens. That horrible day haunts me. I remember so vividly you and me sitting inside the fishbowl. I watched Elena's contorted face, glancing up at our parents and back at us."

A tear dropped from Luisa's eye. "God, when those officials entered and announced those words I'll never forget, 'All unaccompanied minors, step this way.' I remember that my legs almost buckled as we were steered toward the exit door, past our bawling mothers and grim-faced fathers plastered to the other side of the glass."

Franklin pulled a box of tissue from the credenza and held it out to her. He nodded. "Yes, I remember their faces every single day. And the pitying faces of the stewardesses as they greeted us and escorted us to our seats. You sniffled and shook. I was trembling just as much as you."

Amelia said, "I don't know if you know this, but I studied social work at the University of Havana and worked in the mental health field. I hope to get a job in that field here, although I need to improve my English first. I think studying and working in that field helped me get beyond the negative feelings I had about the whole family separation. We are fine now."

Franklin was without words for a moment, thinking of the possibility his father wouldn't recover. And that his sister and he couldn't resolve their differences. He looked up. "I hope Elena and I can come to some kind of peace someday. Actually, at this time of crisis, we need to get over the past. If not now, I don't know if we ever will."

Luisa said, "Do you remember that one flight attendant . . . well, they were called stewardesses in those days . . . the gorgeous one who kneeled down in front of us, put her hands on ours and said sweet things? She kept bringing us more drinks and snacks."

Franklin grinned. "I was young, but I thought all the stewardesses were stunningly beautiful. I was mesmerized especially by that one's looks and her funny way of talking.

Luisa smiled. "Oh, so you weren't even thinking of me then, you little lothario."

They laughed.

Luisa said, "After the plane touched down, my heart was pounding wildly. You took my hand as we walked side by side into the busy airport."

"Mine was pounding like that too. I felt all tingly, like I would faint."

"You were being a little man. The priest, and the nuns appeared and escorted me one way, and you the other. No good-byes"

Franklin shuddered.

Luisa dried tears. "Another separation."

Franklin was quiet for a while, trying to maintain strength in his voice. He looked up at their somber faces. "I'm glad we are all here together. Would anybody like another cup?"

They all said no and arranged to meet at the hospital. Amelia said she'd be sure Elena would visit.

Chapter 28

Elena Morales Lennox

Elena considered the psychology that Amelia tried to instill in her.

Elenita bounded over from across the room and placed a hand on her leg. "Mimi. Macawoni." Elena put a DVD on for her, boiled water, and opened a box of prepared macaroni.

Amelia entered, letting the door slam behind her. "I saw your brother."

"How is my dear brother?"

"He's fine. He has the same sentiments that you do. He wishes you two didn't fight all the time."

"If he'd shut up and stop imposing his beliefs on me, we'd be just fine."

Amelia smiled, looking like she pitied Elena for her lack of understanding.

Elena dwelled on her father, lying in the hospital, perhaps dying. She turned to Amelia. "I'm so afraid to see mi papá. I'm afraid to lose him." She looked into Amelia's eyes, knowing Amelia would think she was being silly. "I just can't make myself go. Losing him to death or his possible incapacity will be one more time that he's been pulled away from me. All I had of him for six years of my youth was a photograph or two, and my mother's constantly crying about him. Then, the day after I'd been rejoined with him, Franklin arrived and took his attention away from me. And yet later, Sylvia took him."

A weight lay inside her. She wanted to shed the feeling that people had pulled her father away. Amelia drew her into her arms.

Elena glanced at Elenita. Her voice shook. "If he dies, or never regains his mental capacity, poor Elenita will have no more memories of him as a great-grandfather than I did of him as my father during those six years. I had no grandfather, no father, and no brother that I could remember, because they all disappeared while I was too young. Your father was the only man in my life, but even he went away after the attempted escape. Don't tell Berta this, but I was never close to mi

113

tío Humberto. Mi papá acts so sweet to Elenita, much more so than he was with me. But she's too young to understand."

"Does Elenita have a grandfather living? Does she know him?"

"I've never met Pedrito's ex's parents. My former husband, Pedrito's father, left long ago and later died. Kalvin's not blood related and doesn't pay much attention to her. And on the great-grandparent front, even if Kalvin were related, his parents disowned us. They refused to acknowledge me or our marriage. Fortunately, she does have her uncle Miguel and … well … Franklin is sweet to her. But she has no grandparent or anybody like that."

Amelia nodded and sighed. "That's rough."

Elena took a deep breath. "I can't wait to see your father, my tío Alejandro, I hope Elenita can get to know him, your mom and your sister."

"Yes. He wants to see you and your father, and he'll love to meet Elenita."

Elena lit a cigarette and blew the first puff away toward the window. Amelia grimaced in disapproval and glanced across the room at Elenita. *Shit. Another person to give her crap about her smoking.* Elena went just outside and spoke through the screen, while trying to blow smoke the opposite way. "Maybe he could go to the hospital when we do. That could remove pressure from me."

Amelia smiled. "Okay, I'll convince him to come at the same time."

They sat silent for a few minutes.

Amelia took a sip of water, and said, "Do you recall that back in the time we were discussing, there were very few men in Vista Alegre? And very few teenagers. Those like your brother and my sister were gone. Teenage boys were in the army. Then, after you left, young people who were old enough to be away from home went to country villages and farms to work or to instill literacy in the populace. A lot of kids a little older than I was willingly went away to promote literacy and teach. They dressed in uniforms, like a literacy militia. It was a grand and successful effort."

Amelia was silent for a few minutes. Elena could see that she was trying to decide whether to say something, or maybe how to say it. Amelia sighed. "Elena, how do you feel about your mother? You said earlier that she was sullen and withdrawn during those years. Did you get along with her when she was alive?"

Elena considered the question. Naturally, they didn't always get along, but she decided their relationship was pretty normal. "Yes, we got along."

Amelia said, "Your mother suffered a lot during that time. She was trying to handle things on her own. Mima never realized that she had any less than before. Our mothers knew that wasn't the case. I think all of them were traumatized."

Elena hadn't thought of it that way before. She mashed her cigarette in the ashtray and stepped back into the kitchen. "So, now you're being the social worker again. Saying my mother was a little off, but that there's a reason for it. Maybe she was just crazy and maybe I got my unease from her." She poured the powdered cheese-like substance into the cooked macaroni, stirred it and set it on Elenita's tiny table.

She turned back to Amelia. "Amelia, I do think that losing our home because my father left without permission and didn't return was traumatic for her. We did just move next door, into Mima's house, but it was like a step back for my mother. It's interesting that you didn't lose your home after your father was caught in the escape attempt."

Elena placed a cup of juice in front of Elenita, who said, "I wanna see Julia."

"I'm sure your mommy and daddy can arrange that, honey." She turned back to Amelia. "I'm happy that Elenita has friends. I wish my friends when I was young had stayed around. Do you remember it like I do? My best friends, neighbors and schoolmates would be on the streets and in their homes one day and gone the next. I would never have any idea that their families were planning to leave. I imagine they didn't either. I'd never hear their names again. Their houses would suddenly be dark and vacant. New families would appear in the abandoned homes."

Amelia said, "Sure, I remember that, even after you were gone, but every year the numbers of those who actually left decreased."

"Whenever new families moved in, they were mean," Elena said. "A woman and two children moved into half of an empty house. You know they always divided larger houses into several dwellings. The first thing the new neighbor said to me was, 'Where are your father and

115

brother? They're not working for the Revolution, are they? They aren't in the military or out in the country-side teaching farmers to read and write. Those *gusanos* have fled, haven't they?' I froze, wondering whether she was one of those people my mother had warned me could report us."

Amelia said, "Of course, people called mi papá a worm too."

Elenita was engrossed in television. Elena said, "Is there color television in Cuba now? And fun, educational shows for children? Do Cuban stores sell plastic cartoon characters that take after those on television and in movies? All I remember is the drab, slow, documentary style programs, showing 'our leader' walking between rows of sugar cane, or describing how wonderful our country was, and going on and on with his long, long speeches."

Amelia snickered. "Many of us still have the old, small, black-and-white televisions, connected to rusty, broken antennas with frayed wires. Just like most computer screens. But color television programming exists now. With the help of friends and relatives who don't live in Cuba, people are able to get modern, flat-screen color televisions. Few programs are of interest to young children though. One can buy bootleg DVDs with the latest movies and shows. Now, it's better to buy televisions in Cuba, rather than those that friends and relatives bring in. One can buy a television in Cuba with a built-in digital box, which converts antenna reception, even poor rabbit-ear antennas, into clear digital pictures."

Elena said, "Are students still instructed to chant anti-American sentiments like, *'Cuba sí. Yanquis no.'*? I never knew why we had to refer to people of the United States as Yankees, or why we were not supposed to like them. I used to try to imagine how I would know if I saw one."

Amelia smiled. "Yes, younger children do."

"And how about the rallies? God, I hated having to go. I remember my mother dragging me to them."

Amelia smiled again. "Yes, even now, we have to sign attendance sheets for rallies at our workplaces or schools. We join the other apparently enthusiastic participants and act the same. But don't get me wrong. Many, many Cubans are very supportive of the Revolution and the rallies. They believe their position in the world is good, and their free lodging, medicine and schooling is a great benefit that arose from the Revolution."

Elena looked again at Elenita. A child of her age or a few years older couldn't have a clue as to what a rally was all about.

Amelia said, "I've seen plenty of U.S. activities on television. People here in the U.S. think the Cuban kids singing and chanting on the streets is some big pro-government demonstration that they are forced to do. I don't see it that different from the way people here, young and old, stand for your National Anthem and put their hands on their hearts for the Pledge of Allegiance at public gatherings. Sometimes here in Miami, you can hear kids yelling the Pledge with gusto. Every country is the same. Cuban kids are taught to express their love of their country. It doesn't mean they are brainwashed, at least not any more so than your children are."

Elena nodded slowly. "You are totally right, again, madam social worker. You have such a broad, wise view of everything."

"Oh, don't be silly, Elena."

"But you might as well abandon your idea of making me get along with my brother."

Chapter 29

Sylvia Morales

Sylvia felt so helpless. She wished there was something she could do to wake Louis or to find out if he was aware.

His sunken cheeks and cloudy, slightly open eyes made him appear to have aged years since yesterday morning. His eyes quivered from time to time behind paper-thin eyelids. Caressing his pallid, bony hand, she said, "Louis, honey, can you hear me?" She thought an eye twitched. "You don't need to worry about a thing. I'm taking care of you."

His eyelids moved again, like window blinds on a defective roller. He emitted a guttural sound. She jumped. What was that? Was he trying to talk? Was he in pain?

Franklin blew into the room. She tensed. It seemed Louis's hand in hers did the same. She was glad he visited his father, but he always raised the anxiety level. She wanted to inquire about whether he'd learned anything. After a hesitation, she said, "Franklin, can we step outside and talk?"

Franklin shot fiery eyes at her. "Why can't we talk here?"

She looked at Louis. She was sure he twitched under the sheets. "I don't want to upset him."

Franklin approached his father and grasped his hand. Louis' eyelids fluttered. "Papá, do you want us to leave? I think you are aware and can hear. Am I right?"

At least she and Franklin agreed on that count. She moved to her husband's other side and placed her hand on his. She looked at Franklin. "I know he can hear. You and I may be the only ones who see that. I know that in my heart that if he could communicate, he would say that he wants me to help him. Has George Murphy even been here?"

Franklin shot his hateful scowl at her. "Yes, he has. The doctors told me. Listen, Sylvia, my father is a proud man . . . a thoughtful man. He does not leave things to chance. You know that, from what he told us just the other day. He said he was planning to change his documents. But he didn't have time. I'm not going to question his choices."

She stewed but decided not to ask more.

Franklin turned away and looked out the window for a moment. Then he spun back to her. "The documents do not designate you at all. And, as I understand it, you signed a prenuptial agreement, which I'm sure waives your rights to be involved."

The bastard angered her so intensely. She wanted to fight back, wanted to say something rude and nasty. But she decided there was no sense.

She felt another presence, then heard the grating, nasally voice of Doolittle. "Aw, Louis. How could this have happened?"

Doolittle placed a hand on Franklin's shoulder. "I'm sorry, Franklin."

Then he strode toward Sylvia, with the air of an aristocrat, held her by both shoulders and kissed her on the cheek.

She tried to avoid his riveting eyes, but they sought her out.

"How lucky he is to have you by his side, Sylvia." He looked down at the slight figure of her husband in the bed. "Has there been any change in his condition, any sign of recognition?"

Louis's head seemed to rise slightly and bob as though on a stick. His eyes squinted, like he was trying to see through a thick film. His head collapsed back into the pillow.

She turned to Doolittle. "He just lifted his head. Did you see? I think he just isn't able to communicate."

She watched Doolittle's expression. "Yes, well . . .," Doolittle said, his voice trailing off.

"Mr. Doolittle, I believe he can hear and is aware of our presence."

Doolittle turned back to Franklin. "Will you be in later? We need to talk."

Franklin sighed.

"Did your dad create a will? We need to know about his estate plan."

Franklin did not answer.

Sylvia said, "Gentlemen, no legal talk here. Please take your discussions outside."

Franklin took Doolittle's arm and led him away. Doolittle whispered loudly, "Did he give you his vote in the firm?"

Franklin barked, "What do you know of George Murphy's involvement?"

Doolittle grimaced and pursed his lips. "We're working on a guardianship to get some access," he offered, with authority.

Sylvia was sure Louis jerked this time. Franklin seemed to notice it as well. She looked at Doolittle. "Please do not discuss such matters in the room. You can still be heard. Out."

Doolittle put an arm around Franklin's shoulders and moved him toward the door, speaking under his breath. "I suggest we use your sister as guardian, since she has no interest in the firm."

They still stood inside the room. Franklin pulled back and glared at him. "My father has signed documents. Guardianship is not necessary, and even if it is enacted, the court will name the designees of those documents as guardians. Finally, who could be more incompetent to speak for my father than my sister? She will not even visit. You know the court would never appoint her."

Doolittle gritted his teeth and tugged Franklin's elbow, pulling him farther away. "Take it easy, Franklin. We'll control her. We need a family member."

Franklin hissed, "No way! My father appointed people he trusted. And anyway, she's not the only family member. I'm a family member. I'm a lawyer. I've handled guardianships."

"But you have an interest as a potential shareholder in the firm," Doolittle pleaded.

Franklin glared at him. "Are you aware of the priority to serve as guardian under Florida statutes? First, whoever holds a power of attorney will have priority. If there were no power of attorney, Sylvia, as his wife, would have next priority, unless she waived that right in a prenuptial. Then, his children have equal rights to serve."

"Shhh, Franklin. Don't let Sylvia hear that she could serve."

Sylvia said, from across the room. "Well, I did hear that, and I've heard the rest. Get out."

Franklin shook his head and pulled away from Doolittle, sneering. "I can't believe any of this." He strolled back across the room, looked down at his father, said a few words in Spanish and marched out of the room without considering her or Doolittle.

Chapter 30

Luis Morales

It's so disheartening that Franklin and Sylvia are at odds over me. I'm glad he's at odds with Braxton Doolittle though. My trust for Doolittle's ethics has vanished. If I'd known that Franklin would become an attorney, the kind of brilliant, astute, honest, hard-working attorney that makes the legal profession honorable, I would have kept all the stock for him.

Sometimes I think Franklin and Sylvia are on the same wavelength, but then one of them, usually Franklin, becomes obnoxious. The way he marched out was unpleasant, although since he was battling with Doolittle, maybe it was all right.

Lying in this position is so uncomfortable. Distant luminescence sneaks into the room and mixes with pins of colored lights flickering in the room. I'm confused. I try to relax.

Now the light is coming through gaps in wood, as I try to rest, while half sitting and half lying on the hard wood of the chicken coop loft outside the Siboney Farmhouse. The ruckus outside continues. The house seems alive, jam-packed with men talking loudly. Groups of men continually venture outside to urinate, talk, question the plan or argue. Each time the talk seems particularly interesting or particularly contentious, we crawl around looking for a way to see through gaps between boards.

My brother has grabbed my arm, waking me again. Hearing shouts, orders and the clatter of rifles banging together, we crawl again along the floor to the side facing the farmhouse, where most of the cars are packed together, and again peer out. All the men are dressed in khaki army uniforms, like official government soldiers.

Fidel Castro has mounted a wooden box. He proclaims, "Comrades, we may win, or we may lose, but in the end this movement will triumph. If we win, tomorrow will fulfill what Martí aspired to. If we don't, the gesture will have sent an example for the people of Cuba."

I say to my brother, "It's a 'gesture?' The movement will triumph, even if they lose?"

Abel Santamaría, standing near Fidel in the yard, announces, "We must all believe that we will win, but if fate is against us, we will have to bear defeat bravely because one day everyone will know what happened. History will record it, and all young Cubans will follow our example of dying willingly for Cuba. That will make our sacrifice worthwhile and help ease the sorrow of our loved ones and our parents. To die for one's country is to live!"

Fidel steps up on the box again. "You already know the objectives of the plan. Without any doubt, it's dangerous, and all those who leave this place with me tonight must do so voluntarily. You still have time to make a decision. Those who are determined to go, take a step forward." All but four step forward. He orders that the four be locked up.

Assignments are shouted. Rifles are handed out. The sounds of footsteps, rifles banging together and car doors creaking open and then slamming shut vibrate through the small space. Men pile into cars, start engines, rev up, and roll out in a line, leaving a huge cloud of dust.

Silence.

"Let's go," my brother says.

I try to get my bearings. "How? Where?"

Two of the other men pull up floorboards and drop through the floor onto the ground inside the fake chicken coop. My brother scrambles to the hole they've made, saying, "Come on." He plunges through the hole. Felipe and I do the same, but more carefully, to avoid breaking a bone on the fall.

I'm not sure it's good to leave or what we should do, but at least we haven't been shot. As we walk out of the chicken coop, I say, "Are you ready to abandon this nonsense and come home?"

Miguel stops and stares at me in disbelief. "Fidel will lead by the end of today. You heard him. Cuba will be in flames. I have every intention of being a part of it. This country needs this Revolution. That speech was unbelievable."

I shake my head, dismayed. "I'll call it unbelievable. True, Miguel. This is doomed to failure. Most of the guys that were locked up with us knew it. They were the wise ones. You must come home and forget this ridiculous plan. Anyway, the so-called Revolution abandoned you. They didn't want you."

He laughs aloud. "You go home and live with the *status quo*, imprisoned by tyranny."

Felipe hasn't said a word, but now whispers to me, "We've got to get out of here. Let's leave your brother. I don't think we should stay with him."

My brother runs into the farmhouse.

I look around. "Where's your car?"

He spins around, wide-eyed. "Shit. They must have taken it."

I follow my brother into the farmhouse, saying, "You go, Felipe. Thanks for bringing me. I owe you gratitude forever. But I can't leave my brother."

"And what am I going to do? walk to Santiago?" Felipe follows me into the farmhouse.

Tables, chairs, beds and the floor are strewn with civilian clothes, uniform shirts and pants, boots, shoes, personal belongings, empty suitcases, canvas bags and wooden crates. My brother scrambles around the room grabbing military pants and shirts, holding them up to himself, dropping them and grabbing others. He pulls a pair of pants on over what he's wearing, but they are so huge, they drop to the floor. He tries another but can't get them higher than his knees.

I grab his arm. "Let's go, Miguel. It's not safe to stay here. We don't have a car, so you won't be able to get to the Moncada in time to fight."

He keeps trying on pants.

I grab his arm. "Miguel, we are leaving." He turns and wrenches my hand away. I motion to Felipe, and we start leaving.

Then Miguel runs toward us, hopping on one foot, as he tries to pull on another pair of pants. Finally, he abandons the pants he can't possibly put on and follows us as we trudge through the dusty yard, turn north on the dirt highway and pad along toward Santiago with the light of stars and the moon shining intermittently through the overhanging trees. The quiet is broken only by our footsteps, occasional hoots and chirps of night wildlife, and the buzzing of mosquitoes and dragonflies.

Every few minutes, Miguel shouts, "We will prevail," and then, "Cuba will be in flames," and then, "Fidel is the grand leader."

We come upon two men, dressed in wrinkled uniforms that don't seem to be the right sizes in the process of changing a flat tire.

Before we reach them, another car occupied by three men comes toward us, makes a U-turn and screeches to a halt next to the car with the flat. The men abandon the car with the flat, jump into the other car and zoom off, leaving the car with the flat tire and the keys in the ignition. We complete the change of the tire.

In twenty minutes, as specks of dawn peek between buildings, we are entering the city. I point. "That way. Let's go to your house, Felipe."

Miguel leans over the seat, grabs the steering wheel and tries to keep Felipe from turning. "Straight. Go toward La Moncada."

Felipe keeps trying to turn, and I try to help. Miguel lights into Felipe, pummeling him about the head and shoulders as Felipe tries to drive while imitating a turtle.

Miguel keeps striking, yelling, "You son-of-a-bitch. You fascist."

Felipe fights back, flailing his left fist while steering with his right. He breathes hard between punches. "Mark my words, Miguel. If the so-called Revolution succeeds, it will be like every revolution worldwide before it." He pauses when Miguel strikes his temple and then continues. "The one who takes power will become arrogant and rule like a fascist, or a communist, or a dictator. A coup by the military results in a military state. A revolution by a revolutionary becomes a dictatorship."

"You are a fool," my brother hisses, pounding Felipe's head again.

Finally, Felipe skids to a stop, barely avoiding hitting a tree on the side of the road. He jumps out of the car. "That's it. I've had it."

I hear the sound of gunshots. "Where is that coming from?" It must be coming from the Moncada. It's amazing that we can hear them from here, blocks away.

"The Revolution is succeeding," my brother shouts triumphantly. "Get back in and drive. I want to be a part."

125

Felipe says, "How do you know the gunfire is from the revolutionaries? I thought the plan was to take over by trickery, not shooting."

Miguel shoots him a look. "Fidel didn't say there would be no shooting. He said we wouldn't shoot the soldiers or kill without reason. It has to be our men shooting the soldiers."

"It could be that your little band of pathetic losers is getting its ass kicked," Felipe says.

A car full of apparent revolutionaries zooms by, heading away from the Moncada, the occupants disrobing and tossing uniform shirts out the window. Miguel runs and grabs a shirt, which he tries to put on. A man runs down the street, dressed like a physician or other hospital employee.

I look around, hoping the police or soldiers aren't following the escaping group. "Felipe, we need to get off the streets. We're going to get caught up in this."

Two cars race toward us from the area of the Moncada. I freeze. The cars veer in front of us and screech to a halt. Armed soldiers leap out, brandishing machine guns. They appear to be real soldiers, because their uniforms are thicker, darker in color and pressed, unlike the mildewed, old, incredibly wrinkled, yellowish ones we saw strewn around the farmhouse. They aim at us. "Halt. To the Ground." Felipe and I go to our knees and then our stomachs.

But headstrong Miguel runs, yelling, "The Revolution will prevail. Fidel will take power."

Bursts of machine-gun fire interrupt the quiet morning, and the unmistakable sound, like a sack of flour hitting the ground, tells me my brother is dead. My face on my crossed arms, on the hard, rough, asphalt, I sob.

One of the men kicks me hard in the ribs. "Get up. Now." He kicks me again.

Two men pull my arms from behind. It feels like they'll be ripped from their sockets. A man spins me and shoves me against the car. I strike my chin on the roof above the rear door.

One laughs. "Your little revolutionary mission is not going well. Many of your slovenly, so-called soldiers have died. Your leader is nowhere to be found. Where is he?"

I struggle against the pain. "Who?"

"Don't be stupid. Your leader, Fidel Castro."

"We are not revolutionaries."

He whacks me behind the legs with a hard rod, and I fall to the ground, groaning in pain. I am kicked in the ribs again.

"Where would we find the command of the operation?"

I shake my head again. "No, let me explain. My friend Felipe and I went to locate my brother, to convince him...."

I'm struck again, this time in the lower back. The pain is excruciating. I can't speak.

They begin on Felipe. He says, "Look, we aren't wearing uniforms."

The soldier says, "We've seen many other cowards fleeing in stolen clothes, and even no clothes. You can't fool us."

I hear Felipe groaning and sobbing, and I feel sorry for having brought him here. Something heavy drops next to me, but I do not look because I know it's my brother.

We are forced into the car. My brother is seated next to me, his lifeless head and body leaning on me. I do not move him away because he is still my brother. Sadness and desolation engulf me. My brother's skin and clothes, still moist with his drying blood, stick to me.

One of the guards sits in the back on the left side, next to Felipe, while the others sit in front, one with a rifle permanently trained on us. Jammed into the back seat, we sway and bounce roughly. I worry that a weapon will discharge accidentally. I want to try again to explain that our arrest is in error, but the constant rocking and discomfort make communication impossible.

The car screeches to a halt in front of the Saturnino Lora hospital, across the street from the Moncada, where soldiers rush in. The man riding shotgun stands and asks a sentry, "What's happening here?"

"The last of the pitiful revolutionaries thought they could trick us by acting like patients and medical personnel. But we have rooted them out. The end of the fruitless attack on the Moncada is near."

We hear a gunshot, and then another within the walls of the Moncada, and then one from within the hospital. Soldiers run from both areas toward the courthouse, which stands on the street corner next to the Moncada.

The soldiers in the car laugh. One turns and points to Miguel. "I guess your comrade here won't be helped in the hospital."

An army officer orders the soldiers out. They stand beside the car, pointing across the street, and then down toward the harbor.

"If the dissident is dead, take him to the other side of the Moncada and drop him on the parade ground so it appears he was killed there."

Another officer comes up and says, "No, we need some bodies deposited back at the Siboney Farmhouse, where it started." He points, "Those troops are going there now. They'll take the body."

A searing scream echoes from within the hospital walls. I'm petrified with fear.

Two soldiers open the door on the right and pull my brother's body out. They heft him toward a truck with an open truck bed, lift and drop him over the tailgate. A loud metallic sound penetrates the air as the body crashes on the truck bed.

I think of having to report my brother's death to my parents and siblings. Then, I think it's unlikely I will ever have the chance to talk to them about anything. My future is not promising. I might be incarcerated, for who knows how long. Or worse.

Voices bring me to. Two doctors appear next to me, looking at charts. One is reading aloud. "Ischemic stroke," one says.

"Multiple strokes," says the other.

"The pons was affected. Perhaps the strokes affected multiple areas. Here, here and here." They are apparently looking at a printout. "No lesions. But multiple bleeds."

"Is it coma?"

"Maybe. It almost seems more like Locked-In Syndrome, but everywhere, including vision. His eyes are usually half open like this, as I understand it, but non-responsive."

"That's contradictory to the definition of L.I.S. He would have to be conscious in some way."

"I'd say the only reason one knows a patient is in L.I.S., is if he's alert enough to disclose it. That doesn't mean this patient isn't in that state. Could he have had a stroke in the supranuclear ocular motor pathways at the same time?"

"Need more tests." Papers shuffle. "How can we get a test on the ocular movement control if he can't communicate?"

One peers into my eyes, and then shines a blinding light into my brain. With one hand, he pulls my lids open and seems to manipulate the eyeball. "Contraction," he says.

Dammit. That hurts. Stop it, please.

"I'm not getting anything. I'd still say coma. Why are you thinking otherwise?"

"I don't know. Family and some nurses have noted odd movements."

I'm looking back. *Blink, damn it.* They leave.

Chapter 31

Franklin Morales

Franklin pulled to the curb in front of Murphy's Plumbing, a drab and beat-up building among many others in a fringe neighborhood. Within sight were two pawn shops with tacky decorations and teasers hanging in windows, a liquor store, a furniture store stocked with used and cheap-looking furniture, and a wig shop. Two groups of black men and one group of Latin-American-looking men stood in front of the stores watching him. A large truck zoomed by, so close his car lifted a bit. He grabbed a pad and some papers, stood in the warmth of the day, nodded at the three gawking groups and headed inside.

Nobody attended the nicked and filthy reception counter, so he rang a little bell. A haggard older woman with a cigarette hanging from her mouth came around the corner and raised an eyebrow at him.

"Hi, I'm Franklin Morales. Is George Murphy around?"

"Who wants ta know?"

"Uh, I'm Franklin Morales. He's a friend of my father, Luis Morales."

She thought for a moment, squinting through the haze of smoke. Then, the name seemed to be familiar to her. "He ain't here."

Franklin hesitated.

The lady spoke more softly. "Want me ta try ta call 'im?"

He nodded. "Thanks."

She picked up an odd-looking microphone and yelled, "Hey, George. George, come in."

A scratchy voice came back. "George here. Come on."

"Someone here ta see ya. Son of Lou Rallies, or something like that."

"Huh? Oh, is it Franklin?"

"Uh, yep. Over."

There was silence for a moment. "Send him over ta Claude's Diner. I'll meet him there. Over."

The diner was not exactly Franklin's kind of place, but old George, belly extending above and far beyond his almost invisible belt and a toothpick dangling from his teeth, stood at the front door like it was his home.

They shook hands. Mr. Murphy put an arm around Franklin and pulled him inside. "I'm so sorry about Lou's condition." Franklin cringed at the way he said the name.

Mr. Murphy motioned toward a booth and they sat. "What can I do for you?"

"Sylvia and I are searching for answers, but doctors will not talk to us. The heart surgeon told us early on that he had a heart attack, due to a blockage in his heart, and they had to operate, and that apparently, he had several strokes. We can't get any information out of the neurologists. I'm hoping you know more than we do." He shook his head and stared at the table, thinking of his papá lying in bed like a corpse.

Mr. Murphy frowned. "They're still doing tests."

"When will you hear more?"

"I don't know."

"Will you go the hospital today? Can you inquire and tell us?"

"Yeah, I was gonna go later if they didn't call."

An old, sad-looking waitress dressed in a yellowish dress approached. George made some weird hand motion toward Franklin like lifting a can or bottle and drinking. He wrinkled his brow. Franklin didn't get the motion at first, but then said, "Uh, Coke."

"Coffee," George said. Franklin couldn't imagine drinking watery gringo coffee in a diner like this.

"Anyway," Franklin continued, "My father told me that he designated you alone to make medical decisions, for a time, but that another person and I join you in deciding whether to discontinue life prolonging procedures."

Mr. Murphy nodded silently and swirled his finger on the table-top. "You know, your dad is a special man. I've never known anybody quite like him. When I first met him, I was impressed with his uh, what was it? Uh, his grace. Yeah, he was just so humble, so gracious. So polite. A nice man."

Franklin hadn't always thought of his father as gracious. But he did have a gift that caused people to love him. That's why he'd been so successful. He'd never gone out just to hobnob and attract clients. He didn't play golf or hang out in bars. He just attracted them naturally while being himself.

The waitress brought the glass and cup and banged them on the table. Mr. Murphy's eyes misted as he stared out the window. The silence made Franklin uncomfortable; he strummed his fingers on the tabletop, looked out the window, and then glanced around the room. He hated diners.

Mr. Murphy sighed aloud. "He's a good man. I'll do anything I can for him. I hadn't realized how large a plan he had made and what I was supposed to do."

"Mr. Murphy, are you aware that you cannot make end-of-life decisions alone? Are you aware you are part of a committee on financial documents as well?"

"I know that you and somebody else are going to be involved with me. I'm not sure when. I heard something about some other documents from his secretary, Ruth, but I haven't seen anything."

Here he was sitting in a diner with Bubba, the plumber, who was picking at his teeth with a wooden toothpick. This man was in charge of important decisions but had no clue what he was to do. He had no education, no knowledge of the law office, no knowledge of the intricacies of the family, no knowledge of trusts, no knowledge of anything but wrenches and pipes and eliminating clogs in the plumbing. Where in the hell had his father's mind been? Then he thought of how aggravated he'd gotten at Sylvia for expressing the same misgivings.

"Franklin, your dad told me years and years ago that if anything ever happened to him . . . if he died or couldn't take care of himself . . . I would receive instructions from unknown persons, and that he hoped I would do what the documents said to do."

The waitress returned. Mr. Murphy ran his fingers together to indicate he'd take the check.

He leveled his eyes on Franklin. "We'll talk again soon, probably after work today. Don't worry. It's all under control."

He stood, and Franklin did too, dissatisfied with the complete lack of information or comfort he had hoped to obtain.

Chapter 32

Elena Morales Lennox

Amelia said, "Come on. Come on. My father is meeting us at the hospital. We need to get moving."

Elena questioned having consented to visit her papá. She carried Elenita's things to Amelia's Volkswagen and strapped her car seat in place.

Amelia clutched and shifted through gears. Elena said, "I thought all the cars in Cuba were American. How'd you learn to drive stick?"

Amelia shrugged. "The old U.S. cars in Cuba are mostly used as taxis. If anybody can afford a car, it is usually an older Russian model, like Lada or Moskovich. Most are manual. A boyfriend had a Lada and taught me. I don't know many Cubans who have ever driven a car. By the way, you people in the United States shouldn't steal the name America for yourselves. We are all Americans. Maybe you can say you are North Americans, but Canadians are that too. We even have a collective noun for you, *estadounidenses,* like United Statesians or something like that." They laughed.

Elena said, "Do you remember being taught to fear the U.S. bombing and invading us?"

"Sure. What the *estadounidenses* called the *Bay of Pigs*, and *The Cuban Missile Crisis*."

Elena smiled. "People in Miami who were children at the time say they had to practice getting under their desks at school because they thought Cuba, or really Russia from Cuba, was going to bomb them."

Amelia said, "Yes, the kids of both countries were taught they were in danger and needed to be prepared for attack from the other country."

Elena searched her memory banks again for recollections of events that occurred long ago. "Amelia, I don't like going back in time like this. I guess it's just seeing you. I was thinking of the time my mother, a shovel over her shoulder, pulled me to the rear yard of Abuela's home one night, in darkness and dug a deep hole.

"After laboring for a long time, she rushed to the house and returned, dragging a blanket, bunched at the top. She let it fall open on the ground and began removing silver chalices and crystal pieces. She wrapped each piece in a fine, white linen napkin, laid them all on a tablecloth, wrapped and tied the cloth and gently placed it into the hole."

Amelia made the final turn before pulling into the hospital's parking lot.

Elena continued. "'My God,' she said, carefully placing one piece into the ground. 'This was my grandmother's. She would die if she knew that all her special pieces had ended up like this.'

"Her face was streaked with dirt, tears and worry. After filling the hole, she dragged the shovel around, trying to make the area appear natural and undisturbed. Suddenly she froze. 'Shhh. Lie down. I hear somebody.' We lay silently, in the darkness, listening, but nobody appeared."

Amelia parked the car. As they got out, Elena said, "Just a minute. I need a cigarette," and lit up.

Amelia said, "Are you serious? Your mother really buried things? Are they still there?"

"As far as I know."

"Once we were in Miami, she'd say, 'I wish I had my silver and crystal to adorn the table. This house is so plain, Luis.' My father would shrug his shoulders and say, 'Cari, dear, just forget it.'"

Elena felt tears streaming down her cheeks. She puffed quickly and flicked her cigarette onto the asphalt.

They reached the elevator and rose to the floor of the Intensive Care Ward. Elena inquired at the nurses' station but was told the number of people in the room was at the limit.

"God, I hope he's going to be all right. Maybe he's alert and talking now."

They sat. Amelia looked at Elena. "I hope so. My father should be here soon."

Their attention was drawn to the television, which showed Raul Castro and others standing on a large stage in front of thousands of people.

Amelia said, "That's *Plaza de la Revolución en La Habana.* All those men, oh, and a woman or two, are world leaders who've gone to pay their respects. You see who's notably missing, don't you?"

"The President of *El Imperio,* and in fact, anybody from our country."

"Ha-ha, you're getting it now."

Amelia walked over and turned off the television. "You look gloomy, Elena. I'm sorry to raise bad memories."

"No, I'm sorry for being melancholy. Do you know about the jewelry?"

"What jewelry?"

Elena smiled. "One day, mi mamá set all her jewelry on the bed. She wrote a list of the items in longhand with her fountain pen. After categorizing each of the eighty pieces, she carefully placed them into a box and sealed it. Then she wrote the entire list again.

"She concealed the box in a canvas bag and said were going shopping, which was odd, because we'd never been shopping before."

"We set out for a march around town. She stopped in some of the bodegas I'd been in with Abeo, but she didn't buy anything. I think she was checking to see if spies were following. Then, we stopped in front of a large building. 'Elena, that is the flag of Spain, the country where I was born, and where your brother Franklin is. Don't ever forget this place. If I die without my jewelry, I want you to retrieve it.'

"Inside, a guard called somebody on a phone. A man dressed in a dark suit emerged, greeted us and took us down a hallway to an office. We entered, and he closed the door. My mother looked around nervously.

"She opened the bag and handed the box to the man. He reviewed the hand-written list, which she'd taped on the outside. He signed and dated the duplicate sheet she'd written and returned that one.

"Sometime later, before we left Cuba, she said that the jewelry had been moved to the Spanish Embassy in Havana. Over the years, now in Miami, she beseeched the Spanish Embassy here in Miami to return it, but they denied her each time. She kept the handwritten list.

"She'd fallen from her origins as a rich debutante. She spent all her years, expecting that something would happen that would result in her being able to return to her homeland, to her old house, which she had to relinquish when she left the county, and to retrieve the buried items and her jewelry."

"Elena, we could go back, and get the jewelry and dig up the yard for the other things."

Elena laughed aloud. "Sure, you think the people in the house would let us dig up their yard? The embassy would just let us in? Customs would just let us walk out with a bunch of porcelain and jewelry?"

Amelia smiled. "Well, maybe not. Have you seen the movie, *The Twelve Chairs*, about a Cuban man who finds riches in the fabric of dining-room chairs after the revolution?"

"No, I've missed that movie, but it sounds like fun."

Amelia touched Elena's wrist. Elenita played with dolls on the waiting-room floor.

Elena said, "I have another story that haunts me." She hesitated for a moment. "Quite some time before I was to leave Cuba forever, my mother and Mima took me on a long train trip. I asked, 'Mima, where are we going?'"

"'To see your grandfather, mi amor.'

"I was shocked and confused. I'd seen photos of my grandfather, but I had always thought he was dead.

"I gazed at landscape flying by, trying to imagine where we were going to this man I'd never heard of before. The trip to Havana was interminable. Then, we changed trains and headed to the southern coast, where we boarded a ferry for a slow trip across bumpy water. We went by taxi to a building on a semicircular driveway. Out a window inside the building, I saw a number of huge cylindrical buildings.

"Inside the visiting area, men in uniform reviewed and stamped official-looking documents, and others patted and squeezed our bodies. Then, we were seated at shiny metal tables and stools standing in neat rows. Prisoners in gray outfits entered and sat with visitors.

"A tall man with silver hair limped toward us. Mima cried out and pulled herself up. 'Dear. Look at you,' she said, as she and he embraced. When she disengaged from him, my mother stood halfway, and he kissed her.

"'Elena,' Mima said, 'This is your grandfather.'

"I wasn't sure what to do. He leaned down, kissed me on the cheek and said, 'It's a-pleasure to meet you, *nieta.*'"

Amelia said, "I remember when your grandfather was released and came home. He never talked. He had the appearance of an incompetent. I think your Mima suffered more once he was home."

Elena looked down. "I knew he was finally freed, and that he died. Mi papá never talked about him. I feel that I lost a whole relationship with somebody else . . . another man . . . I could have been close to. I never saw him again."

Wiping tears, she looked at Elenita playing peacefully on the floor, thinking again that the child had a great-grandfather, for the moment, and wondering if she should take her in to see him. But what good would that do? She wouldn't understand why he's unable to touch her or speak to her.

Tío Alejandro entered the waiting room, broke out in a big smile, and yelled, *"¡Mi sobrina de ojos verdes favorita!"*

Elena grinned. They shared a cheek kiss.

"I'm still your only green-eyed niece."

He'd aged considerably since the last time she'd seen him. But his eyes still had the same sparkle.

"Yes, but you are my favorite."

"Uncle, you look wonderful. Welcome to our country. How are you?"

"I'm fine, *gracias a Dios.*" His grin was intense.

They hugged for a long time.

Tío Alejandro said, "Elena, I'm so sorry about your father. I hope he gets better soon. I am only here in the States because he performed his legal magic."

Elena smiled. "I didn't know that."

Then he turned and kneeled. "I am told I am to meet a lovely child. I'll bet it's the little girl here." He kneeled next to Elenita. "Hello, Elenita."

She looked timid and unsure.

"You remind me of your grandmother when she was your age."

He hugged her. "Can you women please help an old man up?"

Chapter 33

Luis Morales

I feel the presence of Sylvia and Franklin. They provide me peace, in spite of the strain between them. I understand the common issues between stepparents and stepchildren, especially when the stepparent comes into the marriage late in life and is younger than the adult children. I want Sylvia, Franklin and Elena to all get along. As a matter of fact, why hasn't Elena been here?

I drift back to prior unhappy times. I'd like to stop, but it's like a story that my brain needs to relive.

I'm in the overflowing courtroom, in the courthouse next to the Moncada. Everybody who was arrested is here, in front of three magistrates. Some lawyers represent multiple defendants. Felipe and I have a lawyer who represents only us and three others. Because so many defendants are being tried together, we sit in the spectator seats, as lawyers are spread around multiple tables in front. Lawyers cannot confer with their clients.

During the first day of the trial, some defendants have been called as witnesses.

Now, Fidel Castro rises. "I wish to be placed on the witness stand."

The magistrates look at each other and nod. One says, "Very well."

He swaggers to the stand. A lawyer for the government asks him questions about the Moncada attack. It seems to me that he's just admitted and bragged about being the organizer, but in the next sentence says he knows nothing about it.

I wish I could ask my lawyer what he thinks. I lean over and whisper to Felipe. "What is he saying? That he organized it, but wasn't present? Being not present would make him not guilty?"

"I guess."

The prosecutor asks, "Mr. Castro, you have indicated that you were the chief promoter of the Moncada attack. Were you the leader?"

Castro seems to nod *yes*, at the same time as he shakes his head *no*. "José Martí was the intellectual author."

"Sir, was Martí present? Oh, of course he could not have been. He died in the previous century."

The day drags on as all twenty-four defense attorneys interrogate Castro. Each one points to his client or clients and asks whether they were involved. Fidel denies that any of the defendants was involved.

Our lawyer stands and approaches the dais. "Mr. Castro, I ask whether you are familiar with two of the defendants, Mr. Luis Morales and Mr. Felipe Salvador Llorente."

"I do not recognize those names."

Our lawyer turns to the judges. "Your honors, may I have these two defendants stand up?"

The magistrates nod. We rise.

"Mr. Castro, do you know these two men."

He shakes his head. "No, I've never seen them.

"Were they involved in the Moncada attack?"

"I have no idea."

Our lawyer tries a few more questions and sits.

The prosecutor stands. "Mr. Castro, how many of the defendants do you know."

Castro smiles and looks around the huge group of defendants. He shakes his head. "I've seen a few."

"How many is a few? How many people do you recognize?"

Castro shrugs. "I may know ten."

"How many of these people were at the Moncada during the attack?"

Castro smiles again. "Are you trying to trick me? I've never stated that I was there. How would I know?"

Several defendants snicker and guffaw. A magistrate bangs a gavel.

The prosecutor then says, "All right. You've stated that you don't know or recognize these two defendants and have not heard their names. But you've also said you know and have seen very few of the defendants. Is that correct? It's not a very helpful statement, is it?"

Castro smiles and shrugs.

Castro is dismissed from the witness stand. He turns to the bench and bows. "Magistrates, I am a lawyer. I wish to represent myself."

The justices look at each other. One answers. "Not now. We are not going to allow that at this time. Maybe later. And while we are speaking of this, we intend to administer this trial in a judicious manner. There will be no grandstanding. There will be no political reference, one way or the other."

The lawyers for all the defendants continue to fight for their own clients, interviewing other defendants.

At night, as I sit on my bunk in the Boniato Provincial Prison, about an hour from the Courthouse, Castro talks and talks to his admiring followers. How can they be so supportive? Don't they recognize that his faulty plan caused them all to be jailed?

I hear him explaining his plan again. "Tomorrow we begin to turn the trial into a tribunal condemning the atrocities of Batista. That is what this must be about. We will veer the focus away from ourselves." Then he goes on and on, practicing what he plans to say.

We are on the bus, with guards around, like every morning. Out the windshield I see police cars and army trucks with officers and soldiers holding rifles. Out the back window I see the same. We turn onto the street between La Moncada and the courthouse and pass through files of well-armed police and soldiers. We are ushered through a side door and along hallways of the courthouse. Then, we sit for hours in the heavily guarded third-floor legal library until the court is ready for us.

Fidel Castro rises, uninvited, and again says, "Magistrates, I ask again that I may represent myself, to be my own lawyer, as I am trained as a lawyer."

A magistrate says, "We will allow it, but you must maintain the decorum of this proceeding. No grandstanding. Is that understood?"

Fidel Castro smiles and nods. A man stands and says, "Your honors, on behalf of the Bar Association, we have these robes for Fidel Castro and the other two defendant attorneys to wear."

The trial momentarily seems to be some kind of awards ceremony, as they don their robes in front of the audience.

Then, Fidel Castro begins to take over the proceedings exactly as the magistrates said not to. He struts around, making speeches, interrupting and dragging unrelated issues before the tribunal. The magistrates look annoyed.

Spectators comment, "The audacity of that man. You'd think he was presiding over the tribunal."

In the afternoon, Haydée Santamaria, sister of Abel, is called to the stand. Her attorney asks her whether she was at the Moncada on the morning of the attack.

"I came to Santiago from Havana to see my brother Abel and to attend the *Carnaval*. I knew nothing about an attack. I went to a party with him and learned that the men were planning to participate in a peaceful intrusion at a military base. I agreed to go along, to be a nurse."

The prosecutor says, "If it was to be peaceful, why would they need a nurse?"

Then he tries to get her to admit that she knew what was to occur, but it leads to nothing.

Now it's our turn to testify and for our lawyer to try again to show that we truly were not involved. I'm not confident. Our lawyer calls Felipe to the stand. He says we were trying to find my brother and to remove him from the Siboney Farmhouse.

The prosecutor smiles. "Well, you were not found sequestered at the Siboney Farmhouse, were you? You were found within five or six blocks of the Moncada, early in the morning, as many dissidents were fleeing. Isn't that right?"

Felipe does not answer.

"Miguel Morales was in the car with you, and was killed by police as he ran, ranting for the Revolution. Isn't that true?"

I see no hope. Our story is little different from that of any other defendant.

Our lawyer has now called my former friend Ernesto as a witness. He asks Ernesto what he was doing that afternoon and evening.

"Standing on the streets, watching the *carnaval* activity."

"Isn't it true that you were the contact who greeted rebels and directed them?"

He shakes his head. "No."

"Isn't it true that you came across Luis Morales and Felipe Salvador Llorente in the early evening on that day?"

Ernesto hesitates, then nods. "I did."

"And did they not tell you that they were looking for Luis Morales' brother, Miguel, to get him away from the group that was planning the attack?"

He smiles. "I don't remember that very well."

"Will you not verify that these two defendants made it clear to you that they were not part of the dissident group?"

"I cannot verify anything about their intentions."

Our lawyer looks frustrated. "Was either of their names on the lists of revolutionaries you maintained?"

"What lists?"

"Are you afraid, sir, to tell the truth? Are you afraid you will be prosecuted if you admit you were part of the plan?"

Ernesto shakes his head.

The magistrates are yawning, looking at their watches and reading papers. One's head keeps fading and jerking like he's trying to stay awake.

"Haven't you known Luis Morales for many years?"

"Yes."

"Did you ever talk politics with him?"

"I don't recall."

Our lawyer looks at his notes, obviously trying desperately to find a question that Ernesto will answer truthfully and helpfully. He looks up a few times but seems to decide against the questions.

Our lawyer sits down, and the prosecutor rises. He asks a number of questions of Ernesto, trying to get him to say that Felipe and I were involved, but fortunately Ernesto does not confirm anything helpful to the prosecution either.

Our lawyer calls one of the policemen who arrested us. "Officer, these two defendants were in street clothes when arrested. Isn't that true?"

"Yes."

"Then, what made you think they were part of the attack?"

"Many of the attackers fled wearing street clothes they had stolen at the hospital or in the barracks."

Our lawyer points at us. "These men had no weapons, did they?"

"They probably abandoned them when things went awry."

"These men were not dressed in the uniforms of the attackers. You found no uniforms in the car. And you found no weapons in the car. Correct?"

The cop shakes his head. "There was reason to arrest them. The third man ranted about the success of the attackers and ran. One of these two men had been the driver of the car, and the other was the brother of the man who yelled about the success of the Revolution. It was obvious they were all attackers."

Our lawyer summarizes to the panel of bored magistrates, claiming that we were not attackers and that our arrest was a mistake. Our story is no different from any other defendant's. I know from the judges' faces that our lawyer's attempts have been fruitless.

At night in our jail cells, like most nights since the trial began, Fidel Castro says, "Did you see them squirm today? They cannot prevent me from bringing up the atrocities of the Batista government. The prosecutor is unable to gain control. Magistrates are listening to me. No matter what they ask and what they say, I can twist the words to help our cause."

Then he begins practicing tomorrow's speech.

That night, guards come in and say, "Fidel Castro, you have been ordered to solitary confinement."

On the sixth day of trial, Fidel Castro does not join us on the bus. In court, a prosecutor announces that he is ill.

In the evening, although we cannot see him inside his solitary cell, he can speak and listen. He interrogates his followers about what occurred in the trial during the day. He coaches them as to the next day's action. He reports that he will not be returning, as he has arranged for his own private trial after the mass trial is concluded.

Castro is released from solitary confinement, and now has his own jail cell. Every night as the mass trial continues, he prepares for his own, private trial. He creates, recites, revises and practices his closing argument in front of his admiring audience, as he tries to get the beat just right.

> *"HONORABLE JUDGES:*
>
> *A lawyer has never had to . . . No. Never has a lawyer had to practice his profession under such difficult conditions; never have there been so many . . . .. No. Never have such a number of overwhelming irregularities been committed against an accused man. In this case, counsel and*

defendant are one and the same. As attorney, he has not even been able to take a look at the indictment. As accused, for the past seventy-six days he has been locked away in solitary confinement, held totally and absolutely incommunicado, in violation of every human and legal right.

He who speaks to you hates vanity . . ."

I try not to laugh. I don't believe the last statement at all. I wish he were really locked away in the solitary, so we would not hear him.

". . . with all his being, nor are his temperament or frame of mind inclined towards courtroom poses or sensationalism of any kind."

He goes on and on, detailing every piece of testimony given by every witness while he was present. Then he begins,

"As the trial went on, the roles were reversed: those who came to accuse found themselves accused, and the accused became the accusers! It was not the revolutionaries who were judged there; judged once and forever was a man named Batista—monstruum horrendum!"

Night after night he practices.

Most of us defendants are convicted in our trial and sentenced to El Presidio Modelo on the island called the Isla de Pinos.

After Fidel Castro has his private trial in a room at the Saturnino Lora hospital, he explains how spellbound the magistrates were, but he has been convicted and sentenced as well.

Chapter 34

Elena Morales Lennox

Tío Alejandro put an arm around Elena and pulled her with him. "Let's go and see your papá."

In the hallway, he said, "Your father is going to be happy to know you are here. Don't be nervous."

She stopped near the door, trying to gather strength, resisting his pull. Her heart pounded, causing her to wonder what happened to her father's heart, and his brain, and if it pounded like hers was pounding now when he had the attack.

Dread and discomfort always came to her with hospital visits. Today, she'd come only to show her father that she cared, and maybe to cause her arrogant, know-it-all brother and her father's wife not to think badly of her. She wanted them to know she'd come to visit, but at the same time hoped neither Sylvia nor Franklin would be in the room.

She didn't know what to say to her father, how to act, or what to do. Whatever she would say to him, she didn't want those two to see her or listen to her.

She could picture herself walking in and saying, "Hi, Sylvia, how's mi papá today?"

Sylvia would look her up and down with apparent bewilderment and mistrust, and say, "If you had been to see him, you would know."

Once, before Elena's father married Sylvia, Elena stood next to him in the front yard on a sunny afternoon as he raked leaves. It took a while to gather strength, just like it was taking her a while to enter the room now. He raked, looking at her, like he was expecting something. "Papá, are you and Sylvia planning to sign a prenuptial agreement?"

Her father stopped raking. His eyes darkened and riveted on her.

"I wasn't trying to be rude, papá. I'm sure she's a nice lady. But what if you die, or get divorced?"

Anger, surprise and hurt blended on his face. "How dare you question Sylvia's scruples! If I want to leave her everything, I can, and I will. We will never discuss this again."

He glowered, turned and abruptly marched away, leaving her feeling like a heel.

God, love was sickening, especially when an old man was being manipulated by whatever she was doing to him. The joy and utter childlike fascination in his face whenever his bride entered the room was revolting. He'd never looked at her mother that way.

Her uncle looked at her several times, a question mark on his face. She knew she was acting strange. He pulled her arm into the crook of his and tugged gently. She took deep breaths and allowed him to usher her in.

Just inside the door, she halted as she found her papá's ridiculously young wife sitting there looking all sorrowful and holding his hand. Sylvia looked up and dabbed tears away from under her eyes. What the hell was she crying for? She was probably hoping he'd kick off early when she married him.

Franklin stood and hugged tío Alejandro. Turning to Sylvia, he said, "This is our Uncle Alejandro. Before the other day, I hadn't seen him since I was seven-years-old and left for Spain."

Tío Alejandro nodded and shook Sylvia's hand, while he grimly looked at Elena's.

Sylvia rose and approached Elena, reaching for her shoulder, but Elena frowned and shrank away. "Here, Elena, sit and talk to him."

Franklin pointed to his chair. "No. It's okay Sylvia. I'll be leaving in a minute. Elena, you can sit here."

Elena froze. Both looked at her inquisitively. Elena looked at the shell of her papá, so shrunken, attached to machines with blinking lights and tubes in which fluids flowed. Dull eyes looked blank between half-open eyelids. She didn't recognize him.

Her papá's bride stepped to the foot of the bed, put her hands on Elena's shoulders and pushed her toward her chair. Elena felt like a stone statue, fighting the push. But Sylvia maneuvered her to the chair and sat her down. Franklin seated tío Alejandro in his seat.

Sylvia grabbed Elena's wrists and put both of her hands on her father's hands. "There. Talk to him. I believe he can hear. Hold his hand. He feels more comfortable when somebody touches him."

Elena looked at her. Why would her step-mother be talking like this? Her papá obviously had no idea what was going on. She remained frozen, her heart pattering wildly. She felt Franklin's and Sylvia's glares. She wished she hadn't come. This wasn't for her. She couldn't touch her papá's hand. She couldn't talk.

"Honey, Elena is here," his wife said to him. "She's sitting next to you. Everybody cares about you, my love."

Finally, Elena managed a whispered, *"Hola, papá. ¿Cómo estás?"*

Seconds later, she reached the breaking point that would lead to tears. She fought against it. But suddenly, a horrid feeling overcame her. She sobbed, "Will he go to a nursing home?"

Her uncle had a hand on her father's forearm, eyes downcast. Her brother and step-mother stared at her.

Still weeping, she blurted out, "I can take him to my house."

Finally, her stepmother answered, "If he's able to leave for home, I'll take him to our home. But we don't know when he'll be leaving yet."

Elena sat there uncomfortably for a few minutes, never doing what her papá's wife ordered her to do.

Discomfort overruled reason. She leapt from the chair and fled the room, leaving Franklin, Sylvia and tío Alejandro looking bewildered.

Chapter 35

Sylvia Morales

Franklin strolled into the hospital room. "Sylvia."

"Franklin."

He looked at his father, and then at her. "Can we talk outside?"

He put a hand on her back as they moved toward the door. "Sylvia, I think we are finally getting some movement. I've clarified with Mr. Murphy that he no longer can work alone. The committee is scheduling meetings with the doctors. I will assure that you are included in all decisions."

She felt tears well up in her eyes. She nodded.

They hugged. "Thank you, Franklin."

She went into the corridor and telephoned Elena.

"Hello."

"Elena, it's Sylvia."

"I know."

"How are you doing, Elena?"

Silence.

"Well, I'm sure you are suffering, worrying about your father."

Silence.

She tried to decide what to say. "Elena, if you would just come and visit him again, I think it would be good for both of you. I can make it a point not to be there if you prefer."

Silence. But she thought she heard sniffles.

"Elena, is there something I can do to make you more comfortable?"

She heard a very meek "No."

"Okay. Well, Elena, we can talk anytime you want to. Okay?"

She heard an almost inaudible squeak of, "Okay."

"All right, Elena, I'll let you go now. Call me."

Silence.

Sylvia hung up, exhausted. It was hard to imagine a sixty-something year-old woman sounding like a lost child.

In the room, she rested her hand on the bed next to her husband's. He twitched. His eyelids fluttered. He groaned lightly. She wanted him to react, but still felt the need to comfort him, not knowing what he was feeling.

She hated the thought of talking to Louis' law partner, but she had to get some answers. She exited again and called the office. She got through the receptionist and Doolittle's secretary without too much difficulty.

He picked up. "Yes, Sylvia. What is it?"

"I want to know more about this court proceeding you were talking about. I can't get any details about Louis's health. I just want to find out how I can help my husband."

After some hesitation, he said, "Sylvia, I'm frustrated too. That's why I'm filing the guardianship."

"Do you have a copy of the prenuptial agreement that Louis and I signed? Do you know if it says anything about if I can speak for him?"

"No. I don't have it and I am not familiar with the terms."

"You represented him. You prepared it. How can it be there's not a copy in the office?"

"He actually prepared it. I didn't."

She didn't know what else to say or ask. "All right. Thank you for at least talking to me."

Why had she bothered calling him? She knew more than he did. She disconnected.

Chapter 36

Luis Morales

I can vaguely see my secretary Ruth's face looking down at me, the wrinkles around her eyes trembling. "Mr. Doolittle has been questioning me about everything," she says.

I tense, but of course nobody realizes it.

Franklin says, "I'll have a chat with him."

The television is on. Raul Castro is saying, "Fidel dedicated his whole life to solidarity . . . with the poor, and for the poor he became a symbol of the anti-colonial and anti-imperialist fight, for the emancipation and dignity of the people."

Turn it off, please, I plead in my head. And then I hear Fidel's voice, "*Hasta la victoria siempre!*"

My anxiety fades as my Cuba pulls me back to my roots. I sift through memories of Vista Alegre, the neighborhood of my youth, nestled in a slight decline beyond the highest point of the city of Santiago de Cuba, far from the harbor and commercial areas.

I'm running along its streets, with cousins and other children, past the few massive homes and the many modest ones. We race into someone's yard, scramble around the bushes and trees and rush into a house. In some homes, we slow down and walk quietly past rooms with fancy, rarely-touched furniture, while in others, we ramble straight through, from the open front to the open rear. Often, we stop in the kitchen on the way, where a maid or nanny greets us, smiling and humming, and treats us with *malta* or fresh fruit juice.

We race outdoors again, past neatly cut yards and gardens, sprinkled with healthy verdant ferns, hedges and *malanga* plants. A dark-skinned chauffer maneuvers a large automobile between long

151

lines of palm trees on Avenida Manduley, the widest street of the subdivision, separated by a well-manicured median, as the automobile's owners sit in back, heads held high.

A tram with a sign saying *Vista Alegre–Alameda* clatters into the neighborhood from the lower part of the city. Dark-skinned maids, nannies and other workers disembark. Later, a nanny might mount the tram with younger children to take them to a park, or the club, or another home. At the end of the day, workers line up at the stop to be taken back down into the city, although several of ours reside in the neighborhood.

Vendors pull wagons or sit on the benches of horse-drawn buggies, crooning, "*malanga,*" "*huevos,*" "*pan*" or whatever they have to offer.

I sit at the dining room table, waiting for the cooks to bring in plates and bowls filled with food, as my grandmother says, "Do you children remember where we lived before moving here to Vista Alegre? In the city, where all the homes were attached to each other, surrounded by little or no open area, perched directly on the narrow, twisting streets, filled with noisy automobiles, horses pulling wagons and trams? It was your grandfather who knew of the farm that occupied this land, *Arroyo Hondo*. When they first started talking of converting it from a farm to a neighborhood, he said we would build homes here in this, as he described it, 'high, fresh oasis, giving such a pleasant view that it brings a smile to the viewer's lips.'"

I'm playing tag and fútbol with the dark-skinned servants' children, along the grass that surrounds and separates twin cobblestone tracks leading to the garage and servant's quarters behind our home, or on the street in front of the servants' small, wooden homes across the street.

I enter a room in our home, where Abeo, a large, perpetually smiling, dark-skinned woman, speaks with a lilting accent to my youngest sister Clara, while cradling her in her arms. Even though I'm about seven, Abeo still likes to grab me and pull me close, just as she did when I was my sister's age.

Abeo takes all of us, from the youngest infants to the five and six-year olds, to the park in the center of Vista Alegre and to visit nearby homes. She and the other maids push the younger ones in strollers along Avenida Manduley.

I shift from past to present. I look up to find my secretary Ruth regarding me. "Mr. Morales, I expect to have you back in the office very soon. Things are fine. But you *are* the law firm."

I try to nod, to no avail.

Chapter 37

Franklin Morales

Franklin was surprised not to see Sylvia as he arrived at his father's room again after a stint in the office.

She walked back in, looking down at her phone. She stopped abruptly and looked up, making a face as though she was surprised to find herself holding it.

"Franklin, I still haven't seen Mr. Murphy."

"Right. I had expected he'd be here by now. Maybe he's eating pancakes at his favorite diner."

"Well, I already stuffed my fat ass with pancakes today, so I'm right here."

Hearing Mr. Murphy's drawl, Franklin spun around in horror, only to find him leaning against the doorjamb, grinning and chewing on a toothpick.

"Sorry for my language, ma'am," he said, nodding at Sylvia. "I know I'm a bit uncouth. Mr. Lansing Armstrong would have called me a Barbarian I suppose."

Sylvia rushed toward him, holding out a hand. "Mr. Murphy. What can you tell us?"

"Well, Sylvia, the doctors haven't figured out much yet. They say they fixed his heart, but they don't know what else the strokes have done."

Sylvia scowled. "Well, what are they doing? What tests have they performed?"

"Uh, a lot of tests that sound like a jumble of letters."

"What are they trying to determine?"

"What's wrong with him."

Franklin could see that Sylvia was put off by Murphy's speaking with such authority, while disclosing nothing. He decided to lend support to Sylvia. "Mr. Murphy, we want to know exactly what tests have been done. When are the doctors scheduled to give a prognosis?"

With an annoying wry grin, Mr. Murphy shook his head. "I've talked to them several times. They are working on it."

Sylvia said, "We are not satisfied. Are we Franklin?"

"Right. Listen, Mr. Murphy, as I think I told you earlier today, my father told us on Sunday that the documents as currently written appoint another person and me to step in with you."

Mr. Murphy turned his twisted grin toward Franklin. "I don't know that we are at that point yet."

"I think we are. I'm going to contact the other designee."

"Lansing Armstrong's dead."

"I'm aware of that. I meant his alternate."

Sylvia sat and held her husband's hand again.

Murphy said, "I don't think there's much hope."

Sylvia flew to her feet like a sprung jack-in-the-box, pointing at the door. "Do not say such things in this room."

Mr. Murphy grinned and said, "Aw, Sylvia, you know he can't hear."

"Out," She demanded, loudly.

Looking sheepish, he made a harrumph noise and walked over to the bed. After looking at Franklin's father for a moment, he turned back. "Your buddy Doolittle is trying to get one over on all of us you know. He asked me if I wanted to join his little plan."

Franklin's stomach tensed. "That ass called you?"

"Yep."

Franklin said, "He told you about a guardianship?"

"Yep. He wanted to know if I'd go along and just give up, so he wouldn't have any resistance."

Sylvia asked, "What did you tell him?"

"To kiss my ass. Pardon me ma'am. Ya'll might think that I don't care about Louis over there, but I do. And I'm not gonna be pushed around by that sleazy bastard."

"All right, Mr. Murphy. We are going to fight the guardianship. Even if my father is found incompetent, they fail on being able to appoint Elena. And I am to be involved in my father's health care decisions. Will you please make an appointment, so we can all meet, including Sylvia, and talk to the doctors in detail?"

"I reckon," Mr. Murphy said, as he drifted out.

Chapter 38

Elena Morales Lennox

Elena stewed about her father's plight as she spoon-fed Elenita a thick, blended concoction of vegetables. As a child, she'd watched Abeo prepare it so often she had learned the technique.

The previous evening, she'd prompted and spoon-fed Kalvin about what to say to old, balding, arrogant Braxton Doolittle.

She'd said, "This is critical. My dad might not return to work. He may not even live. You need to position yourself to become a partner. You've still got a lot of good years ahead of you. Doolittle and Franklin would have no reason to give you partnership. We need to make it happen."

He'd looked at her like he didn't get it. "Oh. Of course. Should I ask Franklin?"

She sighed. She should be the lawyer. She'd married this man, younger than she, with high hopes for the future. Yet, they'd just plodded along. He seemed to have no ambition. "No, Kalvin. Don't ask Franklin. Make a stand. Position yourself. Figure out plans for firm management in his absence. Look for files. Look for word processing documents."

It was her papá, not Doolittle, who'd arrived in Miami, unable to speak English or to use his law degree, yet he succeeded in creating an amazingly successful law firm. Although she wasn't sure what kind of succession planning her papá had created, she felt certain that he would have arranged to get stock into Kalvin's hands—not for Kalvin's benefit—but for hers. He couldn't just let the firm go to her brother and the other partner. Could he?

Elena handed Elenita the iPad, already set with one of her favorites. She clicked the T.V. remote to *Days of Our Lives*. She wondered whether her papá would come back to reality, or remain like so many soap opera characters, ill, with an unknown and undiagnosed condition, and then dead, and written out of the future series. As she considered her papá's unfortunate circumstances, and indirectly, her own, she lost contact with the soap opera.

She decided to call her husband for an update.

The receptionist, a sixty something year-old woman who'd been with the firm for years, answered, "Morales and Doolittle. May I help you?"

"Kalvin Lennox, please."

"Who's calling, please?"

Now that pissed her off. That woman knew perfectly well who was calling. *God give me patience.* "This is Mrs. Lennox, his wife."

"Just a moment please," and she dropped Elena into silence.

Finally, the secretary for Kalvin and another associate came on. "Mr. Lennox' office, may I help you?"

"Lynn. Is Kalvin available?"

"Who's calling please?"

Elena fumed. She'd tried referring to the bitch by her first name. "This is Elena Lennox, Lynn. Is he available?"

"One moment please," and Elena was floating in nowhere land again.

An eternity later, Lynn returned. "I'm afraid he is not currently available."

"Not available?"

There was a hesitation. "Uh, he's not at his desk."

"Where is he?"

She hesitated again. "Mrs. Lennox. I'll have him call you as soon as he is available."

"Fine," she said, too loudly, and clicked the hand-held to off. Incompetence. She simmered. She placed Elenita on the floor to play with toys.

Kalvin called.

"What are you doing?" she demanded.

"Huh? . . . I'm working."

"Take my calls."

She knew he was rolling his eyes.

"What have you done about the partnership issue?"

"Well, uh, I asked Braxton this morning what he knew about your dad's estate plan. He doesn't know anything."

"What do you mean?" She was seething. "He's the goddam estate planning lawyer there, isn't he?"

157

Her husband hesitated. "He says your father did the estate plan on his own. Maybe used a lawyer friend from Daytona Beach. He knows nothing about it. But, as I was leaving his office, he received a call from some guy named Murphy."

"That's the guy. Find out what he's doing." She clicked the phone off again.

A while later, Kalvin called back. "Doolittle wants to see you."

"What does the bastard want?"

"I think to talk about you being the guardian."

Elena arrived at Morales and Doolittle with Elenita on her hip and approached the front desk, where the bitch she'd dealt with on the phone sat.

"May I help you," the haughty woman asked. Why did legal staff have to act so uppity, like salesladies in department stores that sold high-priced items?

"I'm here for a meeting with my husband and Mr. Doolittle."

The woman looked down. "Mr. Doolittle's calendar does not indicate an appointment."

"My husband called me."

"What's your name?"

She tried to control herself. "Listen, goddammit. I am Elena Morales Lennox, wife of attorney Kalvin Lennox and daughter of Luis Morales, the senior partner and your boss."

The lady glared at her, unafraid. "I am sorry Mrs. Lennox. I didn't recognize you."

"Buzz my husband."

She sat like an intruder in the lobby for far too long before Kalvin finally emerged from the netherworld, smiling and stepping grandly, his heels clicking loudly on the tile. He leaned and kissed her on the lips, ignoring Elenita. She half pecked back. A kiss from her husband wouldn't appease her.

"Mr. Doolittle is expecting us," he said as he escorted her to Doolittle's office, not bothering to greet or carry Elenita.

When they arrived at Doolittle's office, the old lady who acted as his guard looked up over half glasses and frowned.

Kalvin stuck his head in the door. "She's here."

A blondette walked out of a cubicle and seemed to grin at her.

Elena followed Kalvin into Doolittle's office. Doolittle stood and approached, but stopped just short, obviously trying to decide whether to kiss, shake hands, or what. She offered neither, so he finally settled for a meek, awkward little mechanical bow of the head.

He motioned for them to sit in the leather chairs, as he remained seated behind the fancy desk. Elena seethed at the opulence of this office compared to her husband's. The old fuck could just sit and watch the sailboats and cruise ships going to and fro.

"Elena. We wanted to talk with you about your father's affairs."

No '*I'm sorry your father has taken ill*' or anything like that. She looked at him, disinterested, glad he seemed nervous.

He looked down. "Uh, the time has come to take some action."

No shit, Sherlock. She glared at him.

"Er, Kalvin and I were trying to decide who was the most logical person to handle his affairs, and we decided it was you."

"Why? Because I'm nobody?"

The poor man was struggling. It was nice to see a litigator rendered speechless.

"No, Elena. Because you are family, but not a member of the firm."

She scrunched her nose. "I'm married to a member of the firm and the daughter of the senior partner."

"Yes, but there is no other family member who is not an employee of the firm, except of course Sylvia, and she has waived her right to serve."

"How did she waive?"

Her fidgeting husband jumped when she kicked him in the shin. "We believe she signed a prenuptial agreement."

Doolittle's success as a litigator consisted of pushing people around by strongly stating what he wanted to be the law, whether or not there was any law to back him up. "You believe? You haven't seen a copy of it?"

"We're working on it."

The guy was a total idiot. She couldn't fathom why her papá had made him a partner. She looked out at a cigarette boat flying along, bouncing over light waves.

"So, you figure that we'll file for guardianship, the court will appoint me, without objection, and I will do whatever you say."

His flummoxed look gave her pleasure. He cleared his throat. "Uh, Elena. Hopefully, there will be little objection. We don't expect that anybody more suitable than you will petition. And upon appointment, you will be the guardian. All we want is for you to vote his stock in the firm and to sign assignments so that they will transfer into the right hands upon his death."

"And whose hands would those be?"

The man looked over his silly little glasses just like his secretary had, appearing displeased.

"Well, his stock would be sold to members of the firm, or the firm itself, as specified in the shareholders' agreement." He watched her and waited.

Her useless husband, who had learned who-knew-what in law school, had the jitters, but otherwise was as useful as a corpse. She was on her own. "Two issues there. One, how much do you pay for the shares? And two, how does this benefit my husband and me. I guess I can give some shares to Kalvin, right?"

Doolittle looked like a porcupine had snuck up his ass and was backing out. He sputtered, "We need to join forces . . . to . . . uh . . . to be sure your father's wife doesn't get involved in firm activities. You and your brother, as your father's rightful heirs, will receive the value of his shares."

He looked scared again. She was loving this.

"I may not be a lawyer, but I know that getting . . . .," she made quote marks, "value," and she made them again, "is not the same as getting the shares themselves." And I'm sure his wife does have some rights. I'll tell you what," she said, getting to her feet and despising the fear in her husband's eyes almost as much as she was enjoying it in Doolittle's. "You get the papers together, with an agreement showing me how this will benefit me and Kalvin, and then we'll see."

As the two powerless men sat dumbfounded, she swung Elenita, who had slept through the whole thing, kind of like her wimp of a husband, onto a hip, and marched out the door.

Chapter 39

Luis Morales

I recognize the smooth touch of hand on my arm as my blood pressure is checked. I can make out her rich, chocolate skin, kind eyes and bouncy reddish hair. She looks into my eyes. "Hi, Mr. Morales. How you feelin' today?" She waits for an answer, which I cannot produce. She puts a hand on my face and smiles at me. I feel the warmth of compassion and mercy.

Is my inability to stay in the present an indication that I've lost control over my mind, just like I've lost control over my body? Am I nearing the end? I don't want to lose my grip on reality. I don't want to die. I vacillate between believing my thoughts are completely logical and realizing they are irrational. I struggle to be in the present and to understand better what has happened and what might happen to me, but I keep reverting to prior times, in the grasp of my Cuba, my Santiago de Cuba, my Vista Alegre.

I'm a boy, riding in the back seat of the family's brilliantly polished Buick Roadmaster Estate Wagon, as our chauffer, Rafael, a thin, wizened man of African origin, drives us through city streets. Residents of the lower city stand gaping, like we are visitors from another planet.

Now, I'm standing with my father on La Alameda Avenue, facing the docks and the dark water of the harbor of Santiago de Cuba, crowded with ships bringing supplies from afar, and loading sugar, rum and other products for transport to foreign ports. Workers unload trucks, steer horse-drawn buggies, or pull and push large pallets on wheels to and from the harbor docks where many ships float on the water. Many of the crates display the insignia and the name of Bacardí. I think how exciting it must be to work on freight ships, traveling to far-away lands.

Beyond the water of the harbor, the green foothills and mountains of the Sierra Maestra mountain range climb to the sky. I picture myself

161

tramping upward through the wooded areas of the mountain and looking down on the bustling harbor from above.

The Hotel Casa Granda and other buildings along the streets nearby feature long, rectangular windows, with huge wooden shutters, many of which are propped open. We stride a few blocks up from the harbor and arrive at Parque Céspedes. The Hotel Casa Granda, the Cathedral, Velázquez's elegant historic home, and the Ayuntamiento, impose their presence around the park.

I imagine myself on the rooftop of the Casa Granda, the venue for parties and events I've attended with my parents, hosted by the Bosch family, the Bacardí family and other wealthy families of the city and our neighborhood, looking down at the harbor and out to the sea.

My memories shift to a day when we Vista Alegre kids sneak a ride on the tranvía, its metal wheels screeching loudly on the tracks, as it grinds its way down toward the waterfront. We exit the tram several blocks above the harbor and walk along the streets, jumping out of the way of men carrying barrels and pulling wagons loaded with provisions. We meet up with kids we knew from when we lived in the lower part of the city, including Alberto, the son of our chauffer Rafael.

We enter a large door leading to an enclave surrounded by buildings, like a city within a city, where residents mingle on balconies and circular staircases leading to upper floors. The smell of fires and aromas of food cooking fill the air.

Inside Alberto's family kitchen, the scent of spices and seasonings mix with the aroma of baking bread. His mother smiles. "Sit. I just made a stew of sweet potatoes, chicken and fresh vegetables."

Even though we aren't hungry, the aroma is so wonderful that we sit and eat.

I feel that I'm smiling, feeling the air, listening to the sounds and smelling the aromas of my tranquil, luxurious youth in Santiago de Cuba.

I'm surprised to find Sylvia leaning in and scrutinizing my face. Does my contentment show?

Chapter 40

Sylvia Morales

"So, your husband is eighty-four. How old are you, Mrs. Morales?"

Sylvia sipped watery coffee from a dainty, elegant white cup, feeling like she should hold her pinky out to the side, just so.

"Fifty-two."

"Hmm." The lawyer, a plump, balding man named S. Crandall Warnock, raised one eyebrow, seemed to smirk and silently leveled his eyes at her.

Choosing this lawyer may have been a mistake. Maybe she should have chosen a female, or one married to somebody quite older or younger. She wondered whether she should tell him anything about her history and relationship with Louis; about having earned a bachelor's degree in paralegal studies; about moving to Miami specifically to have a long career working at the prestigious law firm of Morales and Doolittle; about becoming the paralegal solely dedicated to Louis, the senior-most partner; about never expecting that Louis would ask her out on a date and to get married to him.

She snapped back to the lawyer's office and looked up. Warnock continued staring at her. She wished he could witness how she and her husband regularly engaged in discussions about national and world news, literature, music and the arts, how they both enjoyed a whole world of interests and activities, which this lawyer could probably not even visualize.

She sipped her coffee and tried to be calm. "You seem to be focusing on our age difference. Do you know my husband? If you do, you know that he is vibrant and sharp, young in body, mind and spirit. Even at his age, he is a hard-working, brilliant, passionate and compassionate attorney. That's why I married him."

"Mrs. Morales, I was not implying anything. I was merely inquiring as to details I need to know."

It seemed that the lawyer ended his sentence with a turn of his lips and maybe a wink, something she often perceived when the age difference was the topic.

"My husband and I signed a prenuptial agreement. I did it gladly. I was marrying the man, not the money." She struggled to avoid getting choked up. "We've been married, happily married, for fifteen years. I never expected him to suffer a medical crisis. Not even now. I knew from the start that I might only have twenty or thirty years with him, but I love him." She fought to hold back the tears. Two large droplets oozed out and splashed onto the desktop. She hurriedly dried it with her napkin. Her stomach rolled like a churning sea.

The lawyer sighed aloud. "Mrs. Morales," he said, his jowls jiggling, "being that you signed a prenuptial agreement, and you say you have nothing to gain financially, why do you consider it so important to control your husband's affairs?"

Her stomach twisted at the thought of her husband's children and law partner. She was certain that her stepchildren thought of her as a meddling bitch, yet she had to make a stand.

"My husband needs me." She felt the floodwaters coming again. She was *not* going to cry again. "I'm interested in his welfare, not his money."

"When you signed the prenuptial agreement, did you also sign estate planning documents? Or did he?"

She looked up at his cold glare, shuddering at the memory of the prenup ordeal. "No. It became a very difficult situation. I didn't want anything from him but his love. I'm sure his children suggested the prenup."

When Louis had mentioned a prenuptial agreement, he was almost apologetic, acting as nervous as he had on the early dates. Although it hurt her that he might have some apprehension, she swallowed her pride and accepted it. "Sir, my husband's lawyer, actually his law partner, Mr. Doolittle, prepared a massive document. When he asked me to sign it, I said fine. Then he told me I had to get a lawyer. I said I didn't even care about it and would sign it without a lawyer. He said to make it legal I had to have one."

Mr. Warnock nodded and stuck his pen between his front teeth. "How did that go?"

"I met with the lawyer. I said I'd sign the prenup. I didn't care. But the lawyer said, 'But what about this?' 'What about that?' He suggested adding some provisions to protect me. Then he and Doolittle communicated with letters, phone conversations and ridiculous negotiations over perceived issues that did not even matter to me, and probably not to Louis. I felt like the lawyer made me look greedy."

She looked out the window again, remembering an evening during the fiasco, when she said to Louis, "I told you I'll sign the agreement. I didn't tell that lawyer I wanted anything. I feel awkward. Just give me the document and a pen, and I'll sign it. Forget all this legal posturing over our marriage. It's a marriage, not a business deal."

Louis' face turned red. He shook his head. "I am so sorry to have even suggested it. I trust you. I'll tell my lawyer tomorrow to forget it."

"No, I don't mean I want to abandon it. I don't want your children to think I'm after something, or I've talked you out of it. I will sign it as it is."

As though he hadn't heard a word she'd spoken, the lawyer said, "Did he create a will?"

She avoided his look and gazed out the window at a parking lot packed with cars. "I never saw any estate planning documents, and I never asked. But Louis is a meticulous lawyer. He has this thing about organization and maintaining control."

"Have you had any conversations with his children or law partner about it?"

It amazed her how the mere mention of any of those people could sour her stomach and raise anxiety. "His children and I do not communicate very well. I understand that stepmother-stepchild relations are often strained. If I inquired about the estate plan, they would see me as being interested. That's the furthest thing from the truth. But Louis had a meeting with his son Franklin just the other day . . . uh, Sunday. the same time he suggested I have documents, and he told us that he has documents, and that Franklin plays a role. He asked Franklin to make some changes, to include me too. But that was the day before the heart attack."

Warnock's pen entered the mouth again. "I need to see a copy of the prenup, so I can see what you waived. You may have waived your right to be his guardian."

165

"I don't know if I have a copy," she said, shaking her head in disgust. "My husband needs me and perhaps let me sign a document that will prevent me from helping him."

She was just swaying in the wind, like a dandelion whose seeds would soon scatter.

Chapter 41

Franklin Morales

Wednesday, November 30, 2016

The receptionist announced on the intercom that George Murphy was on the phone. Franklin slipped the earphone over his ear and hit the button.

"Franklin, it's George Murphy. I've asked the doctors to evaluate your father's long-term prognosis and whether to invoke the living will."

"Mr. Murphy, I don't believe your authority extends to enacting the living will."

"I have authority to have him evaluated."

Franklin felt a rumble of unease within. "Have the doctors said anything?"

"No. They are still evaluating. They set another type of brain scan for this morning. They are also talking about taking him off life support. They think his heart will beat and he'll breathe without it."

Franklin winced. "They *think*?"

"They say they do it gradually, to see."

"Have you talked to Sylvia?"

"I didn't think you much cared what she would think."

Franklin let out an audible sigh. "Mr. Murphy, there's not much love lost between us. But I have the impression that she actually cares about him and wants him alive. She's with him all the time. She thinks he shows some cognitive activity, on which I agree. We need to include her. What time are they planning to try disconnecting equipment?"

"I think this afternoon, after the tests."

"I want a meeting, *before* they disconnect anything. I'm going to try to locate Roosevelt Harris, the other designee. And I want to know exactly what they intend to disconnect."

Mr. Murphy cleared his throat. "I guess you're right."

Franklin clenched his jaw. "I won't agree to disconnect or remove nutrition and hydration before a good long study by all the doctors and input from us, including Sylvia."

"I agree."

Franklin was pleasantly surprised at how logical Mr. Murphy came across.

"Also, Franklin, the doctors have suggested that we consider putting a Do Not Resuscitate in place, so if he goes, he won't be revived."

"Mr. Murphy, I would agree to a DNR order much sooner than I would agree to pulling his feeding tubes, but I still want to know the result of the tests."

Franklin scrolled through his contacts to Jude Armstrong's number and called.

The call connected on the second ring, followed by several seconds of noise, then, "Hello, Jude Armstrong here."

"Jude, this is Franklin. How are you?"

"Hey, Franklin. I'm good. Sorry about dropping the phone. It was under stacks of file folders and papers. I'm hopping around boxes. You know we've moved our offices?"

"How are the new digs, Jude?"

"Out my window, I see the hard-packed sand of Daytona Beach. What an improvement over railroad tracks, which was all we saw from our prior corporate office. I just hung a framed photo of cars and people on the beach, which was taken just blocks from here in 1958. And I have another one from many years earlier. I put one on either side of a large window, so I can look out at the people enjoying the sun and sand, and compare then versus now. Old cars versus current cars. Different bathing attire. And I'm trying to decide where to hang my law degree and Bar admission certificate."

"Congratulations on the move and graduating law school, Jude."

"Thanks. Listen, I was also just looking at the title commitment on the out-parcel we've contracted to buy in Kendall for our new up-scale concept restaurant. There's an old agreement that could be a problem. Do you know anything about it?"

"I ordered a cleaner copy of that document because the one we received was blurry. But I wasn't calling you about that, Jude."

"Oh, what's up?"

"My dad's had a medical crisis. We don't know if he'll survive or be able to return to work."

"I'm sorry to hear that. Your father is one of the most kind, sincere, honorable men I've ever known. What can I do?"

"My father and I felt the same about your dad. Do you have access to your dad's files?"

"Yes, I have his files, and originals."

"Okay. Your dad was named a personal representative, trustee and agent in his power of attorney and in his health care documents. Roosevelt was named alternate for anyone who couldn't serve."

"I don't have the computer set up yet and don't know where everything is. But, there's a box someplace. Uh, hang on. Here. The box says, 'Lansing P.R. or Trustee.' Okay. Here's the file, with copies of those documents. It says the originals are in a safe. The safe is in the other room, still on a dolly. Where's the combination? Oh, here. Let's see . . . ." Franklin heard sounds of walking, moving things, paper crumpling, and metal grinding. "Yes, here they are."

Franklin said, "They name your dad, George Murphy and me, right? And Roosevelt as alternate?"

"Yes. Murphy's the guy who fixed up the plumbing on our restaurant on *calle Ocho*, right?"

"Right."

Jude said, "Roosevelt is away today. I'll connect him."

After a moment of silence, Jude said, "Hey, Roosevelt. I've got you on conference with Franklin Morales."

"Hey, Franklin, how are you?

"I'm good, Roosevelt, but my father is in a medical crisis."

"Aw, I'm real sorry to hear that, Franklin. Mr. Morales is as dear to me as Mr. Armstrong was."

Jude said, "Did you know that Mr. Morales named you as an alternate in all his estate planning documents?"

"No, I didn't. I wonder why."

"He probably asked my dad to suggest somebody, and, as you know, my dad trusted you more than anybody, even me."

Roosevelt's voice turned somber. "So, what's going on? Is your dad in a hospital? In Miami?"

169

"Yes. George Murphy was designated to make medical decisions alone first, but now you and I join him as a committee. Can you come, or at least communicate with us by phone or video chat? They are doing more tests today and considering some serious actions that I believe require our input."

"I'm in Naples, just across Alligator Alley from you. Give me an hour or so to wrap things up here and I'll drive over."

Jude said, "I'll head down from here with the documents."

"Thank you, guys, so much. Text me when you're close and we'll meet at the hospital."

Chapter 42

Luis Morales

I hear a voice, saying "No change," and focus on a man dressed in scrubs.

Sylvia is sitting next to me, rubbing her thumb along my hand and wrist. She sighs loudly. In a raspy voice, she says, "He reacts. His eyes see. They move. He is alert."

The man says, "I'm sorry. We see no evidence of that. We've performed every possible test. EEG, CT Scan, MRI, blood tests, urinalyses. There were apparently multiple strokes and multiple bleeds. Are you familiar with Hospice? A palliative-care nurse could help. Maybe it's time...."

"Stop," she says, loudly. "Just stop." She points forcefully toward the door. The man turns to leave. She calls after him, "Maybe you should spend more time here to see what's really happening instead of relying on tests and mechanical observations."

Snippets from the past are flickering through my thoughts like vintage images displayed by a clattering movie projector. The color of my memories dulls the light of the room. Warmth comes with the color. The warmth of love. My roots, deep in the soil of my Cuba.

I am thirteen, in May of 1945. My father puts an arm on my shoulder and says, "I have business to attend to in Havana, Florida and Washington, D.C. As the oldest, I think you should learn about business."

We travel by train toward Camagüey along the outskirts of the Sierra Maestra mountain range, past farms, herds of cattle, sugar cane plantations, coffee plantations, pastures with livestock and vast, hilly grasslands.

As the train rumbles along, I gaze out the window, where I see dark-skinned workers, fully dressed in long pants and long-sleeved shirts, cutting sugar cane.

I glance at my father. "Hard work in the hot sun."

My father frowns. "They are accustomed to it. And by the way, I've been noticing that you talk to our servants like they are your equals. You must learn that they are not."

A peculiar, unidentifiable feeling comes over me.

My father continues, "We are different. We are not like the natives of Cuba. We are not like those who were brought in from Africa and Haiti. We are of Spanish heritage. Our blood is pure. Remember that."

His statements make me sick. I do not look at him. Then I smile, thinking we might have a little Moorish blood in us.

He continues, "I treat them with respect, but I do not socialize or discuss personal matters with them. Now that you are a teenager, you must maintain your position and cease acting like they are your friends."

I maintain my silence, wishing he would stop talking like this.

He continues, "You will see more white-skinned, European-blooded people and fewer Negroes and mulatos in Havana than in and around Santiago de Cuba. That is because the Oriente area is and has always been the main location of sugar cane and coffee cultivation. Slave ships from Africa landed in this area. Later, French colonists brought their slaves here from Haiti."

Finally, he tires of dwelling on this unpleasant talk.

I again watch the landscape slide by, glimpsing little towns and villages first being a speck, and then coming into focus, and then buildings slipping by as we pass by and continue, to the next one. I imagine the lives of the people, young and old, involved in the activities of everyday life. Everywhere there are people on the roads, carrying cut crops on wagons or on their backs, with the help of oxen and other beasts of burden. Dry dirt swirls in little clouds as the train's speed pulls it along.

In Camagüey, we board a commercial plane for my first airplane flight, to Havana. The plane roars down the runway and suddenly climbs. I stare out the window at the vast, pure, uninvolved green areas below. As we roar over hills and mountainous slopes, I see less rich, green vegetation, and more red dirt, dotted with dry vegetation.

I'm exhilarated by the roar of the engines and the vibration of the plane, changing as it climbs, steadies, and sometimes moves higher or lower or one way or the other. The pilot veers out along the coast. Iridescent, blue water becomes turquoise near shore, and laps at sand.

The wheels squeak as we touch down at the airport in Havana. After we climb down, men grab our luggage and take it through the building and outside. A lanky, dark-skinned man with short-cropped hair and a thin mustache hugs my father and grabs our bags.

"Angel, this is my son, Luis."

The skin around his eyes crinkles in a way that makes him seem devilish, happy and kind. As we shake hands, he takes a small bow and says, "I'm pleased to know you, Luis."

I wonder how my father can be so friendly to this man, since he has the darker skin and tight-knitted hair of the Africans my father says are not our equals.

We get into an open jeep and head into the city. Angel says, "I was at the Marrero plantation yesterday. Their crop is being damaged severely. No insecticide is working. I'm sending the team from Bayamo over to see if they can figure it out."

My father nods. "They had a similar problem with locusts at some of the northeastern fields."

"Yes, the same crew I'm sending found the resolution to that problem."

Once it dawns on me that my father works with this man, and he's more than just a driver, I am more surprised about my father's attitude.

On the long ride into the city, we pass a multitude of people standing and walking along the roads, trucks carrying plantains, tractors carrying straw and big, shiny, new cars from the United States, like those that cruise through Vista Allegre.

My father lights a cigar. "Angel, how's the new distribution center coming along? Will it be in operation by first of the month?"

"I think so. There's some delay in receiving the specialized conveyor belts."

Puffing and blowing out, my father says, under his breath, "I heard of an uprising of cane field workers in Bayamo. What's going on?"

Angel blows cigar smoke into the air. "I think we have them back under control. They say they are underpaid and overworked. But it's no different from anywhere else."

My father flicks an ash out the window. "I think labor union organizers are pushing them. Is there any evidence of organized labor involvement?"

"Yes, we're taking action to appease the workers while trying to keep the union organizers out."

I fade out. After what seems like a long time passing haciendas and farming areas, homes and businesses begin to sprout. Then, we are on wider city streets, between rows of stately buildings with elegant architecture at the eaves.

Angel pulls to a stop in front of a stylish hotel near Parque Central. "Here we are. I think Mr. Bosch's driver is transporting you tonight. I'll see you tomorrow."

Bellmen take our bags. My father waves at Angel as he pulls out. "See you tomorrow, *amigo*."

After unpacking our clothes in the hotel room, we walk outside and take two turns to the right. I try to keep up with my father's march down the smooth, open walkway between two parts of a wide street toward the water. "Luis, do you see the name on the street sign? Paseo de Martí. It's been known by that name for many years, but the people call it Paseo del Prado, or just El Prado."

He marches for a while before making a sudden about-face and strutting back toward where we started. Soon, we turn to the left and walk under walkway with arches to our left past a hotel with a sign saying Hotel Sevilla on the front.

He says, "See how this two-story building looks different from the four story one coming up. They were originally separate, but have been joined. And the tall, plain-looking building behind it was built in recent years. There's a nice view from the top, but you'll see another great view from where we are going. We cross another street behind a large, elegant building with a dome on top. My father explains that this is the Presidential Palace.

Then, he turns right again and struts up to a tall, brownish building, decorated with large pieces of reddish tile dotted with speckles, topped by towers. The sign outside says "Edificio Bacardí." Inside, we find gleaming, light brown, dark brown and reddish marble floors and walls, decorated with brass. Prominent designs of the letter 'B' adorn the walls and the impressive front desk.

The man at the desk says, "Sr. Morales. It's a pleasure to see you. The elevator operator will take you directly up. Mr. Bosch will be arriving shortly."

An aged, uniformed black man closes the gates and swings a lever. The ornate, caged elevator rises.

As we emerge, a man in a suit appears, embraces my father, shakes my hand and ushers us into a huge office with windows covering two sides.

"Sr. Morales, how have you been?"

"Fine, Manuel. And you? How is the family?"

"Very well. How long will you be in La Habana?"

"A few days. We're on our way to the United States to handle some business."

"Would you like some rum?"

My father nods. After delivering my father's rum, Manuel looks at me, "What a lucky young boy, getting to visit the United States. I hope I can see it someday. Come, you have to see the spectacular views of Havana."

We step out onto a balcony. A strong breeze cools the air a bit. I can see a sliver of El Prado between Hotel Sevilla and the building to the left. Old people walk and sit under hovering trees. Children play. I move along the balcony, gazing downward.

Manuel goes inside. My father joins me at the wall, a rum drink in one hand and a lit cigar in the other. He says, "Do you recognize where we are and where you've been? He points to the left. "You see *El Capitolio*? You will be surprised when we get to Washington because our congressional buildings look almost identical." He laughs. "We will spend a lot of time in *El Capitolio* tomorrow, in the United States Capitol in a week."

"Why?"

"Because the governing bodies of both countries make the laws, and much about the sugar industry is affected by laws. We must be involved in congressional action."

Mr. Bosch arrives. My father smiles broadly. "Pepín, how are you?" The two embrace.

175

"I'm fine, thank you. You are looking well." Mr. Bosch turns to me and shakes my hand. "Luis, how are you? You are getting taller and looking quite grown-up. How old are you now?"

"Thirteen, sir."

"A young man. We expect to have you as an executive here someday. Study hard."

Mr. Bosch joins us as we return to gaze across the city. "Do you see where *Paseo Del Prado* converges with *El Malecón*? Tonight, we will drive along the water to the affluent area of Havana, called *Vedado*, and beyond that, across a little river that joins the sea, to even more affluent areas, where you'll enjoy a feast."

I nod, looking at the long, concrete walkway running along a wall that separates the street from the sea.

My father drops a hand on my shoulder and points back to the left. "That's *el Gran Teatro*, just before *El Capitolio*. We will attend a concert there tomorrow night. Isn't it magnificent?"

Manuel returns with fresh drinks and stands next to us, as my father continues pointing and describing the city. "Directly past El Prado lies the large residential area with its majestic buildings, lining narrower streets. It's hard to make out the architecture from here, but when we are inside that part of the city, I want you to look up at the eaves and the fascia of those grand buildings."

I look into the streets and become lost in my imagination, picturing people bustling around, families living and shopping and kids playing.

They walk with me to another side of the building, pointing down again. My father says, "Can you see the cathedral with two towers that are not the same size or height? We'll go see it maybe tomorrow or the next day."

I nod.

We walk again. "Do you see the plazas, there, there and there? See that large building right there?" He pointed. "That's *Hotel Ambos Mundos*. Ernest Hemingway wrote several of his books there."

I'm not sure exactly what he's pointing at, as I see a lot of large buildings, but I nod as though I do.

After the men drink several drinks, a man in uniform comes in and makes cups of espresso. As they drink, they light up fresh cigars.

I remain glued to the railing, my thoughts swirling as I try to imagine the lives of the people of this magnificent city. I learn about Havana, but although my father has said I am on this trip to learn of business, I've learned nothing about it yet.

Sylvia is sitting beside me, holding my hand and humming a soothing song. I suffer over her frustration that she's not named to make my medical decisions, but at the time I prepared the documents, I had to keep peace.

She leans close. "I know you're there. I hope you know I'm here, and I'm waiting for you."

She is quiet for a few moments. I recognize the sound of Franklin's shoes shuffling.

"Sylvia."

"Franklin."

I become anxious, anticipating terse words, but this time, none come.

Chapter 43

Sylvia Morales

Sylvia sat again at Warnock's desk, tapping her fingers on the arm of the chair. She'd searched through Louis' desk drawer and located a folder with her name and a copy of the prenuptial agreement.

She did not wait for him to finish reviewing it. "Mr. Warnock, does Florida law not say that the spouse has priority to serve as guardian?"

"Well, yes, but . . . "

"And you do not see anywhere in the prenup where I waived the right to serve as guardian, right?"

"Well, that's true, but . . . "

"So, I can file guardianship and anybody else would have the burden to prove why I can't serve as guardian. Is that right? I want to file first."

He looked at her, lost in her words. A young woman entered and dropped a couple of files into his in-box.

He watched the girl leave. "Even though you aren't prevented by this document, the law provides that a person named as pre-need guardian or as agent in a power of attorney will have priority."

"Mr. Warnock, are you able to represent me and file a guardianship? Or, if they file first, can you represent me to become guardian instead? You have such a defeatist attitude that I don't have much confidence."

He grimaced. "Mrs. Morales, the law prescribes burdens of proof and presumptions."

She dropped her fist a little too hard on his desk. "Isn't it your job in court to know what the burdens of proof are and prove our case? And a presumption is not the final answer, right? It can be overcome with proof, right?"

He looked down and shook his head. "We can file for guardianship and see what happens."

She knew her face showed anger. "I'd like to hear something a little more convincing, Mr. Warnock."

"I'll do my best, Mrs. Morales."

His sheepish expression did not convince her that he could handle it. She rose and headed out, saying, "I may have to seek other counsel."

Chapter 44

Elena Morales Lennox

Elena sat in Doolittle's office, boiling with anger. Her dear husband Kalvin was nowhere to be found, as usual. Doolittle bragged about a golf game on the phone with somebody. Then he went on and on in his pompous voice about Jane and Melissa and Rachel somebody or other.

Finally, he dropped the phone on its cradle and looked up at her. "Here are the guardianship documents for you to sign."

He placed them on the desk in front of her. After pointing with his fancy pen at names, addresses and other data, he turned to the signature page and handed her a different pen. "This is the petition to have your father declared incapacitated and to appoint you as guardian. Sign here. And this is the petition for emergency temporary guardian."

"What is emergency temporary guardianship? How does that work with the guardianship?"

"The procedure to appoint a permanent guardian takes time. The examining committee and the lawyer all have to examine the alleged incapacitated person and file reports. If we can show an emergency, the court will appoint you quickly, with just a short hearing and little or no testimony."

"What emergency are you planning to show?"

"The office cannot function without the president there."

She signed and dropped the pen on the desk. "What's next?"

"We'll submit it all to the court. The judge will appoint an examining committee and a lawyer for your father, and the court will set a hearing at which we will present our evidence of an emergency, and hopefully the court will agree. Whether or not we succeed there, there will later be a hearing to determine incapacity and, hopefully, the court will appoint you as permanent guardian."

Elena shifted Elenita from one knee to the other, bouncing her lightly. Elena was going to play the stupid game Doolittle had in mind, for her own benefit, not for his. She was going to push her worthless husband into general partner position. She'd already contacted a lawyer, and she knew that once she became guardian, she could fire Doolittle as the attorney and hire her own attorney, with court approval, which would undoubtedly be granted. Wouldn't it be funny to watch his reaction when he realized he'd been bamboozled?

Kalvin walked in, looking surprised at her presence.

"I already signed."

"Okay, great," he said, nodding too happily.

She shook her head. What a loser. How could she ever propel him to be the leader of the firm and keep him there?

She marched out, without saying a word to either, and almost bumped into Franklin coming around the corner from the back hall.

"Whoa, Elena. What's up? Hey, Elenita." He tickled Elenita's ribs. She giggled and hid her face behind her hands.

"Nothing, Franklin. I am our father's daughter too. I can come into his office."

"Don't be silly, Elena. I was merely making conversation. Are you here about the guardianship?"

She stared at him, unsure what to say. "Ask Doolittle."

Franklin reached into the bag Elena was carrying and pulled out one of Elenita's toys, a rubber blow-up doll that makes noise when it's squeezed. He squeezed it. Elenita giggled and reached for it.

He whispered, "I don't trust Doolittle. He's up to something."

Elena smiled. "I've never known you to be paranoid."

"I wish you'd drop the guardianship case. But if you don't, we'll get it thrown out of court. And if we don't, you won't be the guardian. Be careful with Doolittle. He's not concerned about you. He's doing this just to get control of the firm."

"Don't you worry."

Chapter 45

Luis Morales

My father and I sit in the back of a large United States car driven by a uniformed chauffer as we cruise up the *Malecón*. A heavy, grim-looking man sits in the passenger seat. A wave shoots a shower of salty water onto the road as we continue past *Hotel Nacional*. Later, the road swerves to the left, passing a large Roman-looking structure with a waterway beside and behind it, where people in swimsuits lie in the baking sun and bathe in the water lapping in from the sea.

We cross a bridge and skim along a boulevard separated by a median with trimmed trees and shrubbery. Large, imposing homes stand along each side of the road. Eventually, the car slows and pulls into a long driveway. Two guards open the gate and signal us to pass. At the end of the driveway, men dressed in uniform open the car doors for us, and others escort us inside. The grim-looking man shadows us.

The guests are all dressed fancy. Women, their faces looking like white plaster has been caked on, wear long dresses adorned with bright sequins, and hold their chic cigarette holders, some with sequins and jewels. Men wear pinstriped suits and shiny shoes, and have their hair slicked back. I look around for children my age but see none.

My father introduces me to several men and women. One woman, with a husky voice and silver hair, sticks her hand under my chin and lifts it. "You are adorable. One day you are going to be a handsome charmer, just like your father." Then she grabs my father's arm and squeezes, causing me to wonder whether she knows I have a mother at home.

My father smokes cigars, drinks, laughs and moves around the room.

After a period of mingling, snacking and drinking, the guests are seated at a long table. People laugh and talk all around me. I feel alone.

More items of silverware than I have ever seen in my life surround my plate. My father informs me which unique item to use with which food item. With great flourish, dark-skinned waiters in uniform present the plates simultaneously. I can't identify the vegetables or flavors, but everything is delicious. I take a bite of the chicken. It seems to melt in my mouth. I lean over to my father. "This chicken is incredible!"

My father smiles. "Roasted ostrich breast."

After dinner, my father returns me to the hotel and goes out again. Once he returns, I am awakened throughout the night by his groaning and snoring. The room smells strongly of alcohol and stale cigar smoke. I awake long before he does, but I remain in bed, waiting. Eventually, he drags himself out of bed.

After an early lunch, together with others from my father's work, we climb the numerous steps of the *Capitolio* toward the portico, supported by granite pillars. At the top, as the men try to level their breathing, I admire each of the three massive doors with bronze bas-relief depictions of scenes of the Spanish/Cuban/North American War and one of Jose Martí alone, speaking to a crowd.

Inside, we are greeted by a bronze statue that resembles a statue of Athena from Greece I've seen in books. In the floor in front of it is a diamond that my father says originally belonged to a Russian Czar.

Directly above us is the circular interior of a dome with colored designs framed by square gold-colored borders. To the left and the right are long hallways with shiny patterned tile floors and an arched ceiling with the same design as I saw when looking above.

I stay in the hallway outside the room where Congress is in session. Sometimes I look out the window onto the streets of the city, and sometimes I watch the goings-on.

Just inside the door, on either side of red-carpeted stairs men, mostly large and all looking to be of Spanish heritage, as my father would describe them, seem to argue as they sit at or stand around mahogany chairs with burgundy-colored leather seats and backs, each behind an individual desk. To the left is a long desk with many chairs and official-looking men. Above the main congressional area, behind pillars, are rows of seats for spectators.

Often my father and the others are in the main area, sometimes standing, sometimes kneeling next to a seated congressman. Sometimes he leaves the hall, and appears on the second floor, always talking seriously with somebody or other. Hour after boring hour, he moves from place to place.

The next day, in the lobby of the hotel, my father, smiling broadly, greets a man dressed in a white suit and sporting a bow-tie. "Luis, this is *el Señor* Lobo, the most influential man in the world when it comes to sugar."

Mr. Lobo shakes my hand. "I'm pleased to meet you, young man. Are you going to follow in your father's footsteps?"

I shrug.

Sr. Lobo waves towards the outside. "Come on. We are going to a baseball game."

Angel waits outside in his jeep. I head toward it, but Sr. Lobo ushers us to a large enclosed car instead. My father motions for Angel to follow in the jeep.

At the ball field, Mr. Bosch rises from his seat in a box and shakes my hand. "It's nice to see you again, Luis. Are you enjoying your time in Havana?"

"Yes sir."

Mr. Lobo, Mr. Bosch and my father chat about sugar and the apparently related topics of coffee and rum production. I sit behind them in the box.

Angel arrives and sits on bleachers behind me. He whispers, "Luis. Do you like baseball?"

"Yes, sir, I do. Do you?"

"Don't use all that formal talk with me, Luis."

I look at him, confused. I've been taught by my father to call everybody older than me '*señor*', so I can't refer to him as '*tú*.' He is '*usted*' to me. My father would have a conniption if he saw me talking to an adult so casually.

"Okay, sir."

"Luis, you are still calling me sir."

I just stop talking.

Angel pats me on the shoulder. "You know this guy coming to the plate? If he gets on base, I assure you he'll steal."

"Yes, sir. He always steals."

Angel shakes his head. "Oh lord. I give up."

Other white-skinned men dressed in suits arrive and enter the box, flanked by others who seemed to be guarding them. Nobody acknowledges Angel, who remains behind me with not-so-well-dressed men, most of whom have darker skin.

A man introduces the newcomers to my father, Mr. Lobo and Sr. Bosch. "This is Mr. Lansky and Mr. Siegel." My father and Sr. Lobo stand and shake the newcomers' hands. The new arrivals lean down to shake Mr. Bosch's hand. He shakes without rising.

I stick out my hand to shake, as my father has taught me, but either they do not see my hand, are too engaged in their own deep conversation, which seems close to an argument, or are not interested in talking to a boy.

Mr. Bosch grabs my father's arm and pulls him down, whispering. "Did you invite these guys, Lansky and Siegel?"

My father shakes his head and says, "I don't even know them."

Mr. Bosch whispers, "We don't want Mafia here. We cannot be seen together, to have people thinking we are affiliated. We produce and sell rum, legally."

My father, Sr. Bosch and Sr. Lobo converse. Sr. Bosch speaks to another man, who then speaks to Mr. Lansky and Mr. Siegel. Lansky moves in front of Mr. Bosch again, states something emphatically, while pointing his finger at the other men. Then Lansky, Siegel and their bodyguards slip away.

My father, Sr. Lobo and Sr. Bosch huddle, shake their heads, and earnestly discuss what I presume is business. They seem to have no idea they are at a game.

Sr. Bosch leans in to my father. "Batista is too close to Lansky. When you get to Washington, promote our interests, but don't let the names of Lansky or Siegel be mentioned in regard to our interests. You aren't going to have Batista there with you anyway, are you?"

"No, we'll obtain information from him, but we are not taking him along."

Angel and the other men behind me talk loudly and boisterously, as they smoke cigarettes and cigars constantly, while drinking Bacardí rum and Hatuey beer. They all continue patting me on the back, causing me to turn around.

"Luis," says one of his friends, "I'll bet you have a lot of girlfriends, don't you?"

I feel my face turn red. "Not really."

"You want to come with us this evening and we'll find you some nice girls?"

The thought horrifies and frightens me. "Uh, thank you, but I'm sure mi papá has plans for me."

I know the names of the baseball players because I love the sport and read about national and international players and games in the newspaper at home. I can recite statistics and characteristics of all the players on both teams.

Some of the alleged facts those behind me spout about baseball players and games are completely untrue, but I remain silent. When not talking about baseball, Angel and his group talk loudly of women and fishing, and then whisper about plantations, sugar, rum, politics and politicians.

Angel says to somebody behind me, "We are going to Washington, D.C. But we're stopping to see General Batista in Florida on the way."

A man mutters, "What does *El Hombre* have to do with anything? He's not president anymore."

Another almost whispers, "He probably invented the nickname himself. I think the other nick-name, *El Mulato Lindo*, is his style, although there's nothing pretty about him."

The men laugh. The first man says, quietly, "He does have connections, here and there. He's made arrangements for Sr. Morales to meet congressmen when we get to D.C."

I know from reading newspapers that Batista hates the "*Mulato Lindo*" nickname, because it refers to the fact that he has some African blood. I think of my conversation with my father on the train, which seemed to indicate he thought Cubans whose veins don't contain pure Spanish blood are inferior. I wonder how it can be that he is so entrenched with a man who has what he calls inferior blood. I remember during the last election seeing a poster showing Batista seated in a car, marker on the side saying, *Este es El Hombre*.

I try to pay attention to the game, but the conversations in front of and behind me are distracting.

A man whispers, "I can't imagine what Batista has to offer. It seems a waste of time to stop to see him."

Angel replies, "Probably is."

Chapter 46

Franklin Morales

Franklin texted Roosevelt and Jude as he entered the hospital. He started for the elevator, but changed his mind and veered for the chapel, where he sat on a pew, prayed and meditated. What would happen to his father? Why were things so difficult dealing with his sister and Sylvia? He closed his eyes and drifted.

Six years after his arrival in Spain, after seeing his cousin and godmother in the little town where the old matron had a cottage for a month each summer, he received a letter.

It said:

Dear Franklin,

The time has come. I have been working in Miami for quite some time, first as a law clerk, but now again as a full-fledged attorney. I'm preparing to create my own law firm and leave the firm where I have been working since the beginning. Tu mamá and sister have finally risen to the top of the waiting list to be able to leave Cuba and join us.

I am sending you a plane ticket and arranging with your school to take you to the airport in Madrid for the trip to Miami, Florida, our new home.

Franklin. I cannot wait to end this long separation and have all of us together.

Franklin hardly knew what to think. He could not imagine what his mother, father and sister would look like. Elena was only two when he last saw her, so she'd be eight or nine now. And she wouldn't remember him anyway.

A few weeks later, he was an unaccompanied minor again, but this time, at age thirteen, treated almost like an adult. The flight attendants smiled at him but didn't act like they felt sorry for him.

On the long flight, he thought, imagined the future, and dozed from time to time. What would Miami and their home be like? Would his parents act like they did when he was seven? Would Elena be happy to see him, or not?

Eventually, the plane landed. He walked with a representative of the airline and the other passengers off the plane and down a long hallway. An immigration official reviewed his passport and stamped it. Then he emerged into an area where people stood facing the arriving travelers.

His mother shouted shrilly, "Franklin. Franklin. My Franklin," and ran to him. Shaking violently, she engulfed him in her arms.

Once she freed him, his papá embraced him. Elena looked at him blankly, like she didn't know him, which of course she didn't.

Franklin approached her, leaned down, put an arm around her and kissed her on the cheek. Then he placed a hand on her head and said, *"Hola, hermana."*

She didn't react. Feeling like a stranger in a strange land, he walked with his family to retrieve his suitcase and then outside into the warm Miami air.

They entered an immense automobile, with the name Continental on the side. He sat on the wide, red-leather back seat. His sister hovered by the other door, seeming far away.

His father started the car and slowly moved out of the parking lot and down a street. Franklin gazed out the window at single story, flat-roofed, concrete-block buildings and homes on either side as they slid along. Soon, his father pulled into a driveway and stopped the vehicle. Then, Franklin stood on a tile floor in a small living room.

His father led him down a short hallway, pointing each way. Elena stood in the doorway to her room, an odd, mistrustful look on her face.

Soon, Franklin sat alone on his new bed in his own bedroom, feeling like an alien in a world where he was not sure he could become comfortable.

When Franklin reached the hospital room, Sylvia whispered. "You've spoken to George Murphy, right?"

Franklin nodded. "Roosevelt and Jude should be here very soon. I've been texting with them."

Sylvia frowned. "And George Murphy?"

"Yes, Sylvia. He said he's coming."

Jude Armstrong and Roosevelt Harris strolled in. Franklin did a half embrace with Roosevelt. Roosevelt said, "I'm so sorry, Franklin."

Franklin shook hands with Jude and they did a short man-hug as well. "How are you guys doing? How are the families?"

Roosevelt nodded. "Fine. Gloria sends her love and prayers."

Jude said, "Joyce does as well. But what's important now is what we can do for you and your family."

Putting a hand on Roosevelt's shoulder, Franklin said, "Sylvia, you knew Lansing Armstrong, I believe. I don't know if you know his son Jude, who's now a lawyer and has his father's files, and his business partner Roosevelt Harris."

Roosevelt approached Sylvia, extending a hand. "I'm Roosevelt. I'm so sorry Luis is so ill."

Jude also gave condolences. Sylvia shook their hands and looked from man to man, saying, "I was so sorry to hear that Lansing passed on. He was a great, great friend to my husband."

Stepping over to Jude, Franklin asked, "How's your sister Jenny doing?"

Jude, smiled. "Fine, just fine."

Roosevelt sat next to Franklin's father, rested a hand on his chest and shook his head. "Don't you worry, Mr. Morales. We'll take care of things. Your beautiful wife, your children, your business . . . all will be all right, waiting for your return. Just get better." He touched the top of his head.

Roosevelt stood, turned back to Sylvia and took her hand. "Lansing would have done anything for your husband and for you, which means that we will as well."

Her eyes shifted away and back again. Franklin smiled, thinking it was funny that Roosevelt, the black surrogate son to white Lansing Armstrong, seemed to have more of Lansing's characteristics than his own son did.

Chapter 47

Elena Morales Lennox

Elena flipped through channels with the remote as Elenita sat on the couch to her right. She lit a cigarette and walked to the kitchen, where she prepared a rum and coke and squeezed some lime into it, saying aloud, to nobody, "At least I can drink a *Cuba Libre*, even if I cannot make my Cuba a free place." The doorbell rang.

She flicked an ash into the ashtray and went to the door. Her unbearable brother cheek-kissed her. "Sis. Jesus, you're asphyxiating poor Elenita here," he said, as he leaned down and kissed the child on the cheek. "*¿Cómo estás, niña?*"

She giggled.

Elena crossed her arms and fumed. "What do you want?" Amelia's attempts to improve her outlook didn't seem to be working.

His eyes showed hurt. Probably just for show.

"I love you too, sis. Listen. Have you been to see papá again?"

He pissed her off with every word. He knew how it hurt her to see their father wasting away and shriveling into nothing, swallowed by sterile bed sheets. And he knew that the step monster was always there. How could she visit? What was the point? She ignored the question.

He stared at her. "You understand he's seriously ill, don't you?"

She felt tears well up. "Of course, I know that."

"He knows who goes to see him."

Her gut turned. "How do you know what he knows? Does he talk to you? Are you the privileged one who can channel his thoughts?"

"He talks with his facial expressions and body movements."

A salty tear entered the corner of her mouth. *Great. The bastard always pissed her off.* She felt her head nodding like a bitch as she spouted, "Okay Mr. Know-it-all, is he still happy having that woman at his side? She's just biding her time, waiting for him to kick off so she can go get another old man and raid his children's inheritance."

Elenita began to whimper. The discord was upsetting her. Elena dropped her cigarette into the ashtray and snatched her up.

Franklin said, "Look. I've never cared much for Sylvia either. I've always thought she manipulated him. I've been changing my mind though. Anyway, I know he entered into a prenuptial agreement with her."

"Those things aren't worth the paper they're written on. He probably owns things jointly with her, and she's going to move everything into her name. Just like what happened to my friend Maribel's dad. You know her, right? Her stepmother did exactly that. She put everything the old man had in a joint account while the old man was out of it. And that was it. She got it all. Prenup. Bullshit."

Her brother strolled around the room investigating, invading her space. "Papá knows, or at least knew, exactly what he was doing. He designated people to be in control."

"Hah!" she exploded. "What does that old man Murphy know? He's a goddam plumber. The bitch'll probably take care of his plumbing and then he'll just lie there and get manipulated like papá."

"You've apparently given this some thought."

"Fuck you."

Franklin laughed. "Please watch your language around sweet little Elenita and stop smoking cigarettes with her in the room."

"Get the fuck out."

Elenita began to cry.

He said, in a lower voice, "Sis, I'm trying to figure out what to do to protect papá and the estate. Would you like to be involved?"

Her tears were all gone now. "You aren't the one to handle it. You're a wimp too. She's probably sucking you off."

He glared at her. His jaw clenched, and for a moment she feared she'd gone too far, and he would strike her. Instead, he turned abruptly and stormed out, slamming the door behind him.

"Asshole," she said.

Amelia wouldn't be very proud of the way she'd handled that.

Chapter 48

Luis Morales

I'm glued to the window for my second airplane flight and my first out of my country, watching the distant large buildings of Havana, the inlet, *el Castillo del Morro* and bare land as we slowly veer away from the coast. Sr. Lobo, my father and others talk loudly over the drone and vibration of the propellers about their plans once we arrive in the United States.

My father sticks his finger on the window glass. "The Florida Straits, separating Florida from Cuba." I gaze down at deep blue water alive with rolling waves, dotted with occasional ships.

After a while, my father points out the window at a long line of islands, connected by a long bridge. "Those are the Florida Keys. A key is really just a kind of island, like Cayo Smith, next to our cottage." A short while later, we are above a big swampy area, and my father points again. "Those are the Everglades."

Finally, the plane turns. He points down. "The airport is coming up. Those buildings are downtown Miami."

After we land and go through a building where people look at paperwork, men pick us up and whisk us away in large automobiles.

Before long, we are seated in a restaurant with long, metallic tables covered with white tablecloths, eating roast pork, red beans and rice, sweet plantains and everything else I'm accustomed to eating.

A nurse enters my hospital room, takes my pulse and looks at my charts. Sylvia says, "Do you know when one of his doctors will be in?"

The nurse says, "No, I imagine sometime after five."

"Do you think they'll do another brain scan?"

"You'll have to ask one of the doctors."

"As his wife, I have a right to know."

The nurse says, "Just stick around. A doctor will be in."

I move back to the trip, now rocking and fighting sleep as we glide on a train from Miami to Daytona Beach. Vast pastureland, dotted with horses and cows, zips by.

Angel is not with us. He was singled out and told he had to go to another car as we boarded. Rumbling northward, I'm surprised to see people with very dark skin, like those in Cuba, toiling in orange groves, dressed in long-sleeved shirts and long pants, just like the sugar cane pickers in Cuba.

The train stops in little towns along the way, where a few people board or get off. During a brief stop at a train station, I see advertisements of orange-growing companies, with photographs of white-skinned girls and men, all dressed up, standing by trees, smiling, with oranges in their hands. None of the advertisements shows the true pickers.

In the early afternoon, the train stops at a building, larger than many we'd passed or stopped at, with a sign saying, Daytona Beach. Like other stations we've stopped in, I see 'White Only' and 'Colored Only' signs at the bathrooms, water fountains and areas of the waiting room.

I look at my father. "What is *colored*?"

"Negro."

It dawns on me that while the workers on the farms as we've traveled north reminded me of those in Cuba, the separation of the races here seems to be considerably stronger than in Cuba. Looking across the railroad tracks from the station, I see what appears to be a village of unpainted wooden houses, lining dirt streets in which only dark-skinned people walk, sit and stand.

As we walk down the steps from our train car, I'm surprised to find Angel walking back from the front of the train. "Where were you, Sir?"

"Please, Luis, call me Angel, not *sir*." He points toward the first car behind the engine, which looks dirtier and older than the rest. Something like soot darkens the windows.

Angel frowns. "I know my skin is not like yours, and I know that's why I can never hold your level of work in Cuba, but I've never before been told that I couldn't travel in a train car with people with lighter skin."

My father grimaces. "I'm sorry that happened to you, Angel. It didn't seem there was any problem eating dinner together in Miami. Maybe it's just a rule about trains."

Angel nods. "Maybe it was okay to eat together because the restaurant was Cuban, and they are used to Cubans of different races."

I'm trying to digest exactly what I've heard and what these signs I'm seeing are all about.

On the street, men from our group stand near a line of large, shiny, black cars.

A man appears and escorts Angel, my father and me to a car. Cars begin to move away.

The driver says something, looking at all four of us. I understand the word *English*.

My father and I shake our heads no.

Angel answers something I don't understand so I imagine he speaks a little English. The driver and Angel converse.

Finally, the driver exits the car. Angel turns to us and explains in Spanish. "It is happening again. I don't think I like this country so much. I am not permitted to cross the river with you, or to stay in the same hotels where the light-skinned people stay. I am forbidden to attend anything you will attend because all are east of the river. Even General Batista's home is there, so I will not be able to attend the festivities."

My father says, "I'll try to talk to *El Hombre* to see if anything can be done."

I've always heard that General Batista himself is *mulato*, although he does not have such dark skin or African features. I wonder if the residents do not realize it.

The driver comes back with a copy of a tiny green booklet with black print with the title, *The Green Book, 1945*. He holds it open to a page and points. "Here's a place that we can take you."

We follow other cars a few blocks, but then the others turn right, and we turn left. We head into the area I've seen from the train station, with narrow dirt streets and unpainted, weather-beaten wooden homes and stores. The driver stops in front of a small building.

An old black man is swinging back and forth on a porch swing. The driver and Angel get out and walk up to him. The older man points to his right. The men return to the car.

"No vacancy. He is sending us to a college, where he says they have some rooms."

My father looks surprised. "A college?"

"Yes, Bethune-Cookman. Apparently, it is a college for Negro students. They have rooms for non-students. Negro entertainers who perform at hotels on the beachside can't sleep on the east side of the river, so they stay at the college."

The driver drives a few blocks and stops in front of a large brick building. They go inside, leaving us in the car. After fifteen minutes or so, they come out and retrieve Angel's suitcase. We say goodbye and leave without Angel.

I wonder whether my father has a feeling about the discrimination in this place, being that he seems to discredit dark-skinned men, although he seems to like Angel, and President Batista.

My father and I are driven across a wooden bridge spanning a large river, to a street called Main Street, which is lined with little shops, restaurants, a pool hall and banks.

The driver stops the car just before a coquina bridge joining a large wooden pier standing on pilings above the ocean and a concrete structure, under which we could see a wide expanse of hard sand, fronting beautiful, blue water. A large wooden building with a sign saying, Ocean Pier–Casino–Dancing, stands in the middle of the pier.

To our left is a grand, white, wooden hotel, with a sign indicating is it the Seaside Inn. We get out of the car and walk toward the water, then turn back to look at the entrance of the hotel. I see windows facing the water. I imagine gazing out at the magnificent sea, smelling the salt air all night and listening to waves crash as I sleep. We enter the huge, tastefully decorated lobby and soon have the key to our room.

After leaving our things in the room, we walk back along Main Street and step into a clothing store. My father buys bathing trunks, light shirts and sandals for himself and me.

Back in our room, while changing clothes, I stand at the window. Strong waves, cresting with white froth, roll in and slap the shore. This beach is like nothing I've ever seen. The waves are huge, more uniform and longer-lasting than those at Siboney Beach. On the sand below the pier, people stand, sit and lie among cars on the sand. It seems the sand is very hard-packed because cars are driving just like on a paved street. I recall hearing the men talking about cars racing here.

I notice that what I've heard about Negroes not being allowed to cross the river must be true. No dark-skinned person is to be found.

After changing into our swim-trunks, we go down to the beach. My father sits on the sand as I walk into the warm, soothing, ocean water. I let the strong waves sway me. Then I float, looking at the sky. I stay in the water for a long, long time, sometimes lying on the sand in shallow areas, sometimes romping in the crashing waves. From time to time, my father enters the water for a bit, and then returns to sit on the sand.

Later, we walk up a large concrete ocean-front park, past a coquina stone tower with a clock at the top, to a coquina-stone, shell-shaped outdoor concert stage.

As we get closer, I can see and hear a band of four men playing a cello, trumpet, trombone and drums, much like those of Cuba, but without the lively Cuban rhythm. Finally, we enter an underground tunnel near the clock tower and cross under the street on the way back to the hotel.

Chapter 49

Franklin Morales

Thursday, December 1, 2016

Franklin arrived at the office, catching Kalvin wandering aimlessly through the halls. What was wrong with this guy?

At Ruth's desk, Franklin said. "Ruth, I need some more details about my father's trips to Cuba. I understand that he had you schedule me to go with him this week. I'm considering going since he cannot."

She nodded. "Yes, what did he tell you?"

"How he got started, how he goes legally, and I can too, that a driver would pick us up and take us to places where we would deliver money according to a list. How much money do I need to take, and what about expenses?"

"Here is the entire file." She opened the folder. "Here's the Table of Contents, the list of the current beneficiaries, each showing the person's total bequest and periodic distributions. We write a check from the trust account applied to each one, and he cashes it at the bank before the trip. He converts it to Canadian money or Euros before he goes, because there is an extra ten percent penalty on converting U.S. money. There, the driver converts it to Cuban money, part in one kind of pesos and part in another. The driver will explain." She placed an accordion folder on the table and pulled out several smaller files with labels. The smell of stale smoke came from either her or the folder.

"I make reservations, if needed, but he generally just stays in the same private dwellings each time since he goes regularly. There's a folder on travel arrangements, including lodging and drivers. You will find more folders with other important details, including the fees your father charges and how his expenses are paid."

Franklin nodded.

She continued, "We could postpone the trip, but if you do, you'll have to double up. The beneficiaries count on the income to supplement their meager salaries."

"Please postpone my father's flight. Hopefully he will be better and able to go next time."

Franklin thought he should explain the trip to his sister. But, as soon as he thought of it, he became aggravated. She'd be sitting there in her cluttered living room, smoking cigarettes, her poor grandchild enveloped in second-hand smoke. She'd watch soaps over his shoulder as he tried to talk to her.

Franklin popped into the firm library looking for a volume of *Florida Jurisprudence*. Kalvin sat at the long, oak table, behind an open book of *Florida Statutes*, another of case law, and a treatise. He scribbled notes on a legal-sized yellow pad.

"Kalvin, no laptop? What are you working on?"

Kalvin looked up. "Oh, uh, I'm researching something for Mr. Doolittle."

"Oh. What?"

"Uh, well, uh, something about guardianship."

"Oh, really? Who's the client?"

"Uh . . . uh, I don't know. He just asked me to research."

Franklin nodded, certain that it was his father's case.

Oak shelves surrounded the first part of the room, with ancient, leather-bound tomes of the *Jurisprudence* series. Franklin went behind the books on display to the rows of metal shelves on rollers, hiding other shelves. He shoved one aside, located the book he needed, and leafed through the pages. He could find the same book on-line, but he loved the smell and feel of actual pages.

He heard whispering in the front area and walked back out. Kalvin and Samantha, a twenty-year-old blond with bronzed skin, the only blond, blue-eyed, completely Caucasian looking person in the office, were looking at each other. Franklin had seen what looked like flirtation progressing for a few weeks.

She glanced at Franklin and blushed. "Oh, hi, Mr. Morales."

A bit later, he went back to the library to return the book and found the newest associate, Ramón, saying, "Hey Kalvin, you back there?" He walked around the shelves. "Kalvin?"

Gertrude walked down the hall. "Have you seen Samantha? I can't find her anywhere."

"No," a woman answered.

"Where could she be?" Gertrude said.

Samantha strolled out from behind the shelves, adjusting her skirt. Ramón said, "Hey, uh Samantha. You see Kalvin anywhere?"

"Huh, no, uh-uh."

Ramón muttered to himself as he walked away. "Where is that lazy-ass son-of-a-bitch?"

Franklin walked to the back row of the rolling shelves. The rollers sounded on another row. He heard Ramón's voice again. "Kalvin, where the hell you . . .?" He stopped short. "You son-of-a-bitch. In the goddam library. Is there room between the shelves like that? Un-fucking-believable." He laughed. "Ah, the sweet aroma of pussy."

Doolittle's voice came from the hallway. "Where have you been? I've been asking for you."

Kalvin answered, "I've been right here, researching."

As Franklin walked back down the hall, a staff person said, "Franklin, you have a phone call."

Franklin sped up his steps. As he reached the office, his secretary said, "Your uncle Humberto."

Franklin slowed down. Tío Humberto was always harassing his father, and probably was now going to harass him. He grabbed the receiver and shifted to Spanish. "Hello, Uncle. How are you?"

"Fine, Franklin. Listen I want to talk to you about your father's trips to Cuba."

Franklin was taken aback by Humberto's not even inquiring about his father's health.

"All right, Uncle. What do you wish to say?"

"That it's wrong. Wrong. You know it is. Your father takes money into that country, and you know whose pockets the money fills."

Franklin tried to calm himself down, but he was defensive of his father. "No, Uncle. I don't exactly know what you are talking about."

"Fidel! Every penny you take to Cuba or send to Cuba benefits him, not the people."

"Tío Humberto, I don't agree with that feeling at all. I know my father didn't. We believe that the Cuban people need what we send them. It's not benefitting the government. Our government has imposed plenty of penalties that cause that government *and* its people difficulties. Not that I agree with that either, but we are not going to leave the people to suffer."

Tío Humberto snorted. "When they have money to purchase things, it benefits the government."

"So, you would have them suffer just so the government doesn't get a penny of tax or whatever it is you think benefits it? Is that it?"

"Exactly, and when your father travels there, he stays in government hotels and eats in government restaurants. That's even worse."

"Are you so sure that's where he stays and eats?"

Tío Humberto's voice rose. "You and your father are communists, aren't you? You don't see anything wrong with what happened, do you?"

"Tío Humberto. Don't label us with any such word for helping people. And, as a matter of fact, this isn't really us personally helping the people anyway. These people inherited the money. They own the money. My father simply delivers it."

Tío Humberto's voice vibrated. "Your father even created that non-profit corporation to send more. He's benefitting the Cuban government with his own money and donations he receives."

"Uncle, I'm not going to talk about this anymore. I'm following in my father's footsteps on this, including the non-profit, tax-exempt corporation that you mention."

Plastic pieces of a home phone crash together as the phone goes dead.

Chapter 50

Luis Morales

In the evening after a day in the warm ocean water, I'm again dressing up. I try to tie my tie alone but need my father's help. I gaze out the window and amazed at how many people are still out enjoying the water. I'd rather stay at the beach into the evening.

A driver picks us up and drives back along Main Street toward the river. Just before the bridge, he turns right. After passing not too many houses, he turns to the left, passes a stone wall and stops in front of a large house with a tiled roof.

General Batista greets us just inside the front door. He and my father hug. "Luis, I have a friend of yours here. Angel, come."

Angel, grinning from ear to ear, comes around the corner, dressed in a suit, like the waiters.

My father grins. "How'd you do it, Fulgencio?"

"A driver went to the mainland to pick up the workers who would serve the food. They dressed Angel up just as nice and brought him." He laughs. "We won't make him work, but he looks nice, doesn't he? I'd let him sleep here, but I don't want to displease Mrs. Bethune by not returning him to the college."

As the sun sets, leaving a fiery orange glint on the river water, the crowd lingers on the lawn, enjoying drinks and appetizers served by uniformed Negro men and women. The home has the feel of the homes of Vista Alegre in Santiago de Cuba, with an airy flow, large carved-wooden tables and chairs and large decorated tiles covering all the floors. The walls are adorned with paintings. Two swords with colorful handles hang crisscrossed over the mantle in a sitting room.

General Batista smiles proudly as my father admires the main room. "Fulgencio, this is some beautiful home. Have you spent most of your time here since your presidency ended?"

"Yes, although I also have homes in New York and West Palm Beach. I love fishing in the ocean right here in Daytona Beach, in front of the Boardwalk."

My father says, "I heard you plan to run for office again. Is that true?"

Batista laughs. "I probably stand a better chance of getting elected as a senator from here."

Batista turns to another, and my father attempts a conversation with a man who doesn't seem to understand Spanish. A translator helps. Then my father introduces me. "Luis, this is Mr. Ransom Olds. Race car driver. He lives next door." We shake hands silently. The translator drifts away, as does Mr. Olds.

My father introduces me to several other men, Mrs. Batista and their young son, Jorge.

One of the men who accompanied us from Cuba asks an English-speaking man who also speaks broken Spanish, "I thought there were thousands of sexy army women marching around on the beach. Where are they?"

The man smiles, "They certainly weren't all sexy, although some were very enticing. They're gone. With the war winding down, they closed the program. But it sure was great when they were here. I dated a couple."

Another Cuban says, "I guess the German prisoners of war are gone too?"

"Yes."

"I heard the prisoners constructed and made very intricate architectural designs on part of the hospital."

"True."

My father and General Batista wander away.

Angel looks at me and smiles. "How was your day, Luis?"

"Fine, sir."

A Cuban man walks up. "Angel, I've never seen you so dapper. In fact, I haven't seen you since we arrived in this city. What have you been up to?"

Angel grimaces. "See the color of my skin? I'm not allowed on this side of the river. I now know that anybody with skin as dark or darker than mine is treated much worse here than at home. Sure, at home I'll never be an executive, but I can go anywhere I want. The only reason I'm at this house on the beachside tonight is that they put me in a car with these workers, dressed like I was going to work as well."

The other man glances at a waiter and says quietly "What is it, a law or something?"

"Yes, as a matter of fact it is. I've learned all about it."

"I don't understand, Angel. The waiters look more like Africans. They have much darker skin than you do. You aren't much darker than General Batista himself. Mixed bloods with slightly dark skin are treated the same as those with black skin? How is it Batista can live on this side of the river?"

Angel snorts. "He was president of a country and has a lot of money. He is very generous to the city."

The man shakes his head. "Where are you staying?"

"In a dormitory room at a college for negro students. It's called Bethune-Cookman College. A lady named Mrs. Bethune founded it. She created and operates the college and is allowing me to stay in one of the dormitory rooms. The word negro, they pronounce it like nee-gro, but it seems to have a stronger meaning here. It doesn't just mean dark skin. It's a race. And there seems to be a separation, a resistance of both races to blend with the other. It's odd, and uncomfortable.

"Negro musicians who entertain white people on the beachside can't sleep on the east side of the river, where the beach is, so they stay in the college dormitory rooms."

The man seems fascinated. "Is this Mrs. Bethune *una negra* herself?"

"She is. Years ago, she created a school for black children, many of whose parents worked for wealthy white people; she later convinced the city to give her an old garbage dump to create her dream of a college, so black students had a place to study, since even education is separate here."

"How did you learn so much about this?"

Angel smiles. "I had tea with Mrs. Bethune."

The other man laughs. "Oh, you did, did you?"

"She learned there was a man from Cuba on campus and she wanted to ask me a million questions about education in Cuba, from elementary school through university. And she asked many questions about whether people with dark skin studied in the same places with those that have light skin."

The man nods.

Angel continues, "We drank the tea in a room at her home, which is on the campus. There were photographs on the walls of her with all these rich-looking white people, with the wife of the President of the United States and even President Roosevelt himself. I understand she freely crosses the river to meet with the wealthy white people. She's one of the most influential people here. I understand that with her relationship with the President and his wife, the people of the city have to respect her. Oh, something else I learned is that even though I, with my dark skin, can enter a store in the shopping area, I cannot try on or return clothing. Also, I may not eat in any eating establishment except those near the college. Mrs. Bethune's students, because she makes them dress up in uniforms, look impeccable and act like good citizens, are treated much better than other dark-skinned people in the downtown area.

"Earlier, you were talking about the lady soldiers in town. I learned females in this country aren't allowed to be in the real army, so they created this special army corps just for ladies. Mrs. Bethune suggested to President Roosevelt's wife to let some of them train here, so they did."

"I had to learn some of this stuff from others or by asking her about photos I found, because Mrs. Bethune is quite modest and doesn't readily talk about her accomplishments."

A black man dressed in uniform holds out a tray to me, and I take a piece of bread with ham and cheese.

Angel turns to me. "What have you done since we arrived, Luis?"

"We went to the beach. Our hotel is right in front of the sand and water."

Angel frowns and nods. "Since the negro people can't cross the river except to work, they also can't enjoy the ocean. I heard that Mrs. Bethune said something like, 'That's God's water, isn't it?' She and some others purchased beach-front property in another town, so they designated it as a beach for the people who weren't allowed on the beach here. One of the men at the college took me to it. We drove for quite a while and then crossed a river in a different city. On the beachside, we drove for a long time along a badly maintained dirt road because *coloreds*, as they say it, cannot drive on the street near the beaches.

"Once we finally arrived at the beach, small shacks where you could change clothes stood along the shore. The sand was white and soft. The water was a beautiful hue. I guess that was the same water you swam in here in the racist city, God's water." He smiled. "We swam for a few minutes. It was nice."

I'm perplexed by the complicated procedure that people with different colored skin have to follow here. I leave the conversation to gaze out over the veranda.

After a while, I'm with my father and others in a car behind a motorcade led by a car that says 'Daytona Beach Police' on the side, with its lights flashing. We travel in the direction opposite Main Street and then turn towards the beach along a wide boulevard lined with palm trees. In front of us as we near the beach is a hotel grander than the Seaside Inn, with a sign in front that says 'Clarendon'. Through an above-ground tunnel at the bottom of the building, I can see the ocean and the beach. Then we turn north on Atlantic Avenue. Soon, the caravan of cars pulls into a long, semi-circular driveway. We pile out and climb steps to a concrete-block house high above the street. In the house, numerous sliding-glass doors allow a full view of the beach. I am encouraged to follow other kids down to the beach and stand around on the hard-packed sand.

Later that night, we drive back south, past our hotel, to a mint-green-colored hotel behind a sign saying, 'Streamline'. As we climb out of the car, one of the men tells my father, "I understand that we are likely to find Bill France, the founder of local, modern-day auto racing, here."

We go to the top floor of the Streamline and enter a room under a sign saying, 'The Ebony Room'. Several of the men who traveled from Cuba with us are also here. I look out a couple of windows, trying to get an image of Daytona.

One of the men says, "Let's go up to the roof for a better view. There's a bar up there."

From the roof viewpoint, I see the pier in the ocean, and try to locate the coquina rock structures near it. I can see the wooden bridge over the river. Looking northward, I try to figure out where General Batista's house is, but trees obscure the view. Angel takes me a level higher, and I can see a little more.

After being mesmerized by Daytona Beach from above, I go back down, into the Ebony Club. Through a translator, my father introduces me to a tall man with black hair, Mr. France, who says, "I'm pleased to meet you."

A man puts a hand on Mr. France's arm, whispers to him, and pulls him away.

My father tells the interpreter he wants to speak with Mr. France about sugar and rum.

The interpreter brings another man to talk to my father. The man says, "Your Cuban Rum is smooth and tasty. Yet we have no need for sugar as a product. And alcoholic beverages already exist here. We are not interested in promoting those businesses. Our mission is auto racing."

One of the Cuban men says, also through the interpreter, "How do we bring in wagering as an official part of the races? I see several casinos in Daytona Beach."

The man seems to turn his nose up as my countryman speaks. The interpreter translates his words. "The Ocean Pier Casino and the Burgoyne Casino on Beach Street are dancing and party locations, not gambling businesses. We are interested in automobiles and racing. Organized racing and racers; not organized crime. Not what you seem to be getting at. We don't need sugar. We already have rum. We don't need gambling in conjunction with racing." He walks away.

The friendliness and acceptance seem to fade. A while later, I hear a man say something about 'the Cubans,' and waving his hands like we should go.

My father and the others get the message, and we depart.

The next day, we stop in a small gasoline filling station on Main Street, close to the river, near a large cemetery. I hear one of the men say, "This is France's station." My father and others walk in. I can see them talking to somebody. Their arms wave in the air as they attempt to explain. They come out, looking sullen, get into the car and drive away without a word.

Chapter 51

Sylvia Morales

As Sylvia sat, holding her husband's hand and stewing over whether he was breathing properly, an unshaven man, dressed in wrinkled blue scrubs, entered the room. Without acknowledging her or speaking, he approached Louis, stretched his eyelids open and stared into the whites of his eyes. He tapped a reflex-testing device on his knees and elbows. She wondered whether that was useful in the position that Louis lay. The doctor's eyebrows rose; he pursed his lips.

"Excuse me, are you one of his doctors?" she asked.

He looked at her as though he'd just realized she was there, as he moved Louis' gown aside and listened to his heart with a stethoscope. "I've been asked to do a consult."

"Doctor . . . uh . . . Straight," she said, reading his name tag, "Who asked you to do a consult."

Straight looked at her. His grooming was as pitiful as his scrubs—his silly comb-over revealed a freckled scalp, with gray and white hairs poking out among the few brown ones. Gray hairs sprouted from his ears like a grove of alfalfa sprouts. "The hospital's Ethics Committee."

She knew this was not good. "What is that? Who is that?"

He cleared his throat. "It's the committee that becomes involved when something serious occurs, such as invocation of a DNR or inquiry about whether life-prolonging procedures should be withheld or withdrawn. The Committee designates one of its members, a hospital physician, to examine the patient and file an opinion."

Sylvia was stunned. It took a few seconds to find her voice. "Who has suggested withholding or withdrawing anything?" She held up a hand. "No, don't even tell me in front of my husband. Let's talk outside."

He looked at her like she was some kind of nutcase. "Well, uh, please let me finish my examination." He held both Louis' hands, took his pulse and pushed down in various places.

She marched from the room and stood, banging closed fists on the wall, waiting for him to exit.

When he did, he said, "Uh, Miz, uh . . . "

"Morales," she said. "Mrs. Louis Morales. Sylvia. I am his wife."

"I'm sorry, Mrs. Morales," he said. "These matters are never easy." He looked like an old weasel.

"I don't care about 'these matters.' I care about Louis Morales."

He stepped back. His left eye twitched. "Ma'am, it does not appear that you are the health-care decision maker. But I will say anyway that I have not made a determination. I need to review all the records before I conclude the inquiry."

She glanced into the room, where her husband lay silently. "Doctor," she said, "I believe he's still here. I see his twitches. I feel his quivers. I do not believe they are automatic. Please give him some time. Please."

He looked at her, stone-faced, and rambled down the hall without a nod or a smile.

As she reentered the room, she was surprised to find a young man with very dark skin standing over him.

"Excuse me. Mrs. Morales? I'm Desmond. I just wanted to come by and see Mr. Morales. I work in the law office."

She shook his hand. "I'm pleased to meet you, Desmond."

He took a seat, put a hand over Louis' and shivered. A tear rolled down his shiny cheek. His voice shook. "Get better, Mr. Morales."

"How long have you worked in the office, Desmond?"

"Uh, about nine months, ma'am."

"What do you do?"

"I'm a paralegal."

"What did you do before you worked there?"

He looked at Louis's face. "I came here a year ago from Haiti. Mr. Morales came to the facility where I was housed and spoke to us about making our way in the United States. Afterwards, we spoke individually. I guess he was impressed that I'd taught myself English before arriving. He offered me a job on the spot as a clerk. He got me into a course to obtain a certificate as a paralegal."

"Really?" She was surprised to learn of this volunteer work.

She felt a tear sliding down her cheek as well.

"I'm sure that my husband is aware of what's going on and that he appreciates your coming to see him."

Chapter 52

Sylvia Morales

Franklin, Roosevelt, and Mr. Murphy walked into the hospital room together.

Franklin said, "Sylvia, the doctors say he's breathing on his own. They are going to slowly remove the ventilator and see if he's able to breathe without it. But if there's a problem, they'll reengage it."

"Are you sure it's safe?"

"The way they've explained it, yes."

A nurse entered, followed by an orderly. They moved her husband onto a gurney and took him away, with equipment trailing.

Tension remained in the room.

"All right," Franklin said, "Let's talk about other things while we are waiting. The guardianship has been filed. The judge will appoint an attorney for him and the examining committee."

Sylvia stared at him, mouth open. "Your father will have an attorney?"

"Yes, when a guardianship is filed, the court appoints three people, such as doctors, nurses, psychologists or similar professionals to examine him separately and file reports. The court also appoints an attorney to represent the 'alleged incapacitated person' or 'A.I.P.'. If the A.I.P. has the ability to contest the case, his lawyer would present his defense. If the court determines he is incapacitated and appoints a guardian, then all those expenses, including the fees of the attorney who filed the guardianship, are paid from the incapacitated person's funds."

Sylvia's mouth dropped again. "Really? So even though we don't think this guardianship is necessary, all the fees and costs will come from our funds? That hardly seems fair."

"The law is set up to protect the A.I.P., but yeah, if the guardianship is implemented, the A.I.P. pays for it in the long run."

Chapter 53

Luis Morales

Far too many people have been in my room lately, evaluating me, talking about me, sometimes showing animosity toward each other. It raises anxiety, although, of course, most don't realize that I am alert. Sylvia tries to protect me from uncomfortable situations. Franklin also attempts to promote only positive, peaceful talk, but not to the extent that Sylvia does.

A nurse just left after switching the television channel to Univision. The announcer explained that Fidel's ashes were in a vehicle that is part of a caravan, traveling from Havana to Santiago, following in reverse the route Fidel and the Revolutionaries took when the Revolution prevailed, after he'd made his first speech in Santiago de Cuba on January 1, 1959.

Another worker walked in while the news was on, saying, in Spanish, "Why do you have that shit on?"

A live video trailed the vehicles of the caravan passing along country roads and entering villages along the way. In the countryside, crowds of people lined highways, and inside pueblos and cities, people lined the streets, waving flags, singing and chanting something new. "*Yo soy Fidel. Yo soy Fidel. Yo soy Fidel.*"

The nurse answered, "I was looking for a show."

"Well, don't let them keep on boosting him up even now that he's dead."

The celebration somewhat upset me, but I was also intrigued at the government's ability to bring out the crowds to honor him in this way. A whole country announcing that each and every person is Fidel. "I am Fidel. I am Fidel."

She switched off the set, leaving me in much-appreciated silence. Now, in solitude, I'm at peace. During the night, nurses enter infrequently. There's little sound out in the halls. It's dark. It's quiet.

After leaving Bill France's gas station, we board a train and head north to Washington, DC.

Again, Angel is directed to one of the first two cars right behind the engine, darkened with soot, with signs above the doors, saying, "Colored Car."

I stay awake most of the long trip, looking out the window. While the sun is up, I watch negro workers picking cotton balls and green leaves, which Angel informs me are tobacco, as we clatter northward.

The following morning, in Washington, we travel to the hotel in a parade of large, well-polished, black cars. I see no Colored or White signs. I see some black men who seem to be working for whites, but I also see some who are well-dressed, like professional men or businessmen. Is this the same country where I woke up yesterday morning?

Inside the hotel, we stand in a huge open area with plush chairs, large tapestries and colorful rugs over tile floors. White and black marble adorn the room. Angel is assigned a room in the hotel, just like all the rest of the people in our group.

We are transported in a motorcade to the U.S. Capitol building. The streets seem wide and busy.

As I learned in Havana, the dome of the Capitol looks almost identical to that of *El Capitolio* in Havana. I wonder which country created and which copied the other.

Just like I did in the *Capitolio*, I stand around in the hallways while my father and the Cuban contingent linger and converse in hushed tones with official-looking men. My father and Sr. Lobo smile broadly.

I hear Spanish-English interpreters talking of importing sugar, of import taxes and how and where the sugar deliveries will arrive in the United States. They also talk of importing rum, coffee and cigars and increasing gambling activities in my country. I'm ready to return to my home and forget all this business.

The fog embedding my brain shreds again. More doctors, looking at me, touching me, murmuring with each other just inches from me. What's happening? Have any of the tests shown something positive, or negative? My throat is still so raw. My chest is still so tender. My behind hurts like when I lay on the wooden floor of the chicken coop at the Siboney Farmhouse and the tiled floor of my tiny closet-turned cell at the prison. I hope I don't get one of those killer skin lesions that are so dangerous in hospitals.

I burst awake, shocked by my own snoring. That hurts too. But I feel better without that damn plastic wedge intruding through me.

Cari, where are you? I can't stand it without you. Please wait for me. Please wait.

Chapter 54

Elena Morales Lennox

"Come on, Mom. Let's go in."

"Go see who's in there."

"Mom, don't be silly. Sylvia will be there, and maybe Franklin."

"I need to know."

Pedrito huffed and went around the corner.

"Sylvia is there. I told her you were nervous about visiting. She said she can step out."

Elena trembled. She breathed deeply several times, trying to prepare herself. Sylvia came around the corner and walked straight toward her, arms outstretched. "Elena, I'm glad you've come back. Your father will be happy."

Elena kept her arms wrapped around her midsection, but Sylvia hugged her anyway, then stepped to the side with an arm still around her as she moved her toward the room. "Come on. He wants to see you."

Inside the room, she found him lying like a phantom. But now, he looked more natural as some of the medical equipment had been removed. She gazed into his drawn, grayish face. He did not look like a living being.

The bitch was still holding her. She wanted to run again. She grabbed Pedrito and pulled him close.

Again, Sylvia pushed her to a chair. "Here, sit. Hold him. Touch him."

Elena tried to hold back, but found herself sitting, with a hand on her papá. His breathing seemed to accelerate. She shivered uncontrollably. Noises emitted from his mouth. Parts of his face and jaw seemed to move. Horrified, she looked at Sylvia.

Sylvia smiled. "He reacts to pleasure, pain and unpleasantness. His look means he's pleased that you are here."

Elena sobbed. She dropped her head on his midsection, but suddenly jolted away, worried that she was hurting him.

Pedrito sat on the other side of the bed and touched him too. He cried quietly.

Sylvia left the room. Elena stayed for what seemed like hours, watching him twitch and make facial movements and wondering if that meant he was aware.

Finally, she stood, looked around to see if Sylvia had returned, leaned down to kiss her papá on the head, and, with Pedrito following, left the room.

Pedrito dropped Elena at home. She ate leftover *arroz con pollo* and fretted over what would happen in the hearing on the emergency temporary guardianship. Kalvin and Doolittle were treating this too casually. Did they have any idea what they were doing?

Kalvin should have been home by seven. Here it was eight-thirty, and she'd heard nothing. This behavior was becoming a habit. Finally, almost two hours late, he banged through the door and staggered into the room, carrying the stench of alcohol.

"Where have you been? What have you been doing?"

"Uh, just talking to the guys from the office."

"Working on tomorrow's hearing?"

"We don't need to. It's just a short hearing. It's no problem. Really routine."

"Your dinner is there on the plate. You can microwave it."

He put the plate in, slammed the door and punched digital buttons. She glared at him, as he watched the turning plate.

"What's going to happen tomorrow? How are you going to present our case?"

"Oh…uh…well, we'll just tell the court why we filed the guardianship and why it's an emergency."

She wanted to laugh. "You think that's going to do the trick? You think Franklin is just going to sit there and let it happen?"

"Well, he shouldn't be guardian."

This time she did laugh. "What are you going to present to counter him? Does he really have documents that actually name him and give him priority as guardian?"

"I think he's just blowing smoke. And anyway, the priority will go to you."

She shook her head, this time not laughing. "You and Doolittle are losers, and we are going to lose. I'm going to be embarrassed. I'm planning on switching my attorney right away. I should have done it already."

"What are you talking about? You can't change attorneys."

"Oh, really?"

He'd only eaten half his meal, but he tossed the plate into the sink with the remaining food still on it and marched out of the room.

Chapter 55

Franklin Morales

Roosevelt, Jude, Mr. Murphy and Franklin sat at the counsel table on the left side of the courtroom, while Doolittle, Kalvin and Elena sat at the table on the right, and Sylvia and Mr. Warnock sat at a table near the empty jury box.

The bailiff said, "Please rise," as Judge Reynolds marched into the courtroom. The judge flopped into his seat and said, "Be seated. Let's see. We are here on the Guardianship of Luis Morales." Glancing up after rifling through the file, he said, "I see that we have several apparently interested parties in the courtroom. Let's see. Mr. Doolittle and Mr. Lennox, it appears that you represent the petitioner, Elena Morales Lennox. Is that right?"

They nodded.

"And Mr. Franklin Morales, are you not with Mr. Doolittle and Mr. Lennox on this?"

"I am not, Your Honor," Franklin said, partially rising.

"I certainly hope we do not have different members of the same law firm on opposite sides of a matter appearing in front of this Court."

Franklin stood and stated, "Your Honor, I am here in my individual capacity as one of the nominated agents named in powers of attorney and a health care surrogate form executed by my father while he was competent. The other gentlemen at this table," he said, waving a hand toward them, "are Mr. George Murphy, and Mr. Roosevelt Harris, who are also named in the same capacities with me in these documents and attorney D. Jude Armstrong of Daytona Beach, Florida. Mr. Armstrong can speak for me as my attorney to the extent that is necessary to avoid conflict. I was unaware until recently of the fact that these members of my law firm filed a guardianship, which was completely unnecessary, being that my father executed documents designating persons to handle his affairs in the event he would be unable to do so."

Appearing perplexed, the judge looked at the third table, and said, "Mr. Warnock, I see that you appear to be representing another. . .. Who is this?"

Warnock half stood and said, "Yes, Your Honor. This is Mrs. Sylvia Morales, wife of Louis Morales."

Judge Reynolds shuffled files and said, "All right, we will proceed in the normal fashion in asking the Petitioner to state a case and see who, if anyone, wishes to object to the petition for appointment of an emergency temporary guardian or offer other arguments. Mr. Doolittle, you have filed a Petition for Guardianship and a separate Petition for Emergency Temporary Guardianship. I will enter orders appointing an examining committee and an attorney to represent Mr. Luis Morales."

Franklin stood. "Your honor, I move that the case be dismissed."

The judge frowned, but then smiled. "Mr. Morales, as I stated, since the petition was filed by your firm, you and all attorneys in your firm are disqualified to represent your father. Do you not agree?"

Franklin shuffled his feet, uncomfortable. He finally formed a statement. "Being that my father has not yet been appointed an attorney and has not yet been served, I believe we can simply ask at this point to have this case dismissed. If I am allowed in my individual capacity, I would move to have the petition dismissed on the basis that it was filed by an attorney with a conflict of interest."

The judge shook his head. "Franklin, you know I can't do that. There's no requirement that would affect the validity of the filing of the petition, even if there was a conflict. Once it's filed, it's in the court's hands. However, it is a bit difficult for either of you to make an argument."

Franklin remained on his feet. "Your Honor, regarding the appointment of an attorney to represent my father, I am sure my father would prefer to choose his own counsel rather than having one appointed from the rotating wheel. On behalf of my father, I suggest that Mr. David Jude Armstrong here should be appointed."

Judge Reynolds smiled. "The statute does state that the alleged incapacitated person can substitute his own attorney, but Mr. Morales has not made such a request."

"Your honor, my father is unconscious. We three, Mr. Murphy, Mr. Harris and I stand in his shoes as agents under the power of attorney he signed. The power of attorney is still in effect as of now. Thus, we, as his agents, hereby request that Mr. Armstrong be appointed. That's the same as his requesting this himself."

"Good points, Mr. Morales." The judge pulled out his Florida statute book and studied his computer screen. "Yes, as I thought, 744.331(2)(b) says, and I quote, 'The court shall appoint an attorney for each person alleged to be incapacitated in all cases involving a petition for adjudication of incapacity. The alleged incapacitated person may substitute her or his own attorney for the attorney appointed by the court.' I may have to appoint somebody from the wheel and then you as his agents can request to substitute. It does not say I can appoint the attorney of his wishes initially."

Franklin was frustrated. "I acknowledge that the statute reads as you state, Your Honor, but it just makes no sense to go through two steps when we all know what's going to occur."

Judge Reynolds said, "I take it that attorney Armstrong has not applied for and become part of our county's list of approved attorneys for such representation."

Franklin replied, "Judge the attorney chosen by the AIP does not have to be on the list."

"All right, I'll take this under advisement."

Glancing through the file, the judge chuckled. "I suppose we can back up a step. The Notice filed by the Petitioner's counsel indicates the sole purpose of this hearing is to determine whether an emergency exists that would require appointment of an emergency temporary guardian. We are not dealing with the main case yet, as the alleged incapacitated person has not been served or examined by the examining committee. Mr. Doolittle, state your case for an emergency."

Doolittle stood. "Your Honor, we filed the petition on behalf of Elena Morales Lennox, daughter of Louis Morales, because it is clear that a guardian must be appointed immediately to handle various important matters."

The judge plopped his chin on his fist. "Nothing is clear to me, Mr. Doolittle. Can you provide more detail on the nature of the emergency?"

"Your Honor, Mr. Louis Morales is the managing partner of our law firm. Urgent matters need his attention."

Judge Reynolds furrowed his brow. "Well, considering that Morales and Doolittle is a law firm made up of lawyers who practice estate planning and corporate law, I would expect the lawyers to have a good background in planning for incapacity and handling corporate matters when one is absent. And Franklin has stated there is a power of attorney. Speaking of an existing power of attorney, are you familiar with the concept of least restrictive means?"

Doolittle looked at Kalvin, who rose, perspiration dotting his forehead. "Uh your honor, it means the court should not take away more rights than necessary."

The judge nodded. "That's true. We should not automatically create a plenary guardianship if reasonable limitations are available. But it also means if the party has executed documents such as powers of attorney, unless there is some reason not to honor them, the Court is to consider ordering that they be honored. Besides that, I am surprised that the law firm has put itself in a position that the temporary absence of a partner causes the firm to freeze up. I cannot imagine what the emergency is that the agent on the power of attorney cannot resolve."

Doolittle stood and stammered. "Significant financial matters must be attended to."

"We'll need to have testimony about the nature of the emergency, but let's also get to the other big question here, which is why, if Mr. Morales did specifically name these gentlemen as his attorneys-in-fact and agents in various documents, is it necessary to have a guardianship at all? Franklin, do you have a copy of the power of attorney with you?"

Franklin stood and said, "Yes, Your Honor. Here is the original financial and property power of attorney."

The judge motioned for Franklin to approach and hand it to him. The judicial assistant and sheriff's deputy both flinched at a lawyer marching to the dais, but, looking at the judge, understood it was an invitation.

The judge studied the document. "Durable. Full powers. Dated quite a long time ago. Signed, witnessed, acknowledged before a notary. I can't imagine how you would be able to state that this is not a valid power."

Doolittle replied, "Your Honor, these gentlemen have not been forthcoming with what authority they might have, and have not shared a copy of the power of attorney. We do not know whether they actually have any authority; they have not offered any assistance to the law firm on these issues, and we would suggest that they are unwilling to do so. Furthermore, we would propose that it is a conflict of interest for Franklin Morales to be involved as attorney-in-fact for his father, when he is a member of the law firm in question."

The judge shook his head slowly. "Franklin, do you have another copy to show Mr. Doolittle?" Franklin nodded and handed him a copy. As Doolittle looked through it, obviously trying to figure out what to do, the Judge continued. "How is it a conflict for an agent to be a member of the firm? I don't know that a conflict argument applies to appointments voluntarily made by the principal. Can you cite law stating otherwise?"

Doolittle said, "Judge, we feel that it would be much better to have a disinterested family member handling these matters."

The judge sighed aloud. "The court cannot overrule documents based on your feelings, Mr. Doolittle." He glanced at the third table. "Mr. Warnock, would you like to weigh in on any of this?"

Warnock stood and said, "Your Honor, on behalf of the wife of Mr. Louis Morales, we believe that neither Elena Lennox nor Franklin Morales would be appropriate as the guardian. Mr. Louis Morales loves his wife, Sylvia, very much, and has confided in her many things about certain . . . "

Doolittle and Franklin simultaneously leapt to their feet and yelled, "Objection. Hearsay," at the same time.

"Sustained."

"He told her these people could not be tru . . . "

"Objection, Your Honor," the two hollered again.

Warnock said, "Mr. Morales would want Sylvia Morales as guardian, and she would have priority under Florida law."

Sylvia placed an arm on Warnock's wrist and made a facial gesture.

Franklin stood. "Your Honor, as you have wisely stated, the examining committee has not yet been appointed, so there is no evidence regarding my father's capacity or lack thereof. And there can be no determination affecting his rights until an attorney has been appointed to represent him. We have heard no argument or testimony as to any emergency. Before the court even considers appointing an emergency temporary guardian, we request that an evidentiary hearing be scheduled to review the nature of the alleged emergency. As you have also stated, Your Honor, my father has appointed people of his choosing in valid documents to handle his affairs. Whether or not there would be a conflict of interest is not applicable to that appointment. A guardianship is not appropriate."

The judge nodded. "Mr. Doolittle, you have not convinced me that there is an emergency or that Mrs. Elena Lennox should be appointed. Please bear in mind that Florida law requires that we try to use the least restrictive means, which means allowing one to create documents such as powers of attorney, which would make resorting to guardianship unnecessary. And the law provides priorities as to who should be guardian. Designees under a valid power of attorney, especially one with a preneed guardian designation, would have priority. It is premature to discuss who would be guardian when Mr. Morales has not even been declared incompetent. I would suggest that before coming in here again, the parties should meet and review the documents to which Franklin refers and decide whether this proceeding is appropriate." He banged his gavel and the crowd moved out.

In the hallway, Franklin said, "I invite everybody to the office one hour from now and we will do as the judge suggested."

The others wandered off, grumbling, without acknowledging they would appear.

Chapter 56

Sylvia Morales

Sylvia sat alone on a dark-brown, soft-leather sofa in the lobby of Morales and Doolittle. Dressed in the navy-blue dress she'd donned for the hearing, she felt like her attire was more appropriate for a funeral than a meeting. The large formal conference room, shielded by heavy, smoked glass, was directly across from her. A staff member entered the conference room and placed a tray with a pitcher and glasses on the credenza.

From behind a high, mahogany desk near the front door of the reception area, the receptionist said, "We are missing Mr. Morales very much. I hope he is better soon and able to come back into the office. He brings warmth and . . . I don't know how to describe it. But he is the backbone and spirit of this firm."

Sylvia's eyes burned. She managed, "Thank you. We hope he will be better soon and able to return."

Mr. Warnock strolled in and nodded to the receptionist. "I'm here for a meeting with Franklin Morales."

He sat on a chair with a carved wooden back, a bit higher than Sylvia. "Well, Sylvia. I hope that Franklin is truly going to be open and helpful today."

Sylvia regarded him. "I don't want to fight. Let's just listen. I think Franklin and the others may be handling it correctly and we need to support them, as opposed to those who are trying to do a guardianship."

"As you wish, but I think we need to show some strength, so they don't run rough-shod over us."

"Mr. Warnock, as I explained when I told you about the prenuptial agreement, I've already been through the problems of having a lawyer try to show that I am not a pushover. Let's see what they say."

She looked straight ahead through the smoky glass of the conference room. Franklin entered the room from a rear door, picked up a remote control and flipped through buttons while watching a screen.

Doolittle and Kalvin also entered from the rear door, approached Franklin and seemed to exchange words. Doolittle glanced through the dark glass into the reception area, walked to the side of the large window and drew the curtains closed.

Elena sauntered into the reception area, passed by the receptionist without a word or a look and dropped onto the other couch, not even looking at Sylvia. The stench of recent and stale smoke came with her.

Sylvia regarded the gaps in makeup and uneven line of lipstick on her lower lip. "Hello, Elena."

Elena glanced at Sylvia and back at her cellular phone. "Hi."

"What's happening next on the guardianship, Elena?"

Elena shot an ugly, defiant stare at her. "What do you care? You are on the other side."

Sylvia strove to maintain cordiality. "I'm on the side of my husband, your father."

"Oh, bullshit, Sylvia. You're on your own side."

Sylvia felt the attack. "No, really, Elena. I'm not."

Warnock put a hand on Sylvia's shoulder. She flinched. He leaned over and whispered. "Sylvia, there's no point in getting riled up over this, and certainly not in irritating Elena."

Sylvia fought to regain her composure. *Relax. Relax. Let Elena be. All right.* She was composed.

Chapter 57

Franklin Morales

Franklin invited Elena, Sylvia and Mr. Warnock into the luxurious conference room. Elena took a seat next to Doolittle, who sat at the head of the table opposite the door, with Kalvin on his other side. Franklin, flanked by Roosevelt and Jude on one side, and Mr. Murphy on the other, sat at the head of the table near the door, below the screen where he would project documents from his computer. Warnock and Sylvia looked somewhat out of place, sitting on one side, in the middle of the long table, like spectators at a ping-pong match.

Franklin said, "I had planned to hold this meeting anyway, but since the judge specifically stated that we should meet, I figured I'd fulfill his request so that we can put an end to this unnecessary guardianship."

Doolittle piped up. "It is not at all unnecessary . . . "

"Ah, but it is," said Franklin. "I will set forth the documents that my father has created, which are intended to avoid court involvement."

Franklin pushed a button to display documents from his computer on the screen above him. "The first document is this durable power of attorney. As you can see, it names Franklin Morales, Lansing Armstrong and George Murphy as attorneys-in-fact, or agents, and names Roosevelt Harris as alternate if any designee is unable to serve. It is signed and acknowledged by my father in the presence of witnesses and a notary public. We have used this binding document to handle my father's financial matters as to any asset owned by him, including his stock in this law firm."

He switched to a second document. "This document contains a health care surrogate designation and living will, which follow samples suggested by Florida law. The surrogate form designates Mr. Murphy alone initially to make health care decisions. Then it states that if there is a question as to life-prolonging procedures, or if my father is unable to communicate for a term of seventy-two hours, the three of us are to make such determinations together, as a committee. The living will provides that if he is determined by two physicians to be in a terminal or end-stage condition or in a persistent vegetative state, he wishes life-prolonging procedures to be disconnected, or not connected, and the three of us make that call together. The next document is a health-care power of attorney, which is intended to supplement the other health-care documents in case any medical professional or other interested party for any reason refuses to honor the basic statutory documents. Finally, there is a HIPAA release, authorizing the same people to obtain information from doctors and medical providers under federal privacy law."

He switched documents again. "The next document is a Do-Not-Resuscitate order. This document was not signed by my father, because it would not have been appropriate for him to sign it at the time that he signed the other documents. It's intended for somebody who already has some condition that's going to end life in the near future. It is different from the living will in that it says that if the person expires for any reason, then the person will not be resuscitated. Florida law provides that to be valid, the DNR must be signed by the party, or by an authorized person on his behalf *and* the patient's doctor. Just yesterday, we and his primary physician, Dr. Jeffreys, executed it."

Doolittle stood up. "This is outrageous."

Franklin glared at Doolittle. "What's outrageous is your filing a proceeding to circumvent legal documents executed by a member of this firm and your partner. Please sit down. I have more."

Doolittle glanced at Kalvin and Elena and sat down.

"This next document is page one of a revocable living trust, which names Luis Morales as grantor and trustee. This is page seventeen of said trust, which states that upon his death or incapacity, the same three people and the same alternate named in other documents shall act together as successor trustees. As to all assets that are owned by the trust, we are already in charge. Even if a guardianship is implemented as to my father's property, the trust and the trustees will remain in place." He looked at Doolittle and Kalvin. "You do know that a guardianship will not generally result in control over trust assets, don't you?"

Doolittle glanced at Kalvin, an eyebrow raised.

Franklin pushed the button again. "This next document is a stock power, executed by Luis Morales, granting me the authority to do whatever is necessary with his stock in the law firm, which, by the way, is assigned to the trust upon his death."

Franklin turned off the projector and scanned the room. "At this point, we do not see a need to make any drastic change in the firm. We do not intend to take any action to terminate my father's life, because there's not been an actual determination yet that there's no hope for recovery. We have the power to take all necessary actions to preserve my father's wishes and his rights. We will contest this guardianship attempt if you pursue it." Looking at Doolittle's corner, he continued. "I hope that you'll simply withdraw the guardianship petition and that will put an end to that matter. You know you're not going to be able to prove any kind of emergency to the court. If you don't withdraw it, you should amend your petition to appoint the designees of the power of attorney instead, because the court will undoubtedly appoint us."

Elena banged her fist on the table and stood up. "You pompous ass. Who in the hell do you think you are? Franklin Morales, heir to the throne...the heir apparent...the air-head...the full of air...the full of hot air." She pointed a finger at him and wagged it. "You are the most obnoxious, controlling jerk I've ever known. When you walked into the airport as a teenager, I could not stand that sneer, that smirk, that assuredness. You think you can come in here and just parade all these documents like *papi* loves you and act like *papi* doesn't love me." She stood and marched back and forth, pointing at Kalvin, then Doolittle, and then Franklin. Through gritted teeth, she hissed, "All of you are a bunch of blowhards, with no knowledge of the law and no ability to do anything. You are the most pitiful excuses for lawyers I've ever seen in my life. I could run this firm better. I could handle this case better." She swept her hand toward her lawyers. "Since my attorneys are incompetent to assist me, I will go find another attorney." Looking at Jude Armstrong, she said, "Mr. Armstrong, I've always admired your father. He was a fine gentleman. I'm sorry you've been brought into this mess. My father did not do you right in making your father or you, or you," she said pointing to Roosevelt, "parties to this situation. Same goes for you, Mr. Murphy."

Doolittle stood and stammered. "We believe we have a good . . . uh, really good . . . chance of having Elena appointed."

Kalvin nodded tentatively.

Elena said, "That's it? That's your argument? Jesus Christ. Useless. Incompetent. I already announced I'm replacing you. If you think that would change my mind, you're just plain stupid."

Franklin sighed, glancing at the elegant painting of the founding partners of the firm that graced the far wall. His eyes roamed the room and settled on Doolittle. "Braxton, there are all kinds of issues with this proposed guardianship. You know full well you won't prevail."

Sylvia leapt to her feet as well. "My husband would not want to see this travesty. He would be appalled that his family and his law partners are at odds and trying to take over from each other. It's completely ridiculous." She surveyed the room. Doolittle's and Kalvin's eyes focused on the table. Only Franklin, Mr. Murphy, Jude, Roosevelt and her own attorney looked at her with interest. Elena glared.

Sylvia sat back down, sighed and collected her thoughts. Wiping a tear from her cheek and looking back and forth between Franklin and Elena, she said, less forcefully, "Let's all please just be reasonable . . . for him. Although I am a stepmother, I am truly involved in this only for your father's best interest. I have nothing to gain here. I only want what is right . . . for Louis." She paused again, seeming to focus on her husband's portrait at the end of the room. "I've been unhappy because I felt left out. But now, I feel better about it."

Franklin said, "Sylvia, I do believe that you have our father's interests at heart. We have not intended and do not intend to keep you in the dark. You know from our meeting with my father the day before his heart attack that he intended to change it this week, to add you and another and remove non-family members. He created these documents much for you. He wouldn't want you to feel that his children had control over your future. And he didn't want to risk that his children would question his placing you in charge. And you know that he also has suffered in the past because of governments, people and circumstances not turning out the way he anticipated. He needed a feeling of total control, without putting all his wishes into the hands of any one person."

Sylvia nodded, smiling slightly. "That is a very wise and well-put analysis, Franklin."

Franklin nodded and, pointing at her, said, "He did it for you."

Elena stood up again, pointing around the room. "You people. Franklin, you just go ahead and kiss her ass. Sylvia, you just go ahead and kiss Franklin's ass. The two of you being all mushy and sweet with each other is disgusting."

Then she addressed her husband and Doolittle, "You're fired as my attorneys." Then, addressing Franklin, she said, "You, my dear brother . . . you can take all those documents and shove them up your elite ass." She marched from the room.

Tension permeated the air. Kalvin and Doolittle rose, like they were no longer certain of their roles, and slipped away.

Franklin cleared his throat, tried not to grin, and said, "Well, Sylvia, we scheduled this meeting to bring some things to light. And we want to answer your questions."

Warnock looked at Sylvia, and then at the others. "We are concerned about the ownership of the law firm, who will be in charge, who will own the stock, what will happen with the firm and exactly when."

Franklin looked to his left and right and said, "I don't want to be rude, Sir. I'm trying to make this a conciliatory meeting. We have a copy of a prenuptial agreement that my father and Sylvia executed. In it, Sylvia waived all rights to his assets and income." He glanced at Sylvia and Warnock. "Now, this does not mean that he omitted her from his plan. He provided for her well. All the prenup means is that she has no rights as a spouse based on any law. The shareholders' agreement requires that the firm provide income to her. The same agreement contains a buyout provision for the firm to purchase my father's stock after he is deceased. Part of the cash received is destined to benefit her."

Warnock said, "To what extent?"

Franklin said, "Mr. Warnock, the buy-out provisions on death are not relevant until my dad is dead. Currently he is alive. Thus, only the income provision is applicable." Franklin stopped and considered the audience again. Then he continued. "My dad has taken great efforts to take care of Sylvia, because he loves her and is fully aware of her assets and work status. We will honor his trust agreement as well as the shareholders' agreement."

Warnock asked, "When are you planning to schedule a reading of the will?"

Franklin was taken aback. "Mr. Warnock, I just said he's not dead. Are you listening? Anyway, they only read wills aloud to beneficiaries on television. Generally, a copy of the will is mailed to interested parties. In this case, the will is the pour-over type of will, which gives everything to his revocable trust, to be distributed from one pot. My dad apparently funded his trust with all his assets or made the trust the beneficiary of every asset. Therefore, even when he's dead, the will is irrelevant."

Warnock said, "What income will she receive?"

Franklin's patience level had been reached. "Are you listening? It's a rather complicated calculation, based on net profits in the firm. As the co-trustees, we are obligated to pay bills and make life-time distributions."

Warnock started to speak, but Sylvia put her hand on his forearm and said, "That's okay, Mr. Warnock. Let it go. I'm satisfied." She looked at Franklin and said, "Franklin, I don't know what to say to you. In some ways, I've always felt you were so arrogant . . . I mean that you come off looking like you think you are better than me . . . I mean, better than everybody. That's obviously what Elena sees too."

Franklin shuddered. "Wow, thanks, Sylvia."

She smiled. "I wasn't finished, Franklin. I wanted to say that I believe that you are a trustworthy man . . . a good man. I believe you have a lot of your father in you. I am going to trust you that my situation is being reviewed and that I will be taken care of. I do not have any desire, or need, or wish to become involved in the firm . . . or to know anything about the firm . . . so long as what Louis has provided for me comes to me. My primary concern right now is his health. I am satisfied that he has chosen the right people to be involved with those decisions as well."

Tears came to her eyes. Any bad thoughts of her that he ever held were flitting away.

She continued. "I don't know what to make of all this. I feel like I cannot get a straight answer about his health. I'm suffering. I want the three of you to do your utmost to take care of Louis. I'm confident you'll make the right decisions. Will you do that?"

He said, "Sylvia, I want you to know that Mr. Murphy, Roosevelt and I will do whatever we can for my father, and we will follow the documents he created."

They all stood. After a slight hesitation, Franklin and Sylvia embraced.

Chapter 58

Elena Morales Lennox

Friday, December 2, 2016

Elena fidgeted in the reception area of Barker & Cummins, P.A., a law firm in West Miami. She checked her watch every couple of minutes. The receptionist dealt with phone calls, had a laugh or two with employees and ignored her, unconcerned by the length of time she'd been waiting.

Maybe this was a mistake. Maybe she should just continue with the way Doolittle had planned everything.

Yet, she had the distinct feeling that Doolittle was playing her, and playing Kalvin, and that they—more importantly, *she* would end up screwed.

A woman emerged from the inner sanctum and asked her to enter. She picked up Elenita and followed. The woman ushered her into a small conference room with a single round table in the middle surrounded by four cushioned chairs.

Soon, a man of about forty entered the room. His looks, manner, and dark eyes, framed at the top by bushy eyebrows, attracted her.

"Ms. Morales, I'm Manuel Salazar. What can I do for you?"

She explained the facts and the plan of naming her as guardian. Then she sighed and said, "I'm not stuck with Doolittle and the firm after the guardianship commences, am I?"

"You'll have to obtain court approval to change counsel."

She hoped her face didn't reflect her thoughts. God, he was adorable. His upper lip curled sensually when he spoke.

She concentrated. "I understand that the court will approve a change of counsel if I request it, as long as I have competent replacement counsel. Is that right?"

"Most likely."

She inquired into Mr. Salazar's experience with guardianships, his attitude about going against Morales and Doolittle and the expected procedure.

He laughed. "If you're asking whether I'm afraid of Braxton Doolittle, or have some allegiance toward him or the firm, the answer is no on both counts. I'll be happy to take it over. But you need to get appointed first, which may not be as easy as you think."

She glanced out the window at a parking lot filled with cars. Elenita fidgeted, standing next to her chair. She pulled her onto her lap. "I'm family. I'm not a member of the law firm. The wife signed a prenup. This guy George Murphy is not family. This other guy, Roosevelt Harris, is not family and not even a resident of Miami. How hard can it be?"

"Did your father sign a power of attorney naming these other people?"

"Apparently."

"I hope your lawyers advised you that the persons designated in a valid power of attorney probably have priority."

"My brother keeps saying that. My lawyers don't seem to have a clue if that's true or not."

Salazar tapped his fingers on the desk. "Your brother is right, unless there's something else to the story. Your attorney may have to prove why the power of attorney shouldn't be honored. I can't tell you whether or not you'll prevail. I'd need to study the prenup and whatever other documents exist. Can you get copies of documents? I could become involved earlier if we think your lawyers aren't prepared to properly handle the case to get you appointed, but I'm not going to commit to that without seeing the documents and knowing more."

"Will you represent me after I'm appointed?"

He smiled that adorable smile again. "Of course."

Chapter 59

Luis Morales

I relax.

I'm sitting on the hard floor of my tiny prison cell, writing letters to Cari. Being in the perpetual silence of solitary, away from Castro's incessant monologue, is a blessing.

The brutish guard, *El Asesino,* comes into my cell and shoves me. "What are you doing?"

"Writing a letter to my beloved."

He grabs my missive, crumples and drops it onto the floor. He moves around the tiny cell, dragging his hands along the walls, searching for evidence of an escape route. He shoves my shoulder, knocking me from my knees to the floor. Then, he kneels and looks under the cot.

On his way out, he stomps on the crumpled letter, grinding it with his boot, and kicks me in the ribs. I remain curled on the ground, trying to hold in the pain, dreaming of Cari.

I believe that my dear Cari will wait for me, but who knows how long she can do so.

Life drags on, day after long, hot, hard day. A tin cup of putrid bean slop, and another with water, speckled with floating debris, is passed through the bars. In the perpetual solitude, I sip the slop with a thick metal spoon. Should I try to go back with the others, so I can eat the food they eat, which is quite decent? I sit, sleep and wait desperately for any opportunity to exit the cell, and especially to enjoy the outside air for any length of time.

A guard enters, says, "Visitor," and escorts me roughly into a room. Cari sits at one of tables, where visitors sit on one side, and prisoners sit opposite. As I walk toward the table, smiling at her, trying to look nonchalant and comfortable, the guard strikes me strongly in the kidney area and pushes me into the chair. Cari sees my reaction with silent alarm.

I smile. "It's all right, darling. How are you?"

"I am all right." She wipes a tear with her wrist. "I miss you so, so much."

We speak about the people at home, how things are in the neighborhood and what she is doing in her life. She tells me that her sister, Isabela, is entering the university. Her brother Alejandro, the one who initially protected her so staunchly from my attempts to approach, has graduated as a civil engineer. She speaks of her job at a pharmacy and says she is simply waiting for me to be released. She cries again. "You have to be released . . .. You have to . . . some time. I don't know how much longer I can take it."

I say, "I know, my darling. I don't know how much longer I can take it either."

We speak of getting married, of raising children, and of enjoying the cottage at the beach where we met.

Before I know it, the visit is over. She is ushered one way, and I the other way. Soon I am back in my cell on my knees, hands clasped in front of me on the cot, crying like a baby.

Now in my hospital room, I suppose I've dozed off for a few minutes, because suddenly months have passed in my prison cell.

A guard opens my door and grimaces. "Your sentence has been commuted. You are free to go." He hands me a bag containing my clothing.

I stand, looking at him, unsure what to do. I look across the courtyard to see if anybody is outside the room where the others sleep. I dress and gather up my toiletries and the few personal objects from under the cot. I question whether this is a trick, and whether I will be shot for escape, but he stands looking at me, waiting for me to make a move. I guess they won't shoot me dressed in my street clothes.

Another guard escorts me outside and points to a Jeep. The driver slams the gear into first and jerkily drives between large treeless areas. Off to my left is the hill, on which perch some of the pine trees for which the island is named. We pass between the first two mammoth cylindrical buildings that house thousands of prisoners, around the large one in the middle and between the other two. Over the rough engine noise, I feel the hum of activity within the prison walls vibrating through me. After passing the last of the buildings, we approach the gate. The driver stops in front of an administrative building, in the middle of a semi-circle of other buildings. He takes me inside, where I am required to sign a document. They give my belongings and some pesos.

Finally, I am free. I walk along a country road, asking directions from men swinging sickles at weeds. After maybe an hour, I near the small buildings of the town of Nueva Gerona, where I ask how to find the docks for the ferry to the mainland.

While waiting for the ferry, I plan my route to Cari and imagine the excitement of our reunion. The ferry arrives. I board on foot, alongside other pedestrians and vehicles. The ferry slips out, cruises down the narrow waterway, moves into open water and forges through the churning froth from the strong current and battering waves. The wind, splashing water and bounce of the ferry are delightful, because I am free. How long it has been to be able to feel this, to hear water smacking on the hull of a boat. I cannot believe that I can go on my own to find my Cari.

After disembarking on the mainland, I trudge in the late afternoon heat, and finally arrive at a small building on the train tracks. The agent informs me that trains go only to Havana, and that I have missed the last one of the day. I ask the cost to take a train to Havana and also from Havana to Santiago and determine I do not have enough money.

I wander through the town, find a diner and order the cheapest food on the menu, an egg, a piece of bread and coffee. After so many months of watching the other men in the barracks being served tiny cups of strong sugary coffee, like they were in a lodging house instead of a prison, I savor the tiny cup of frothy espresso.

I count my remaining money and decide I need to find my way to Santiago by asking for rides. Maybe along the way I can find a bus or train that travels along the southern coast rather than going all the way north and west to Havana and then heading southeast from there.

A truck with two white drivers and workers in the back stops and lets me climb onto the bed with the dark men with Caribbean accents. I worry for an hour or so whether I have perhaps just been recruited to cut cane. Finally, the truck pulls off the highway, apparently heading into a farm, stops and lets me out.

Between rides, at some point after dark has fallen, I sleep in the bushes near the road, being disturbed constantly by frightening sounds of wildlife. I have to move several times because I am bitten by ants, then mosquitos, then gnats. What I presume are animals and reptiles crunch through the dry, broken branches, leaves and sticks around me.

Many, many hours later, through a combination of car rides, truck-bed rides and horse and buggy rides, I arrive in Santiago. I begin my trek through the city, searching for the pharmacy where Cari works. She's told me what it's near. Eventually, I see a lone pharmacy at an intersection, just blocks from La Moncada and am sure I have found her.

Inside, I am delighted to find my beautiful Cari, dark hair hanging around her lovely face, lips moving as she earnestly counts pills. She glances up, shrieks and rushes around the counter to embrace me. The old pharmacist looks aghast for a moment, but then seems to understand that although I look like a derelict, I probably am not. I am free.

After two weeks of planning, we are married. Nobody questions the apparently impetuous nature of setting and holding a wedding so quickly. It is common knowledge and accepted among our friends and acquaintances that Cari and I have loved each other for a long time and were made for each other, and that I was imprisoned, not as a criminal, but because of political beliefs, even though I actually had no 'beliefs' at the time of my arrest.

My father sits at the head of my grandmother's dining room table, a lit cigar pouring smoke around, as the cooks prepare dinner. Cari, my mother and my grandmother are at the table.

My father turns to me. "Miguel deserved to have been killed for being involved in that attack. I will always question your claims of innocence too."

Mi mamá, constantly mourning Miguel's death, scurries from the room, crying. My father continues. "That stupid plan to attack the Moncada, expecting to take over the whole country, was just ridiculous. How could you and your brother get involved? Both of those Castro boys talking about a revolution. What revolution?"

"Father, I do not wish to discuss this."

"That's because you know I do not approve of that Castro fellow that you follow."

I keep my mouth closed.

He continues, "As you know, I am a great follower of General Batista, but releasing the Castro brothers and all of you was a great mistake. Now, I hear they are in Mexico, planning to return and raise havoc."

I remain quiet, as always, as he stares at me, waiting for me to defend myself, or perhaps to jump on his bandwagon.

"Mark my words, if the Castros come back, they will destroy this country." He glares at me, then lights a cigar. "You won't talk because you are a follower, a complete embarrassment to me and to the family. You act like you are apolitical, but you are one of them."

I remain silent.

Of course, he does not stop. "You were part of the Moncada attack. You were arrested on site. You were tried and convicted with the rest of them. You spent time in prison, in close proximity with the rebels. You are one." He tokes on his cigar and downs some rum. "As a matter of fact, you are studying to be a lawyer, so you can protect them. Isn't that true?"

After being wrongfully convicted and imprisoned, I want to be a lawyer even more, to protect the downtrodden, to keep people from being imprisoned for no reason and to fight for what is right. I am still not a *fidelista*. I am not a rebel, but I want to fight for what in my conscience represents the good of the people.

I ignore his glare, silently thinking I need to protect my wife, and as soon as the child comes, to protect the child, from this.

At our home, in the same block as my parents' and grandmother's homes, I ask Cari, "Do you want to move away from my family? Do you want to stop eating there?"

She smiles and kisses me. "No, darling. We cannot do that. Your mother and your grandmother should not suffer because your father is like that."

I ask myself how I could have let my father put a damper on that time of my life. My father's incessant negativity rises to the surface of my mind and counteracts the beautiful relationship with my wife and child.

Chapter 60

Elena Morales Lennox

Elena sat outside her home smoking a cigarette, wondering what the three kings were deciding about the fate of her father. She couldn't bear to visit him again, yet.

Her cell phone rang.

"Yes."

"Hola, Elena. We are meeting with doctors again in a few minutes. I think they are going to say our papá is stable."

She struggled to decide whether she could say anything. She couldn't. "Elena, are you there?"

"Yeah."

"All right. Well, presuming they say he's stable . . . uh, I don't know if you know he made a plane reservation for me to accompany him to Cuba Saturday morning . . .. I think I should go."

She started boiling with rage. "What the hell, Franklin. You're going to just leave? What if something happens? How dare you?" She could feel herself screeching.

"Listen, Elena. This is important to him. He's never missed a trip. The people are counting on him. He's the one who made my reservation, so he could teach me what to do for when he couldn't. I can't just abandon his wishes."

She pictured him, traveling around Cuba, visiting family he never met before, being the savior for the poor people, just like her papá. He *wanted* to go. He wanted to be the great man. She couldn't wait to tell Silvestre this bullshit. "Yes, you can, Franklin. You can choose not to go. You don't have to go. You *want* to go."

"I've wrestled about this, Elena. I really have. If the doctors say it appears nothing is going to happen in the next few days, I have to go."

She said, "We have a hearing on Tuesday." Then, she smiled. "Actually, it would be great if you weren't there. You're the only one not on our side. So, just go and don't come back. I'll take over."

He started using his fake, soothing voice. "I'll be back Tuesday morning. I'll be at the hearing in the afternoon." He hesitated. "Elena, you should visit him. Maybe while I'm gone it will be easier."

She pictured the room, with the wench always at his side. "Maybe, if you take that bitch with you."

"Elena, Elena, Elena. Calm down."

"Calm down? Me? I'm trying to do the right thing and you're trying to prevent me."

"You know that's not true, Elena. You are welcome to come here and meet the doctors with us. Please, come."

She clicked off the phone. *Son of a bitch. Sneaky little bastard.* He wasn't going to Cuba for her papá. He was going for himself.

She searched for Silvestre's number and dialed him.

"*Dime.*"

"You'll never believe where my brother is going tomorrow."

"Hmm . . . Let's see. Cuba?"

"Yes, he says he has to fulfill the obligations of *mi* papá to deliver money to the poor people who are stuck there. Stuck there because they want to be. If they wanted a better life, they should have left."

"*Qué carajo*! Just like his father."

"And if something happens to my father this weekend? He won't even be here. Asshole."

If she were talking to anybody else, they'd be saying 'Well, Elena you don't even visit him.' But Silvestre would never take that position.

"Where's he going? East or west?"

"I don't even know. Who cares?"

"Well, if he's going to Santiago, he can join in the celebration of Fidel's life as the dictator's ashes arrive in that city to be entombed in a mausoleum."

She almost choked. "He'll probably be right out front, waving a flag and chanting."

"Elena, what's your father's prognosis?"

She didn't want to talk about prognoses. She didn't want to think that things might go badly. "I don't know. My brother says he's meeting with the doctors soon and he thinks they are going to say he's stable. Stable? I want him to wake up. What good is it to be a stable vegetable?"

She disconnected with Silvestre and tried to decide who else to talk to. There was nobody else to share this news with. Nobody would care.

Chapter 61

Sylvia Morales

Sylvia was daydreaming about the happy times with her husband when Franklin, Dr. Jeffreys, and two doctors from the hospital showed up. She stood, accepted a hug from Dr. Jeffreys and shook hands with the other doctors. Franklin looked to be in pain.

Dr. Jeffreys said, "Sylvia, I know you prefer to talk medical matters outside the room. Would you like to step out?"

She nodded, let go of her husband's arm and followed him out and toward the family consult room. Mr. Murphy, Jude and Roosevelt arrived at the room at the same time.

"Sylvia," Dr. Jeffreys said, "We've asked these doctors to give us some insight into what they have determined."

The doctors looked like fish gulping air.

One finally managed, "We do not have a definitive cause for his apparent comatose condition. He's breathing on his own, as you know. His vital organs are working. There does not appear to be any shut-down of organs. The blood tests all look good."

The other one said, "He could come out of this at any moment, or it could take weeks, or even longer."

She felt a crying jag about to come and struggled to squelch it. "Is discontinuing life support being discussed?"

"No, ma'am," the first one said. "Not at all. As you know, he was removed slowly from the breathing apparatus. Everything is functioning. Discontinuing life support now would mean ceasing to provide nutrition and hydration. That would not even be considered at this point. In any case, it's not the doctors who make that decision. The doctors can only give an opinion about the condition. Then, the surrogates make the call on what to do."

She looked at Franklin and the other surrogates. "You are not considering that, are you?"

"No, Sylvia," Franklin said. "Not even thinking about it."

Roosevelt asked, "Doctor, I'm wondering if it's reasonable for the two of us to return to our homes, at least for the weekend. We can be reached by phone if something occurs. It's a four-hour drive to return."

A doctor answered, "I would say at this point, that's fine."

"I have ordered a hospice worker to come in," Dr. Jeffreys said. "Sylvia, I recall that you were upset about that word previously, but believe me, it can be quite helpful, for Luis and everybody else. It does not mean he is going to die, but if he takes a turn for the worse, having that person already involved will make everybody more comfortable. Is that all right with you?"

Her stomach clenched, but she managed to say, "The word just sets me off. I'm sorry. But I know from you and others that it's not negative. It's not a death sentence."

Franklin said, "My dad is a big fan of Hospice. They helped very much when our mother died."

Sylvia whispered again, "You don't think he'll believe that we've given up hope?"

Franklin replied, "No. He won't feel that way."

"All right."

"Uh, Sylvia, there's something else I want to tell you."

She knew her look showed anger.

"Whoa, Sylvia, you don't even know what I'm about to say."

She breathed in and out. *Relax. Relax.* "I'm sorry. What is it, Franklin?"

"Do you remember that on Sunday one of the things we discussed was my going to Cuba with my father tomorrow?"

Her insides raged. *Calm yourself, Sylvia.* "Yes, Franklin, I remember."

"And you know he made the reservations for us to go, right? I think it's important for him that his obligation is carried out."

"So, you intend to go?"

"Yes, now that we know he's stable, and that nothing is likely to go wrong this weekend, I think it's important. For the people he cares about down there, and for him."

She struggled with this apparent lack of concern for Luis' health. What would Luis say if he could speak? She stewed over the answer.

He'd agree that Franklin should go. Of course, he'd never acknowledge that his health could take another bad turn.

"What if something goes wrong while you are gone?"

"I understand that now my telephone service works in Cuba. I can receive calls unless I'm in a rural area at the time."

She resigned to the fact. "All right, Franklin. Tell your father. He will be relieved."

Chapter 62

Luis Morales

A woman with dark-brown skin and a round face enters the room and touches my arm. "Hello, Luis," she says, pronouncing my name correctly, although with a slightly island-flavored, non-Spanish accent, "I am Georgina. I'm going to spend time with you. How are you feeling?" She looks deep into my eyes. Her forehead crinkles. She delicately traces her fingers, then rubs her palm and closed hand up and down my arm. It tickles. I feel that I flinch, or shudder. She does not appear to notice movement.

She looks back into my eyes, studying, moving in and out, still rubbing my arm. "Luis," she says again. "I'm going to be with you." She picks up a chart and reads, still touching me.

Sylvia and Franklin enter—together—like friends. Franklin sees Georgina sitting next to me. He holds out a hand and says, "Hi, you must be the hospice nurse. I'm Franklin, his son. This is Sylvia, his wife."

Sylvia whispers, "Franklin, don't say that word."

"Georgina," the nurse says, with her sweet, lilting accent. "It's all right to say the word. Luis is comfortable. Hospice isn't bad. We are here to spend time with him, to be sure he's comfortable."

Sylvia whispers to her. "I still worry that he will see this as giving up hope on him. Don't you think so?"

Franklin and Georgina shake their heads no.

Sylvia and Franklin take seats on opposite sides of the bed, I relax again and resume my dream.

Georgina is speaking to the others. Her words and look merge into another rising from my memories.

A lady with dark skin and a Haitian accent holds Cari's hand. "There's nothing to fear. There's nothing to fear. And for you too, Luis. Cari is at peace. Look at her face. There's no struggle. There's nothing but love and peace."

245

I gaze into Cari's soft, aged face. The sparkle of her eyes is missing. But the nurse is right. She appears to be relaxed. Her dull eyes close. She clenches my hand. I relax.

It's a blazing summer day shortly after my fifteenth birthday. The servants carry provisions across the dark-green grass to where the Buick is parked on the long two-strip driveway. Rafael, in his chauffer uniform and wearing a beret, chocolate skin shining from slight perspiration, buffs the round fenders and bright, silver-colored bumpers. He puts the convertible top down.

We kids are running to and fro, making sure our new water toys are packed, although most are stored in the outdoor closet at our cottage on La Socapa, the strip of land bounded by the bay, the inlet and the ocean.

Our father, who's usually traveling on business throughout Cuba and the world, is at home and going to the beach house with us.

We pile into the car. Our father, wearing a brown hat that feels soft as velvet, a white short-sleeve, button-up shirt and suspenders to hold up his khaki-colored pants, sits in the front passenger seat. Our mother sits in the back on the left, all dressed up in a summer frock, white and dotted with flowers, our youngest sister Clara on her lap. She wears a pink scarf to protect her hair from the wind. My brother Miguel, my sister Emma and I, excited as can be, are crammed with our mother into the back seat between provisions that don't fit in the trunk.

Rafael pulls out, glides through the streets of our neighborhood of Vista Alegre, moves along Avenida Manduley, and then winds down meandering city streets to the water, passing laborers painting buildings, pouring asphalt on the streets, sweeping sidewalks and swinging sickles at grass and weeds, women leaning out windows to hang clothes on clotheslines, and children playing. Occasionally, we glimpse the water of the bay. Then, Rafael takes a little highway, paved well in some places, but scattered with occasional potholes, gravel and unpaved areas, toward the inlet. Rafael drives fast when the road is smooth and slow when it is beat up.

Our father taps cigar ashes out the window, causing us in the back to duck from the racing embers. Occasionally, he fiddles with the ends of his full, black mustache, which always has the rich odor of cigar leaves and smoke.

Rafael stops at the landing where the boat to transport us to La Socapa waits. Rafael, our father and I pull provisions out of the car, stack them on the road then carry them down the stairs and out the platform to the boat. Emma and Miguel lean on the metal railing overlooking the water and then run down the stairs and leap aboard. Our father goes back up to help our mother down the stairs while holding little Clara.

A large, white freighter with rust-colored stains on the sides eases out the narrow, deep-blue channel, heading toward El Morro and the darker blue seawater. I sit on the bow, legs dangling over, as the small boat forges across the freighter's wake, toward Cayo Smith, a hill rising from the water, with seemingly every square inch occupied with well-constructed, mostly wooden, homes. The island is capped by a white, stone church at the highest point.

On the eastern rocks at the mouth of the inlet, opposite La Socapa, the centuries-old fortress, Castillo del Morro looms high above the water. Behind us as we cross the water is the Ciudamar Yacht Club, an elegant private club, where our father entertains powerful national and international businessmen, while we enjoy the long swimming pool and small, private, sandy beach.

The boat churns through the light wake of a trawler. White waves crisscross from the wake of another vessel, producing a roiling chop as the waves smack the shore and sea wall from different angles.

In the small channel between Cayo Smith and La Socapa, the water is smooth and quiet. My siblings stand on the deck, holding the railing and watching the beach, where a few other children already play.

We dock in front of our family's rustic, wooden cottage perched at the top of the bank of La Socapa, and thus protected from ocean storms. I help my father and Rafael carry supplies up the hill.

Inside, I unload boxes and bags and hand things to my mother. She deals with mundane household chores only while here since there is no room for servants to stay. She trots around, clicking heels on the wooden floor as she pulls curtains and windows open, allowing baking sea air to creep through the house.

247

The younger children raid the outdoor storage closet, grabbing tiny shovels and toys to play in the wet sand of the beach. Their yells and shouts pierce the air as they reach the shore. I am anxious to join them. My father and Rafael finish bringing things up. Then, Rafael leaves on the boat to head back to Vista Alegre. My father stands outside, puffing a cigar and gazing at the water.

Finally, my mother realizes that I'm too anxious to remain, so she dismisses me. I go out the back door, to escape the gaze of my father, and slide down the hill to the shore. My younger brother Miguel is romping in the water with a kid I've never seen before. My sister Emma stands, drawing in the sand with her toes, talking to a young girl. I wonder who they are.

As I walk toward the other kids, my eyes fall upon the most stunning girl I've ever seen. My heart leaps to my throat. I've never talked to any girl besides those with whom I've been in school for years. I've never thought anything romantic about any of my classmates.

The girl smiles at me. I guess I kind of half smile back, but my eyes go to the ground because I am simply unable to look straight at her. I glance back at the younger kids and then back toward the girl again.

I find myself walking toward her, wondering what I will say when I arrive. Soon, I stand in front of her, speechless. Her bright-green, dancing eyes and wry, one-sided smile draw me in, but still don't promote speech.

Her voice is light and airy. "*Soy Caridad.*"

"*Hola, Caridad. Yo . . . Yo soy . . .*" I finally manage to say, "*Soy Luis.*"

She wrinkles her brow and gives me that amazing smile again. "Where do you live?"

"Vista Alegre." Then I realize I should ask the same. "Where do you live?"

"A few blocks outside the main entrance of your fine neighborhood."

We watch the kids play for a bit. "You are rich," she says, with almost a question in her voice.

I don't know how to answer. I've never really thought about it, but then I guess my family does have much more than those who live outside our neighborhood. I shrug.

She laughs, a sweet, high giggle. "You live in Vista Alegre, the most magnificent neighborhood in Santiago. You have to be rich."

My face burns. I look down at the light sand.

I feel the presence of a visitor. I look up to find a boy, perhaps a little older than I, peering at me through dark-brown, intense eyes. He holds out his hand. "Alejandro."

"Luis."

I glance at Caridad. She's looking down. The boy does not remove his eyes from me.

"My sister is not permitted to be alone with a boy." He looks at his sister and then out into the water. "What is your last name?"

"Morales."

"Where do you live?"

"Santiago. Vista Alegre."

The boy considers me again. A new look seems to come to his face. Caridad looks from me to him.

"Who is your family?"

I tell him my parents' and grandparents' surnames.

"Where did they come from originally?"

"My father was born in Spain. My mother right here. Her parents came from Spain too."

"What was her maiden name?"

"Ortiz."

The boy's brow wrinkles as he tries to place the name.

I have questions too, but don't feel invited to ask them. I can feel the ethereal presence of the girl standing to my left. Our siblings play in the cool water not far away.

The boy nods at me, puts his arm on his sister's shoulder and silently leads her away. They stand on a landing where they can keep an eye on the children, but at such a distance that I cannot taint her. It is probably all in my mind, but I think she likes me. I am enamored with her.

Franklin speaks, interrupting my dream. "Papá. I want you to know that I am flying to Holguín in the morning, just like we'd planned. Your driver is picking me up and we will do all that you would have done. I hope you don't think I'm abandoning you, but I think this is what you would want. The doctors say that you are stable and nothing bad is likely to happen. I hope you are happy with this decision."

Sylvia weeps silently. But Franklin is right. I am happy.

Chapter 63

Franklin Morales

Saturday, December 3, 2016

Franklin checked in to his flight at the Miami International Airport. Procedures for flights to Cuba had apparently changed very much in the preceding two weeks since charter flights were now replaced by direct flights. His father had explained to him how checking in under the charter flight scheme was like already being in a Latin-American country. Passengers would roll in numerous duffel bags, boxes and other unofficial-looking packages, containing gifts and items to sell and have them sealed in plastic wrap. Now, with passengers pulling suitcases and purchasing the visa form at the airline ticket counter it seemed like any other flight.

He checked "Family Visit," which was true, but he considered the other general license for "Humanitarian Projects" as the reason for a future trip.

At the gate, he sat among residents of Cuba who had visited the U.S., Cuban-Americans visiting Cuba, and non-Cuban U.S. travelers most of whom traveled in groups. He had an odd feeling of nostalgia, coupled with trepidation.

Television news in Spanish showed the caravan carrying Fidel's ashes toward Santiago de Cuba, passing cheering crowds. Many in the awaiting area made comments or at least looked uncomfortable about the news. One said, "I cannot believe we are arriving the same day as this staged celebration." He knew his father would say the people's love for Fidel was legitimate.

After take-off, Franklin gazed down at his office, the Freedom Tower and other large buildings of downtown Miami, cruise ships at port, and deep-blue water lapping beaches and surrounding islands. Sail boats glided on a slant through the bright sea. Cargo ships steamed off shore, smoke spewing above.

251

Soon they were passing other islands in the stream, bounded by even clearer, turquoise water. And before much longer, they floated above the exquisite white sands and turquoise water of the shores of eastern Cuba. His heart fluttered.

Then they hovered over different-colored squares of farmland, sporadic houses and the specks of farm animals grazing. The airport landing strip was off to the left. The plane veered and began its descent. Here he was, returning to his homeland. How did he feel? He could not identify the emotion.

Franklin completed his customs form, noting that he had to disclose how much money he was carrying only if it exceeded $5,000, which it did not. He filled out his health form, marking that he had no symptoms of anything, had not been around anybody suffering any symptoms and had not been in any other country recently.

The other passengers talked incessantly, pointing out the view to others. As the plane touched down, the Cubans applauded. A sign on top of the airport building said, "Frank País – Holguín." They disembarked and entered a large room with line of kiosks with immigration officials. He stood in a line, awaiting his turn.

The official examined his documents, looked at a large, old computer monitor, told him to look at the camera and asked his purpose for visiting.

"Visiting friends and family."

She motioned for a man in uniform to come to the cubicle. She handed the man Franklin's passport, and the man said, "Come with me."

Franklin meekly followed, worried about what was going to happen? *Would he be forced to return home without having accomplished anything? Or worse?*

They sat in an office, where the man began typing slowly on a keyboard connected to an old, large computer monitor, like those used in the U.S. years ago before flat screens were invented. "Purpose of your visit?"

"Visiting friends and family."

"What family?"

"Cousins. In Santiago de Cuba."

"What are their names?"

Franklin nervously searched his memory for the full names he knew and spouted them out. The man typed.

"How do you have friends here if you haven't been here before?"

"Uh, they are friends of my family."

"How much money do you have with you? You did not complete that section of the form."

"I thought I didn't have to if I had less than five thousand. I have about four thousand."

"What do you do for work?"

"I'm a lawyer."

The man looked at him, eyebrows raised. "Who is your employer?"

"I am a member of a law firm, with my father."

"Do you have a business card? Who is your father?"

"Luis Morales."

Franklin handed him a card, and he studied it. "Your father visits regularly. Delivering money to people. Is that why you are here, with so much money? Why are you here instead of him?"

"Yes. He's gravely ill."

The man stared at him without compassion.

"Will you stay in a hotel?"

"No, in *casas particulares.*"

"You mean rentals? Are you aware that you may not stay in a home other than a licensed rental?"

"Yes, I understand that."

The man rose, motioned for Franklin to follow, walked back to the cubicle where Franklin had first been interviewed, handed the passport to the agent and stood aside.

The agent exchanged nods with the man, slammed her seal on his passport and visa, handed them back, said *"Bienvenido a Cuba,"* and signaled with her head for him to exit the gate opposite where he'd entered.

He was in. What a relief.

On the other side of the door, he got into another line, this time to go through a security check, just like in Miami before boarding the plane. He had to remove everything from his pockets, run his carryon through an x-ray machine and walk through one.

It took forever for his checked bag to arrive on the belt. A man speaking U.S. English said, "They x-ray all the suitcases in the back. That's why it takes so long." Franklin had checked luggage because he'd brought peanut butter, canned tuna, canned sardines and other delicacies that Ruth had instructed him to take. He'd feared that such items could be confiscated when passing through security on the way to the plane if they were in a carryon bag.

Finally, they exited the airport. A somewhat tall, well-built, white man with silver hair, said, "Franklin. *Aquí.*"

As he approached, the man smiled. "You look just like your father when he was your age. I couldn't miss you." They shook hands, and the man embraced him.

"*Soy* Daniel. *Bienvenido a* Cuba. I hope you speak Spanish, because my English is poor."

Daniel led him to a large, blue station-wagon type vehicle, with all its windows open, opened the rear door, placed his suitcase inside and seated him in the front passenger seat. "*Vamos a Santiago de Cuba.* Do you need to eat or anything?"

"*No. Estoy bien. Vamos.*" Franklin wondered whether his Spanish would roll off the tongue and whether vocabulary and verb declensions would be readily available to his mouth. In Miami, he and his compatriots spoke it every day, but it wasn't ever pure Spanish. It was sprinkled with English and slang in the unique accent of Miami Cubans.

Franklin asked, "What type of car is this exactly? A Land Rover? A Jeep?"

"It's a Willys. A kind of jeep your country used to use in the military."

"It's much larger than any jeep I've seen. And the blue color makes it more unusual."

Daniel smiled. The engine rumbled as he shifted through gears. "A jeep wagon style Willys. They are very common here in Cuba." He drove through the quaint and quiet city of Holguín, passing small houses, some with inverted anchor symbols on signs in front. Franklin asked in Spanish what the signs meant.

Daniel answered in Spanish. "They are rentals...*casas particulares.* Blue means rentals for foreigners, and red means for nationals. Under the red anchor, it says, "*moneda nacional*," which is Cuban pesos, also referred to as CUP, the kind of money you will not use. I believe, but am not certain, that rentals for foreigners have higher standards, like hot water and air-conditioning." He pointed. "See that little eating establishment over there, with two different prices for everything on the sign?" Restaurants like that are called '*paladares*'. They are private, as opposed to government-operated. Some, like that one, take both kinds of money. A peso cubano, what you will not use, is about one twenty fifth of a CUC, which you will use."

They traveled along country highways, sometimes smooth, sometimes rough and through little towns and villages, always seeing people on the roads, walking, riding horses, or sitting on seats of buggies behind horses, trucks and pre-1960 U.S. cars. They talked of the places and people along the route. Many of the buggies had signs indicating they ran specific routes, like buses.

Daniel said, "Normally, we would go first to Bayamo, which is the westerly route into Santiago de Cuba, but I fear we'd end up behind the caravan with Fidel's ashes, so we'll take an easterly route instead and backtrack to Bayamo tonight."

"Daniel, do you mind if I ask a question about the feeling of the people and the government as the result of his passing?"

Daniel looked at him. "Go right ahead."

"People in Miami say that the people here are not happy. That they are all trapped here. That they go to these rallies by force. That they don't really mean it. That they are secretly happy he's dead. My father, on the other hand, has always said that there's a saying, 'Life is hard in Cuba,' but that in general the people really are content, even if they complain about shortages and lack of income. And that they loved Fidel. What is the truth?"

Daniel smiled. "All that you hear on both sides of the Florida Straits has some truth. The majority of us Cubans were born into the Revolution or were children when it began. We were raised pledging allegiance to Fidel. We have shortages, but we also have *la libreta,* the ration book that provides various items at subsidized prices. Outside the city of Havana itself, it's much more difficult to find chicken, or eggs, or any kind of meat. And they rarely have such things in a bodega that takes *pesos cubanos,* meaning one has to go to a CUC store, which is very expensive for the common person. Anyway, that's a lot of detail. We Cubans are all right. We are industrious, adaptive, resigned to our fate, loving and courageous. And don't forget, we are taught from early years that all our problems stem from you. The Embargo. *El Bloqueo*. That's the big problem. You won't give or even sell us anything, and then you criticize our financial status. And the atrocities your CIA has pulled. Shameful." He roars with laughter.

Franklin said, "Yes, I've heard. Unfortunately, I believe most of what you think our government, especially our CIA, has done is true, although the people of our country are unaware."

Franklin had a lot of questions about *pesos Cubanos, pesos convertibles* and *la libreta,* but chose to wait to inquire. Now, he marveled at the views of the countryside.

They crossed rickety bridges over thin, brackish waterways and passed farms, small groups of horses and cattle, barren areas, palm trees, and crops of sugar cane and corn and other vegetation. Later, Franklin glimpsed the peaks of mountains in the clouds. Buildings, vehicles and people seemed so beat up. It appeared that the saying was true. Life is hard in Cuba.

Daniel's phone rang. "*Dime.*"

Franklin knew that Cubans often answered the phone that way, saying, "Tell me."

"*Hola*, Luz, we are approaching your fine city. Are you with your mother? Shall we go to your house first? You know I have only Franklin, Luis' son, with me because Luis is ill."

He nodded, said *sí* a few times, *no,* once or twice and finally, "*Está bien*. We will see you at *Plaza de la Revolución.*"

He clicked off. "Your cousin, or maybe second cousin, Luz, and the rest of the family cannot wait to meet you, although they are very worried about your father. The family is at the Plaza of the Revolution, a couple of blocks from their house, cheering with the crowds, waiting for Fidel's ashes to arrive."

Franklin smiled. Wouldn't Elena be pissed to hear this. Maybe he'd be caught on T.V. cameras and shown to the people of Miami. That would go over well. He smiled to himself.

Mountains became closer. Open land diminished. More people and buildings began to appear. "Ahead is the lovely Santiago de Cuba, birthplace of your parents and you and your sister. It is such a special place, the jewel of Cuba, where everything happened. The July 26th Movement was born here. The Revolution was born here. Fidel made his first speech after the Revolution prevailed here. And centuries before, this was the site of significant occurrences of the War of Independence from Spain."

Nostalgia arose in Franklin again. This was it. Returning home. Seeing family for the first time. How did he feel? How should he feel?

Daniel pointed again. You see those big rusty-looking chunks of metal pointing to the sky, and the huge crowd? That's *Plaza de la Revolución*. We haven't missed the arrival of the motorcade. He punched into the phone, asked where the family was standing, and said, "We'll drive to your house to park and walk back."

He wound his way around people crowding the streets and entered a neighborhood. "This area is generally called *Sueño*, although that's not its formal name." Franklin knew that word meant 'dream' in English.

Daniel parked, and they walked downhill a couple of blocks, arriving on a wide street, lined with throngs of people, jutting flags in the air, singing and chanting. They merged into moving crowds and neared the metal shards, which Daniel referred to in Spanish as '*machetes*'.

Some were leading the crowd, which was morphing into one chant, which became, "*Yo soy Fidel. Yo soy Fidel. Yo Soy Fidel.*" It began to dig into his being, reminding him of when he'd eaten daily at a Hari Krishna setup outside the library at the university. Every day, as he ate, the chant of 'Hare Krishna, Hare Krishna, Rama Rama, Hare Hare,' would embed itself in his brain.

"*Yo soy Fidel. Yo soy Fidel. Yo soy Fidel,*" chanted the mass of people, moving, shaking small Cuban flags. The deafening clamor vibrated through him.

"*Aquí están,*" Daniel said. He went up behind a group of people and started kissing women and hugging men. Suddenly, several women shrieked, "Franklin, Franklin," and rushed to him, all kissing and hugging. Then, men turned and embraced him as well. He did not know who was who, but the outpouring of love was overwhelming.

"*Y tu papá?* I'm so sorry to hear. You have to tell me everything. We love your papá."

The chant turned into a roar again. The family turned and shook their flags. A young woman who Franklin recognized from photos and Facebook turned back to Daniel and Franklin. "Franklin, I'm Luz. I'm sure you are overwhelmed by the welcome from people you don't even recognize. You'll get to know us soon. Listen, I don't know if you want to wear them, but you see these armbands? They say M-26-7. You know what that is? The July 26 Movement, the beginning of the Revolution, from that day that Fidel and the others made the historic and valiant attack on the Moncada barracks here in Santiago. It's the symbol of the Revolution. Will you wear one? I have two extra."

Franklin glanced at Daniel. They both nodded. She tied one on Franklin's arm and another on Daniel's. Then, she handed each a Cuban flag. She exclaimed, "*Yo soy Fidel. Yo soy Fidel.*"

Franklin hesitated, not wanting to insult his family by not expounding the sentiment, but not sure he could truly relate to the enthusiasm.

Luz turned back again, reached an arm around Franklin's shoulder and said, "You look just like your father. I feel that you are your father. I cannot tell you how much he means to us . . . not because he brings money and things we need, but because he is such a dear man."

Franklin didn't know what to think. He had no idea that his father was so loved, admired and needed. All he could think was that he had to fulfill his father's legacy.

"*Aquí viene. Aquí viene. Mira, mira. Yo soy Fidel. Yo soy Fidel.*"

A police car, a single blue light spinning, led the way, followed by a truck with television cameras facing front and back, and cheerleaders helping the crowd to chant in unison, trailed by a Jeep, pulling a trailer with white flowers surrounding a square glass enclosure, in which sat a wooden box, covered by the flag of Cuba. The caravan slowed as it passed the larger crowd. The chanting rose to a crescendo, pulsating through Franklin.

Did these people really care? Was this man really revered like that? Amazing.

Soon, the caravan was gone. The crowd wound down, some smiling, some crying, walking away, some still with the flags raised, others with them at their sides. Family members walked beside Franklin with arms around his back.

Walking up the incline of the narrow streets in the neighborhood, Franklin admired homes that resembled those built in Florida in the 40's and 50's. Most were nicely kept. He was startled by a dog that ran to the edge of a flat roof, barked and growled viciously. He guessed that was their yard. Arriving at the family home, he was again startled by a black dog hovering above and barking loudly.

"Luz said, "That's our dog, Frida. One time she fell from the roof and had to undergo surgery. But as you see, she is not afraid to go to the edge."

Luz unlatched the locks to the gates at the street and the porch. She unlocked the front door of the home, and they entered the tiny front room. Franklin walked along the terrazzo floor, past 50's-style plastic couches and chairs, coffee tables and rocking lawn chairs such as they had in the States in the sixties. "Franklin, have a seat. Would you like a beer? Do you need the toilet? We have a feast of pork and many other things, just for you."

Luz introduced him to an older, white-haired woman, sitting in a rocker in front of a television, watching the caravan still rolling through the city. "This is Isabella. Your mother's sister."

The lady looked a bit confused at first. "Luis?"

"No, Nona, this is Luis' son, Franklin."

Franklin realized that all Cuban women kissed, and men kissed the women when they met, even on a first encounter, so he leaned and kissed her. She studied his face and smiled. "Pleased to meet you, young man."

The middle-aged woman said, "I am Lolita, her daughter, and Luz's mother. Luz' father, my husband, Jorge, is no longer with us."

Luz said, "Are you getting who all these people are, or should I repeat?"

He nodded, "Yes. I've got it. Isabela, Lolita. You are Luz. Your father was Jorge. But there were more people I thought were family on the street."

"The others are like family to us and know your father well, but we are not related. They will all be here soon to eat with us. We will introduce you."

He asked to use the toilet and was ushered through a bedroom and into the restroom. He was surprised to find the toilet handle broken, requiring him to reach into the dark water to pull up the chain to flush. How could it be that there wasn't enough money to replace this? Oh, maybe there were no toilets for sale.

He exited the bathroom and the bedroom, into the dining room. To the left was the kitchen. "Come in," Luz said. "You are family."

In the kitchen, he found a hodgepodge of small, worn appliances—a toaster, a blender, and a counter-top electric burner. Pots of food stood on a traditional combination gas oven and stove.

Luz said, "The stove-top hasn't functioned for years, which is why we have the countertop burner. You may wonder why this seems like half a house. That's because it is. Just behind this wall is the other half of the original house, occupied by another family. That's the Cuban way. Many, many houses were divided at the beginning of the Revolution. But this was a family home, divided in recent years by the heirs of my grandmother."

Outside the kitchen was a concrete enclosed area, bounded by a wall and metal stairs leading to the roof. The family dog, a large, black mix that seemed to have a bit of shepherd in him, had climbed down, and now leapt back up the stairs.

Franklin walked around the dwelling, pondering photos of people, looking at the worn furniture and the poor condition of the walls, doors and windows. He kept thinking that with the money they received on a regular basis, these people should be able to upgrade everything. Then, he remembered that they cannot obtain any products from the United States because of the Embargo. Why would his country insist on hurting the Cuban people in a lost effort to punish the leadership?

They sat for a sumptuous meal. The pork was tender and nicely flavored with garlic and spices. Lolita poured rich gravy from the pork onto his rice. A garlicky mojo covered the *yuca*. Fried malanga was drenched in flavorful Cuban honey. He downed two rich, dark Bucanero beers.

After the meal, Lolita served flan and coffee, just like the sugary *cafecito* he enjoyed at Versailles. The roar of conversation reminded Franklin of family in Miami, in those little terrazzo-floored homes near the airport, where the adults would yell louder as a large plane passed over, rattling the walls.

Daniel had gone out to exchange money, some to *pesos cubanos* and some to CUC. When he returned, he ate quickly. Then, he said, "We hate to leave so quickly after your hospitality, but we have deliveries to make, and I want to show Franklin some places that are meaningful to his father."

Luz grinned and asked, "May I go with you? I know all those places too."

Daniel said, "Of course."

After a while of kissing and hugging goodbye to the rest of the family and friends, they made off.

Chapter 64

Sylvia Morales

Sylvia whispered sweet nothings into her husband's ear. Was he reacting, smiling, moving? She couldn't tell. His cloudy eyes remained half open, blinking occasionally, probably involuntarily, as usual, but the eyeballs did not seem to move in the sockets. They did not produce tear drops, no matter what she said.

Two men dressed in doctors' gowns entered. "You must be Sylvia," one said. "I'm Dr. John Neil, and this is Dr. Dennis Martin. Has anybody told you we were coming?"

She nodded. "Are you the ones providing a second opinion? Or maybe I should say an opinion because it does not appear any opinion has been rendered?"

"Well, yes," said Dr. Martin. "We are looking at all records, examining your husband and interviewing doctors and personnel. We cannot say that we will be able to render an opinion either. But we will report what we find . . . or don't find."

"All right. Should I leave you alone?"

"Yes, please."

She walked out into the hall and slowly traipsed toward the visitor's area. Elena came around the corner toward her father's room. "Good morning, Elena."

Elena grimaced. "Hello."

"A couple of specialists are in the room examining him, to see if they can determine what's wrong."

"Oh. Who ordered that?"

"The committee . . . Mr. Murphy, Franklin and Roosevelt."

"Well, as of Tuesday afternoon, I expect to be in charge of it all."

Sylvia gritted her teeth and took a deep breath in an effort to remain calm. "Do you really think you are going to win? I have serious doubts."

Elena frowned, then grinned. "I've engaged another lawyer to handle the hearing."

Sylvia wanted to step back, away from the overwhelming odor of cigarette smoke. "What does your new lawyer think about your chances?"

"He needs to see documents. As a matter of fact, do you have a copy of my father's estate planning documents . . . all the things that were shown the other day in the office? And your prenuptial agreement?"

Sylvia's stomach sizzled. "No, I don't. And why would he need to see the prenuptial agreement?"

"To see if you waived your right to serve."

Sylvia had trouble putting together reasonable thoughts. "Listen, Elena, I'm not on your side with this guardianship proceeding. I'm not filing a guardianship proceeding myself. I'm not trying to become guardian, so my prenuptial agreement is irrelevant. But I'm certainly not giving you any ammunition to help you win your case."

"You're on their side. Franklin's side."

"I am not on any side, except that of my husband. The documents Louis has put together give his wishes, and they should be honored."

Elena stared at her with red, piercing eyes. Her face pulled back into a horrendous mask of demon-like fury. "You are swept into Franklin's domain. He's manipulating you, but he won't get anything over on me." Elena turned and marched out of the corridor.

Sylvia felt overtaken by a vibration of rage. *How could this woman be like that? How? Was she just born hateful?*

Chapter 65

Luis Morales

Two doctors examine me, shining lights into my eyes, taking my vitals and murmuring things I don't catch. But they are not hurting me, so I do not tense up.

On the beach below our cottage, my brother, Miguel and I load fishing gear into the small, wooden rowboat and shove off from shore. I row between the peninsula and Cayo Smith, heading toward the channel to the inlet, as Miguel readies the equipment for fishing, untangling line and preparing the crude rigging. He's the fisherman. I just like to be in the water.

I row to the south, past the high, stone walls of El Morro that guarded the east side of the inlet in past times. A military ship passes Ciudamar Yacht Club on its way into the protected harbor area at the foot of the city of Santiago de Cuba. I navigate the churning froth left behind by a tugboat that just passed on its way out to sea.

I continue rowing until we are about a hundred yards offshore, then move west of the main channel, away from mouth of the inlet. Farther to the west, the green hills of the mountain range merge into craggy, steep walls rising above the water. I drop the oars, banging wood on wood, and sprawl on the uncomfortable rib-like wooden frame of the boat bottom, one leg propped on a wooden seat and the other hanging over the side.

Miguel talks incessantly, as always, rambling on about the weather, the color of the water, nibbles on his hook, fish he thought he'd hooked, things that took his bait—on and on and on. I pay little attention to him.

I reminisce about my too-short, fortunate meeting with Caridad, who has occupied my thoughts ever since I met her the day before. I can picture her standing on the beach smiling. I stretch the truth into thoughts of her taking my hand, putting her arms around me, kissing me with those luscious lips. I'm not the kind of boy to think of a girl in this way, and especially to imagine intimacy. I've always been serious, with my feet on the ground. But I'm lost over her. Maybe my infatuation is due to the newness, as I've never seen or talked to any girl I didn't know from my school or neighborhood. I want to be with Caridad. The water pops and snaps against the hull. I float in my dreams.

Miguel yanks on the pole and lifts it over his head. "I got a big one."

I'm sure it's not as big as he's implying. If it were, it wouldn't fit into the boat anyway. I ignore him. We bob in the water. The sun climbs higher, baking my skin. I prop myself up, so I can look at the beauty of the inlet and the harbor. I gaze up at the small openings and cannon turrets in the face of El Morro. A little farther inland, and around to the left, is the cottage, out of view from here. I imagine boating all the way through the harbor, past all the land masses, to the right, where the city is perched and climbing above the harbor. If I were on top of El Morro, as I've been many times, I could see all the cottages on La Socapa, and much of the way through the harbor.

What could Caridad be doing now? Thinking of me? I try to picture exactly where her family's cottage is and how I can nonchalantly arrive there sometime, while avoiding the intense protection of her brother. I hope that she is still down here at the shore and that I can happen upon her again. I hope it's today.

Eventually my exuberant brother tires of fishing, but not of gabbing. He says, "Let's go," takes a seat and grabs one of the two sets of oars. Great, I'll have help this time.

I drag myself from my torturous bed and row toward shore, enjoying the strain of my upper-arm, chest and shoulder muscles and imagining a meeting with Caridad. Miguel continues talking, but I'm not listening.

As we turn back into the calm strip of water between La Socapa and Cayo Smith and approach shore, I turn and see a sole swimmer, dark head bobbing above the water. My heart accelerates. Could it be her? Can my luck be this good? I row faster and faster, leaning so far back that I almost fall into the bottom of the boat. But I keep working, working, working. Nearing shore, I peer over my shoulder, but I can't get far enough around to even see if the swimmer is still there. I don't want to run her over. My brother has stopped rowing and is facing the shore.

I ask my brother, "Is there anybody in the water?"

He laughs. "Girl of your dreams."

I don't know how he knows, but I don't care. "Continue straight?"

"Yes."

I must display my strength. I lean into every pull, well into my methodical breathing routine. "I won't run her over, will I?"

"She's leaving the water, not looking back at you. You can forget about showing your muscles." He laughs.

Shortly, the boat slides a little way up the soft sand onto the beach.

I stand immediately, scoping the shore and the water. Where the hell has she gone? My brother laughs again.

I try not to look too anxious. "Where is she?"

"There." He points with his head toward the embankment and one of the pathways leading up to where the cottages perch above the beach. Caridad and a young girl walk into the trees and begin climbing the dirt walkway toward the little houses at the top. I don't hesitate. I evaluate the different routes and run toward a path to the left of the one she has taken, hoping to get to the top before her, and nonchalantly intercept her as I walk down. Of course, if she admired my musculature in the boat, she will know the encounter is not by chance. Maybe she has left on purpose to avoid me. It just doesn't matter. I must take the risk. My feet hardly touch the ground as I sprint upward.

I hear her and the other girl giggling as they trek up the path to my right. At the top, I slow, try to breathe and relax so it will not be apparent that I have run. I turn onto the path she is climbing, only to walk smack into her brother, who stands, arms crossed, with a smirk on his face. "*Amigo*. Why were you running? You should slow down." He laughs. "I saw you coming to shore. I knew you would chase my sister up the hill."

"Huh?" I ask lamely, captured like a fly in a web. Branches rustle on the path where Caridad is obviously climbing towards us.

"Turn around and go back down your path."

And, like a fool, I do.

Chapter 66

Franklin Morales

Luz bubbled with explanations from the back seat as Daniel drove through the Sueño neighborhood. "Daniel, go to the Moncada first, okay?"

He turned down a street.

"Actually, pass along I Street." He turned again. "Franklin, do you know about the Moncada attack and what happened with your father and uncle there?"

He regarded her. "Uh, no. I know I had an uncle ... Miguel ... who died long ago. What happened?"

Luz said, "Uh . . . maybe I shouldn't tell you if your father didn't."

Daniel remained focused on the road, his jaw clenched.

Franklin looked at the uncertainty on their faces. "What? Did something significant happen that involved mi papá?"

Daniel sighed. After a few moments of looks at Luz in the mirror and jaw muscles working, he said, "I imagine that his father would have told him and showed him all of this on this trip."

Luz, now subdued, remained silent, looking at Franklin and then out the window. "I'm sorry. I'm so stupid."

Franklin said, "If Daniel thinks my father was going to reveal something to me about his past, since now he cannot, and perhaps will never be able to do so, I would appreciate hearing it."

A tear flowed down Luz's cheek. "All right, I want to show you a house, and then, Daniel, can we stop for a few minutes at the Moncada to explain the story?"

Daniel nodded, his face muscles like knots.

"Okay, slow down here. Franklin, there's a sign by the door. Can you read it?"

He read aloud. "In this house #218 were thirteen young people who participated in the historic attack on the Moncada Barracks."

Luz said, "Three or four houses in town and the Hotel Rex were pre-staging areas of the attack, before the revolutionaries went outside the city to another staging area, which I'll tell you about."

Franklin nodded. "Pre-staging areas for what attack?"

They drove a couple of blocks. Daniel stopped in front of a large concrete building, painted a mustard shade of yellow.

"Let's get out and walk. In July 1953, the people of Santiago de Cuba were preparing for *Carnaval*."

Daniel added, "Nowadays, we still have *Carnaval*, but people no longer have money to dress up. It's still a party even today though."

"What happened to mi tío and mi papá?"

Luz nodded. "You will understand shortly. Seven years before the Revolution succeeded, in 1953, Fidel had created a plan to attack the Cuartel Moncada, this building right here." She waved her arm around the parade ground. "It was a military garrison, with administrative buildings, army barracks, a military hospital and officer housing... those identical wooden houses that are now residences right over there across the street...were officers' quarters. This large area was the parade ground. Those guard towers on the corners are obvious. At the same time they attacked here, they would attack another military garrison in Bayamo, where we are heading in a while, on the other side of the Sierra Maestra mountain range.

"Fidel's theory was that taking over these military bases would allow him to initiate a coup to overturn the coup that had occurred just months before, which placed Batista back into power.

"The revolutionaries rented a farmhouse about halfway between the city of Santiago and the beach town of Siboney, a little less than an hour from the city in those days, as their headquarters to prepare for the attack and dubbed it *La Granjita*, or *La Granjita Siboney*. Almost two hundred revolutionaries, mostly from Havana and nearby towns, arrived here in Santiago de Cuba, mostly unnoticed because of the influx of revelers. In early morning on the 26th of July . . . remember that date? . . . when they expected all the soldiers would be sleeping off the effects of alcohol, they would sneak in, dressed in uniforms that looked like official army uniforms and trick the real soldiers posted to protect the Moncada.

"Felipe Salvador Llorente, a friend and neighbor of your father, went to your father's home the afternoon before the attack to inform him that your Uncle Miguel, who was a teenager, was trying to involve himself in the attack, which Felipe thought was a dangerous mistake. You are going to meet Felipe.

"They searched for your uncle at some of the houses and the Hotel Rex, and then went to *La Granjita Siboney,* where all the revolutionaries from the other sites had merged for the final planning and to receive uniforms and guns. Your father, your uncle and Felipe were locked up because they weren't believed to be true revolutionaries. Later, after the revolutionaries had left for the attack, they escaped, and, somehow ended up near here. They were caught and believed to be revolutionaries. The Batista police shot Miguel to death."

She pointed at the building. "Supposedly, the guards in the towers shot at attackers, resulting in those holes in the building. I say *supposedly* because the holes are quite large and seem quite high if the guards were shooting at revolutionaries. Bullet holes in the front of *La Granjita Siboney* were reportedly added after the event. Anyway, a number of revolutionaries were killed here on the parade grounds or inside. Some were caught and tortured, and some bodies were supposedly moved to other places, like *La Granjita Siboney*."

She looked at Daniel. "Can we show him the museum?"

He nodded.

She pointed to a sign. "As you see, it's a school now, but there's also a museum inside, with some of the real and fake blood-stained uniforms, maps, drawings and other items of interest. If you get a chance to go to *La Granjita Siboney*, see the museum there too."

They entered. She paid for the three. "Oh, you have to learn the money here. It's quite strange. We Cubans who work for the government, like me because I work at a university, earn Pesos Cubanos, or CUP, and you use Pesos Convertibles, or CUC. All museums have two prices. You pay two CUC here, which is about two dollars, and more if you want to take photos. We Cubans pay two CUP. A CUP is about one-twenty-fifth of a CUC. That means we pay about eight cents, which is still a lot for us."

When she'd finished showing him the museum items, she ushered him along the sidewalk beside the building toward the wide street behind it. At the intersection, she pointed to the left. "That large square building is the courthouse, where all of them, including your father, were tried, and most were convicted. Fidel's final speech and determination of guilt did not occur in the courthouse with the others. Instead, they worked out some deal and held his over there at the hospital."

She pointed to the right. "And I understand that your father was right here on this street the morning your uncle was killed, and your father arrested." Franklin tried to imagine the horror his father must have experienced. They crossed the street and walked through the hospital grounds. A number of separate rooms stood along a long outdoor walkway. They stopped in front of a sign indicating a tiny room where Fidel's final trial was held. Franklin had trouble imagining that the impetus of so much history occurred there.

Upon exiting, they walked to the rear of the property, and stood, looking down through the city, to the water. "Your father and most of the rest, but not Felipe, went to prison on an island off the southern coast of Cuba, far from here. Your father was released before the others. Apparently, they decided Felipe was truly not guilty at the trial and later decided the same of your father. But your grandfather was a close confidant and henchmen of Batista, so he might have pulled strings. The real Revolutionaries weren't in for long either. When Batista let the others out, he made them leave the country, but that apparently was not very smart of him. Since the attack was on July 26, 1953, even though it failed, it became the foundation of the Revolution . . . the July 26 Movement. Remember the armbands this morning, M-26-7?"

As they walked back to the car, Franklin's brain tried to make sense of what happened and to determine whether anything he knew about his father was related to this traumatic event, which he'd kept a secret.

Daniel said, "We must go to Bayamo, so we can return before it's too late to visit a couple of contacts here."

Luz put a hand on Daniel's arm. "Will you just drive by Hotel Rex?"

Daniel drove past the courthouse and turned right. He stopped two blocks later.

"Please, Daniel, let us just run up the stairs for a moment."

He grimaced silently.

She jumped from the car. "Come on."

She ran across the street, under the sign saying, Hotel Rex, entered and skipped up the first flight of stairs. Although Franklin kept up with her, he gasped for breath at the top. "I'm a little older than you, Luz . . . like over thirty years."

She breathed deeply and beckoned him to follow. "You look to be in great shape." She stopped in front of an open door and pointed to a sign, saying '26-7'. "You already know that's the July 26 Movement. And this name, Abel Santamaria, was one of the attackers. He and a number of others were here that evening. There's a copy of the food bill downstairs. I believe your father was here that evening too. Let's go before Daniel gets angry."

They ran back downstairs and hopped into the car. Daniel maneuvered to a fairly-well-paved six-lane highway, passing along a ridge that offered a nice view of the city and the harbor. They passed less occupied areas with more farmland, where horses and cows grazed. Inside and outside of towns, people walked and waited along the road, many holding out hands for rides. In little towns, people stood in line to fill natural gas tanks, men rode horses and multiple-passenger buggies with signs saying what route each took, kids played with balls, rocks, marbles or jacks, men sat at worn tables playing dominos, mangy-looking dogs scoured for food and chickens and roosters pranced in the streets.

They passed a concrete sign saying *Granma*, under a depiction of a boat. Luz said, "This is the province of Granma. That was the name of the boat on which Fidel, Raul, El Ché and many others landed here on their return to fulfill the quest of the Revolution. The city of Granma is on the coast in this province. The government changed names of locations after the Revolution."

They circled a square in the center of the small city of Bayamo, passed a street or two, stopped and piled out. Luz led them to a dwelling where the front door stood open. An elderly man using a walker emerged from the darkened interior, greeted them and stepped aside to let them enter a front parlor. A frail woman sat in a rocker. A younger man rose to greet them.

Daniel hugged the men and leaned down to kiss the woman on the cheek. He stood back, extending his hand toward Franklin. "I'm sorry to report that Luis has taken ill. This is his son, Franklin."

Franklin shook the hands of both men, while putting his left hand around their shoulders, and shook the woman's hand, while kissing her on the cheek.

Luz kissed all of them, saying, "I'm Luz, a cousin of Franklin. My grandmother is a sister of Luis's wife, Cari, who died some time back."

The younger man asked, "Would you like a coffee?"

Daniel said yes and nodded to Franklin in a way that made him understand he should say yes, so he did

As the young man worked, the old one said, "We pray that Luis will recover soon."

Franklin looked around the apartment, taking in the outmoded appliances and furniture.

"Thank you. I will return with or without mi papá in the future."

Daniel brought out the list of people and what this family was to receive. Franklin pulled out the bank bag and set the stipend on the table.

Shortly, they had bid the first family goodbye and entered two other homes to make deliveries.

On the highway back to Santiago de Cuba, Franklin asked, "Does my father ever purchase items that people need? I mean, couldn't you ask people if they need something, purchase items in the bigger cities and deliver them?"

Daniel grimaced. "We have done that, but not on a regular basis. There's not much time to do so, and there's no room in the car for large items or many smaller ones."

"You or somebody could have an extra paid job to learn what people need and purchase them. Kitchen appliances, for example. And consider Mario, the computer programmer, dealing with that old technology. He could benefit so much from something more modern. Money spent on items would reduce their cash gifts but would be very helpful."

Luz, said, "I could help with that, and I would not charge money. I can pick out the items, and you," pointing at Daniel, "could retrieve them."

Daniel grimaced. "I don't know. I can't fit anything large in here, and don't have another vehicle. But, if you want to implement that, I could help find somebody."

Franklin looked at Luz. "Luz. You have a full-time job, don't you?"

"Yes, but I have time. Please, I'd love to be involved."

"That would be great," Franklin said, smiling.

They visited two more families as they entered Santiago de Cuba. After the last delivery of the day, they went to a restaurant a block from Luz's family's home. "This place just opened. Few know about it, but I hear it's quite nice. Kind of expensive for Cubans though."

They stopped in front of a three-story building on 1st street, between 6th and 7th, in the *Sueño* neighborhood, with a sign on the wall saying, *Marbella* and a depiction of a marlin leaping into the air.

They climbed to the third floor, which was open-air. They sat at a railing, with a view of shadows of the mountains in the distance, standing above the neighborhood homes of flat, concrete roofs, on many of which dogs pranced and barked.

Franklin and Luz ordered octopus cooked on the grill, and Daniel ordered filet of fish cooked in white wine. They also ordered a side of fried *malangas* and honey.

Franklin wiped *Bucanero* beer foam from his mouth. "This meal is so good. You say it's expensive, but most dishes here are six dollars, and even the beer is only a dollar fifty. That's cheap for us."

Luz said, "I guess I haven't explained how much money we subsist on if we work for the government. As a professor with not too many years of experience, I make seventeen dollars a month. My mother, also a professor, but close to retirement age, makes twenty-eight. If we came here for a meal for four, that would take her entire monthly salary and part of mine. And, of course, my grandmother could never climb the steps, so we'd have to take hers home. To get take-out or to take leftovers, you must generally bring your own bag or container. Some restaurants offer take-out containers, for a charge."

Franklin nodded. "I understand."

Luz said, "I'd like to attend the rest of your trip, to continue this thought about helping the people with products. Don't worry, you can just leave me in Holguín at the end, and I'll take a bus home. Please?"

Franklin said, "What about your work on Monday and at least part of Tuesday?"

She said, "Don't worry, I have time off. I don't teach classes on those days."

Franklin looked at Daniel, who offered a tilted-head acknowledgement.

After the main meal, they ordered a *Copa Lolita*, a dessert of mouthwatering flan and ice cream together, and a couple of extra plates and spoons. Franklin said, "Oh my God. Exquisite."

Then they walked Luz to her home, returned to the jeep and drove a few blocks away to the *casa particular* where they would stay. A friendly, middle-aged couple greeted them. "Come in. Come in. Where's Luis?"

"He's ill," said Daniel. "This is his son, Franklin."

"Welcome, Franklin. We pray for your father's swift recovery."

Daniel explained that the couple was on the list of recipients, so they made the distribution, as well as paying twenty dollars for each room and five dollars for each breakfast, which would be ready at six-thirty a.m., as requested. Franklin's room had an open window, overlooking the same view they had from the restaurant.

Chapter 67

Elena Morales Lennox

Sunday, December 4, 2016

Elena had downed two Cuba Libres during the long evening as she speculated where her husband could be. She'd been pissed ever since the fiasco of a hearing. No word from him since mid-afternoon when she'd jumped on him, saying, "You and Doolittle are peas in a pod. You can't run that firm. You'll never have stock in that firm. You have no idea what you're doing. You're a sorry excuse for anything."

"Elena," he said, placing an arm on her shoulder. "We couldn't have won that hearing. The judge was right."

"You two idiots should have known what would happen. You were unprepared. You were bullied. You have no idea what you're doing. I'm sorry that I ever trusted in your legal abilities. I always knew Doolittle was a blowhard. He may be even more pompous than Franklin. But he was relying on you to know the law. The judge didn't fall for his hot air and gave you no credence because of your lack of knowledge."

"Elena, it wasn't like that."

"Yes, Kalvin, it was like that. You're a sorry excuse for everything you are."

He'd stormed out in a huff, saying, "If you do not appreciate my work on your father's case, then you can just kiss my ass."

Now, after midnight, he still wasn't here. She lay on the couch, imagining and wondering. Was he drunk in a bar? Was he with a woman? Could something have happened to him? Could he have been arrested for DUI? Could he have been in an accident? Worry and anger merged together. Goddamn him. But what if something happened? It would serve him right if something happened. But what if he was hurt? He's not hurt.

Damn that bastard for making her have these emotions. It's his own fault for being so standoffish. Let him rot in whatever he has gotten himself into. Bastard. Should she check hospitals? No, dammit.

The rolling wheels and squeak of the automatic garage door opener sounded. She should act like she was asleep. Don't give him the satisfaction of thinking she gave a shit. She didn't give a shit. Asshole. She moved into the bedroom and got into bed, turned her back to his side of the bed and pulled the sheet over her head.

He stumbled into the room, sat on the bench at the foot of the bed, dropped his shoes on the floor loudly, wandered into the bathroom and took a loud piss, dropped clothes on his way to the bed and climbed in, reeking of booze, and—and—what—weed? Why had she married this jerk? And—what?—the smell of a woman—of sex? Mother-fucker.

She tried to remain still to avoid the possibility he'd want sex. That would be unlikely anyway. He never wanted her anymore, unless he was really drunk, and he'd probably already fucked some young bitch. Yuk. Bastard. When he bothered to have sex with her, she would lie there, stare at the ceiling and just let him do it.

He farted loudly and turned toward her. Which was worse?—the gas or the rancorous breath? He mumbled something, but she couldn't make it out. Soon, he snored loudly. She tried to sleep for a few minutes, but it was no use. She marched out to the kitchen, poured a stiff one, went outside and lit a cigarette. She lay on the chaise lounge, staring up at the stars. This was nice. She could do this. Look at the stars. So peaceful.

Her father's face came to her. He was so handsome when he was young. He still had that, but not this week. This week, he looked like hell. Like he was on death's door. How could this happen? How? Here she was, all alone, with a dying father, a dead mother, a bitch of a stepmother, an asshole of a brother, and the biggest asshole of all snoring next to her.

She had to take over her father's affairs, or she would be left in the dust. If she didn't have Kalvin around, what kind of money would she have? If the firm fired him, being her age and with no good work history, what chance was there of ever finding a job at all? He'd never been a work horse, had never produced anything beyond a mid-range salary and certainly would not do anything like that now.

Her only hope was to take over. She could charge a fee as a guardian, couldn't she? If she threw asshole Kalvin out, she would get a good portion of his income. But knowing him, he'd stop working so he wouldn't have any income to share. If her papá did die, certainly she'd receive something. She did not expect that her husband would receive anything, because her papá probably thought their marriage was tenuous anyway. He'd probably give stock in the firm to Franklin and give her cash to equalize them. But how much would go to that wife of his? How much? Her stomach constricted.

And Franklin, down there cruising around Cuba giving out goodies and money like her papá did before. Walking into little shacks and huts, with that overly-proud smile, his hand held out like he was a fucking politician, saying, "Hi, I'm Franklin Morales. I'm here to save you from your misery."

Mother fucker. Mother fucker. At least her father was humble. This didn't go to his head. He probably sat with the people, drank some coffee, talked of their needs, felt their pain. But not Franklin. Bastard, bastard, bastard.

Suddenly, she came to a conclusion completely off topic. Her alcohol use, her smoking, her vulgar language and her negativity had gotten out of control. It was due to her unhappiness. The first thing to do was to get rid of Kalvin. And then she needed to quit smoking. But right now, she needed another smoke.

Chapter 68

Luis Morales

The new doctors are back, murmuring about something. One writes on a clipboard. They shine that awful light into my head like the others did before. I try to escape my fears and evoke happy times.

Caridad and I, both seventeen years old, sway on the front porch swing of her home. We are going out on our fifth official, authorized date. We are required to be visible, as we await our chaperones, Ernesto and Margarita, a married couple only a couple years older than we. We touch hands from time to time, not as much as I want to, but within the acceptable range. All this vigilance drives me crazy, but I don't think Cari thinks anything of it.

The chaperones arrive and leap from the car. Ernesto, tall and debonair, with a thinly trimmed mustache and slightly curly hair, and Margarita, a beauty, with a kind and gentle face, rush to the porch as we step down. The women and men exchange cheek kisses.

Ernesto turns and embraces me. "You look good, Luis. It's the girl that causes your enthusiasm, true?"

I grin. "Yes, I'm great. How go things with you?"

"Excellent."

The women chatter as we move toward the car. Ernesto has his arm on my shoulder. "I tell you, Caridad is a very special woman."

"Do you think I would have pursued her for so long if she were not?"

He laughs.

Caridad and I sit in the back seat, close, but not so close as to cause concern. The chaperones talk and laugh, looking to the back seat from time to time, eyes going up and down. I would be just as happy to have Ernesto watch the road instead of spying on us.

We arrive at a square in mid-city, where the concert, an eclectic mix of Latin classical, with a little *charanga* and some *son* influence as well, has just begun. People sit on wooden benches around the

278

square. On a permanent, wooden, covered gazebo at the center of the square stage, middle-aged men blow trumpets and trombones. One plays a cello, one taps a snare drum and one sings. Sometimes, they are joined or replaced by others with bongos, flutes, clarinets and guitars. We sit together on a bench.

Caridad taps her feet. After a while, when a good rhythmic Mambo band is playing, in which the musicians rap the timbale, conga and bongo drums, others scrape the guiro, as still others pluck the bass, beat on piano keys and blow the trombone, trumpet and sax, I ask Cari to dance. She pulls me onto the grassy dance area beneath the star-spotted sky. The touch of her hand is electric.

The song is fast, full of good Cuban rhythm and a strong beat. She knows the Mambo. She moves all around, takes my hands at appropriate times, moves in, moves out and keeps me moving. I'm so enamored.

At one point when I have her close, I whisper, "I love you." I gaze into her eyes.

She looks at me, perhaps shocked, perhaps confused. "What?"

At first, I figure she just doesn't want to acknowledge what I said, but now I have the impression that she truly did not hear me. I decide not to try again. My emotions are constantly tugged like this when I am with her. It's not her fault. It's just the tight morés of our culture. I concentrate on how I can get her alone, only to kiss her. I'm lost in love as well as in lust.

During a break, Ernesto and I go to get punch. He looks at me seriously. "What do you think about Eddie Chibás for President?"

I shake my head. "Why do you always want to talk of political crap? But I will say he can't stay on theme. He vacillates too much. His moniker, *El Loco*, is appropriate. He's too outspoken, always making outrageous statements on his radio shows."

Ernesto laughs. "For somebody who cares nothing about politics you seem to know something, even though you are wrong. Chibás is steadfast and serious. He abandoned the Auténtico Party and created the Ortodoxo Party because he was against the rampant corruption. He promotes honest government."

I wonder how I allowed myself to be pulled into a political discussion. "Ernesto, you are trying to bait me. You want me to get riled up about your political objectives. You're right. I don't know much about Chibás or any of this. I don't care. But I will say that Chibás hasn't offered any true social or economic reforms or controls. He never offered a single bill in Congress during the seven years he served. How long ago did he say he would never leave the Auténtico Party? Then he left, because Grau wouldn't promote his wish for a presidential bid. Corruption, gangsterism and discord will continue even if he is president." I smile, wondering how I even developed this opinion or gained this belief.

Ernesto frowns. "You are so wrong, Luis. Chibás will run this government in a way that will eliminate all the corruption of the past."

"I'm tired of talking about this nonsense. Chibás is not his own man. He's another puppet of Batista, and if he's not, he will be. I doubt if Batista could win the election himself, but I think he has the machine in motion and it's in his control."

The women stand near a circle of thin trees, laughing. I walk toward them.

Ernesto grabs my arm, and leans in. "I think Eddie is the man who can lead our country to greatness. He's been groomed for it. Batista had his turn. Why would we want him to rule again?"

"I told you. Batista's been ruling the whole damn time. Our country remains in turmoil under his hidden control."

Ernesto lights a cigarette.

"This reminds me of so many conversations with my father. He would always complain about the current government and all the prior ones. But when Batista was in power or ruling from the sidelines, my father was a strong proponent."

Ernesto blows a smoke ring in the air as if he's bored from hearing me.

I continue anyway. "My father is the one who taught me of Batista's control even though he's not president anymore. He said Batista, with United States' support, put Grau St. Martin into power at the conclusion of Batista's presidency. But then, according to my father, graft and corruption turned the land into a war of gangsters. He always says, other than Batista, the country has been in the control of one corrupt president after the other; one reason to kill and imprison people after the other. I believe business and financial interests are behind my father's beliefs."

Ernesto blows another smoke ring that drifts over my head and asks, as if I haven't said a word, "What about Fidel?"

"What about him? People say his followers are a bunch of fascist thugs."

He shoots me a look of disdain. "Who says that? Your father, I presume."

I sigh out loud, not meaning to. I want to dance with Cari, not talk useless nonsense about politics my father always insists should interest me.

Ernesto grinds his cigarette into the ground. "Anybody is better than what we have now."

I shake my head. "I'm not so sure Fidel is going to be the savior. People say the grass will be greener every time we've had a change. It's all still a mess."

He glares at me. I regret that I've continued the conversation, but now I take advantage of the short lull. "Listen, Ernesto. I've had enough of this. I don't want to waste another minute that I could be enjoying with Cari."

I walk away, knowing he's standing behind me scratching his head, wondering, like my father always does, what is wrong with me that all this political stuff doesn't get my blood churning. I know what will make it churn, and I can hear her beautiful voice and see her silhouette in the shadows.

Chapter 69

Franklin Morales

After a sweet night's sleep, a strong run around the *Sueño* neighborhood in the dawn of the day, taking care to stay on streets of the same level as the home, above the main roads around the Plaza de la Revolution, so he could find his way back again, and then gorging on a marvelous breakfast of pineapples, bananas, guava, mango, eggs, chorizo, bread and strong Cuban coffee, Franklin decided to try to call home. He'd learned he could send and receive calls and texts while in Cuba, but he should turn on data to check e-mail only occasionally.

He decided to call Miguel first because he would know about everybody.

"Hey, Pops. How's Cuba?"

"Interesting. I'll tell you all about when I get home. How's your mother?"

"Fine. We ate with her last night."

"Please tell her I called. Do you know anything about your grandfather's health?"

"I checked in last night. All seems the same."

"Are Jordan and Alisa well?"

"Dad, you've been gone about two days. They're fine."

Franklin laughed. "It feels like I've lost a century since I've been here. You know I'll be back on Tuesday and will head straight to court. Let me know if anything happens."

He called Sylvia's cell and got the same update he'd gotten from his son. For a moment he worried that he had not called his wife, and that many wives would be upset that he'd called others. But Diana would not.

Ten minutes after picking up Luz, they were in the first house within Santiago. After introductions followed by the recipients' expressions of concern about Luis' health, they transacted business, graciously turned down coffee after saying they'd already had a couple of cups and went to the next house.

Outside the seventh house, Daniel said, "This is the home of Felipe, who was with your father at the time of the trouble. I don't know how much he remembers or is willing to discuss."

Felipe opened the door, looked around for Luis and set his eyes on Franklin. "Franklin, I'd know you anywhere. Where is your father?"

Franklin and Felipe shook hands and hugged.

"I'm afraid he's very ill. We do not currently know whether he will recover or not. He's been unconscious for a week."

"I hope he recovers soon. I know he will."

Daniel said, "Listen, Felipe, it turns out that Franklin never knew about what occurred at the Moncada and its aftermath, until we told him the little we know."

Felipe's face turned grim. "Hmm. I'm sorry he didn't tell you, but isn't that just like him?"

Franklin smiled. "Yes, it is."

"So, what have you learned?"

Luz gave a quick rundown of the facts she'd told him. "I don't know any of the details about that night and day, the trial, the prison situation or anything else, so I couldn't tell him."

Felipe put a hand on each of Franklin's shoulders. "I'd be happy to tell you, although it pains me to talk about it, but I fear that you don't have time on this trip. If you come back here in a month, which I hope you are able to do *with* your father, we'll schedule some time and talk and talk."

Although disappointed in Felipe's response, Franklin thanked him, and they left.

As they finished the last visit in the city, Luz said, "Do we have time to show Franklin his original home, and then drive around the inlet, so he can see La Socapa, and then go around El Morro and show him Siboney Beach and *La Granjita Siboney*?"

Glimpses and distant memories of the family's cottage came to Franklin. It occurred to him that he'd rarely thought of it. He always remembered his father's descriptions but seemed to have blocked out his early memories of being there, just like he could hardly remember his own home before leaving the country as a youngster.

Daniel passed through a few streets, and drove along a long, four lane street divided by a median, with some impressive houses on both sides.

"This is the subdivision, *Vista Alegre,* where you and my father's family lived. Turn here, Daniel."

Daniel turned a couple of times, and then Luz said, "This was your grandparents' home, where I believe you lived at least part of the time, and you also lived in that home across the street."

Franklin exited the vehicle and stared at the home, surrounded on two sides by a covered porch. The mango tree of his youth still stood. In what was once a driveway to the left stood a three-story building.

Luz said, "Let's knock at the door."

A woman answered, and Luz explained that this was previously Franklin's home. The woman looked hesitant, but then opened the door wider. Franklin looked into the dwelling but did not recognize any of the rooms. The woman said, "The house was divided into two dwellings. The principal door to the other part is on the other end of the porch."

Then Franklin looked down at the floor, and suddenly remembered sitting on the tiled pattern, pushing around tiny metal cars and trucks. Yes, this was his home. Now the porch came back to him.

After knocking at the other door, but not getting an answer, they crossed the street to the other house. Nobody appeared to be in. Franklin struggled for memories of being here as well. He began to feel a tremendous loss. At first, he'd had no memory. Then, he had a fleeting sense of nostalgia, which evaporated as quickly as it had come. Nothing was the same. He trudged back to the car, not sure he wanted to relive more memories.

Daniel drove out of the subdivision and down through the city, rounded the harbor and passed between dusty buildings of a cement plant. Finally, he cruised along a winding road passing houses, apartment buildings, a park on a hill, and finally a couple of coves with sandy beaches, packed with swimmers and sunbathers.

After passing the last cove and winding back towards the wide waterway, Luz said, "Do you remember that island with quaint, colored houses and a church on top? That's Cayo Smith. But they changed the island's name from Smith to . . . guess what?"

"Uh, I don't know. Fidel?"

"No, remember the name of the boat?"

"Yes, in English it would sound like the nickname of a grandmother. It's also the name of one of the official newspapers, *Granma*," Franklin recalled.

"Right. Now the island is called *Cayo Granma*. The significance of this to your family is not the island itself. See that peninsula across the small strip of water? Do you remember *La Socapa*? That's where the family had a cottage, actually more than one. It's where your father met your mother as kids."

Daniel said, "Yes, he often has me bring him out here, so he can just sit for a while. How'd you know that, Luz?"

"Something he mentioned to me once. Franklin, as you can see, there's not much there now. But in those days, and even when you were young, I understand there were quite a few houses along the large inlet channel. Your family's cottage and a number of others were on the inside just opposite Cayo Smith. Families brought the kids and spent most of their summers here. Do you remember?"

Franklin nodded slowly. "Yes, it's coming back to me. It looks so abandoned now."

Before long, they continued along the road to El Morro. "Of course, you remember El Morro, which is also the name of the fort at the mouth of the Havana Harbor. This road goes around El Morro, past the airport, and then joins with the Siboney Highway. So, we can stop at the Siboney Farmhouse before we go to Guantanamo."

Franklin was happy to leave these memories behind and continue with the mission of meeting people and making deliveries.

Having joined the Siboney Highway, heading toward the coast and town of Siboney, Luz pointed to a dirt road leading up into the trees. "One day, we'll take you up there to see the view from *La Gran Piedra.*"

Just a mile or so later, Daniel stopped across the street from a white wooden building with red trim and a red roof. Large bullet holes had punched through the wood, as Franklin had already learned. They crossed the street, paid the two kinds of pesos for admission and entered.

Daniel said, "The night before the Moncada Attack, into early morning, there were over a hundred and fifty people in here and around, working on the uniforms, handing out weapons and studying maps. Cars lined the drive and the street outside. These little wooden lean-tos in the yard are flimsy models of the structures that existed. They were constructed to look like chicken coops but were used to hide cars. Apparently at least one had a small room above the open area below."

Franklin gulped. "This is where my father and uncle were kept locked up when the group left to attack the Moncada barracks?"

Daniel and Luz nodded.

"Incredible," Franklin said, meekly.

Back in the car, Luz pointed one direction. "Can we take him to the beach?"

"We have stops in the pueblo of Siboney, Baconao and other little places on the way to Guantanamo anyway." Daniel looked at his watch. "We're behind schedule. We can enjoy the beach for a moment only. All right?"

Franklin nodded.

In the town of Siboney, Daniel turned right just before the rolling waves of the beach, and they made a delivery in an several-story-tall building. In the village, they walked on the walkway near the sea among abandoned concrete structures. "All this damage is from Hurricane Sandy," said Luz.

They went back to the turnoff and stopped on the road above Siboney Beach. Daniel said, "This is another place I always bring your father. He always wants to sit on a rock and silently gaze at the water, I believe remembering his youthful jaunts here with Cari. In the past, sometimes he walked on the beach or even swam, but not lately."

Franklin wondered whether his papá really remembered his mamá now that Sylvia was so much a part of him. He had the feeling that yes, he did.

They stopped at a home along the Baconao highway. Luz said, "Some beach around here is where my great uncles Alejandro and Humberto tried to escape by raft with your mother and sister, and tía Yiyi and Amelia."

"Really?"

Franklin glimpsed the deep blue water, as they zipped by patches of trees and bushes. He dwelled on how that failed trip and the other events they suffered had haunted his mother and Elena for so many years.

The road finally climbed and turned inland. Daniel said, "You can't see from here, but to your right, beyond those hills, is Guantanamo Bay, and across the water the Guantanamo Military Base owned by your Empire." He smiled. "If a Cuban wanted to leave the country, especially here in the south, he'd try to arrive by swimming or taking a boat or raft because once on that soil, it was the same as arriving on the mainland of the U.S.

As Franklin, Luz, Daniel and an elderly man sat on small wooden seats on a dirt floor in a home of worn, unpainted wood, sipping rum, a tall, thin, dark-skinned, man limped in abruptly and took a seat. The host ceased looking at his guests and hung his head. Finally, he said, "This is Reinaldo. He was one of the attackers in Bayamo the same day as the attack against the Cuartel Moncada. He was a colonel in the army until he retired. Franklin and Daniel shook his hand, which he allowed, while grimacing. Luz kissed him.

Gazing at the guests through shades of tangled eyebrow hairs partially covering his eyes, and then focusing on Franklin, the colonel said, "We've had enough of you people coming here. Do you think we need you? If you'd just end the Blockade, we'd be fine. Those of us who understand your country, and," he shot a look at the host, "aren't tainted by receiving money, know that you want to be the empire of the world. I believe that you are sent here by your CIA, just like that Alan Gross was. Your CIA has nothing to do but dream up stupid ploys against us. Doesn't the term CIA mean it's supposed to address internal matters to your country? Why is it always trying to manipulate the world? We aren't the only target, but we have been the brunt of your ploys for so long it's ridiculous. You make it look like we want and need something from you, but you are really just infiltrating for your government."

Franklin glanced at the host, wondering what to do. The host asked, "Reinaldo, would you like some rum?"

The colonel shook his head. "The examples are endless. You brought us the mosquitoes with dengue. You tried to kill Fidel many times. You blew a plane of our people out of the sky. You imprisoned the Cuba Five. You made a fiasco out of the story with Elian. You put bombs and poison on the beach around your military base. Only a few years ago, you created that stupid Twitter fiasco. And now, I'm sure you are doing much with our people's ability to have Internet. You made it appear that our people wanted to send their children away on those Peter Pan flights, and act like those who took our children in were so holy and kind, but that's not true at all. The whole rumor about our government intending to send children to Russia was fabricated by your CIA. No child was ever sent to Russia. Nor was it ever even imagined by us. It was implanted."

Franklin sat quietly, waiting for the opportunity to get on the road. He glanced at Daniel and Luz. They wouldn't look up.

The colonel sat, moving his jaws like he was chewing something. "Martí recognized your need to rule the world. You had nothing to do with the situations involving any war you've ever been in. The world wars. Wars in other countries. They were never about protecting your country, except maybe your financial power. Always about spreading your tentacles. Showing your power. Our war, which you call the Spanish-American War, was our war of independence. It's the Cuban-Spanish war and you infiltrated yourselves and tried to say you were helping us.

"You use that word 'American' like it's you. Like you are America. We, and many other countries, are America too. Even your term, Cuban-American to describe our people who moved to your country is trying to steal our identity. We are Cubans, and we are *americanos*.

"You say our people who left were 'escaping'. There was nothing to escape. They wanted to leave because you instilled lies in them about how they'd have it so nice in your country. You didn't tell the truth. You didn't tell them they wouldn't be able to find work in the fields they had studied and worked in here. Remember in the 70's when those who'd arrived there were hijacking planes to return, desperately trying to erase their mistakes of going to your Empire? And then you jailed them in your jails."

Streaks of sweat now poured down the man's wrinkled forehead and soaked the underarms of his shirt. He seemed to relax.

Franklin managed, "Sir. I understand your wrath against my country and our CIA. I assure you that I have nothing to do with that. I do not doubt that it committed many of the acts you refer to."

The colonel looked up. "All of the atrocities, and probably many more."

Franklin nodded. Then he and Daniel stood, as did the host and the colonel. All four shook hands and patted backs as though nothing negative had been stated, and Franklin, Daniel and Luz departed.

After leaving the house, they stopped at four more dwellings in and around the city of Guantanamo, and then traveled along a rocky and hilly route along the southeast coast. They had one stop before leaving the coast and heading north. As they climbed to higher elevations, lusher, greener vegetation encroached on the highway.

Daniel stopped in front of a roadside wooden cabin, where a family sold food and drinks on a small table in the yard. Daniel went to an out-building, which obviously was a toilet.

Luz said, "Do you know this, Franklin? It's *cucurucho*."

Franklin laughed. "Not *cucaracha*?"

Luz laughed aloud, slapped him on the shoulder, made a face of disgust, and said, "That's disgusting."

"Try it." She broke off a piece, held it in front of him and waited for his reaction.

He bit into a moist, strangely textured, explosion of smoke-flavored coconut. What a flavor. He needed more. A lot more "I've never had anything even close to this unbelievable delicacy."

"I would say that's correct."

Daniel came up. "You like it?"

"Unbelievable." Franklin unwrapped another, bit and chewed. "The only problem is I can just picture the calories building up." He chomped in again, feeling guiltier with each bite.

"You look like you take care of yourself. This won't hurt you."

He grinned. "If I ate as much of this as I want to and did it more than once, I guarantee you it would have an effect." He tried to take smaller bites as they took off again, but it didn't last long. The smoky, amazing flavor floated through him and the sugar high gave him a buzz.

Eventually, the road began to drop, and the vegetation changed again. As they descended, Franklin saw a town on the coast. "It's Baracoa," Daniel said. They passed along ocean-front concrete buildings, but they'd either not been completely built or were badly damaged from a storm. Daniel said, "Hurricane Sandy destroyed a bit, but then in October Matthew did the rest. This area got it rougher than Siboney."

They stopped at three houses to make distributions as they passed through the quaint village. Finally, they pulled around a little bay fed by an inlet from the ocean. Daniel turned down a tiny one-way street and stopped in front of a two-story home with an open-air terrace on top. "Here's where we stay."

They exited the car, met the matronly hostess, signed in and were assigned three rooms. "You want dinner, as usual, don't you, Daniel? I have some marvelous fish"

"Absolutely. We're going to stop in our rooms, perhaps clean up a bit, grab a beer on the top floor and then make a delivery to one of the guides at *El Yunque*. He's usually not off work this early, but we'll go before dinner."

They met on the roof-top patio and drank mugs of Bucanero. Daniel pointed across the small bay to a flat-topped mountain. "That's *El Yunque*. It's named that because of its shape . . . flat . . . like-an-anvil top. In Columbus' early writings, he describes Cuba as the most beautiful land that humans have seen, and specifically refers to a table-top mountain in this area of Cuba. Scholars believe this is the second place he and his crew landed, and that *El Yunque* is what he described. If we had time, we'd hike up. Maybe on a future trip. They have guides at the base who walk you up. There's a guy in the middle of the hike cutting fresh fruits from within the mountain and serving them up. We wouldn't be able to deliver to the guide in the morning because we have a lot of stops to fulfill by tomorrow night when we finish in Holguín."

They downed their beers and drove down a few streets and across a small, rustic bridge. Daniel pulled up to the log entrance gate. After being admitted by the guard, Daniel drove along a little road among log cabins and stopped in front of one. A tall, tanned, bare-chested, black-haired man came out and hugged Daniel. "Where's Luis?"

Daniel explained.

The man hugged Franklin, saying "I'm Francisco. Pleased to meet you. I hold your father in the greatest esteem and pray for his recovery." Turning to Luz, he said, "And you, young lady, what is your name? You look familiar to me."

"Luz Sierra Nasiff."

"You are from Santiago de Cuba, aren't you?"

"Yes."

"Daughter of Jorge and Lolita?"

"Yes, how do you know?"

"I worked at the university with both of your parents in the past. Your father, God rest his soul, was a brilliant botanist and a wonderful man. How is your mother?"

"She's fine sir. I'll tell her you asked for her."

They finished the delivery and returned to the house. They had another beer on the patio. Then, the meal was brought up from downstairs a few plates at a time. The fish was succulent. The vegetables and fruit were interesting and exquisite.

Franklin gazed at *El Yunque*, as the sun set behind it. Sitting under the stars in this company, with good beer and delicious food, was like heaven. He wished Diana could be here to enjoy it. He looked at Daniel. "So, this is the way my father eats and sleeps every two weeks?"

"Sí."

Chapter 70

Elena Morales Lennox

Monday, December 5, 2016

Elena contacted Manuel Salazar's office from her cell phone as she drove toward the hospital.

"Barker & Cummins. How may I help you?"

"This is Elena Morales Lennox. Is Mr. Salazar available?"

"One moment, please."

Within seconds she heard, "Manuel Salazar."

"This is Elena Lennox, daughter of Luis Morales."

"Yes, I remember."

"At the recent hearing, my lawyers proved what I thought, that they know nothing about what to do."

"What was the nature of the hearing?"

"Whether a temporary emergency guardianship should be created."

"Was there testimony?"

"No, but at tomorrow's hearing there will be."

"Tomorrow?" His voice registered surprise. "Is it a continuation of the prior hearing? How did the judge seem to be leaning?"

"I think he was favorable to our side, except that the guardianship was filed by the same firm that my brother is in."

"I need to see copies of the pleadings. Did the judge issue a ruling?"

"No, just that we should talk and then come back."

"Did you speak at the hearing?"

"I didn't have a chance."

"How do you expect that I could represent you tomorrow without any prior knowledge?"

"I can meet with you and help. I can provide whatever you need."

"I'll need to take testimony of somebody who can describe an emergency. Who would you suggest?"

"Employees. I'll give you names."

"All right, has anything happened since the hearing?"

She shrugged as if he could see her. "My brother, Franklin, gloating like an ass, showed a bunch of documents, as the judge ordered. But we and my step-mother didn't like what he proposed."

"What kind of documents?"

"Like a power of attorney, a trust, things like that."

"Did your lawyers tell you that those documents could give the party named in them priority to serve as guardians?"

"Well, uh, they mentioned it, but didn't think it was so clear."

"I think I told you that last time. It depends on the details, but Franklin seems to have a point."

"Are you giving up before you start?"

"Mrs. Morales, uh, Lennox, I cannot guarantee an outcome. Even if I were inclined to, the Florida Bar forbids me to do so. Right now, I'm not sure if we have much to go on that will override Florida statute. If I had time to truly evaluate it all, I would advise you. But there's no time."

"You don't sound like you are on my side at all."

"If I represent you, I'm definitely on your side, but I can only do what's possible under the law, with the facts that actually exist. And I don't know what all the facts are now. Even after I look at the pleadings, I don't know exactly what happened at the last hearing, so, I cannot say whether this one will go any better. As for the taking of testimony, there's also no time to take the pulse of the witnesses in advance or to issue subpoenas, so we just have to hope the people show, and that they answer the questions the way we want. There's no way to know. You'll have to tell me what I should ask of whom." He hesitated. "But, Mrs. Lennox, I want you to realize that losing the emergency temporary petition is not the end of the line. That is a special additional pleading and hearing. The judges aren't inclined to grant them unless they are certain there's a true emergency. We have to prove there is. Because of the urgent need to engage me, and lack of time for preparation, I must request fifteen hundred dollars today, which will only cover through the hearing tomorrow."

She told him she'd drop off a check and provided information about proposed witnesses.

She drove to the hospital and sat in her car for twenty minutes with the air running, listening to music on her favorite Spanish language station. She would sneak to the room and only enter if neither Sylvia nor Franklin was present.

She trekked into the corridor, signed in, got a visitor ID and made her way to the elevator banks and upward. Every step seemed to come with more deliberation. Her stomach turned summersaults.

Finally, she was at the door. She glimpsed into the room, finding her father alone. She slowly and silently slid into the room. Her father breathed easily. His eyes seemed half open, like before. Suddenly, something told her that he knew she was there. Did his eyes move? Was his breathing increasing in depth and speed?

Watching—listening—she crept closer. She sat and touched him. His wrist seemed to jump. Did it? She blinked her eyes, trying to stop tears. Dammit. No matter how she tried to hold them in, they leaked out and down her cheeks. She had not realized how much she loved her papá.

What *did* he do on his trips to Cuba? What did he feel? What did he remember? Was it really so bad for him to go? Whoa, what was she thinking? Of course it was. It was wrong, wrong, wrong. But now her son and Franklin's son were communicating with family they'd never met on the Island. And Franklin was down there doing what her papá always did. Could it be beneficial to the family there? Was it reasonable to care about them?

No. She'd always heard that Cubans who remained in Cuba did it because they wanted to. If they were too young to know for themselves, their parents had wanted to stay—had wanted the communist government. So, the kids were communists too. That's what the Cuban exile community in Miami always insisted. Those people wanted what they have. Helping them is ridiculous and helps only their government—helps Fidel. Right?

She gazed into his face. Would he really do it if he felt he was helping Fidel? Would he? That can't be what he thinks.

She jolted at a touch on her shoulder and turned to see Sylvia's beseeching smile.

"Elena. I'm pleased that you have come."

Sylvia grabbed Elena's papá's hand. "Honey, aren't you happy that Elena's here? I can see your joy."

Elena felt a tremendous need to escape.

Sylvia said, "Franklin called this morning to check on his father. He's about finished with the route around Cuba."

Sylvia hesitated. Her look dug into Elena. Elena looked past Sylvia at the door.

"Elena, besides your hearing tomorrow, the doctors we engaged to give a second opinion will report, and Franklin will make a presentation. I hope you will come to all."

Elena fled without a word.

Chapter 71

Luis Morales

Cari and I walk the neighborhood with Franklin, each holding one of his hands. We lift him by his arms as he raises his little legs to climb the couple of steps to my parents' porch. My father and the Batista officials confer loudly. I stand near the door of their war room to listen.

One of the men reports. "The sanitation workers are on strike and other workers will be too. Young men dressed in olive-green military uniforms with armbands saying *26th of July* have set the national police headquarters on fire and occupied schools, hotels, the cathedral and the Maritime Police Station. A number of prisoners have escaped from Boniato jail and have joined the local rebels. The intent is to throw us off the expected arrival of the Moncada rebels' boat on the thirtieth of the month. We are certain the boat is going to arrive late, and we are ready."

My father lights a cigar. "What are we doing about it?"

"A wave of our soldiers will converge on possible landing sites."

My father says, "I usually agree with Fulgencio, but letting Fidel Castro and the others out of prison and making them leave the country made it possible to forge alliances with international rebels and plan the attack. Here it is, only a year and a half after they left, and they are coming back!"

My mind shifts a day or so, to November twenty-nine. Late in the morning, we find ourselves at the table with my parents and grandmother, as servants bring in dishes. Father starts on me. "I expected you out on the streets dressed in uniform like the other rebels. Tomorrow is the day of the landing, isn't it? That's why there's so much activity on the streets. Your boatload of thugs is close, isn't it? All these activities you insurgents are carrying on are known to us. We know País has appointed Celia Sánchez to organize insurrection. Oh, yes, and they have named their movement the 'July 26 Movement'. Is that celebrating the life of your brother who died on that date three years ago? Is it celebrating your being arrested with those thugs? I guess not. Your brother was nothing but a soldier of those fools."

He chugs his whiskey. "All these activities, the closing of the universities, the demonstrations, and even the assassinations in Havana last month, are just intended to steer us off track. We know the boat is expected to land tomorrow, and we know where. They intend to scramble into the hills of Sierra Maestra, just like Martí did at the commencement of the War of Independence." He bellows a deep laugh. "Everything they ever do is based on Martí. We know they have vehicles, food, provisions and men waiting for them. We have troops nearby. They'll be destroyed." He laughs again. "I probably shouldn't be telling you this."

I feel his glare. I glance at Cari, who looks uneasy.

He lights his cigar. "That criminal, ex-president, Prío, from his exile in Florida, is funding your Castro brothers and their band of hoodlums. He is behind the money that purchased the boat."

I shake my head. "How do you know that?"

"What? That Prío came up with the money? We have spies in Mexico and on the boat."

I nod. "If your spies are telling you everything, why are you asking me, and why can't they stop the boat from arriving?"

He becomes pensive for a moment. In a hushed tone, he says, "I hope they do."

Our house is a hornet's nest of activity throughout the night, with officials coming and going and conversing on the phone. The men linger around the maps, faces grim.

As the sun rises on the morning of the 30th, the door opens and closes regularly. I hear one saying, "The insurgents have burned two sugar plantations and seized military posts and ammunition depots. The rebellion is occurring in Guantánamo, Holguín and other cities in El Oriente."

The wait for the boat to arrive continues for several days. On December 2, the cooks prepare breakfasts for the group, but the men hardly slow down. The phone line is blazing. Soldiers and other officials keep entering and leaving.

At noon, my father slams the phone receiver down. "It's over," he yells. "We have control again."

When we are alone, my father says, in a loud voice, "I'm sorry about your compatriot rebels. The boat was forced ashore short of the intended landing, in a swamp. The great majority of rebels did not survive. But they believe your leader, his brother and maybe about ten others are still alive and moving up the hills in Sierra Maestra. They didn't get the supplies that were waiting. I hope they don't have enough power to survive."

I escape the room.

A few days after the landing of the rebels, footsteps sound on the tile floor in my grandmother's house. Voices of the usual group of officials echo in the large room.

One of them looks distressed. He announces, "The July 26 Movement has made an encampment in the hills of the Sierra Maestra. Only twelve made it from the boat. But local rebels are joining them, so the force is growing daily. Here are new maps to post."

My father removes maps of the expected initial route of the rebels from the landing area into Sierra Maestra and replaces them with maps and drawings of believed encampments and movement. He and the others stand in front of the maps, talking, pointing and thumbtacking. Then, they consult other maps and documents on the bed and post some of them on the walls.

One says, "We think Raul is here. We think that Argentinian, Ché Guevara, is here. Why'd they bring that guy here anyway? He's not even Cuban."

Again, those voices are replaced by the voices in my sterile, white, hospital room, speaking in English about my health.

Chapter 72

Franklin Morales

After a few stops in and near Baracoa, Franklin, Daniel and Luz cruised along the northern coast toward Holguín. For a while, every time Franklin looked up, he saw the sea, sometimes darker blue, and sometimes a crystal-clear, turquoise blue over white sand. He'd missed the opportunity to go for a run in the morning, and thus was not feeling his usual self. He imagined sugar from that coconut thing building a fat bulge around his midsection.

Suddenly, he began dwelling on Sylvia's and Elena's statements about his arrogance. He'd never thought of himself as being that way. He thought he was nice, friendly and humble. His father certainly was humble. Everybody seemed to love him, and nobody had ever called him arrogant. If he really believed he was his father, he needed to work on that. He needed to change. Humility was the key. No, he really was not that way, was he? He needed to be forever aware of how he acted.

He woke from a doze. The car ground along rough asphalt. He looked to the back seat and found Luz frowning.

"What's the matter Luz?"

She shook her head. "Nothing."

"I can see you are unhappy about something. What is it?"

She sighed. "Last night, I was looking at the Internet and came across the recent article attributed to your father. I see why the Cubans who left did not like it. But I was irritated by some things he said about my country as well."

Franklin turned to her. "What did he say that you found offensive?"

"It's hard to say. It was more of a tone than actual statements. It was like he thinks the way we live is unfortunate, that we are unhappy . . . that there's something wrong with our country . . . that we should be pitied. I love my country. If we Cubans want to criticize our own country, that's fine. But I don't think your father, who left long ago, should be expressing opinions about our country."

Franklin nodded. "I see. You do realize that he considers Cuba his country too. I doubt that he meant it the way you perceived it. He doesn't feel negative. He was trying to express why he feels it's so important to help the people. It's odd that people on both sides of the issues take offense."

"I know. I still love your father. I'm trying to stop feeling offended." She smiled. "Back to business. Next, we are going to Guatemala."

Franklin said, "I hope you don't mean the country."

She and Daniel laughed. Daniel said, "No, it's a small town. And it didn't always have that name. It's a very historic place for somebody from the U.S."

"How is that?"

"It was the main headquarters of the United Fruit Company. Before the Revolution, that company owned more Cuban farmland than all Cubans together. It produced almost all the sugar. This was a town of workers and executives who worked for that company. You will see the same long, wooden houses standing on blocks as were occupied by executives of the company in those days. Back then it had the very non-Cuban name of Preston. Most are bare of paint now, but some have replicated the bright yellow paint of that time."

They entered the town and stopped in front of an unpainted house. Daniel showed Franklin the names of the occupants on the list of donees. An aged light-skinned man with a kind face opened the door. He looked at Franklin. "Oh, no. *Qué pasó con tu papá*?"

"How do you know I'm the son of Luis?"

"Unless I've just stepped back in time twenty years without knowing, you have to be his son. What happened?"

"He's gravely ill, in a hospital in Miami."

"I'm so sorry to hear that. God be with him. Let's have some rum, and toast to his recovery."

Franklin felt compelled to accept the drink. He and the others nodded.

Their host lifted his glass. "To the quick return to good health of Luis. As great a man as there ever has been."

All acknowledged the sentiment, touched glasses and said, "To Luis."

Daniel said, "You worked for United Fruit Company, didn't you?"

"Of course, everybody who lives here did."

"Franklin has a lot of questions about everything, including that. Maybe on a future visit there will be time to inform him."

"Sure, I will. And we'll go through the photo albums."

After leaving the house and stopping in another, Daniel drove down a beat-up dirt and rock road toward the water, where he stopped in front of a much larger structure.

Luz said, "This was the hotel. Let's walk around and look in the windows."

They walked through tall weeds around the bare, wooden, three-story building, looking through holes that once had been glass-covered windows and windows that still had thin, dirty glass inside faded-white frames. Franklin imagined what the United Fruit Company executives and their families from the United States experienced when staying here.

"Look," Luz said. "A touch of the same shade of yellow paint as we saw on houses."

They gazed into a large room, still containing couches, large chairs, tables and lamps. Franklin said, "Looks like somebody has been living here, and maybe still is."

Luz nodded.

As Daniel drove along a dirt road, avoiding large holes, he said, "Next, we go to the opposite side of this large water body. The town of Banes was the birthplace of Batista. They sometimes called him *El mulato lindo de Banes*. Sometimes, they just said the good-looking *mulato*, referring to his genetic history including African blood, but other times they added his birthplace to the moniker."

They drank coffee in a little farmhouse outside of town, which helped Franklin regain his energy. Daniel said, "Franklin, do you know anything about the coffee that's available to most of us here?"

"What do you mean?"

"When we Cubans buy our coffee, it's mixed with *chicharo*. Do you know what that is?"

Franklin shook his head.

Luz said "Chick peas."

Franklin said, "That doesn't sound very tasty, but if it was in the coffee I just drank, I didn't notice anything odd."

Daniel said, "Yes, you don't taste it, but it makes it milder. See the small holes in the ceiling and walls." He held up the metal espresso pot. "When one prepares coffee with this type of pot the pieces of chick pea expand and can get stuck in the holes, sometimes causing the pot to explode. That's what happened here."

Franklin looked at the holes, amazed, and realized the pot had just been used. "I guess that doesn't happen too often. Do they always flee the room while making coffee?"

Daniel laughed. "Like many things in Cuba, we do not become overly concerned about the unusual standards of our daily lives."

They finished their business and left for the next stops, along the route to Holguín. They stopped at a plain-looking group of buildings on the main highway in Guardalavaca. Daniel said, "Your father likes to change clothes in one of this family's extra apartments, spend a half an hour in the ocean, eat some pizza in a beach-front café, shower and change again, and then continue on the route. Would you like to do that?"

"Whatever he likes to do, I want to do. But I don't have a bathing suit, t-shirt or anything like that."

Luz said, "I didn't bring a swimsuit either."

"Franklin, your father has clothing here, so he doesn't have to take a wet suit on the plane. They always wash his clothes and keep them here."

The owner found a one-piece for Luz to swim in and provided Franklin one of his father's bathing suits.

Daniel drove them to the beach area. They walked to the end of a walkway and looked down on a wide beach packed with Cubans of all races and ages. Daniel pointed upward, to the left. "That's La Maison, the restaurant I mentioned. You can imagine the view. We will eat there on a future visit."

As they trudged along the soft, brown-speckled sand, next to clear, light-blue, lightly-lapping water, they spotted a shaded place, beneath a large tree, where several families and groups of young people sat around, some cooking fish over burning branches.

They laid their things on the ground and walked to the shore. The water was delicious, lukewarm and clear. The sandy bottom gave under Franklin's feet. Luz swam. Daniel joined them and sat in the water. Franklin floated on his back in the baking sun, looking at the clear, blue sky and thinking of home—and his papá.

After a while, they returned to the car, drove back to the apartment, showered, dressed and departed, wrenching themselves away from the owner's tears and love about Franklin's papá.

Forty-five minutes later, they were in the next home and a few hours later, they arrived in Holguín.

Luz asked to stop in the bus station to see if she could reserve a bus the following morning. Daniel took Franklin to one *casa particular* and Luz to another. He went to his own home and, in the evening, picked them up and took them to a restaurant, named 1910. Daniel ate churrasco; Luz ate filet mignon and Franklin ate fish. Franklin said, "I have a cholesterol problem, so I rarely eat red meat."

Luz said, "This beef is so tender. I must say I've never eaten meat like this. My God, it's delicious." She grinned like a child." Can I travel with you in the future?"

Daniel pulled out his phone and showed the screen to Franklin, "When you are home, put the application *IMO* on your phone so we can video chat and exchange messages like texts when we are connected to the Internet, which is not so hard or expensive in the city of Holguín."

Franklin wrote notes.

Franklin said, "Mi papá told me that when he started coming here, the food was always terrible, and he became ill many times, but that the products have improved, and, with so many private eating establishments giving competition, even some state restaurants have improved."

Daniel laughed. "Yes, quite a few times it took us extra days to make the route because your father was out of commission."

They spoke of future plans and Luz's involvement. After dinner, they drove her to the home where she would stay and bid her goodbye. She assured them she could walk the three blocks to the bus station in the morning.

Chapter 73

Sylvia Morales

Tuesday, December 6, 2016

Sylvia sat outside the courtroom, tapping her foot rapidly as she waited for her attorney.

Roosevelt and Jude glanced around, apparently wondering where Franklin was. Then they stepped into the courtroom.

Mr. Warnock arrived and took a seat next to her on the bench, breathing roughly. "Good morning, Sylvia." He took more breaths.

"Good morning."

Franklin rushed up, also seeming out of breath, but in a much healthier way than Mr. Warnock. He nodded to Sylvia and started toward the door, then stopped and turned. He walked over and sat beside her, on the opposite side from Mr. Warnock, leaning close. "I mean what I say, Sylvia. You have nothing to worry about if this guardianship doesn't go through. But even if it does, a trust generally stands alone, so you have nothing to worry about there either. It does not fall within the jurisdiction of the guardianship court. All will be the same as far as you are concerned, regardless." He looked at Warnock. "Do you concur about treatment of a trust in a guardianship, Crandall?"

Mr. Warnock nodded. "Yes, a trust generally continues unaffected."

Sylvia said, "Thank you, Franklin. I'm not worried. How was the trip?"

He smiled. "Actually, it was enlightening and refreshing. You would be amazed at how mi papá is loved there. If it wasn't for their immigration officials mistrusting me, and our immigration officials mistrusting me, and a couple of Cubans who really don't appreciate us going there, it would have been the best trip ever."

"The immigration officials mistrusted you?"

"I think the Cuban officials think I work for the CIA or the U.S. government or something. But they seemed satisfied when they realized I work for a law firm. And they also knew all about my father. And this morning when I arrived home, a Cuban-American immigration official glared at me and treated me like I was a criminal for having gone. It was uncomfortable."

"Luis has never told me about any such problems, although he doesn't tell much at all. I think I'd like to go sometime and meet these people who love him so."

Elena strutted up with a very handsome, young man with Latino features, dressed in a dark-blue suit.

Franklin stood. "Good morning, Elena." He moved as though to kiss her on the cheek, but she shifted away.

Franklin looked at the man.

The man grinned and held out a hand. "You must be Franklin. I don't believe we've met. I'm Manuel Salazar, Elena's counsel."

Franklin nodded. "Can we speak?"

The man shrugged his shoulders. Franklin motioned for Warnock to join them, and they moved around the corner. Shortly, they returned, and Franklin went into the courtroom.

Sylvia grabbed her bag, and, as she stood, said "Mr. Warnock, I'm on Franklin's side. All you have to do is be sure I understand anything significant and step in if necessary to give our support for counteracting the guardianship. We are not opposing Franklin and his crew, okay?"

He nodded.

A sheriff's deputy called the case.

Chapter 74

Franklin Morales

Franklin and Jude whispered to each other as they shuffled files and papers. The Bailiff called for all to rise as Judge Reynolds entered his courtroom and sat.

The judge announced, "We are here again on the petition to appoint an emergency temporary guardian in the case of Mr. Luis Morales, filed by Elena Morales Lennox. The attorney who originally filed the petitions, Mr. Braxton Doolittle, is not in the Courtroom. I see on the computer docket that Mr. Manuel Salazar has filed a notice of appearance. I do not find a motion to substitute counsel. Mr. Salazar, what is going on?"

Salazar stood. "Your honor, Ms. Lennox has terminated her prior counsel and engaged me to represent her."

The judge said, "Is this your wish Ms. Lennox?"

"Yes, your honor, I terminated my prior counsel and engaged Mr. Salazar."

"Very well," the judge said. "This is an evidentiary hearing called in order for petitioner to prove existence of an emergency. If I find there to be an emergency, I may appoint an emergency temporary guardian. It appears there is no longer a conflict of interest since Ms. Lennox' new lawyer is not part of Morales and Doolittle." The judge focused on Franklin. "Franklin, are you now acting as attorney in opposing the petition?"

Franklin rose. "Your honor, just to avoid more confusion, and because I may have to testify, I will have Mr. Armstrong here represent me."

"Fine," the judge said. "Please proceed, Mr. Salazar."

Salazar gave a brief opening statement, explaining how certain critical matters of the law firm required Mr. Luis Morales's input. Then, he said that both his client, Elena Morales Lennox and Mr. Luis Morales' wife, Sylvia Morales, were destitute and had no knowledge of what was going on.

Jude and Franklin shook their heads. Franklin caught the judge looking at him, waiting for an objection. Sylvia looked at Warnock, and both looked at Franklin.

Mr. Warnock rose. The judge nodded at him. "Your honor, I just want to state on behalf of my client, Sylvia Morales, that Mr. Salazar has no authority to speak as to my client's position on this matter."

The judge appeared perplexed. He said, "Okay. Mr. Armstrong, would you like to give an opening?"

Jude stood. "Your Honor, you already very astutely described the situation at the previous hearing. I do not know why we are here again. You specifically instructed us to meet with Mrs. Lennox and Mrs. Morales in order to attempt to resolve issues prior to returning here to take your time. We set a meeting, but Elena Lennox marched out before we had a chance to present much. We have tried to show the parties existing documents that will resolve all matters and are the least restrictive means."

The judge frowned. "Is that true, Mr. Salazar?"

Mr. Salazar got to his feet, glanced at his client with a hint of surprise on his face, and stated to the Court, "I was not officially engaged until yesterday, and I know nothing about the meeting."

The judge frowned. "Did your client refuse to participate?"

Salazar winced and looked confused.

Jude rose and said, "Would you like me to elicit testimony from Franklin Morales about what occurred at the meeting?"

The judge said, "Since the petitioner does not seem to have anything to offer about my request, I will hear from Mr. Morales."

The clerk took Franklin's oath. After Franklin identified himself for the record, Jude asked, "Would you please describe the meeting you arranged in an attempt to resolve the matter?"

Salazar jumped up. "Objection. Settlement negotiations are not admissible."

The judge said, "Overruled. The meeting was based on my instruction and was not a settlement negotiation."

Franklin tried not to smile. "Yes, your honor. I scheduled a meeting and invited all the parties. I showed pertinent pages of all the relevant documents, including my father's trust, durable power of attorney, and health care documents. Elena Lennox became irate and left early, as did Mr. Doolittle and Mr. Lennox, whom she fired during the meeting. We continued the meeting with my father's wife, Sylvia Morales and her attorney.

"We've handled everything with these documents up to now. Neither Elena Lennox's current attorney, nor her previous attorney has asked us for copies of those documents. Although Mr. Doolittle and Mr. Lennox were present during the part of the meeting, they said nothing. There is no emergency."

The judge turned to Mr. Warnock, who stood. "Your Honor, as you may recall at the previous hearing, we indicated we didn't have a strong feeling one way or the other as to whether there should be a guardianship at all, or an emergency temporary guardianship, but if there was to be one, we did not believe that Elena Lennox was the proper person to be the guardian. We are still of the opinion that no guardianship is necessary and re-raise our objection to Elena Lennox serving as guardian. I concur that Mr. Morales did display those documents and did satisfy us in all ways possible that Louis Morales's health and well-being are being addressed properly, that Mrs. Morales's interests are well protected and that her current financial situation is not in any jeopardy."

The judge said, "Mr. Salazar, do you have witnesses to provide testimony regarding the existence of the alleged emergency?"

Salazar stood. "We call Mrs. Betty Olson, the office bookkeeper of Morales and Doolittle, to the stand. She is in the hallway."

Franklin rose. "Your honor, I ask that this witness be excluded from the courtroom until we can discuss whether she should be permitted to testify."

The judge said to the bailiff, "Leave her in the hallway until I can hear counsel."

Jude said, "Your honor, we object to this witness being called. First, we've had no prior notice in order for us to learn the nature of the inquiry or to prepare for cross examination. We object on the basis of her qualification to testify as to firm matters, and we object to her relaying possibly confidential matters in open court. It is not appropriate for Ms. Olson to be interrogated about firm finances at all."

The judge looked at Warnock, who rose and said, "Your Honor, I would tend to agree with Franklin."

The judge drilled in on Salazar. "What exactly is the issue that you are hoping that Ms. Olson can shed light upon?"

"Your Honor," Salazar said, swiping hair off his forehead, "the law firm Morales and Doolittle is in financial straits . . . "

Jude jumped to his feet, grinning and holding back a chuckle. "Objection, Your Honor. How can this man say the law firm is in financial straits? This is a busy law firm. It has never suffered any kind of financial problems. The firm pays its bills. It pays its employees. It pays the attorneys, including the partners. It is prepared to distribute Mr. Morales' income to Sylvia Morales. There simply is nothing to that statement."

"Well," Salazar huffed, "this is not my understanding. I have spoken to Miss Olson. She has confirmed that sometimes there is some difficulty in producing checks in a timely manner, especially now that Mr. Morales is unavailable."

"Objection, hearsay"

"But, Judge," Salazar said, "you asked what we intend to . . . "

"Sustained. You cannot testify. I rule that the testimony of Ms. Olson is inappropriate, irrelevant and unnecessary, and therefore inadmissible. Call your next witness."

Salazar looked exasperated. "I call Mr. Braxton Doolittle."

Franklin turned to find Doolittle had entered the courtroom and was sitting in the back.

"Oh, dear God," Franklin muttered under his breath.

Doolittle approached the witness stand and sat. Salazar said, "Mr. Doolittle, what is the total annual income to the firm?"

"Objection," said Jude. "Irrelevant. Your Honor, this line of questioning is inappropriate. Proving the firm's income can't show an emergency."

Salazar said, "Of course it can when we show that it has declined, and we examine the expenses."

Franklin said, "Your Honor, we have operated this firm for many years. I already explained that we do not have any financial problems or financial crises and asking such wild questions in public about our private finances is inappropriate and irrelevant. There is no difference since my father's crisis. Therefore, I repeat my objection."

The judge said, "Franklin, you are not the attorney and are not giving testimony at this time."

"I apologize, Your Honor."

The judge said, "Mr. Salazar, see if you can find something else to ask that might be appropriate."

Salazar sighed. "Okay. Mr. Doolittle, who's in charge of the law firm?"

Doolittle said, "Well, Louis Morales is the president of the law firm. Therefore, he is in charge. I am the vice president of the firm, and therefore I am set to take over for Louis Morales in his absence or death."

Franklin knew that he himself was also a vice president, of equal stature with Doolittle, but chose to hold that thought for cross-examination.

Salazar continued, "And Mr. Doolittle, are you able to effectively run the law firm in Mr. Morales's absence?"

Doolittle looked at him skeptically, tossed his head and said, "Well, yes. I actually act as vice president quite often."

Franklin wanted to laugh out loud. He put a hand over his mouth and glanced at the others at his table. They all suffered to hold in their delight.

Salazar looked perturbed. "I understood that there was some big problem administering the firm in Mr. Morales's absence. Is that correct?"

Doolittle hesitated, and then quietly responded, "Well, no. Not really. We have documentation such as stock powers, other officers who can handle things, an active board of directors and so on. We're doing fine."

Franklin had to fight to keep from laughing.

"Mr. Salazar," the Judge said, "Your witness seems to have backfired on you. Do you have anything at all to show that there is some emergency? You're wasting the court's time."

Salazar looked around and said, "Yes, I call…uh…. Your Honor, may I confer with my client for a few minutes?"

"Certainly." The judge waved his hand and said in a flippant tone, "We have nothing to do. Just go right ahead and confer with your client for as long as you need to. We'll just be waiting here."

Salazar ushered Elena out the door. His harsh voice poured through the door. She answered just as harshly. Her words, "You are fired, Mr. Salazar," swirled around the large courtroom. After more loud words, they returned. Elena looked livid.

Salazar said, "Your Honor, I have been discharged as the attorney for Elena Morales Lennox. Consequently, I withdraw my notice of appearance and ask the court to release me. As I called this hearing, I hereby end my argument, unless the court wishes for Ms. Elena Morales Lennox to continue it on her own."

Through gritted teeth, Elena said, "You people. This system. This non-system. I will be back. I am going to take over. I am." She marched out.

Everybody in the room, including the judge, glanced around, amusement in their eyes.

Chapter 75

Luis Morales

The new doctors are back in the room, examining me again, for the umpteenth time. I've had more visits from them in about two days than I've had from all other doctors combined since I've been here. Franklin and his crew and Sylvia all show up.

Roosevelt, says, "Do you have conclusions ready for the meeting?"

I see Sylvia tense and shift. I know exactly what will be coming next if anybody says anything about my health. But I'm not so interested in what they say. I drift.

My father and the Batista officials have commandeered the family radio box as they do twice a day. They sit on beds and chairs, frequently jumping to their feet as they strain to make out the details of rebel transmissions. I have gotten tired of escaping every time this group is here, because that is all the time.

Somebody knocks on the door. My father nods to me, as a sign that I am to answer it. Opening the door, I find two of the officials who regularly visit. They know where the others are, and, even if they didn't, the loud radio transmission of Radio Rebelde would guide them. As the men enter, my father looks up, part frowning and part smiling, and waves with both arms toward the radio. "The rebels have gotten a generator and are going to show their hands by announcing their actions on the radio."

I stay in the room to listen. My father adjusts the radio dial. A scratchy tone sounds. Then, in a bold but distant voice, "*Aquí Radio Rebelde,* the voice of the Sierra Maestra, transmitting for all Cuba on the twenty-meter band at five and nine p.m. daily." The national anthem and the *26th of July* hymn play.

Many transmissions mix in my head since I've begun joining the crowd to listen every night. The announcer recites recent battles won and locations of rebel groups in the Sierra Maestra.

My father jumps up. "What idiots. They are telling us. Are you getting it? Write it down."

One of the men scribbles, saying, "How do we know it's true? We can never find them."

Scratch, scratch, static. "Five citizens have been killed in Bayamo. Government planes strafed innocent citizens."

I have trouble imagining planes strafing since I have never seen or heard of anything like that happening. The citizens here in Santiago de Cuba do whisper about the scruffy, unshaven rebels sometimes coming down from the mountains to kill their enemies. But I also have trouble picturing that really happening.

One of the officials taps my father on the shoulder. "The *barbudos* shot three of our men last night on Alameda."

I pick up one of the international periodicals my father has amassed. It shows photographs of the rebels in the woods of the Sierra Maestra. Looking at a photograph on the cover of Paris Match from some months ago, showing Fidel Castro sitting among bushes pointing a gun, I wonder why the government allows these magazines to be sold, and how these foreign journalists and photographers can get so close to the revolutionaries, when our standing government cannot seem to do anything to stop them.

The meetings at our house become more frequent, with more intense discussions. My father speaks by phone with General Batista almost daily. One day, I hear my father say, "It does not seem to me that the rebels have as much power and support as they indicate. I find it hard to believe your ouster is imminent." After a pause, my father continues. "Yes, I know about the battles in which they've prevailed and the villages they are said to control. At least I know what they say about such things. I do not believe that their attacks and holdings are significant."

Whether other officials join him or not, the scratch, scratch. ". . . *Aquí Radio Rebelde,* the voice of the Sierra Maestra," echoes through the tiled home twice every single day.

One day, an announcer says, "Batista has taken control of the public media. The newspapers and radio will not tell you what you need to know about the July 26 Movement. The Movement is gaining strength and taking control of the country, piece by piece. You need to listen to what we announce, because it is the truth."

The announcer states that Batista is committing more atrocities, that the rebels have killed a large number of government troops, that the rebels have lost a few good soldiers, that the rebels have control of a village or have made inroads on certain areas and that Ché Guevara's column of revolutionaries has battled in Pino del Agua.

One evening, the announcer introduces Fidel Castro. Castro begins with words from the speech I heard him create and hone both in the jail cell where we were held before the final court rulings and later in the prison at Isle of Pines, as he put the words to paper, seemingly changing certain aspects.

His voice increases in volume as he reaches the part of the manifesto that accuses the Batista government. I'm back in the prison with him as he forcefully announces, "As the trial went on, the roles were reversed; those who came to accuse found themselves accused, and the accused became the accusers! It was not the revolutionaries who were judged there; judged once and forever was a man named Batista—*monstruum horrendum*!"

Castro swerves around from topic to topic, sometimes maintaining silence about things my father and the other officials want to know and sometimes bragging about successes they have had against the Batista troops.

One late afternoon, Castro announces on the radio, "We know that the hapless Batista army officials are listening, waiting for me to say something useful to them. I'm not that ignorant. But I will say that if you think you know from where the primary radio signal is transmitted, you are wrong. It's been moved." He laughs.

My father bounces from his seat angrily. "God damn it." He grabs the phone and dials. "How do we find this damn radio transmission location? They are making fools of us."

After silence, he continues, "I know. But how do they keep moving the whole transmission system around?"

I hear the voice of David Armstrong. I look around. There's nobody here. His voice remains in my head, almost an hour after he has left the room. I realize that it's the voice and the manner of speaking that affects me. He sounds just like his father. There's something about the delivery. It's soothing.

My father has beseeched me to join him in Havana in the fall of 1958. I've left Cari, Franklin and young Elena, for the first time.

In our hotel, my father harangues me. "We are going for a meal with some of the people we met years ago in Daytona Beach, Florida in the United States. Fulgencio has invited them. Do not let on that you were involved in the Moncada Attack or were in prison with those boys. Be gracious with General Batista."

I wonder why Batista invited people from Daytona Beach. Perhaps he anticipates losing the government and wants to assure that he can return there if he does. I honestly do not remember meeting any adults that evening at Batista's house in Daytona Beach. I spoke no English and still do not.

As we enter the Presidential Palace, guards smile and greet my father by name. Soon, we are in the presence of General Batista. He embraces my father and then turns to me. "Young Luis. Well, you are not so young any more. I have not seen you in quite a while."

He winks knowingly at my father. Something about the look causes me to come to the conclusion that Batista knows all about my having been involved in the Moncada attack and being convicted, and that he is the reason for my extra-early release.

Seven or eight men dressed in suits enter. I don't recall any, but I can tell by the way they walk that they are not Cuban. Then they speak English.

I stand awkwardly as the visitors are introduced. One is the Mayor of the City of Daytona Beach and others are members of the city commission. A couple of interpreters try to help out.

We are served a delicious meal. President Batista gives a speech in which he welcomes the group and talks of Daytona Beach and Havana being sister cities.

Later, the visitors make speeches, which are translated by interpreters. Batista's army marches to the tune of a drum and presents arms. Batista signs some official documents and delivers them to the visitors. My father whispers to me that Batista has transferred a home and some items to Daytona Beach.

This entire event seems rather surreal, especially considering that the revolutionaries are said to be making great inroads into taking over the Cuban government.

Throughout the summer and fall of 1958, my father and the others keep a log of all the reports from the rebels and Batista's army, thumbtacking onto a map on the wall torn pieces of paper, showing locations of encampments within Sierra Maestra and battles in the areas in and around Santiago de Cuba. On the slips of paper, they write the dates of events, codes to indicate what occurred, such as whether the insurgents or government forces prevailed in a battle, or which has gained control.

In December, I'm sitting at the table, as usual, with my father. The reports of battles and the rebel's taking control mount. Very few officials now come around. My father hasn't shaved, showered or changed clothes for days. He totters like an old man, his drawn face looking like he's constantly ready to cry. He's no longer harassing me or saying that Batista's government remains in power.

One of the regulars comes in, shrugs his shoulders and sits. "Batista has decided to give up. He's still petitioning the United States to return there. He has his wife and kid in the home in Daytona Beach writing letters to Eisenhower. But it doesn't seem likely he'll be able to return even though the officials of Daytona Beach truly seem to like him. He's developed several plans as to where he will go."

My father drops his closed fist on the table, but with no force. He shakes his head. "How could he? He's listening to the rebel's reports of success. Why does he listen to those lies?"

Days later, on January 1, 1959, my father says, "He's left. He's given up. Coward."

Two hours later, I stand with my disillusioned, unshaven and disheveled father in Parque Céspedes, below the balcony of the Ayuntamiento, amidst a large, jubilant crowd, as Fidel Castro and his men, all heavily bearded and dressed in olive-green army fatigues and caps, gather. Castro thrusts his fist in the air and proclaims victory.

The crowd yells, "Fidel! Fidel! Down with the assassin Batista!"

My father squeezes my arm unmercifully and mutters, "Lies, all lies."

In the following days, Radio Rebelde continues to transmit, describing victory speeches to wild, exuberant crowds as the victorious rebel army moves northwesterly, toward Havana. My father sits, hollow-eyed and unmoving as announcers talk and talk of the takeover. Within a few days, Radio Rebelde announces that the army has finally arrived in Havana to the largest of the crowds lining the streets, cheering and greeting the bearded, long-haired soldiers of the Revolution. The television broadcasts a long, long, live speech by Fidel Castro.

One afternoon in February, the Revolutionary Guard arrives at my parents' home in Vista Alegre. Our mother allows them to enter. I move Cari, Franklin and baby Elena into a back bedroom. The soldiers talk loudly as they yank drawers open, pull out the contents representing a lifetime of normal living and throw them to the ground. They slam drawers shut and drag the large furniture away from walls, making horrible noise as the wood scrapes across the tile floors. They feel the furniture for false backs and false bottoms and run their hands along walls and the floor.

I watch my father standing, watching blankly. I decide to inquire as to who or what they are after, although I know. "What are you looking for? I was imprisoned as a Revolutionary after the Moncada Attack along with our leader, Fidel Castro. Why would the new government be concerned about me?"

The soldier does not answer. He aims a pistol at my father. "You are under arrest for crimes against the Revolution, as a henchman of Batista."

My father stutters. "I . . . I have never . . ."

They take him away, leaving us standing in the papers and the mess, shaken by our mother's wailing.

Chapter 76

Elena Morales Lennox

Wednesday, December 7, 2016

Elena sat in her car in the hospital parking lot, far from the nearest overhead light. Finally, she could visit her father without Sylvia and Franklin listening and examining her. Visiting hours had ended at nine. The number of people leaving was dwindling. She exited the car, walked briskly to the main entrance and entered. Rather than walk straight past the now-dark reception desk, she turned down a hallway and entered a restroom.

Standing in front of the mirror, she regarded herself. Dear Lord. Why had she even looked? Wrinkles. Dryness. Sagging jowls. Bags under, and almost surrounding, her eyes, dark and heavy. Her hair, dry and unruly. Gray roots overriding the dark. She backed up. Ugh. She looked like a box. She pulled out the visitor's pass from her last visit, on which she'd changed the date with a marker, and affixed it above her breast.

She opened the door, glanced both ways and slid out. She crept down the hall, glanced around the corner at the main hallway, positioned her shoulders, set her determined face and walked like she belonged there.

An elevator door opened. A young woman dressed in scrubs exited without looking at her. She entered, hit the button for her papá's floor and breathed. At his floor, she again glanced both ways, stepped out, and, as quietly as possible, made her way toward his room. His door stood open. She moved inside and closed it behind her. Immediately, she heard from outside the door, "Ma'am. Visiting hours ended at nine, Ma'am."

The woman knocked on the thick door. Elena crossed her arms above her head and leaned against the door, her feet in what she hoped would be a strong stance. The handle turned. The door pushed against her. She turned sideways and pressed against the door with her hip and shoulder.

"Ma'am. Ma'am. Open the door. Margie, call security. I don't know what this woman is doing in there."

"Who is it?"

"I don't know."

Demands kept coming through the door. A man said, "Ma'am, I'm going to have to force the door open. Stand back."

She moved away from the door and cowered by the window. The door opened, and the security guard and three attendants rushed in.

Elena's voice came out weak and squeaky. "Please, let me just spend a few minutes with my father."

One of the female nurses said, in a rough voice, "You should have come during permitted hours."

Elena thought her papá jerked. She pointed. "Did you see him move? He wants me here."

The other nurse nodded at her. Maybe she had seen too. She approached Elena. "Ma'am, what's your name?" She put a hand on her shoulder.

"Elena Morales. I'm his daughter."

The nurse waved her arm. "You all can leave. I'll stay here with her for a few."

"Thank you," Elena said, choking on a sob.

The nurse led her to the chair. Elena sat and tentatively put her hand over her father's. The nurse puttered around, checking things and making notes.

"Papá, I hope you are not hurting."

Tears poured out. How peaceful it was to be here with him alone. She looked into his withered face, trying to see his look from the past. She thought his hand bounced beneath hers. She backed up and stared. Could it be?

"Miss Morales, it's time to go. Say your goodbyes for now. You can return during visiting hours."

Elena placed her head on her papá's midsection and sobbed. "*Te quiero,* papá. I love you so much."

The nurse helped her up and to the door. The compassion in her face was so welcome. "Thank you. Thank you." Elena hugged her. "You were so kind."

Chapter 77

Luis Morales

Cari's sister Isabela proudly proclaims, *"Viva la Revolucón!"*

Cari looks like she's about to take little Franklin out of the room. Cari's brother Alejandro says, "Isabela, would you stop with that stupid pro-Revolution sentiment? Things are no better now. We've been tricked. I cannot believe we fell for the promise that the Revolution would improve our lives. Now, a year after the revolutionary government has taken hold, and things are no better. In fact, they are worse."

Isabela says, "You are so wrong." She turns to me. "Luis, what do you think?"

I clench my teeth. I prefer to keep my thoughts to myself. "As you know, I have never been a follower of either the current or the previous government."

Alejandro says, "The atrocities committed by Batista and even his predecessors pale in comparison to those committed by the new revolutionary government."

Isabela glares at him. "What are you talking about? The revolutionary government kills no innocent people. Counterrevolutionaries, especially violent ones, of course can be killed."

Alejandro turns to me. "I bet the rich people of your part of the city are unhappy. The United States companies are losing their property and businesses. True? Who knows how to run those companies?"

Isabela laughs. "I'm sure our people can handle a sugar mill."

Alejandro says, "The government now will begin taking family farmland. Isabela, soon, the government will be taking your florist shop."

"Don't be silly, Alejandro. The government would have no use for a small business."

My stomach churns with anxiety.

Alejandro continues his focus on her. "Sister, are you making as much money as before?"

"Our income has declined because our customers do not have as much money. But we all have to endure sacrifices for the people. That's what a Revolution is. For the people. The literacy movement is making inroads. Education and medical treatment are free. We have *la libreta*, which provides our needs at very reduced prices."

Alejandro looks sad. "Well, not everybody is happy. People are leaving."

I sit silently, thinking of my neighbors who have disappeared like that. Franklin says there are fewer students in school every day. His school will close for lack of students.

Isabela looks at us. "Luis, Cari, don't you have anything to say? Cari, don't you find things better?"

Cari doesn't like talking about politics either. She shakes her head. "And you, Luis?"

"I am worried. That's all I will say about it."

Isabela smirks. "It's because of what happened to you and your brother that makes you not a fan of Fidel."

I sigh. "What happened to us in 1953 is in the past. I think the government is trying to do the right thing. Whether or not I personally agree with all aspects of it is irrelevant. I don't see a positive future, but I did not see a positive future before the Revolution either."

As the other two continue to banter, I consider whether it's time to get Cari and the children out of the country and to make a new home someplace else.

I wonder whether my criminal history and whom I was alleged to support will cause me problems gaining entry into another country, continuing my education, or working.

Alejandro is staring at me again. "Luis, do you agree?"

"Huh? Uh, sorry."

"Lost in your own world, as usual. Isabela was saying that the Revolution has at its base the teachings of José Martí. I argued that every government has said that, and it means nothing. They say it because the people will follow if they use his name."

I somewhat agree with Alejandro on this count but decide not to say so. I say, "Martí was a great man. He espoused freedom and human rights. Following his beliefs cannot be wrong."

Alejandro bangs his hand again, reminding me of my father, which is not a pleasant recollection. "That's not the point. What I'm saying is that the revolutionary government says it is based on his teachings, but what it is doing is the opposite."

I shake my head. "I don't want to debate this."

"You never want to discuss anything important."

"Discussing it doesn't accomplish anything."

Isabela says, "Fidel has made all the beaches and private clubs public and outlawed discrimination based on race. Dark-skinned and light-skinned people are together now. That's following Martí's teachings."

I revert to my own thoughts. I try to think of a country where I can practice law. I have begun to study English in earnest, spending hours in the library, devouring every book that I can find, especially legal books. I read and try to understand the slang and chummy descriptions in those awful gossip magazines the U.S. travelers left behind when the casinos were shut down and the hotels taken over.

A few weeks later, I'm sitting with Cari late one evening, after days of struggling with a gut-wrenching decision, I take Cari's hand. "Cari, I do not believe our homeland will succeed under the new regime. I believe I should go and try to make a new life for us. I want to apply to attend a seminar in Panama."

Cari silently weeps. "You intend to leave me and the children?"

"Not to leave you, just to go and try to make a new home, in Panama or someplace else, and then have you join me."

She nods, crying.

Days later, we are visiting my father as he languishes in prison. He twitches nervously when guards are close.

I point to a thin, still-healing scar on his face and another on his wrist. *"¿Qué pasó, papá?"*

He shakes his head. *"Nada."*

He immediately starts asking about everybody at home. He whispers a question to my mother about whether anybody has come to

323

the house to interrogate or harass us. She shakes her head to indicate no.

I tell him about my plan.

He scowls. "You've changed your position."

"Papá, you know it's not true."

My father nods.

I whisper. "The government has begun to crack down on everybody who wishes to exit the country. I'm only afraid that if I leave I will never see you again, but I feel I have to leave to open the road to free my wife and children."

My father looks at me, more interested than usual.

My mother says, "Try to make a home for Cari and the children."

My father smiles and waves his hand around. "I may never leave here anyway."

My mother looks at Cari, "What about your parents?"

Tears roll down Cari's face. "My parents want us to make a life for our children, which means not sending them alone to live with an unknown family in the United States, like others are doing."

That same evening, I tell Cari I need to discuss something.

Tears seep from her eyes.

I sigh. "I think we need to send Franklin away too. I keep hearing word on the streets that the new government is preparing to send six and seven-year-old children to Russia."

She hisses, "No. I will not permit you to ship Franklin off on a plane to who-knows-where in the U.S. to stay with who-knows-who, through that *Pedro Pan* project. To possibly be placed with criminals, or at least with people who don't speak Spanish or know our culture. *NO!*"

I'm shocked by her outburst, the most vehement she's ever been about anything. "No, Cari, I think it's best to send him to Spain, to stay in a boarding school, connected to our church. Alejandro is considering sending Luisa to a girl's school there at the same time."

I again feel that I've shifted my body with anxiety. I realize that Sylvia and Franklin are sitting with me, without discord, holding my hands. It puts me at peace.

Cari and I hold hands as we enter Franklin's room to inform him.

His voice trembles. "What do you mean, papá? Will I be alone?"

"Yes, son. Your cousin Maria Luisa will travel with you, but she'll be in a different school. You'll be in Toledo. She will be in Madrid. I hope that in a very short time I will be able to reunite us."

Franklin begins to cry, and I place my hand over his tiny one. "All right, papá, I will do as you say."

Now, in the hospital room, Franklin's strong grip surrounds my bony hand.

Chapter 78

Franklin Morales

Franklin, Jude, Roosevelt and George Murphy finished a meal at Roasted Oak.

Mr. Murphy said, "It's delicious."

Jude said, "My father and some others founded a restaurant in Daytona in the seventies. They beseeched Roosevelt to work for them."

"And," Roosevelt said, "When Jude was in his twenties, he invented the unique cooking mechanism."

"It's very, very good. I'll be back," said Mr. Murphy.

Roosevelt smiled broadly. "Thank you. I'm glad you liked it."

Franklin said, "My father left us a letter asking us to go to the office and locate some hidden documents."

Since Franklin's Porsche wouldn't hold more than one passenger, Roosevelt joined him. Jude went with Mr. Murphy in his truck.

Jude said to Roosevelt, "I'm riding in the Porsche on the way back."

Roosevelt laughed. "All right."

Outside the office parking garage, Franklin hit the button to open the gate, and they drove up the ramp, the Porsche's powerful engine humming in the hollow confines of the garage and tires squeaking on the slick concrete.

As they rounded the last turn, Franklin said, "Interesting. That's my brother-in-law's car."

Roosevelt smiled. "Wow. Somebody's actually working after hours? Isn't it a typical big-city firm with lawyers billing more hours than there are in a day?"

Franklin smiled. "We bill only real hours, and Kalvin would never come close to the number of hours he's even supposed to work. I wonder whose Toyota that is."

The men climbed out of the vehicles. Jude stooped behind the truck, brushing his clothes with his hands. Franklin pushed the elevator button. After a few moments, Franklin leaned in to listen and checked his watch. He pushed again.

After another minute, the sound of the elevator motor indicated it was arriving. As the door opened, Kalvin stood with his back to the door, sliding his shirt-tail into his pants and apparently zipping up, while engaged in a deep kiss with the blond secretary whose name escaped Franklin. Their shoes were in the corner.

The girl opened her eyes, saw the crowd and gasped. Kalvin whirled around, mouth agape. His face turned deep red. His fingers worked frantically at zipping his pants. He stuttered, "Hi … uh … we were just fi-finishing up some work."

Franklin was too horrified to comment. Mr. Murphy laughed out loud. Jude and Roosevelt said nothing.

After a moment, the pair tried to squeeze by, but the men didn't budge. "No, brother-in-law. I think we need to have a little talk. Let's all go upstairs."

The men joined the couple in the elevator and traveled upward in silence. They exited, passed through the lobby and headed toward the offices. Franklin pointed to Ruth's chair. "Kalvin you sit here. And you … what's your name … Samantha? You can sit in Gertrude's chair, so we're all in sight of each other."

In his father's office, he kneeled, removed the false back of the credenza, pulled out the file, opened it and glanced through the contents.

His father had written, "I have discovered some unsavory matters in which my partner, Braxton Doolittle, has engaged. I have not yet finished gathering evidence. I also have determined that my daughter's husband, Kalvin, is not a forthright person. Also, in the past couple of weeks, I've discovered a plot by Braxton to catch and expose Kalvin in something improper. While I want my daughter to benefit from my assets, I do *not* intend to allow Kalvin to take any share of my law firm."

There were several pages of information about both men's activities. When he'd finished studying the documents, he looked out the door, shook his head in disgust and exited.

He pulled a chair from another secretarial area and sat next to Samantha, motioning for the others to come close, so Kalvin wouldn't hear. "Samantha, I have a few questions."

Her face showed fright, mixed with rebellion.

"Samantha, this isn't your first time engaging in such activity with Kalvin. Am I correct?"

She stared at him in silence.

"Are you serious about him? Did he tell you he'd leave his wife for you?"

No response.

"Well, was it just for fun . . . a little sex?"

Silence.

"You were put up to this. Am I right?"

She glared at him.

Based on what he'd just read, he decided to fish. "How much did Doolittle pay you to set Kalvin up?"

She looked indignant.

"Well, did Doolittle tell you to do it in the elevator because of the video cameras? I mean the elevator isn't the most comfortable place for sex. Do I have it right?"

Her eyes opened wide.

"Am I getting close? How much did Doolittle offer you? You know that you're not going to continue working for the firm after this, right? Do you even have law firm experience, or did he hire you for this little ploy?"

She glanced at the other men flanking her.

Franklin asked, "Am I off the mark?"

Kalvin had apparently grown tired of stewing on his own and suddenly spoke up. "Leave her alone."

Franklin turned to him. "Oh, look who's here. Maybe Samantha would like to tell Kalvin exactly why she finds him so appealing."

She and Kalvin shared a glance. Both looked down.

"Tell him, Samantha."

"Tell me what?"

Franklin set his gaze on Kalvin. "You know, Kalvin, you are as incompetent in your own life as you are in the practice of law. You think this chick is all about you? You think she loves you ... has to have your body?"

Samantha squirmed in her chair. Kalvin scrunched his face in confusion.

"Well the truth, dear brother-in-law, is that Doolittle wanted you out because he was afraid my father might give you stock in the firm to benefit my sister and that it would dilute his position. I doubt if my father would have done that anyway. But it appears Doolittle hired Samantha just to entrap you in an illicit activity, so that he could blackmail you and force you out."

Kalvin's chin dropped. He looked from Franklin, to the other men, to Samantha, and back. His facial expression turned from bewilderment to anger to bewilderment again. Leveling his eyes on Samantha, he said, "Is this true?"

She looked at the floor.

"Okay, dear brother-in-law, get on home to your darling wife and act like a good husband for once. Samantha, we need to talk about the next part of your little plan."

Chapter 79

Luis Morales

I'm standing in the sweltering heat of a telephone booth on a street in Miami, meticulously perusing the Yellow Pages and making lists of law firms with Spanish surnames in the titles. Rather than calling, partly because I don't have money for payphones, and partly because I am not confident speaking English, I walk and ride buses from office to office.

In each one, I stand before the disinterested receptionist in my not-quite-so-perfectly-fitting suit, having lost some weight because I do not have money to eat very much. "Good day. I am lawyer from Cuba. I am not licensed in Florida, but I seek work in any capacity."

The receptionist usually shakes her head and grimaces. Sometimes, she will say, "I'm sorry, but we do not have any such positions available." Sometimes, she will leave her desk for a few moments and return, but the answer is always the same.

One day, while reading in a public law library, I see a flyer announcing a seminar for lawyers at the Fontainebleau Hotel in Miami Beach. I decide on one of the boldest actions of my life. I will go to the seminar venue and see if I can meet somebody who can help me. After walking for hours, I cross a small bridge over a river. To my left, I am mesmerized by the beautiful, curving, exterior walls of the Fontainebleau.

Inside, I sheepishly join the registration line for the seminar. When I reach the table, the woman holds out her hand for the admission document. "Excuse me, Miss. I arrive, er, arrived . . . recently from Cuba." I struggle to put my thoughts together in coherent English. "I try to locate work in a law office. I come here to try make contact."

The woman, black hair over an extra-tanned round face, examines my face and clothing. I look down at my suit and at her again, trying not to appear too much like a dog pleading for a bone.

A hand lands on my shoulder. I turn to find a pleasant-faced man of short stature. He sticks out his hand to me, saying. "Welcome to our country, sir. My name is Lansing Armstrong."

I shake his hand, almost bowing. "Luis Morales, Mr. Armstrong."

"Call me Lansing."

He pulls me aside. "Are you aware of the topic of this seminar?"

"No, as I tell woman, I come to meet people."

He asks me what kind of law I practiced in Cuba.

"General civil law."

He nods and asks questions about wills and estates in Cuba and I do my best to answer.

"Have you learned Florida estate law and federal estate tax laws?"

I look down, defeated. "No."

"Well, Mr. Morales . . . Luis . . . without a rudimentary understanding of our basic estate planning and tax laws, I am not sure you will get anything from this seminar."

I look at the ground, ashamed.

Lansing continues. "My friend, I did not mean to imply that you shouldn't be here. I think you had a tremendous idea, and that you could benefit. I would be happy to assist you."

"Assist me?"

"Yes, I will arrange for you to be admitted, and I will introduce you to some people I know in the Miami area. I don't live here."

"Oh. Mr. Armstrong. Lansing. Lansing. I do not know how to thank you." I pump his hand.

Lansing purchases my admission, picks up my books as well as his, strolls into the huge room where attendees are settling in and chooses two seats.

"I do not know how to thank you, sir," I say again.

He smiles. "The appreciation on your face is enough."

"You say you not live in Miami. Do you live in Florida?"

"Yes, about five or so hours north, in Daytona Beach."

I smile. "I visit Daytona Beach as boy, with my father. Beautiful beach. Sand so . . . how would you say . . . durable? . . . hard . . . cars could move on the sand."

Lansing nods. "I'd say *hard-packed sand.*"

"Yes, water so blue. So cool. So rich . . . er . . . *rico. Delicioso.* Waves . . . so beautiful. We sleep . . . er . . . slept at a hotel . . . Seaside Inn. Visit General Batista in his home. You know he lived there . . . 1945?"

"You have a good memory. My parents had a store on Main Street in the same block as the Seaside Inn at that time. I opened my first law office in the same area in 1949. Batista was quite popular. I'm surprised you didn't find Batista fishing in that area of the beach. The City held parades for him on a day they called *Batista Day.*"

We walk out to the reception area and drink coffee, which is close to Cuban coffee, but somewhat weak. Lansing introduces me to a gentleman, and then to another. They ask me a couple of polite questions, but do not seem interested in a Cuban refugee and his life. Then Lansing stops in front of another. "Luis, I would like you to meet Mr. Abraham. He has a law firm in the Miami area with several attorneys."

After a moment, Mr. Abraham flips into Spanish and asks me my background in wills and trusts. But then, as Lansing is standing there, Mr. Abraham, switches back to English.

During the lunch break, Lansing grabs Mr. Abraham by the arm and says, "Let's go to lunch. Do you mind?"

Lansing says there's not enough time to go to the calle Ocho, where he prefers to eat. Abraham leads us to a nearby diner called 'Wolfies'. They help me order a sandwich.

Lansing says, "Tell us your story."

I smile and say, "A long story . . . sad . . . and happy . . . now sad again. My darling wife, Caridad . . . uh . . . Cari. We met young. I fell in love the instant I saw her. Before marriage, I go . . . er . . . went to prison."

"Prison?" Mr. Abraham says, with a look I take as scornful.

"Yes, believe me, I do nothing wrong. Not criminal. My brother . . . believe in Fidel Castro . . . beginning of Revolution. I no. You know about July 1953?"

Mr. Abraham says, "The Moncada attack. The supposed beginning of the Cuban Revolution."

I nod. "My brother Miguel follow. Night *anterior* … uh … before. I find out. Try to find him." I sigh. I explain how my friend and I found our way to *La Granjita* Siboney, how we were sequestered, how my brother was killed, how I was arrested, tried and convicted, along with Fidel and his true followers.

Lansing says, "It's quite ironic that you met Batista as a child and then ended up in his prison."

Lansing turns to Abraham. "Batista owned a riverfront home in Daytona Beach and lived there from time to time after his presidency ended in the mid 40's. He was elected as a Senator to Cuba in absentia, while he was in Daytona, before his second presidency, or dictatorship."

Abraham says, "I never knew he had a home up there. I believe he had one in Palm Beach too."

Lansing continues, "Yes, the City of Daytona Beach embraced him, honoring him with parades and special events. I was at a parade on *Batista Day* in 1956. A group of students from the University of Havana held up a banner saying, 'Batista–Dictator,' until it was confiscated by the police. The people of Daytona Beach knew nothing about his reputation in Cuba. He was wealthy, generous and powerful, and that had a great effect."

I turn to Mr. Abraham. "I told Lansing my father was connected to Batista's government."

Lansing says, "Before he lost control and fled, Batista began efforts to ensure he could join his wife and children in his Daytona home permanently if he had to leave Cuba. Batista treated the entire City Commission, city attorney and Mayor to a trip to Havana and a banquet. He deeded one of his two homes to the City, and later, when he learned he could not return, transferred his other home, artwork and other treasures to create a museum. Many say the artifacts were stolen from Cuba's National Gallery and should be returned.

"Late in 1958, his son, who was still quite young, and living in Daytona Beach, wrote a letter to President Eisenhower asking that Batista be allowed to return. But U.S. immigration rejected the request."

I turn to Abraham again. "I attended the dinner in Havana in 1958, with my father." I hesitate. "My father and my brother-in-law are political prisoners in Cuba now for many years. My brother-in-law,

Alejandro, believed Fidel was going to be the savior, but then he and many others changed their minds."

The men watch me with somber faces. I continue. "I was released from prison in 1954, some months before Castro was." I feel that my English is becoming more fluent as I speak.

"I married my darling Cari. We had two children, and there was a short time that our lives seemed positive. Many believed Fidel would improve things, but once he had control, many of us became disenchanted.

"After I left, my wife and daughter were forced from our home, so they moved into the large home of my mother. Fortunately, the government did not take my mother's home even though my father was in prison." I fight to maintain control of my voice and avoid breaking down. I explain about sending Franklin away and leaving for a seminar in Panama. "I determined that I needed to go to a country where I could obtain work as an attorney, in spite of my poor English, and knowing only Cuban law."

I pause to see if they are understanding my English. They are attentive, so I continue.

"I seek work, in a law firm, not as a lawyer yet, because I need to improve my English, learn what I can learn and try to become licensed to practice law here in your country. Then, my goal is to stabilize myself enough to be able to bring my family together again and make a new home here."

Abraham has said little during the long diatribe. The men look at me with faces of utter compassion and understanding. I hardly know how to take it, but I am grateful.

Mr. Abraham swipes his napkin across his mount, drops it on the table and says, "Luis, come to my office on Monday morning. We will find something for you to do, which will help us, but will also help you achieve your goals. Is that alright?"

"Mr. Abraham. I do not know what to say. Yes. Yes."

Lansing smiles at me with a pride like that of a father watching his son hit a baseball for the first time. I am so pleased and relieved.

Chapter 80

Elena Morales Lennox

Elena was sitting at the kitchen table looking through documents when Kalvin wandered in at ten p.m. He tried to kiss her, but she turned her face. His face and his breath disclosed that he'd been drinking.

"Well, well, well. You've come home. Kalvin, I've been questioning our relationship for some time. You're not the man I thought you were. Your foolish arguments in the guardianship court proved what I should have known. Besides that, it's obvious why you come home late, and always intoxicated."

He stared her down. "Did your fucking brother call you?"

She glared back. "Why would my brother call me? About you? He has no respect for you."

He stared back. "He's way off base. Goddam bully. You pretend you don't like him. Your whole fucking family is against me. Motherfucker."

"What are you talking about?"

"You really don't know? Oh, fuck it. I worked my ass off in that fucking firm of your father's. For you. And you never appreciated a fucking thing. I should probably just leave the firm."

She shook her head. "I don't give a flying fuck what you do. My father hired you only because you are married to me. He doesn't respect you. They'll never make you a partner. And I can't stand you any more anyway. I want a divorce, and you certainly won't even be an employee there without me."

His mouth opened and closed several times, but no words came out.

"Go pack some things and go. You can make an appointment to come back and get the rest of your shit."

He roared into the bedroom and slammed the door so hard the wall shook.

Chapter 81

Luis Morales

I'm sitting on the metal bench in the park behind Mr. Abraham's law firm, reading and munching a simple sandwich like every lunchtime since I was a lowly law clerk before I passed the Bar and began work as an attorney. My dog-eared, heavily marked English-Spanish legal dictionary sits on my lap. Why I still study it, I don't know. I'm now far beyond the basic terminology I used to study, when I would say, "A *testamento* is a last will and testament." "A *fideicomiso* is a trust." I still take courses to improve. I still watch television shows in English, from *Sesame Street* to *Three's Company*, to whatever else. I still repeat new structures and words aloud trying to get the pronunciation correct. I still write new words in my notebook.

Braxton Doolittle drops beside me. "Louis," he says, in his southern U.S. drawl, "You're coming up on two years as an attorney here, right?"

I nod.

He lowers his voice. "I'm thinking of opening an office. I was wondering if you've considered such a thing."

Surprised and unsure how to respond, I consider all that Mr. Abraham has taught me and how he has sacrificed by paying me more than I was worth as I learned English and tried to become a lawyer. But, knowing that he intends to name only family members as partners, I have dreamed of opening my own law firm. I nod. "It has crossed my mind."

Just answering feels like the beginning of a conspiracy. How would Mr. Abraham feel if I said I was leaving? He'd be gracious and not mind. Wouldn't he?

Braxton explains how he knows things about running the law office business that I don't know. He's right of course. But, wait. My thinking is shifting too quickly. I do not know Braxton that well. Yet, I guess I'm impetuous because in three months, we open the firm together.

That first day at the Morales and Doolittle law firm, the proudest day of my life at that point, I stand in the lobby greeting every employee, a few from our prior firm, and a few new ones, with "Welcome to Morales and Doolittle."

During those early years in Miami, Cari and I, and our children, were one happy homogenous family, all the prior tribulations behind us. We went to the beach, enjoyed sumptuous meals together and, sometimes with family who had arrived, feasted on roast pork, plantains, rice and beans, just like in our old home.

The second proudest day of my life was the day Franklin earned his law degree, was admitted to the Bar, and joined the firm. Despite his youth, he immediately showed himself to be astute, diligent and forthright.

Thinking of the good work I've been able to do for people, especially the Cuban people who remained in that country, despite the resistance and antagonism I've suffered for doing so, gives me peace and contentment.

Suddenly, my pride and contentment leave me as I analyze Elena's jealousy, anger, and paranoia. It's my fault. Leaving her behind was a horrible thing to do. Sending Franklin away was also, but if he has bad feelings about it, he does not show them. Cari suffered all her life as well, always talking about her jewelry and all that she lost. I think her feelings hurt Elena too. I understand such memories haunt forever.

Back to pleasant thoughts. Sylvia's face comes to me. I am completely in love with her. I do not feel guilty because my love for Cari has not diminished. Cari was taken from me, but her spirit cannot be taken. Those times are forever imprinted as a part of me.

Is it unusual that my mind is flitting from time to time and subject to subject? Am I thinking differently than I have been? Voices in my hospital room escape me because I'm in the past.

My Cuban roots grasp me and pull me back, again.

I'm standing in a line in Santiago de Cuba, having entered a bank to exchange some money on my very first trip back to Cuba. It looks like any bank in the United States, with a marked area where customers would stand to wait for the next teller. But nobody is on any of those marks in front of tellers or standing behind the lines. People lounge on chairs and couches or stand anyplace but where they should if they are in a line. For a while, I stand on one of the lines, looking around and trying to understand. Somebody leaves after completing business with a teller, and another from somewhere in the lobby approaches the teller. Others enter the bank and say something, and somebody signals and points. Finally, it dawns on me that as each new person enters, the person entering says *"¿Último?"* or *"¿Última?"* or *"¿Última persona?"* They are asking who is last in line. The last person to enter raises a hand, or says *"Yo,"* and then often says, "I'm behind him," as that person points to another. Having already lost many spaces in line, I note who is last, walk back to the door and say *"¿Último?"* The last person signals. When the next person enters and asks who is last, I raise my hand and say, "I'm after him," pointing to the one before me.

I smile to myself as I recall the first time in Havana, thinking a dwelling is on fire, as what looked like smoke pours out of a window. My driver laughs. "It's fumigation, not a fire." Later, I realize stores and museums, and even dwellings, are closed for an hour or so regularly as men enter to spray to control the mosquito that carries the dreaded Dengue fever.

In Santiago de Cuba, soldiers in uniform walk through the neighborhoods, ordering people out, while other soldiers carry the small, diesel-operated machines that spew insecticide throughout enclosed spaces. Residents stay out only until the soldiers exit the street, but not as long as they should. Inside the homes, televisions and other sensitive items are always covered with a bed sheet when not in use. The residents try to clean tables, chairs and floors with soap and water, but the oily substance does not clean easily.

A mosquito buzzes around. A Cuban snatches it in mid-air, examines it and holds it up. "Not a problem. Look. No tell-tale white marks on the body. No white stripes on the legs." Then, smiling with that infectious happiness of the Cuban people, the Cuban says, "Anyway, your people are the cause of this infection. You sent us the mosquitoes infected with dengue. In the eighties. Your CIA did it."

And I cannot say it's not true, especially knowing all that the CIA actually did or tried to do in Cuba.

I'm sleeping in a fifth-floor apartment in Havana with windows open and a sea breeze flowing through. I am awakened by a mosquito bite so intense that I jump from bed, turn on the lights and try to locate it for examination. Five days later, at home in Miami, I am unable to rise from bed one day. My doctor asks, "Did you have diarrhea again, like so many times before when you have eaten undercooked food in that country you love so much? You're probably dehydrated."

I shake my head. "No, the food products have become so much better, and the restaurants are cooking more thoroughly lately. So, I haven't been sick like that in quite a while."

"You still might just be dehydrated. Get a number of bottles of some brand of sports drink that supplies electrolytes and drink them."

I do, but I'm still exhausted and cannot rise even the next day and now a red rash spreads across my shoulders and chest. I call again. "Doc, can you examine me for Dengue or Zika, or both?"

After going to a blood-drawing company, and waiting a few days, my doctor sends me a text message with a statement from the county health department, saying "Zika Virus – Positive". The flu-like symptoms are mostly gone by the time I receive the result. An employee from county health department questions me about where I was when I was bit and sends workers to set out traps at my home and office, searching for the *Aedes Egypti* mosquito, because if one bites me, for perhaps up to six months, Zika can be transmitted to another, and God forbid it might be transmitted to a pregnant woman. And I am advised to use condoms when having sex for up to six months. I'm so embarrassed when I go to the pharmacy and purchase condoms, to use with Sylvia, just to protect her from the remote possibility that I could infect her.

I'm on any one of my trips to the Oriente, the easterly area of Cuba. As we arrive in Santiago de Cuba, Daniel says, "The usual route?"

I nod. He knows that I must visit the same places every single time.

First, we cruise around the Moncada and Hotel Rex, where I shiver and fight off tears. He stops at a couple of homes to make deliveries in that neighborhood. Then, he stops in front of Cari's family home, where Yiyi still lives.

Inside, we make a delivery, from my own funds, talk about Alejandro and if he will ever be freed, Amelia and Luisa, and my family in the States. As always, I say how I miss Cari.

Daniel drives into the Vista Alegre neighborhood. I gaze at the nicely painted government buildings that used to be homes and the formerly beautiful homes that have been untreated since the late 1950's. I remember playing with my friends in and around the homes and former homes. We stop in a couple of houses to make deliveries. The last stop in the neighborhood is my former family home. Tears still come to me, every single time.

Daniel pauses the appropriate amount of time in each of the required stops. I am silent, as usual, as we pass along the Siboney Highway toward *La Granjita Siboney*. The docent at the front door does not ask for my Cuban identity card, but charges me the Cuban rate. I ignore the museum pieces in the home. Haunting images of the multitude of people, including now-famous martyrs, moving throughout the house, come to me. Among them are women ironing fake uniforms, men drawing plans, piles of uniforms and stacks of weapons. Another docent explains to foreign tourists, "Our *Comandante* began the Revolution right here in this home by finalizing the heroic attack on the horrible government that controlled in 1953."

I pass by the group and exit through the back door. I look both ways into the yard and see the hills behind. I stand in the former driveway, remembering the view through the slats of the chicken coop as Fidel presented his speech.

I enter the car again. Daniel raises an eyebrow. I nod. We continue to Siboney Beach, where I plod along the rocky sand, remove my shoes and stand in the cool, lapping water, picturing Cari smiling so happily, as we hold each other in the rough waves.

Leaving the beach, we drive around the airport and the coast, past el Morro, to the inlet. He stops once in front of the formerly exclusive Ciudamar Yacht Club, where now youthful Cubans of all races romp in the water. I stare at the remaining houses at La Socapa and the houses and other buildings of Cayo Smith, now known as Cayo Granma, including the church at the top of the hill at the middle of the island. Again, I am with Cari, first on the beach during that fateful meeting, with her annoying brother trying his best to prevent our connection, and then falling in love, and swimming as teens and adults.

Finally, we are back in the city. We move upwards. He parks a block from Hotel Casa Granda. We exit the car and walk around Parque

Céspedes. We enter the newly-opened tower in the Cathedral and climb the narrow steps to the top. I gaze down on the park and the buildings and then up and down the beautiful streets of downtown. I walk around the uppermost part, stop to look out every window and gaze at the mountains and the outskirts of the city. Then we climb down and walk a few blocks and make a delivery.

Faces of the people to whom I deliver flick through my mind like playing cards. Sitting in so many homes, with older people, married couples, children, multiple generations under one roof, almost always in simple dwellings, with older appliances and furniture, some with dirt floors and outhouses, often sipping coffee. Sitting in these homes is magical. The magic of the soul of the Cuban people living on the island. Resilience, dedication, adaptability, honor, love.

I surely hope that Franklin will see fit to carry on the trips to help the Cuban people, with joy and relish, as opposed to obligation. He must see their wonderful spirit. Living in the Revolution. *La Revolución*. The word is everywhere. Daniel and others think I make no sense when I question the use of that word. But I do. What does it mean? I've studied definitions. "Orbital motion about a point, especially as distinguished from axial rotation." "A turning or rotational motion about an axis." "A single complete cycle of such orbital or axial motion." And the other meanings, "The overthrow of one government and its replacement with another." "A sudden or momentous change in a situation."

I still shake my head in bewilderment. The Cuban Revolution simply does not fit any of the standard definitions. It was the overthrowing of a government and replacement, but then, by definition, it would have been complete in 1959. How does it continue? If it continues, it was not sudden. Or maybe it was in fact sudden, but not complete. Then Fidel's own definition of Revolution, I which I rather accidentally memorized after seeing it on the wall of the Saturnino Lora Museum in the Civil Hospital.

"Revolution is a sense of history;
it is changing everything that must be changed;
it is full equality and freedom;
it is to be treated and to treat others as human beings;
it is to emancipate ourselves and our own efforts;

it is challenging powerful dominant forces within and outside
the social and national level;
it is defending values which are believed to cost of any sacrifice;
it is modesty, selflessness, altruism, solidarity and heroism;
it is fighting with audacity, intelligence and realism;
it is never lying or violating ethical principles;
it is profound conviction that there is no force in the world
capable of crushing the power of truth and ideas.
Revolution is unity;
it is independence;
it is fighting for our dreams of justice for Cuba and
for the world, which is the basis of our patriotism, our
socialism and our internationalism."

Politicians of the United States and the exile community would laugh at this. But I find it interesting. And talking to many Cuban people, I understand that they feel it.

Why am I thinking these thoughts? This ridiculous study of a word has occupied my mind too many times. Focus. Focus on family and nice things.

But the linguistic puzzle returns. I like to think of the other use of the word, meaning a rotation, as in coming full-circle—of returning to where one began, as I did when I first returned to Cuba. I was born there. I left. I have returned. Full-circle. Every time I return, I am home again. I'm still Cuban. I'm always Cuban.

Now, I'm thinking of another circle, the cycle of life. Birth, life. And now, for me, maybe the end of my life on earth—death of the human body. Does that begin another revolution? Another circle, in the after-life? Did God have a plan that involves circles, cycles and revolutions, like the shapes of Earth and the planets, and the constellations, and the solar system, about which everything and everybody revolves?

Oh, stop it Luis. Deep, deep, nothingness. How silly to dwell on such thoughts! Is my brain affected by drugs?

But again, I find myself returning to the word. 'Revolution.' I remember Fidel as he created and honed the *History Will Absolve Me* speech. Lately, there are posters everywhere with a long definition of Revolution, Fidel Castro style.

And here I am. Maybe dying. Maybe preparing to meet Cari again. Thinking of definitions and sayings. And studying the words of a man who is reviled in the United States, especially by my fellow Cubans.

I'm in a car, creeping through the streets of Centro Havana, trying in vain to find a street name and a house number. Unlubricated and unserviced car parts creak as the car swerves to avoid, but often bounces through, potholes.

We pass meager shops, displaying the best efforts at making a buck. On small, beat-up tables inside door openings into dwellings, one displays a few pieces of plumbing material, another displays little plastic storage containers and drinking cups and another displays tools. Another man stands at a counter on wheels, offering drinks from some kind of syrup. Another man stands at his door next to wires and cables hanging from the metal gate.

Some residents sit on doorsteps or look out through the bars of metal gates that act as front doors, contentedly chatting with friends, neighbors and family. Others sit on worn, concrete doorsteps alone, looking desolate. But all in all, the people on the streets go about their business, greet their friends with love and do not complain about their difficulties, although they might make fun of bureaucracy and of having to stand in lines for everything. They smile and exclaim, "Life is hard." And if asked why their financial situation is so hard, they will point at me and say, "Your blockade."

I argue, "It's not my blockade." And they smile and nod.

Cubans on the island become annoyed when visitors from the United States speak negatively of their way of life. I try not to do it. But even when annoyed, they still smile. Their resilience and hope enchant me.

My surrogates and Sylvia are in the room again. It's been a constant flurry of activity. Even Elena is coming around and not causing discord. I wish she could know how I appreciate it.

Suddenly, I find myself in a car with Lansing Armstrong at the wheel, on a tour of Daytona Beach, only a few years after I got the rest of my family to the United States.

"Can you take me to the train station? I want to arrive again just like I did as a boy in the mid-forties."

Lansing drives up the long driveway from his river home, on the east side, not far south of where Batista's home was, drives a bit, and then, just before a bridge, points to a house with a tall tower extending above trees. "That is Lillian Place. It's supposedly haunted. Stephen Crane wrote *The Open Boat* there after being shipwrecked off our coast."

Reaching the west side of the bridge, he points to the green, wooden fence surrounding a baseball field. "Jackie Robinson played his first game as the only black player in an all-white league, right there."

He cruises along Beach Street, drives a few more blocks and stops. "The train station. Now closed."

He stops the car, and I climb the concrete steps of what's left of the station, trying to remember.

I return to the car and direct him to Bethune-Cookman College, where I'm pleased to see a few more buildings than the last time. A see Mary McLeod Bethune's home on campus and remember Angel's explaining how he sipped tea there with her and how she was so interested in Cuban education. Lansing then drives back toward the river and crosses another bridge. "This was the last wooden bridge. You probably crossed it."

"Yes. Please turn left."

"You have a good memory, Luis."

He stops at the home that was Batista's, which has a sign outside saying, "The Cuban Museum."

We enter, and I stand, lost in time. I look at the contents, but more at the rooms. I walk to the window and look down to the river. It seems much smaller than I remember. Voices and faces return to me.

We then drive north and turn on Seabreeze Boulevard, toward the beach. At the hotel with a drive-through to the beach below, I say, "Turn left."

He does so, and in a few blocks, I see the place where we ate that evening, which now has a sign saying, *The King's Cellar*. I am silent, stuck in that former time. Then he drives south again. Soon, he jogs a block toward the ocean and passes the Bandshell and an amusement park.

"Wait. Something's missing. Wasn't there a large hotel here?"

"Yes. The Seaside Inn."

"That's where we stayed. Can I get out for a moment?" He lets me out, and I walk down onto the beach, below the pier. I recall floating in the sea.

I return to the car. Lansing turns right onto Main Street.

"Lansing, I would like to see the Streamline Hotel."

"All right, but now it's a rather cheap transient lodging establishment."

He turns left, drives a few blocks and stops. We enter. He gets permission, and we go up to the rooftop, where I walk around silently, recalling.

Chapter 82

Elena Morales Lennox

Thursday, December 8, 2016

Elena didn't sleep well after Kalvin left the house. So many issues came with a break-up. What would happen to her? How would she survive? She knew that Kalvin would never become a partner in the law firm, but would they even let him remain if he was separated or divorced from her? She didn't think they had much faith in his work ethic. She couldn't even ask her father for financial help now. She again thought of her plan to change her life, to quit the drinking, smoking, and swearing and so on.

She dragged herself from bed at six in the morning, dressed and waited for Pedrito to drop off Elenita. She immediately loaded Elenita into her car seat and drove to Versailles, sure she'd find Franklin there.

At seven, she pulled into the parking lot. Franklin stood at the outdoor counter, sipping a *cafecito* and eating a *pastelito de guayaba*. As he bit, he leaned forward and held out the tiny napkin, trying to catch falling flakes. She wondered why he bothered, since he was outside, standing on concrete.

Elena pulled Elenita out of the car, hitching her up onto her hip. Franklin saw them coming up, smiled, grabbed another napkin and cleaned his mouth and fingers.

He kissed Elena on the cheek. She did not try to avoid it. He kissed Elenita on the forehead.

She choked the words out. "I told Kalvin to leave."

"When?"

"Last night."

He nodded. "Did you discuss his position at the firm?"

A tear dribbled down her cheek. "I told him he had no future there or with me."

Franklin hugged Elenita and Elena together. Elenita played with his ear and hair. Again, Elena succumbed and did not pull away.

"Listen, Elena. I know you're probably worried about your financial future if papá doesn't make it, or doesn't return to work, and if you aren't with Kalvin. You don't need to worry. Papá has provided for you. And he anticipated that Kalvin may not be involved or may not be continuing with the firm. Your share of the value will remain in trust, to protect it, and I'm in charge as the trustee."

Tears rolled down her cheek. She looked at him. "You know, in one way it pisses me off that mi papá thinks he can run my life, but at the same time, I'm very grateful."

"Elena, papá had been compiling evidence about wrongdoing by Kalvin and Doolittle. He didn't want to do anything prematurely, but it all came to a head last night."

"I don't want to know. The two of them can go fuck themselves." Then, she remembered she intended to clean up her foul language.

"We have another meeting at the hospital this morning. Do you want to come?"

Elena flinched. "No, thank you. But I'll be by to see papá this morning."

Franklin looked at his watch. "I have to get going. I have to be at the office early."

"Okay." She hesitated, then added, "What's going to happen to him?"

"If you'd come to the meeting, you'd learn."

"I just can't."

"All right." He leaned, picked up one of Elenita's feet and blew onto the bottom, making a tacky noise. She giggled.

"I have to run." He kissed both and left.

Chapter 83

Franklin Morales

At 8:15 a.m., Franklin stood with Jude in the computer control room of the law firm, watching video screens. Roosevelt, whose bulk and muscle might be needed, was across the hall, connected on Facetime.

Samantha stood at the parking garage elevator door, as instructed. Doolittle glided his sleek Mercedes into his space. Samantha held a finger by the button. Dressed impeccably as always, Doolittle snatched his leather attaché case and strutted toward the elevator.

"Good morning, Miss Foster."

Franklin watched the camera inside the elevator. Doolittle pushed the button for the third floor.

The moment the door closed, Samantha said, "I got him."

Doolittle looked alarmed. "Excuse me?"

"As you ordered, I fucked Kalvin here in the elevator, so you'd get it on camera."

His mouth twitched. He leaned in and whispered, "The camera is live."

Samantha pulled the stop button. "Dear Mr. Doolittle. My price has gone up."

"Your price?" He eyed the camera. His bald head started to shine.

"Yes, my price for getting Kalvin into this situation so you could blackmail him as you requested."

Doolittle looked around, and at her. "I don't know what you're planning, Miss Foster, or what you're talking about."

"Mr. Doolittle, your offer of twenty-five thousand to fuck the lazy son-in-law of your partner here under the live cameras was not worth it. He's a lousy fuck, and I likely picked up some disease from him."

Mr. Doolittle stuttered. "M-M-Miss F . . ."

"I think I could make more money charging you with sexual-harassment for requiring me to have sex with one of your attorneys. The new price is a hundred thousand. Today. Now."

"I don't have that kind of money lying around." Looking bewildered, he glanced at the camera again and back at her. He opened and closed his mouth, like a fish gulping air.

He reached for the red button, but she blocked him.

"Unlock it, damn it." He grabbed her by the wrist, twisted her away from the button, and hit the button, hissing, "You fucking little bitch."

"Goddamn it, Doolittle, that hurts. Now you've added battery. The price is climbing."

Franklin said, "If she says the magic words, get ready to intercede."

Roosevelt and Jude said, "Ready."

As the elevator rose, she said, "The new price is a hundred fifty thou, if you give it to me in the next fifteen minutes. Otherwise it's increasing more. And, don't think I'm leaving your side so that you can destroy the recording. Anyway, it's the one with Kalvin and me doing it."

Franklin watched the reception and hallway elevators. Doolittle marched out of the elevator and through the empty reception area, followed closely by Samantha. He stopped outside where Franklin watched cameras. Samantha continued her work. "Is the money in there, Doolittle?"

Through gritted teeth, he hissed, "Shut the fuck up, you bitch."

"No, Doolittle, I will not shut the fuck up. I want my money for blackmailing Kalvin, for sexual harassment and for battery and it's increasing another twenty-five grand in five minutes."

Franklin was pleasantly surprised at her talents as an actress.

Sweat poured down Doolittle's temples. He yanked his coat off and held it over his shoulder with a finger. His shirt was soaked at the armpits.

He grabbed Samantha by the upper arm and pulled her forcefully into the library. Jude switched to the library camera. Doolittle pulled her behind the shelves. The camera showed only part of Doolittle and none of Samantha. Could he be hurting her? Franklin said, "Shit. Get ready."

"Listen, you fucking little whore. I am trying to think of where to get your putrid money."

"Ow, Doolittle. You're hurting me," she said loudly.

Still watching the camera, Jude moved toward the door and hesitated. Into his phone, he said, "Roosevelt?"

Roosevelt focused his phone to his hand on the door handle.

Franklin said, "He knows cameras are everywhere, recording. He'd be so much more stupid if he hurt her."

"Goddammit," Doolittle said. "I need to get checks. I do not have cash."

"Fine. I'll stay with you. Don't even think you can destroy the recordings."

"How do you think it's going to look that you're shadowing me around the office?"

"How do you think it's going to look when I expose you committing blackmail, sexual assault, rape, sexual harassment and battery?"

He glowered. "You're the blackmailer. I never touched your fucking, skanky ass."

She laughed, "And a hundred fifty grand wouldn't have been enough if you had."

He pulled her back into full camera range, grabbed her by both shoulders and squeezed. "Shut the fuck up."

Hallway cameras revealed her following him to the administration office. On that camera, he saw Samantha just inside the door. Doolittle opened file cabinet drawers and removed three different colored checks, one for the operating account, one for the regular trust account and one for the real estate trust account.

Franklin smiled. "There you go, Doolittle. Keep making more egregious violations."

Jude grinned too.

Franklin switched back to the hallway camera, Doolittle and Samantha passed a puzzled secretary. There would be no video inside his office, but the live audio device on Samantha's person continued.

Samantha said, loudly and breathlessly, "Oooh, Mr. Doolittle, what are you doing?"

"Get over here, sit down and shut up."

"Oh, like that. That's what you want? Oh, Mr. Doolittle. It's so big."

"Shut the fuck up."

She said, "Mr. Doolittle, your pen is shaking. I've never seen you so nervous. And, oh my. You're sweating. Why is that check only thirty thousand dollars?"

"I have to take it from several accounts. That one is from the firm trust account."

Franklin shook his head. Doolittle was such an idiot. Writing a check from a client trust account for anything other than what the money is held for is one of the worst violations a lawyer can commit. If it were cashed, that would put the firm in trouble too, but it was enough that he'd written it. He'd sealed his fate in many ways.

"Ah," Samantha said, "… and now one for fifty thousand from the 'Morales and Doolittle Operating Account.'"

Franklin admired her abilities.

After some silence, she said, "All right, that one is for seventy thousand dollars. What is that? Oh, you have a separate trust account called 'Real Estate Trust Account.'"

Franklin and Jude exchanged glances. Doolittle had sealed his fate.

"I think you're still a bit short, Doolittle. Oh. Okay, you're going to give me a personal check for the balance. It's good that you have a little of your own money in this. I don't think your partners will like you using *all* their money. You're writing that for less than you offered me. You were planning to pay me, weren't you, Doolittle? You wouldn't have screwed me over, would you?" After a bit of silence, Samantha said, "You just sit there, twiddling your pen, glaring at me, staring out the window and looking at the checks. What are you thinking?"

"We need to retrieve the recording from the camera. If we leave it there, Miss Nordman will retrieve it. Let's go."

"Not so fast, Doolittle. Hand me the checks." After a hesitation, she said, "Thank you."

Back to the hallway camera, Franklin watched them passing two more employees walking in the door. She fanned out the four checks and held them up to the camera. Franklin removed the elevator video recorder record. He and Jude moved behind the shelves.

Doolittle entered and pushed eject. He stood, mouth open, gaping at the machine. "There's no recording of me or of you and Kalvin. No evidence at all. Give me those checks."

Samantha jumped back. "No way, Doolittle."

He rifled among the shelves, banging things around. Finally, he stooped down and crawled on his hands and knees, reaching behind the shelf, getting dust on his fancy shirt.

"Are you looking for this?"

Doolittle sprang to his feet and turned to find Franklin, flanked by Jude. Franklin held up the recording. "This is our evidence, with your confession."

Doolittle wrenched his arm around Samantha's neck and yanked her into the hallway.

Franklin said, "Braxton, don't make it worse. We've got you."

Eyes darting, Doolittle turned back to Franklin, and then to the exit. Sweat poured down his face. "Fucking bitch."

Samantha's eyes bulged. Her lips pursed as she struggled for air.

Roosevelt rounded the corner, grabbed Doolittle's arm and twisted it backward. Doolittle grunted, losing the grip on Samantha's throat. Jude joined in. They grasped his arms and neck and tackled him. Samantha rolled free, stood, rubbed her neck, and kicked Doolittle in the ribs.

Secretaries and other staff stood in shock, watching the men pulling Doolittle's arms behind him.

Franklin said, "We can add attempted murder to the list of charges." He put an arm around Samantha's shoulders and moved her away. "Are you all right? Should we call an ambulance?"

"No, I'm fine. It was worth it."

Roosevelt and Jude pulled Doolittle to his feet.

Franklin pointed toward the conference room. "In there . . . now." Roosevelt ushered Doolittle in.

Franklin motioned Samantha in as well. Nobody sat. Samantha handed the checks to Franklin.

Franklin stared at Doolittle. "This is it. Nabbed in your own web. Multiple crimes, and other witnesses saw the battery on Samantha. Are you prepared to resign right now?"

Doolittle looked from person to person, sneered and shook his head. "You arrogant fuck. You think you've won. Now you're stuck with that stupid Kalvin."

"Oh, my. Did you try to blackmail him for me, Braxton? Listen, if you don't resign, bad things are going to happen, including losing your license to practice law."

"That's extortion."

"Samantha may file charges anyway, and we may report you to the Bar whether you resign or not. Thus, it's not extortion. It's not a threat."

Doolittle turned and reached for Samantha. She flinched.

Roosevelt grabbed him from behind, inserted an arm through the crooks of both elbows and kicked a leg, which caused Doolittle to fall to the ground again. "Reckon we need to call the cops?"

Franklin said, "Samantha, please go on out and wait." He crossed his arms. "Braxton, what are you going to do?"

Doolittle sighed and clenched his fists again. Then he dropped his arms and shook his head. "I'm going."

"You mean resigning?" Franklin opened a drawer and pulled out several documents. "Sign this resignation as employee and officer of the corporation. Here's an assignment of shares for no consideration. As you know, the Shareholders' Agreement states that a shareholder will give up all shares and waive all rights to receive remuneration for relinquishing shares when guilty of wrongdoing."

"That's only valid if you expel me."

"I thought you were going to resign to avoid our having to expel you. And you are voluntarily waiving remuneration in doing so. See, it's right here." Franklin pointed. "Also, here's an assignment of all ownership interest in the company that owns the building, again for no compensation. Here's a release as to all stock powers or any other authority you may hold on behalf of my father."

A tear dropped from Doolittle's eye and splashed on the table. He signed all the documents, stood, adjusted his clothing, marched out of the conference room, past the horrified employees, and exited through the front door.

At that moment, Kalvin walked in the front door of the office, late as usual. He stopped short, seeing all the staff standing in the reception area.

Franklin opened the conference room door and ushered him in. Kalvin hesitantly stepped in, looked out through the glass at the employees and glanced around at the others in the room, looking uneasy.

"Kalvin, I guess you realize that Doolittle's intent to blackmail you into resigning has succeeded to some extent. What would Elena do if she learned about your transgressions?"

"I would have said my nuts would be fried. But, I'm out of the house anyway. Did you tell her?" He examined the table.

"No, I didn't. Why don't you just nip everything in the bud and resign from the law firm?"

"I thought the girl liked me."

Franklin suppressed a laugh. "So typical."

"Yeah." Kalvin shook his head, looking more like a sulking boy than an attorney.

Kalvin sighed. He looked at the others. "I guess I'll go."

Franklin opened the drawer, pulled out a resignation and other pertinent documents and handed Kalvin a pen. He signed.

As he left, Franklin said to David and Roosevelt, "Thank you for your help. Now I need to handle a couple more matters. I'll see you at the meeting at the hospital."

Franklin walked into the reception area. All the employees' faces seemed bright and relaxed, other than Gertrude's. Samantha looked pensive.

Franklin decided he needed to make an announcement. "I know this is a shocking time here. I want everybody to relax. Nothing but good will result." He paused for a moment. "As I suppose you realize, Mr. Doolittle and Mr. Lennox have both resigned voluntarily, and Mr. Doolittle has signed over all interests he had in the firm. As of now, the firm name is changed to 'Morales and Morales, P.A.' Please begin answering the phone that way." He looked at Teresa, the office manager and said, "Please evaluate all that needs to change, from letterhead to accounts with vendors, to the signage, and talk to me about how to accomplish it. Oh, also, we need to update the corporate record with the state and with the Florida Bar."

After a lull, in which everyone seemed to reflect on that news, he continued. "My father does not appear to be getting better. If he survives, we do not know whether he'll ever be able to return. But we will carry on his firm as he originally planned it. Now that the negativity has left with the bad apples, we'll become more of a family again."

He opened his arms, and, looking at the group again, said, "Now, I think it's time to start our work day."

They nodded, smiled and started to walk off.

"I need to see you, Gertrude, and after you, Samantha."

Back in the conference room, he looked at Gertrude, her usual condescending look replaced by anxiety.

"Gertrude, with Mr. Doolittle gone, we will no longer be needing your services. We will pay you for four weeks from today. You will be entitled to unemployment compensation from the state of Florida."

After excusing her, he telephoned the client whom Doolittle represented in a questionable closing, based on the memo his father left. "Mrs. Pink?"

"Yes."

"My name is Franklin Morales. I am with the law firm in which Braxton Doolittle was a partner."

"Was?"

"Yes, Mrs. Pink. My father, Luis Morales reviewed your file and asked me to set a meeting with you and take whatever action is necessary to make it right."

"How can you make it right, Mr. Morales? I have been interviewed by all types of police agencies. I am being sued. I have lost a lot of money, and my reputation."

"I'm sorry, Mrs. Pink. We didn't know what Mr. Doolittle had done. We will do everything necessary to resolve it and pay for a separate attorney to represent you. Can we meet?"

She said yes, and they scheduled an appointment.

Chapter 84

Sylvia Morales

Friday, December 9, 2016

As Sylvia pulled into a parking space in the hospital parking lot, she was surprised to find Elena exiting her car.

She would once again make an effort even though it was likely to be fruitless. "Good morning, Elena."

Elena turned her head, lowered her sunglasses and looked at Sylvia. In an ordinary, calm voice, she said, "Hi."

Sylvia was so shocked at the lack of venom, she almost didn't know what to do or say. They walked side by side toward the entrance. Sylvia took advantage of the opportunity by putting a hand on Elena's back as they entered the building. "It's nice to see you."

Elena didn't respond, but at least she didn't throw Sylvia's hand off or say anything rude. As they entered the elevator, Sylvia said, "Are you here for the meeting with doctors?"

"No. To see mi papá."

They exited the elevator and walked down the corridor to the room.

Franklin sat at Luis's bedside. He looked up, anguish in his eyes.

Alarmed, Sylvia said, "What is it, Franklin?"

He stood, walked across the room and hugged them both. Elena didn't hug back, but she allowed it. Facing them, so his father couldn't hear, he whispered. "I don't know. He just seems different today. His breathing is kind of accelerated sometimes. The overnight hospice worker just left. Georgina should be here any minute."

Sylvia rushed toward her husband, trying to discern the change. Yes, maybe his face did look different. She wasn't sure if he looked to be in pain. She hoped not. She sat and touched him. "Did the hospice nurse say anything? Did she think something was different?"

"No, she didn't acknowledge it. But it seemed to me that she looked at me in a knowing way. I don't know."

Franklin placed Elena in the other chair. Again, she did not resist.

Elena touched Louis' hand. "*Te quiero, papi.*" She cried quietly.

Franklin moved behind Elena and placed his hands on her shoulders.

Sylvia felt tears coming. She didn't want to show Louis that she was concerned. But she couldn't help it. She yanked out a piece of tissue and dabbed at the moisture beneath her eyes.

"How long until the meeting, Franklin?"

He looked at his watch. "An hour."

Sylvia relived past times, worrying that thinking of the past meant she believed his life may be ending. No, it could not be. It could not be.

Georgina walked in, said, "Good morning," in her lovely voice and rhythm, but slowed as she came across the room. "Why you all look so sad?"

She squinted and walked toward the bed. She leaned in and put her ear toward his chest. "Hmm. How you feelin', Luis?"

A sound erupted from Louis. "Mmmm. Mmmm."

Sylvia studied his face. There seemed to be movement in his eyes and somewhere in his body too. Others in the room appeared shocked too.

Sylvia gasped. "Louis?"

Silence and stillness. She was sure she'd seen something. But maybe she shouldn't be hoping for that. She'd heard that the dying can experience a sudden time of clarity just before the end. No. Better he remain as he was. She had only imagined seeing something different. Tears streamed down Elena's cheeks.

Dr. Neil and Dr. Martin walked in. "Good day, everybody," said Dr. Neil.

Sylvia wanted to ask a million questions. But she held her tongue and watched them. Would they see a difference? Dr. Martin took his pulse as Dr. Neil listened to his heart.

Sylvia couldn't resist. "What?"

Georgina whispered again. "Might be the change."

Sylvia couldn't stop the tears. She stood and walked into the hallway.

Chapter 85

Elena Morales Lennox

Elena sat with her papá, concerned about his shallower breathing. He seemed to struggle to take breaths, and to keep them in. He'd gasp and almost rise each time a breath flew out. His body twitched repeatedly. She was sure of it. His eyes remained open more and seemed more focused. His vocal cords ground.

Feeling utterly helpless, she decided to talk to him. She could speak freely, as the others were in their meeting. She was the one who remained with her papá, to comfort him. "*Papá. Te quiero, papá.* I'll bet you are thinking of mi mamá. I'll bet you'd like to see her, to be with her again. I'll bet you are remembering your early days of love. Aren't you? I know you are."

He grunted, and she jumped. "Papá, you scared me." She focused on his eyes. She thought she could see inside. His shallow breathing increased in speed. "Papá. Are you all right? Am I upsetting you? Or am I making you happy?" He grunted.

Tears came again. She didn't know why. Was she happy to feel she had a connection? Was she worried that he was going? Was she sad? Maybe all these feelings.

She thought about how upset she'd been about his constant trips to Cuba. Maybe it wasn't so bad. Maybe he was reliving his early life with her mamá. "Papá, I'm sorry I've been so angry about your trips to Cuba. I am starting to think you have valid reasons. I know the world is against you. Against supplying money that benefits the regime. But I know you say it's not true. You are such a kind and caring person. You know best. I know you do. Or at least you think you do."

She sobbed uncontrollably. Through the mist of her tears, she saw his body jerk. She looked at his face, "Georgina, his mouth is changing. It's forming an 'o' Do you see?"

Georgina put a hand on her shoulder. "Yes, dear." Turning to Elena's papá, she leaned in and listened. She gazed into his face. She put the stethoscope to his chest. She used a moist cotton swab to dab at his lips and inside his mouth.

He made an *mmm* sound.

Elena shuddered and took in a hard breath. "Something's happening, isn't it? He's changed. His eyes seem clearer and more alert. Does that mean he's getting better?"

Georgina reached over and stroked Elena's forearm. "Yes, something is changing. Just be with him."

Elena continued to stroke his forearm and whisper to him. After a few minutes, she pulled out her phone and texted Pedrito. "Come to the hospital."

Chapter 86

Franklin Morales

Sylvia, now without an attorney, Franklin, Roosevelt, Jude, Mr. Murphy, Dr. Jeffreys, Dr. Martin, Dr. Neil, the Ethics Committee and the Chief of Staff of the hospital, other specialists and representatives and attorneys from the hospital's medical malpractice insurance company took seats in a room.

A woman entered and whispered to the Chief of Staff.

The doctor announced, "It's time for family and friends to go to Mr. Morales' room. He seems to be declining."

Sylvia gasped. Franklin felt like he'd vomit. Even the doctors looked alarmed. All rushed out of the room.

Franklin dropped an arm on Sylvia's shoulder as they raced down the hall. He slipped his phone out of his pocket with his other hand and dictated a group text to Diana, Miguel and Michele. "He may be dying. Come if you can."

Sylvia reached around his mid-section and said, "I hope your sister is still there."

Chapter 87

Luis Morales

I awake with a start, struggling to breathe. Something has changed. I feel like I've been zapped with an electric prod. I try in vain to make my dry lips meet. My face feels contorted. Is my life coming to an end?

Georgina swabs my lips with something moist, but it's not enough. I struggle. Against what? For what? A woman in pink scrubs rushes into the room. She looks at monitors. Shaking, she takes my vitals. Another nurse charges in. Elena sits to my right, holding my arm and sniffling. Georgina sits on my left. A nurse says, "Should I get the doctor?"

Georgina shakes her head. "Just be sure the morphine is here."

And now there's a man, dressed in scrubs. He looks at monitors and considers me. He glances at Georgina. They nod to each other.

Elena starts sniffling louder. Her hand is shaking in mine. She lets go long enough to text somebody. "Franklin isn't answering," she says.

Georgina tilts her head. "They've been informed. They'll be right here."

I don't feel any pain. I simply cannot get my breath, slow it down or hold it in. It races in and out through my open mouth.

Maybe I'm hyperventilating. Maybe it's nerves, imagining that the end is near. Maybe I just need to have a bag put over my mouth, to readjust my oxygen level. I think my vocal cords have finally managed to make some noise. Elena and Georgina have reacted.

The more I try to calm myself, the faster the shallow, quick breaths come and go, like my lungs are forced by a machine. I just want everything to slow down.

Suddenly I get an incredible pain—somewhere—in my chest, and upper abdomen. I guess I jolt, because the attendants, Elena and Georgina jump, alarm on their faces. I can see details of their faces I haven't before. It seems my vision has cleared.

Is this the end? Is this what it is like? Where are Sylvia and Franklin? Where are my grandchildren? Is everything taken care of? Did I forget something? I don't think so. I'm ready.

Georgina directs the nurse to inject something into the tube.

I'm floating—in air—in water. Relaxing. Sleepy. I sink into the mattress.

Cuba. Santiago. Cari. Cari. Grasping me. Pulling me. Beckoning to me. Entangled in her arms and legs. Entangled in the roots of my Cuba. Cari and Cuba are the same. The same comfort. The same warm feelings. Warmed by their grasps.

Do I see the tunnel? Leading to the other world? At the end of a long cylinder, I see a bright light. The light and the cylinder disappear. Floating in the sky.

Vista Alegre. Avenida Manduley. Maids pushing children. Large cars sliding down the street. Running through homes as a boy. Sitting in homes in the unchanged city, just weeks ago, delivering funds, sharing ideas, memories, coffee, comradery.

Traveling rapidly from place to place, time to time, like on a magic carpet. Santiago de Cuba, Havana, rustic pueblos, the green countryside. Vedado, Centro Havana, Playa. Comfort. Comfort. Home. Miami. Home. Santiago de Cuba.

Mind racing. Vignettes rushing in and out.

Architectural grandeur, now unpainted, crumbling—some grand again—some decrepit. Two-by-four pieces of lumber holding up collapsing balconies. Nicely renovated buildings next to worn ones from which rock pieces fall.

Strolling on El Prado, running every few steps to keep up with my father's lengthy stride, and walking much slower on the same walkway, weeks ago. The same. The same. Old people lounge in the shade on concrete benches, talking and enjoying the outdoors, while men in uniform sweep up leaves and rubbish. Youngsters kick balls. Teenagers dance to modern music with a lot of fast talking. Time warp.

Gazing down on Havana from the top of Edificio Bacardí, years ago. From the rooftop bar at Parque Central, recently. From Edificio FOCSA, where vultures hover, dive and climb, as I sip a Cuba Libre and gaze down at the U.S. Embassy—finally, an embassy again, instead of just something like an embassy.

From the apartment where I stay in Havana. Over rooftops scattered with refuse, rusted tanks and pipes, where roosters prance and bring in the morning, for hours—view of the sea—Hotel Deauville—the tall, yellow building of apartments.

In 1960, sitting across from my father as he languishes in prison, looking lost, sad, resigned to his fate. Wishing I could have visited at least once after he was released and before he and my mother died.

Old U.S. cars, bouncing, rumbling, shaking, sputtering, smelling of gasoline or diesel, spewing clouds of pollution, the odor pouring in from the floorboard. Trying to figure out if a window or door handle is actually what it appears to be. Watching men climbing under hoods of cars, using lead plumbing pipes, rubber and pvc to try to replace broken parts. If it were not for *El Bloqueo* and their meager incomes, they could obtain real parts.

Young school children dressed in their burgundy and white uniforms, chanting and chanting, louder and louder, walking hand-in-hand with a parent, before and after school, sitting in hot classrooms. Older students, in their off-yellow uniforms, walking the streets, sitting, laughing, boys and girls holding hands, shopping, kicking soccer balls on El Prado.

Placards, hand-written signs and billboards reciting propaganda, praising Martí, praising dead and living leaders and revolutionaries. Proclamations that every day is the 26th. *Revolución.* ¡*Viva la Revolución!* Long live the Revolution. We have socialism. We will always have socialism. We are still fighting. Down with the *Bloqueo*!! Down with the Empire.

Luis, force yourself back in time. Just try. The horrors of leaving my family behind keep infiltrating.

Push back. Push back in time. All right. Cultural events in fancy buildings. Being with my family when money was plentiful. Baseball games. Roaming the halls of *El Capitolio* while my father worked. Entering the same halls a few years ago and standing among the reddish leather chairs and dark, wooden desks, in awe of the power that once was wielded from there.

Concentrate. Concentrate. Bring Cari to mind during nice visits to Havana as a young couple. Music, dancing, United States citizens dressed–up, gallivanting on the streets. Cari. Cari.

Chapter 88

Sylvia Morales

Sylvia and Franklin rushed into the room together. Elena looked up, anguish in her eyes. Georgina nodded affirmation.

Sylvia's stomach turned. She sat and grasped Louis's hand. His head moved. His eyes, now clearer and more open, pupils swelling and shrinking, seemed to search the room, and focus on her, and then his children, and then straight ahead. Was that a sign of recovery? Maybe not. Probably not.

Franklin pulled a chair next to Elena and put an arm around her shoulder. She didn't resist. He placed his other hand on his father's wrist and spoke to him in Spanish. Elena cried harder.

Sylvia regarded her husband's face. Sallow, empty, gray. Eyes bright though. Shiny. Shallow breaths burst in and out, seeming to increase in speed. His chest heaved with each rapid gasp. His eyes seemed to blend emotions, between fear, discontentment, concern and pain.

"Georgina, could he be hurting?"

Georgina shook her head. "We're dosing him."

Louis' head rose slightly, not even escaping his pillow. From his o-shaped lips exuded sounds. "Il . . . uv . . . uh . . . uv."

He was speaking. She knew it. She hoped it was an attempt to say her name and the word, love.

Louis' head turned to the other side. "Uv . . . v."

Tears streaming, Franklin grimaced and said more words in Spanish. Elena trembled with the force of her crying.

This was it. He was going. His awareness was not a sign he would recover. She put a hand over her mouth trying to hide her anguish. Sobs escaped her.

Franklin gave her a look. All her efforts to keep anxiety out of the room and here she was the one who letting out deep doleful moans.

She struggled to regain her composure. She gazed into Louis' face again and saw what she hoped was peace.

She forced herself remain calm, to speak calmly. "I love you forever, Louis."

Chapter 89

Franklin Morales

Franklin held tightly to his father's wrist. *"Te quiero, papá.* I love you."

Both Sylvia and Elena sobbed.

His papá's beseeching eyes, seeming to focus on him as he spoke, unsettled him. In Spanish, he said, "I have been to Santiago de Cuba and all around the Oriente with Daniel and even Luz, doing your work. Those people love you so dearly. They really do. I have been so moved. I mean it. I understand all that is behind your desire to travel there and help these people."

Elena glanced at him. He prepared for her to criticize. But she did not.

Franklin mentioned individual people, their health, their wishes and their concerns about Franklin's papá. "I've talked to Daniel and Luz about the possibility of expanding the work beyond delivery of money … to help the people buy things, like appliances and telephones to improve their lives."

Elena grabbed Franklin's arm, displaying a quizzical look. "Can I help, Franklin? Can I go to Cuba with you?"

The meekness of her voice and her offer shocked him. He glanced at his father and swore he saw a nod. He looked into Elena's eyes. "Yes, Elena. I'll put you to work with Daniel and Luz. Papá will be pleased."

She smiled.

They both concentrated again on their father. Sylvia's crying lessened as she held onto his hand with both of hers. His papá's mouth and the skin around his eyes tightened and loosened. Was that a show of emotion? Was it a smile? His papá's eyes seemed to focus on him, then Elena, then Sylvia, and then on the distance.

Chapter 90

Luis Morales

I'm jarred by an excruciating pain. I grab a deep breath. Somewhere deep within—some kind of—something artificial—metallic. I think I'm shutting down. Fear grips me, but then subsides.

Sylvia leans and kisses me on the cheek, her soft hair flowing over my face, carrying her sweet aroma.

Elena holds my hand and sets her other hand on my chest. She's calmed down. Franklin has a hand on me too, and another on Elena's shoulder.

All three are crying. I'm surprised and content that Elena has just changed and wants to be involved in my work with the Cuban people.

Franklin goes to Sylvia's side of the bed and rests a hand on her shoulder and the other on my chest. Sylvia puts an arm around him.

I cannot stop the rapid breaths whistling through my stiff lips. I try again to close my mouth, to retain the oxygen, but it escapes.

My belly feels flat and empty. Jesus on the cross. Ribs showing. What a thought. I'm certainly no Jesus.

Good time to think of Jesus\\time to say a prayer. Not so religious. Should pray. I do believe.

Dear God, I thank you for this life that you have given me. All the good, and all the bad, because the bad made the good so much sweeter. I thank you for Cari. I wish she hadn't gone so early. I thank you for wonderful Sylvia. It cannot be the same as a long-time love—a love that begins in youth—but it is love. I thank you for both of my children. Franklin is a bright, promising, ethical young man. And I thank you for Elena. She means no wrong.

I pray for all Cubans, those who have stayed on the island and those who have left. I pray for peace and harmony among them, for the prosperity of the country and its people, for eliminating hatred.

I pray for freedom from pain and suffering.

I thank you again for everything in my life.

He saw himself sitting in a church as a child.

Dios te salve, María.
llena eres de gracia:
el Señor es contigo.
bendita tú eres
entre todas las mujeres.
y bendito es el fruto de tu vientre:
Jesús.
Santa María, Madre de Dios,
ruega por nosotros pecadores,
ahora y en la hora de nuestra muerte.
Amén.

Another intense pain. *"Santa Maria! Madre de . . ."*

Georgina stands above me. A nurse injects something into the tube.

This awful breathing. My breath must be foul. I must look like something from some horror movie, like rubberized lips stuck in some awful, stretched position.

Alejandro, appears. "Luis, *compadre*, I'm here for you." He glances at Sylvia and says, "I'm sorry." He rubs my arm. "You were a fine husband to my dear sister. Please give her a kiss for me when you see her in heaven." He leans down, kisses me on the forehead and fades back.

Georgina strokes my hair. She takes my pulse, then rubs her hand up and down my arm. The feeling is somewhat like pain, but somewhat not like pain. My heart patters like a hummingbird's.

Where's George? Where's Lansing? Oh, yes, Lansing is dead. Where are David and Roosevelt?

I seem to levitate. I am above, looking down on the bed, at my body. No, that can't be. But maybe. Am I leaving the physical world for the spiritual world?

Franklin says, "Dear papá. I just want you to know that we've taken care of everything. Don't worry. Sylvia and I have come a long way. We and Elena have made peace, for you."

Elena gushes tears and blubbers, making me anxious. Franklin moves next to her, puts hands on her shoulders and whispers to her in Spanish, "Elena. Calm down. Papá is going. He's at peace."

She looks shocked, replying, in Spanish, "Are you sure?"

Sylvia says, "Elena, just give him your love."

Elena says, again in Spanish, "*Te amo, papá. Te amo.*"

I peer into a dark tunnel. A light sparks and pulsates, warming me, like the sun pouring in through a window. Glimpses of people at the end of the tunnel.

Cari stands smiling on the warm sand of Siboney beach, blue waves rolling and breaking behind her, the waves humming like the warm-up of an orchestra. She whispers, "Luis."

"I'm on my way, Cari."

My mother appears, smiling. Behind her, my father beams too. Surprising. I hover again above my earthly body and the people holding me. No fear. Strangely comforted.

I'm drawn back into my body, away from the smooth, warm comfort. No, I struggle against the return. No. Was my hovering above a dream? Pain comes again. Franklin and others speak to me. The hum of their voices is pleasant, but not the same as the hum of a few minutes ago.

Breathing more rapidly—sprinting on a treadmill. I'm reminded of a motor—pistons thrusting. Items whirring by on a treadmill, reminding me of the *I love Lucy* episode in which Lucy and Ethel try desperately to grab and place candy on a conveyor belt. Running feet. Trying to keep up. Making me light-headed.

George, Roosevelt and David stand at the foot of the bed, smiling gravely.

Everybody has a hand somewhere on me.

A nurse marches in. "Too many visitors." She approaches and looks at me. "Never mind. I'll send the others in."

My skin hurts. Brittle. Tender. The surface, or beneath? Hurt. But numb.

David says, "Luis, my father loved you like a brother. I'm honored to have known you. And we . . . all of us . . . your children, your wife, Mr. Murphy, Roosevelt and I . . . are doing what you wished. Don't worry about a thing."

George is choked up. Funny, for such a burly man. "Louis, I love you like a brother too. Go in peace, my friend."

Roosevelt says, "It was an extreme pleasure to know you, sir. You and Lansing Armstrong both exhibited the most honorable, caring feelings of anybody I've ever known."

I groan. I'm racked again with an unusual pain inside. I think I make a sound.

The nurse injects again.

Slowing inside. Tears drizzle down faces above me.

Miguel, Michele, Diana and Pedrito rush in, looking meek and scared. They touch me. "I love you," comes from different voices, old and young, male and female, all merging together.

Faces of the living looking down at me—tears and sad smiles. Odd.

The drone of violins and cellos.

Slow pulsing warmth, pulling me in, pulling me up.

No gasps.

Breaths slow to a light, soothing whistle, encircling the loving words of my family, making their words sweeter.

Relaxing. Peaceful.

Heart slowing, like a beating clock, winding down.

Still on the treadmill during cool-down—losing speed gradually, peacefully, quietly.

Slow steps on the sand of Siboney beach, warm granules gliding through my toes.

Sitting on the warm sand swirling in little rivulets in the light breeze.

Feet cooled by the lapping water.

Arms around a teenaged Cari.

Ready to go, in the grasp of Cuba, in the grasp of Cari and even of my parents. Heaven. Peace.

The tunnel opens again, pulsating, like the dark cavities of a heart. Its light sooths me. No more pain. The pulse pulls me in.

Cari's lovely face and soothing voice. "Luis, are you ready? Come on."

My father and mother nod. "Come."

The light welcomes me and pulls me into comfort and warmth.

371

About the Author

Michael A. Pyle is an attorney who practices civil law in Daytona Beach, Florida as senior member of the firm Pyle, Dellinger & Duz, PLLC.

Writing has been a part of his make-up for many years. He earned a Bachelor of Arts degree in English in 1977, a master's degree in linguistics, with specialization in teaching English to speakers of other languages in 1979 and a Juris Doctorate, with honors, in 1982, all at the University of Florida. While studying for his bachelor's degree, he took creative writing classes, and wrote several short stories, one of which was the impetus for his historical novel, *White Sugar, Brown Sugar*. As a lawyer, he wrote a short story called 'Eloise's Day in Court', about an elderly woman involved in the court process called guardianship, which was published by the Elder Law Section of the Florida Bar.

While studying for his master's degree and his Juris Doctorate degree at the University of Florida, he taught English to foreign students as an associate professor, at the same university. He co-wrote *Cliffs TOEFL Preparation Guide*, which was published by Cliffs Notes, and later, individually wrote *Cliffs Advanced Practice for the TOEFL* and *TOEFL Preparation Guide – CBT* (computer-based test.)

He wrote and worked on White Sugar, Brown Sugar for over forty years, and worked on Cuban Roots for almost thirty. In his presentations, he jokes that he's getting faster, and maybe has another book in him.

Timeline of Relevant Events

Batista serves as President of Cuba – 1940 - 1944

Batista and his family reside in and regularly visit a home he owns in Daytona Beach – 1944 - 1958

Batista is elected as a senator to Cuba while in Daytona Beach – 1948

Batista takes control of Cuba again by coup – March 10, 1952

Attack of Moncada army barracks by Fidel Castro and almost 200 others, referred to as the July 26 Movement, and as the birth of the Revolution – July 26, 1953

Daytona Beach celebrates its relationship with Batista with a parade and banquet on what it proclaims 'Batista Day'; some Cuban students march in protest – March 24, 1956

Batista takes Daytona Beach officials to Cuba, culminating with a banquet. During the festivities, Batista transfers home and contents, including vast art collection to City of Daytona Beach – 1957

Batista flees the country. Fidel Castro gives his first speech of victory at the ayuntamiento (government building) in Santiago de Cuba, Cuba – January 1, 1959

U.S. announces the embargo, which is referred to by Cubans as the *Bloqueo*, or Blockade – 1960

Cuban government under Castro rule begins nationalizing businesses and taking property – 1960

'Bay of Pigs invasion' by U.S. sponsored Cuban exiles – April 1961

'Operation Pedro Pan', sponsored by the U.S. government and a Catholic Church organization, in which 14,000 children were sent to the U.S. without their parents – 1960 – 1962

U.S. expands the embargo ('*bloqueo*') to include all exports to Cuba from the U.S. – February 7, 1962

Fidel Castro's Government requests return of art from Daytona Beach, which was denied – 1962

Cuban Missile Crisis, in which U.S. reacts to Russian missiles in Cuba – October 14 - 28, 1962

U.S. imposes prohibition of travel by U.S. persons to Cuba – February 8, 1963

U.S. reopens relations with Cuba, with an "interest section" instead of an embassy – 1977

"Mariel Boat Lift", in which many Cubans leave for the U.S. from Mariel, Cuba, west of Havana, on private boats from the U.S. – 1980

U.S. law allows a Cuban who reaches U.S. soil to obtain residency, later referred to as the 'wet foot, dry foot' rule – 1965 - 2017

City of Daytona Beach transferred the art to its Museum of Arts and Sciences – 1971

'Radio Marti' is created, allowing U.S. to spread its message to Cubans – 1985

USAid, a U.S. government agency, created "ZunZuneo", referred to also as "Cuban Twitter", a social media text-messaging application to help organize the Cuban youth to overthrow the Cuban government – the 90s

Helms-Burton Act signed into law, tightening the U.S. embargo and imposing other restrictions – March 12, 1996

Cuban Five, convicted as terrorists by U.S. courts, arrested in U.S. – September 1998

Elian Gonzalez episode, in which the U.S. government involves itself in a custody battle between a father living in Cuba and other family members living in the U.S. – 1999

Fidel Castro turns over control of the Cuban government to his brother, Raul Castro – February 24, 2008

Alan Gross is arrested and sentenced to prison in Havana, Cuba, for importing illegal communication devices, sponsored by USAid – 2009

Obama administration creates a procedure allowing family in the U.S. to visit family in Cuba via 'charter' flights from Miami – 2009

Obama administration creates a procedure for 'educational' and cultural visits to Cuba via 'charter' flights from Miami – January 2011

Cuban government initiates economic reform laws allowing citizens to buy and sell residences and cars and discharging half a million government employees so that they can create private businesses – 2011

President Obama and Raul Castro announce restoration of diplomatic ties. Many of the promises by the Cuban government required elimination of the Embargo, which did not occur – 2014

Cuba removed from the U.S. "Terrorism List" – 2015

U.S. removes requirement of using a U.S. licensed tour guide for visits to Cuba via the 'People-to-People' rule - 2015

U.S. and Cuba reopen embassies, replacing 'interest sections' – July 20, 2015

Airbnb and other travel compilers begin listings for travel Cuba – 2015

Commercial U.S. airlines allowed to have flights to Cuba without using 'charter' system – 2016

President Obama visits Cuba – March 2016

Fidel Castro dies – November 25, 2016

President Obama ends 'wet-foot, dry-foot' just before leaving office – 2016

Trump administration imposes restrictions, including again requiring U.S. licensed tour guide for 'People-to-People' travel to Cuba – June 16, 2017

Raul Castro turns over control to Miguel Diaz-Canal – April 19, 2018

Trump administration announces that it will eliminate various means for U.S. persons to travel to Cuba and will impose restrictions on sending money to Cubans – April, 2019

Luis' Family Tree

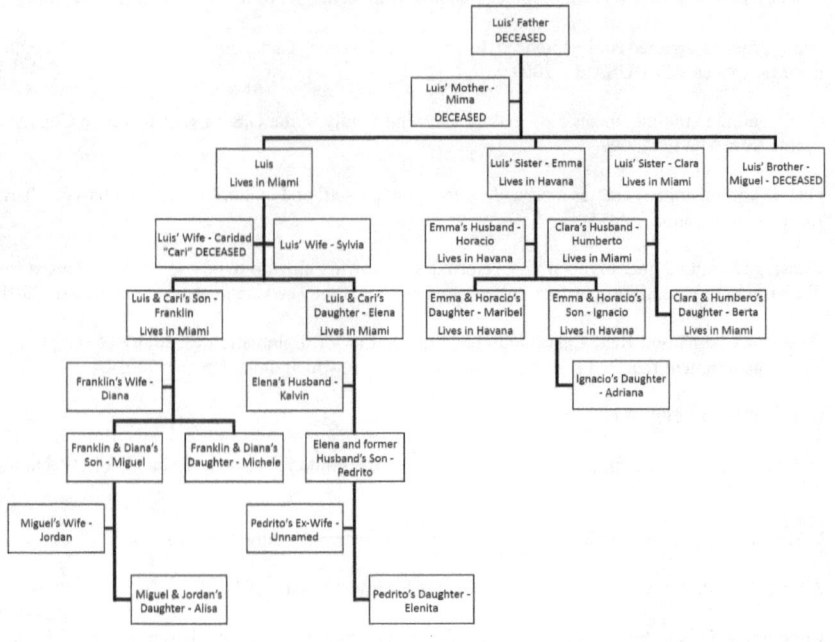

Cari's Family Tree

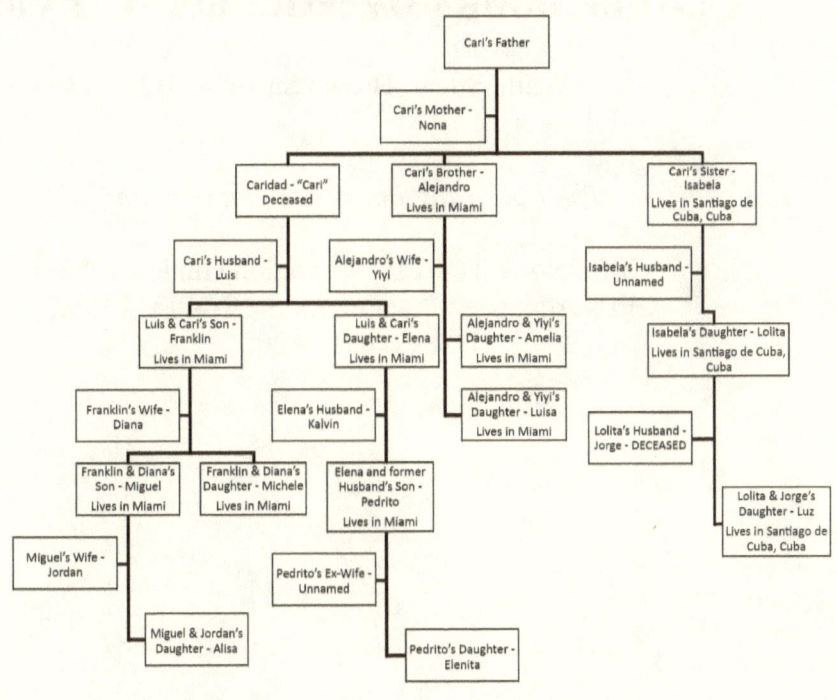

Other books by Michael A. Pyle

White Sugar, Brown Sugar - 2012

The Following Books Are Out of Print:

Cliffs Notes TOEFL Preparation Guide - 1982
Cliffs Advanced Practice for the TOEFL - 1992
TOEFL CBT - 2002